Hazel Fine Sings Along

Hazel Fine Sings Along

Katie Wicks

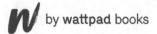

w by wattpad books

W by **wattpad** books

An imprint of Wattpad WEBTOON Book Group

Copyright © 2023 Catherine McKenzie

Published in Canada by Wattpad WEBTOON Book Group, a division of Wattpad WEBTOON Studios, Inc.

36 Wellington Street E., Suite 200, Toronto, ON M5E 1C7 Canada

www.wattpad.com

First W by Wattpad Books edition: May 2023

ISBN 978-1-99077-858-2 (Trade Paper original)
ISBN 978-1-99077-859-9 (eBook edition)

Library and Archives Canada Cataloguing in Publication information is available upon request.

Printed and bound in Canada

1 3 5 7 9 10 8 6 4 2

Cover illustration and design by Elliot Caroll
Author Photo by Fany Ducharme

Interior image © great19 via Adobe Stock

For Elyssa

Chapter One

"I'm so nervous!" Hazel said to Amber as she stared at every outfit she owned, all laid out on the uncomfortable bed of her long-stay motel. "What do you think I should wear to my audition?"

Amber cocked her head to the side. She was one of the sex workers who loitered by the fire escape of the Motel California every night, waiting for customers. Between jobs she loved to show Hazel pictures of her son, Theo, on her phone. They'd quickly become friends after Hazel had moved into the motel a year ago.

"What look are you going for?" Amber picked up a sparkly sequined bandeau top that Hazel's boss at the café where she worked had insisted she wear last Halloween. "This is sexy." Amber held the top against her body, checking her appearance in the grimy mirror. Tall and voluptuous, with platinum blond hair and almost black eyes, she was wearing an all-pleather outfit and five-inch heels. Hazel cringed at the thought of walking around in them.

"I don't think I pull off sexy. Plus, it's a singing competition, not *America's Next Top Model*."

Amber turned around. "Girl, no. They're casting parts, just like everyone else."

Hazel knew Amber was right. *The Sing Along*, now in its tenth season on Fox, was looking for a hundred men and women who could sing *and* fill a role. Hazel only had a couple of hours before she had to show up to the cattle call, where she'd line up all day and maybe, *maybe*, get a chance to sing in front of the judges—Georgia Hayes, the troubled country music star, and music producer Martin Taylor, who'd signed more acts than Hazel could count. They were intimidating and picky, and if she wanted a chance to impress them, Hazel knew she had to pick a lane. She just didn't know which lane would get her where she wanted to go.

"This would be a lot easier if you'd tell me what to do," Hazel said.

Amber laughed and stepped to the door, opening it and popping her head out. The sky was a dusky pink, the sun rising slowly over Venice Beach. Hazel had called Amber into her room for advice and moral support after she'd bolted awake at four knowing there was no way she'd go back to sleep. She didn't usually get to see the motel at this time of day. It was almost picturesque in the washed-out light. You couldn't tell that the sign had two letters that didn't light up anymore, and the cracks in the beige stucco faded into the background.

"Any customers?" Hazel asked.

"Nope. Slow night."

Hazel felt relief. She knew her friend was fine with what she did for a living, but that didn't mean Hazel didn't want more for Amber. That went for herself too. Her last year in this room had been depressing and demoralizing, eroding her hope to a thin flame. With each passing day in this downtrodden life she felt further from her goals. When she'd been approached by a scout to audition for *The Sing Along*, it felt like her luck might be changing. But by the end of today her dream could also be shattered into a million pieces. If Hazel thought too much about it, she'd break out in hives. Definitely *not* the right look.

She picked up a green romper from the clothes pile. She looked cute in it, though it was a pain in the ass when she had to go to the bathroom. "How about this? I could do down-on-her-luck singer-songwriter with a plucky, can-do attitude, which is basically the truth."

"Love it." Amber reached down to the dirt-infused rug and came up with a pair of cowboy boots. "Wear these and do your hair in two braids. You won't look a day past eighteen."

"My ID says I'm twenty-two." When Hazel had obtained her new identity she'd subtracted six years from her real age and deleted her first and last names, leaving only her middle name and her mother's maiden name. Add in a new social security number, and *presto!*, she was an entirely new person. On paper, anyway.

"You get that from Vern?" Amber asked.

"Yeah." Vern was the sketchy front-desk man who always seemed to need access to Hazel's room to "check the plumbing."

Hazel made sure to count her underwear every time he left. "He said it was guaranteed to work, and it better given the five hundred bucks I had to fork over for it."

"His IDs are legit, even if he isn't." Amber rummaged through the old makeup on Hazel's dresser, her bright-red nails clicking against the metal tubes. "This lip gloss should work. And just a hint of mascara."

"Thanks, Amber. I—" Hazel felt him before she saw him. Checkers, her rescue rabbit, was on the run, grazing past her leg as he hopped hopefully out of the room at a surprisingly fast pace. "Checkers!" Hazel called in vain. He never answered to his name. "Hold on!" she said to Amber as she sprinted past her to catch Checkers before he leaped into the scum-covered pool that took up most of the courtyard.

She ran down the rickety metal stairs to the concrete landing and caught up to him right as he was about to jump into the murky water. She gathered him to her chest. His heart thrummed against his rib cage, thrilled by his near escape.

Hazel walked him back to Amber, who was waiting for her by the stairs. A black Toyota Camry pulled up and idled near the bottom of the fire escape.

"Duty calls," Amber said, eyeing the Toyota.

"I could wave him off."

"Nah, that's all right. Break a leg today." Amber sauntered toward the driver's window, then tossed her head back and mouthed "Dad bod" in an exaggerated way.

Hazel laughed, feeling her body unclench around Checkers's soft brown-and-white fur. She watched Amber get into the Camry, then noted the license plate as it drove away, memorizing it like a piece of sheet music. She'd write it down when she got back to her room.

Checkers squirmed against her, and she brought him to her face. "Bad bunny."

Checkers didn't respond, only gave her his patented sad-eyed look with his round black eyes.

Hazel sighed. She only had Checkers because of this kid, Jessie, who'd stayed at the motel with his strung-out mom. She wasn't going to let him bring Checkers to their next stop, and they were going to release him into the wilds of Venice. He wouldn't have lasted a day.

"I'll take him!" Hazel had said, the words out of her mouth before her brain could catch up. Jessie's joyous smile had made it worth it at first, but she had no idea how to take care of a bunny. When she'd googled it, the first thing that came up was: *bunnies typically go to the bathroom two to three hundred times a day*. That, it turned out, was not even remotely an exaggeration.

She'd tried more than once to get rid of him, but she couldn't go through with it. Between the lingering memory of her promise to Jessie to keep him "forever and ever" and the fact that Checkers was her only company, she'd resigned herself to life with the rabbit.

When she got back to her room, she put Checkers in his cage, making sure the door was firmly shut. Then she coiled her chestnut hair into two braids, one on each side of her face, and let them flop over her shoulders. She applied a light coat of lip gloss and mascara. She picked up the romper and held it against her body, the way Amber had, checking herself in the mirror.

A young, down-on-her-luck singer-songwriter stared back at her. She cocked her hip to the side and gave her friendliest grin, trying to project a can-do attitude, then focused until the smile lit up her cornflower blue eyes. She almost didn't recognize herself, but that was the point.

Amber was right. *The Sing Along* was casting parts, and Hazel was determined to get one. She smiled at herself in the mirror again, trying to fill herself with confidence like she'd been taught to do before auditions. Her heart was beating nearly as quickly as Checkers's had been, churning out adrenaline in a way she hadn't felt in a long time.

She could do this. She *could* do this. She was *going* to do this.

Hazel reached for a memory and pulled out the right lingo. "Slate, please!" she said, then mimicked holding up a slate. She rotated through the other voices that would mark the start of filming. "Picture's up!

"Roll sound, roll camera.

"Rolling!"

She slapped the fake slate shut, the clap of her hands echoing off the walls. "Scene one, take one.

"And action!"

"So, Hazel, what are you going to sing for us today?"

Twelve hours later, Hazel stared directly into the camera lens as she stood in the hallway of the Sheraton Grand in downtown L.A. The hall was thick with other contestants waiting for their auditions and the friends and family they'd brought along for support. Only Hazel stood alone. "I'll be singing 'Titanium' by David Guetta."

Keshawn Jackson's mouth broke into an ultrawhite smile. He'd been the host of *The Sing Along* for ten seasons, and had a polished banter that he engaged in with the contestants before they went before the judges. "Excellent choice. A personal favorite."

He said this to most of the competitors, but Hazel pretended not to know that. Instead, she adjusted her guitar strap and said, "It's my theme song."

"Had a lot of adversity in your life, Hazel?"

A highlight reel of her worst moments flashed through her brain. "You bet."

Hazel knew that if she was one of the special contestants who didn't have to wait in line all day, the show would immediately cut to a prepackaged montage about her hardscrabble beginnings and everything she'd sacrificed to get there. But she'd only been approached by a scout after an open mic night. She didn't have a manager or a viral song on TikTok. No special montage for Hazel.

"But so has everyone here, right?" Hazel added, with a winning wink.

Keshawn laughed with delight. He could tell what she was doing, and he loved it. *Finally*, she could see him thinking. *Finally, someone who gets it.* "Where are you from, Hazel?"

"Austin, Texas." That was the truth. Hazel was juggling enough details about herself. She didn't need to add a fake hometown to the mix.

"And how old are you?"

"I'm twenty-two."

"You don't look a day over eighteen."

"I know, right? I get carded all the time."

"I'll bet you do," Keshawn said, his voice warm and deep. "Tell me, have you had a chance to check out the competition?"

"There was plenty of time to do so in that line!" Despite what was shown on TV, the auditions before the judges were the last in a series of steps that took place over the course of the day. Hazel had already sung her heart out in front of a junior producer and an assistant producer on the mean streets of downtown L.A. Then she'd had to sing in a small basement room that smelled like nicotine while they did her camera test. There weren't any windows, but at least a homeless guy wasn't screaming about an alien invasion while a police officer looked on passively as she tried to hit the high note in the chorus.

"We've had an incredible turnout today," Keshawn said. "We've already seen some fantastic talent."

The audition room doors opened and an Asian guy in his early twenties walked out with a well-used guitar slung over his back. He was holding a blue card and sporting a wide grin. He high-fived a couple of surfer dudes who'd been waiting for him, while two girls in slip dresses giggled.

"Oh, look, here's Benji Suzuki—I knew you'd make it!" Keshawn said, beckoning Benji over. They were a sharp contrast: Keshawn in a three-piece suit, his dark hair close-cropped, his nails manicured. Benji's black hair was straight, feathered, and highlighted. Five ten and well built, he was wearing a short-sleeved shirt and multicolored board shorts. "I'm sure you've seen Benji on TikTok, Hazel?"

"Of course!" Benji had mastered cutting his songs into

viral videos that drove teen girls crazy and inspired imitation. There'd even been a Suzuki Challenge a few months back.

"Are you excited about making it through to Universal Week, Benji?" Keshawn asked, moving the mic toward him.

Benji tossed his head in a practiced gesture. "Fo sho."

Hazel hid a smile. Benji knew what he was doing, too, and his brush-off was a bit too casual. He wanted this as much as she did.

"That's fantastic. Benji, you want to wish Hazel luck? She's up next."

Benji rolled his eyes to Hazel's. As they locked in place, he gave her a slow smile. Hazel found herself responding to it, an answering smile on her lips and a fluttering she hadn't felt in a while in her stomach.

"Well, well, well. I'll have to keep my eye on you two." Keshawn gave them a knowing nod then pointed to the audition room. "You ready to go in, Hazel?"

Hazel threw her shoulders back. "Fo sho!" She winked at Benji, and he mouthed "Good luck!"

"Go on then, go!"

Hazel put her hand on the door handle, anticipating what came next. The adrenaline that had come and gone throughout the day was back, her heart stuttering, her palms sweaty.

"Let's watch Hazel's audition," Keshawn said, addressing the camera. "And remember to . . ."

". . . sing along if you know the words!" the crowd shouted with him.

The audition room was a standard-edition hotel conference room—thick multicolored carpet on the floor, beige walls, and track lighting. This room was an upgrade from the last one Hazel had been in, though, with a wall of windows letting in the bright California sunshine that always buoyed Hazel no matter how hard her day was, and freshly piped-in air. There were cameras and key lights set up around the perimeter, and three people sitting behind a long melamine folding table that was filled with an array of headshots and cola. *The Sing Along* logo was blown up on a large canvas behind them, as were the faces of several past winners, including Hazel's favorite, Kate Maple.

Hazel steadied herself and focused on giving the judges her most confident smile. When Georgia and Martin had taken a lap through the cattle call earlier that day, the air had buzzed with excitement. One woman, Zoey Johnson, a Black country music artist Hazel had stood in line with for half the day, had nearly passed out when she'd seen Georgia, who'd been a force in country music for most of Hazel's life.

From a distance, Georgia looked the same as she had when she'd become famous at twenty. But up close Hazel could see that Georgia wasn't aging well. Her bleached blond hair was brittle and split at the ends and her screen makeup sat in the deep lines around her watery green eyes. Rumor had it she had a drinking problem, which might be true or might be a vicious lie spread by the record company that was apparently trying to welch on the back end of a multi-album deal. Georgia was smiling at Hazel, though. She was the nice judge, the one who encouraged even those she sent home.

"What's your name, sweetheart?" Martin asked. British and in his midfifties, he'd manufactured a hundred hits and a dozen girl bands. He was wearing a tweed jacket with patches on the elbows, and his dark hair was bristle-cut, almost military-like. The winner of *The Sing Along* got a record deal with his label. Hazel knew it was important to stay on Martin's good side, which was easier said than done. Unlike Georgia, he'd made more than one contestant cry with his withering assessment of their talent.

"Hazel Fine," Hazel said, trying to keep the quake out of her voice. She'd been through auditions before. She could survive this one.

Martin scanned her body from her scalp to her cowboy boots. His eyes felt like fingers, probing her. "And are you fine, Hazel?"

Hazel slapped on a smile that made her face hurt and her soul die. "As fine as can be!"

"Ignore him," Georgia said in her Southern twang. "Tell us about yourself, darlin'."

"I'm twenty-two years old and from Austin, Texas. A waitress by day, I'm a singer-songwriter by night."

Georgia laughed and the man sitting to her left cracked a brief smile. In his early thirties, with chestnut hair that had a light curl to it and dark-green eyes, he was wearing a black T-shirt and had a stack of notes in front of him. Hazel didn't recognize him, and she thought briefly about asking who he was, but then thought better of it. She wasn't there to ask questions. She was in the witness box.

Instead, Hazel tracked her eyes back to Martin. He was scowling at her as if she was a puzzle he needed to figure out. Hazel could feel the heat of the lights on her neck. A bead of sweat trickled down her back.

"What made you audition for *The Sing Along?*" Georgia asked.

"Singing is my life."

Martin crossed his hairy arms and leaned back in his chair. "Is it now?"

"I want it to be."

"Do you think you have what it takes?"

Hazel lifted her chin. She met men like Martin every day when she was waitressing. Men who thought they could touch her like she was part of the furniture or tell her what to do like she was their child. The only way to deal with someone like that was to meet them with equal confidence. Manfidence, Hazel had taken to calling it. "I do."

Martin gave her a brief smile. "Show us, then, love."

Hazel moved her guitar into place, her fingers falling easily onto the frets. She loved this instrument. When she'd seen it in the pawn shop six months ago, it had beckoned to her like a lover. She'd worked a month of double shifts to pay for it, but it was worth it.

As she got ready to start, Hazel thought back to the seedy motel where she barely made rent. How tired she was when she came home from a shift. How often her sleep was interrupted by someone pounding on her door looking for their dealer. She was tired of living like that. She shouldn't feel this old at her age, whatever it was. Her life was supposed to be more than this. She deserved more than this. And here it was, her chance—her *last* chance it felt like—if she could reach out and seize it.

So, even though she hated it when singers did that, she closed her eyes, focused on the strings she was plucking and the form her mouth had to take to get that first chord right.

And then she sang as if her life depended on it.

Because it did.

Chapter Two

"Hi, I'm Hazel Fine. I'm a singer-songwriter from Austin, Texas, and I'm going to be the next winner of *The Sing Along!*"

"That's great, Hazel," the director of the promo spot said after Hazel's tenth take. Her name was Sheila, and she had a mane of bright-red hair that she wore in a thick braid. "Can we do it one more time? Maybe with the guitar?"

"Sure, no problem."

It was two weeks after her successful audition and the first day of the competition. She and a hundred other hopefuls had been told to show up at a hotel in Universal City with a week's worth of clothes and to be ready for a grueling week of group and individual auditions. Twenty-five contestants would be eliminated each day until they were down to the final group that would make it onto the live shows. But first they had promo shots to shoot—little vignettes in which the contestants danced with their guitars or jumped into the air as they yelled, "I'm going to win *The Sing Along!*"

Hazel walked back to her starting position by the star-shaped pool. The sun was beating down, and sweat snaked down her back. If she stayed out here much longer she was going to start to smell. Maybe they'd let her jump *into* the pool the next go-around?

The nameless guy from her audition was standing at the edge of the pool with her guitar in hand. His name was Nick Barnes, and Hazel had learned that morning that he was the musical director for the show. Six feet tall and trim, he was once again wearing a black T-shirt, though this time he had his ID badge on a lanyard around his neck and a pair of tortoise-shell Ray-Ban Wayfarers covering his eyes.

"You need any help?" Nick asked as he held out her guitar by the neck. He had long, tapered fingers, and the backs of his hands were tanned.

"I got it." Hazel took the guitar and slipped the strap over her head.

"I tuned it for you. Your E string was flat."

"Oh, thanks." That set her teeth on edge. The slightly flat E string was on purpose because Hazel liked the tone it gave to her chords, but he probably assumed she didn't know what she was doing.

He'd intimated as much earlier when he'd started to explain what a mark was. It got under her skin for some reason. So, instead of doing what she'd planned and pretending that she was as naïve about blocking as the other contestants, she'd told him she knew what she was doing and had counted out the steps to the red X made from painter's tape in the grass. When she'd met his eyes in a challenge as she hit her mark, he'd nodded and gone back to scowling at the other competitors. She didn't expect him to give her a medal, but some acknowledgment would've been nice.

She shook her thoughts of cranky Nick away. She probably wasn't going to have much to do with him after this.

"Ready for another take, Hazel?" Sheila asked in her cheerful voice. She could do this all day, apparently, just like Captain America. And by the looks of the number of people lazing around the pool waiting their turn, she was going to have to.

"Ready!"

"You and Miss Johnson will be rooming together?" the desk clerk asked two hours later when she'd finally finished her camera work. Early twenties and still pimpled, his name tag said his name was JASON, and his black suit was loose across his shoulders.

"If that's okay?" Hazel wasn't a fan of communal living, but she knew she'd have to bunk with someone, so she'd agreed when Zoey had asked to room together.

Zoey had texted Hazel the day after the auditions, and they'd been exchanging messages ever since. Zoey talked a bit too much about her girlfriend, but Hazel knew she probably felt that way because she was jealous. Hazel wished she had someone special to leave behind. The only good-bye for Hazel had been the one to her boss. When she'd told him she needed a week off for the show, he'd given it to her—as in, he'd fired her and told her not to come crawling back when things didn't work out.

Jason tapped at the keyboard. "All of the contestants will be sharing a room at first, so it's no problem to accommodate you."

"Great," Hazel said, though the words *at first* rattled her. She'd have a roommate until one of them got eliminated is what he meant.

If she was the one to go early, she was in trouble. She hadn't bothered to let Vern know she was leaving the motel. Instead, she'd snuck out in the early dawn, catching a knowing nod from Amber as she let her last customer out of her room. But he'd caught Hazel rolling her suitcase away anyway, and had started crooning in a painful voice about her being able to check out but never leave.

She'd burned every bridge she'd had left in L.A. with her shady escape from the Motel California. She had less than $500 in her bank account. The thought of having to pawn her guitar for bus fair to Austin made her sick.

No. *No way.* Whatever happened, she wasn't going back there. To *them.*

"Everything has been taken care of by the production company," Jason said. He gave her a smirk. "But there's a twenty-dollar daily limit on room charges like the minibar."

"No problem."

"If you spend more it will be charged to your credit card."

"I got it." Hazel buried a snort. Good luck with that. The card she'd handed over only had enough room on it to let the $250 charge for incidentals go through. Another problem she'd have to deal with if she got eliminated.

But enough. She'd spent too much of her life looking past the good parts to what would happen when it all fell apart. She'd vowed to stop doing that.

"And there's no smoking and no pets."

Hazel kept her features even. "That's fine."

"You'd be surprised how many people flout that rule. The biggest problem is the owls."

"Owls?"

Jason motioned to a poster on the wall advertising the nearby theme park. "Because of the Wizarding World of Harry Potter? We're less than a quarter mile away."

"That explains all the people in capes."

He rolled his eyes. "Imagine what it's like at Halloween."

"I'll bet."

"No owls in there?" He pointed to the battered roller bag that held most of her possessions.

"No, sir."

She wasn't lying. Checkers wasn't in her suitcase. He was in his cage in the backseat of her car. She'd parked at the far edge of the parking lot under a large palm tree and left the windows cracked open, but hadn't quite figured out how to get him into her room without being caught. Zoey said she was cool with it, but she hadn't *met* Checkers yet.

Maybe she could find somewhere to stash him on the grounds? And then accidentally leave his cage door open? No, that was evil. He'd probably get caught and end up as some prop in a magic show at the theme park. And that was the best-case scenario.

"One key or two?" Jason asked.

"I'll take one."

"Most people in the competition take two." Jason smirked again. "Lots of fraternizing."

Hazel knew contestants hooked up—the producers loved to work these showmances into the plot. But Hazel wasn't looking for that kind of complication. *The Sing Along* was work. Hazel wanted to keep it professional. "One key is good for me."

Jason ran a key card through the programmer as Hazel heard a burst of giggles behind her.

She glanced over her shoulder to see what the commotion was about. Benji the TikTok star was standing twenty feet away at the lobby bar. He was surrounded by several girls Hazel recognized from the auditions. A pretty twentysomething with black hair and deep-blue eyes named Bella Moore, who'd been one of the ones to sail past the cattle call, and the two eighteen-year-olds in slip dresses from outside the audition room.

Before she could turn away, Benji caught her staring. He gave her a slow smile and raised his hand in greeting. She waved back, feeling foolish.

He pushed himself off the bar and walked toward her at his surfer's pace. Like he didn't have a care in the world; like he knew he'd catch the wave. "Hey, Hazel. What's up?"

"Just checking in."

"Right, right. You wanna join for a drink?" He motioned to where Bella and the others were now scowling in her direction.

"I'm kind of beat from that commercial shoot."

Benji grinned. "That was a trip, right? First time I've done something like that. I mean formally. Usually I'm the camera-man, lighting crew, and the talent."

"You'll have to show me how to use a ring light without it getting in my eyes."

"I can't share all my secrets."

"Secrets are what makes life interesting."

"That so, Hazel?"

"Benji?" Bella called. "The ice in your drink is melting."

Hazel stifled a laugh. "You better get back."

"Guess I should." Benji held out his hand like he wanted to shake.

"We've already met."

"Just take it."

She put her hand in his and he leaned toward her. "You sounded great in the audition." His breath tickled her neck, but before she could say anything he'd slipped away, and was gliding back to Bella.

She watched him as a blush crept up her neck.

"I'll just put a second key in here," Jason said.

"This way." Hazel motioned for Zoey to follow her. They were in the hotel's back alley, near the garbage containers. Zoey was holding Checkers, looking overwhelmed. She was shorter than Hazel and ballet-dancer thin. She wore her hair naturally, and it framed her face, accentuating her delicate features and soft brown eyes.

"I had a parrot growing up," Zoey said, speaking quickly. "My little sister taught it to say *screw you* and my mom got rid of it. That's where my experience with animals ends."

"I hear you." Hazel was anxious to get Checkers inside. He

didn't like the heat. Well, she wasn't sure about that, but she didn't like it, and she wasn't covered in fur.

"Did you have pets growing up?"

"Nope," she said simply, and hoped they could move on. Hazel didn't want to focus on her messed-up past. And she wanted to tell as few lies as possible. There were already enough to keep track of. "Just a bit farther." They walked down the alley to the service entrance Hazel had scoped out earlier. "Good, the laundry cart is still here. We can put Checkers inside, and no one will see him. We'll cover him with a stack of towels."

Zoey pulled her oversized sunglasses down from the top of her head as if they were setting off on a secret mission. Then she hoisted Checkers in the air and blew him a kiss. "Don't bark, baby. We need to smuggle you into our room so stay very quiet."

"He's a bunny, Zo."

"What does he do, then?" Zoey put Checkers into the cart and arranged fresh laundry on top of him, making sure there was space for him to breathe.

"He poops. You'll see. Don't say I didn't warn you."

"He's so cute, though."

Hazel smiled. Checkers was the cutest. She felt guilty for her earlier thoughts about abandoning him in the parking lot.

"Okay, let's do this." Hazel wheeled the cart toward the door she'd propped open from the inside with a towel. "Remember, act like we're part of housekeeping."

Zoey laughed. "You're wearing cowboy boots and my jeans have rhinestones on the butt. No one's buying that."

"You're right. Let's get a move on before someone sees us."

"Do you mind if we stop and selfie this first? I've got to send a pic to Brooke." Brooke was Zoey's girlfriend. So far, Hazel knew that Brooke was lactose intolerant, could fix any car engine, and was from Nashville, like Zoey.

"Fine, but make it quick. We're smuggling a bunny into a no-pets hotel. It's not a federal offense but we might get disqualified if we're caught."

"Do you think that's a real possibility?" Concern edged Zoey's voice.

"I'd never have asked you to help if I thought that. But if you're worried, I can do this alone."

"No." Zoey tucked her phone back into her pocket. "We're in this together."

"Thanks. Okay, let's get out of here before we get caught." Hazel pushed the cart forward, concentrating on keeping the wheels straight, which was surprisingly difficult.

"What's in there?" a male voice said behind them, startling them both.

Hazel cringed as she heard Checkers scratching against the vinyl basket. She quickly covered him with more towels, praying he had enough air to breathe.

"Nothing," Hazel and Zoey said in unison, then turned and stood at attention to face Nick.

He'd gotten some sun earlier, tanning his face in a way that complemented his olive complexion, but it didn't make him any friendlier. He raised a disbelieving eyebrow and leaned to the side, trying to see behind them. "What are you doing down here, then?"

Hazel felt panicked. She didn't want to get a reputation as a problem and give the judges a reason to kick her off early.

"We were sneaking a cigarette," Zoey said, coming to the rescue.

"I'd have thought you girls would want to preserve your voices."

"First of all, we're women," Hazel said. "And our voices are fine."

Nick held up his hands like he was under arrest. "Sorry."

"What are *you* doing down here?"

"Waiting for an amp delivery." He took a step around them and peered into the basket, touching the towel that Hazel had hastily put in place. If he moved it, he was going to have a direct line of sight to Checkers.

"You need a towel?" Zoey batted her eyes and suggestively bit her bottom lip. Zoey might have been into girls, but you'd never know it from this performance.

"I'm good," Nick said to Zoey, though he was looking at Hazel. She felt uncomfortable under his gaze as he reached his hand farther into the basket. He picked up something small and held it between his fingers. "Not too sanitary, huh?" He held up a brown ball. "A Cocoa Puff. In the laundry." He brought it closer to his face to examine it.

"Don't do that!" Hazel's hand shot out reflexively and knocked Checkers's poop out of Nick's. It skittered across the ground.

"What the—?"

"I thought you were going to eat it."

"Excuse me?"

Hazel's face burned as her heart beat at a manic pace. "Maybe I overreacted."

"You think?"

"Sorry. Anyway, we've got to go. See you around." Without giving Nick a chance to protest or ask more questions, Hazel opened the door and dragged Zoey and the laundry cart inside.

As they rushed down the hall to the service elevator, Hazel glanced over her shoulder, praying Nick wasn't following them. This wasn't the impression she needed or wanted to make in *The Sing Along*, especially not with the musical director. As she stabbed at the Up button for the elevator, she vowed to keep a low profile from here on out.

It was time to let her singing do the talking.

Chapter Three

The next morning, Hazel and Zoey both woke early, nerves poking at them before the alarm on Zoey's phone sounded.

"You awake?" Zoey asked as the light peeked around the edges of the room's blackout curtains. Their room was a standard-issue two-bed queen, with a row of windows overlooking an internal courtyard, and a bathroom with an inviting tub. There was a flat-screen on the wall, built-in dressers, a desk area, and a comfortable armchair in the corner. The air-conditioning kept the room at a perfect seventy degrees.

Last night, it had felt like an oasis, but this morning, Hazel had been staring at the creamy-white popcorn ceiling for forty-five minutes. "Yep."

"I've never performed with other people," Zoey said. "Not since choir in high school."

The first round of auditions during Universal Week was the group round, where they'd be divided into groups of four and given a song to perform in front of the other contestants. Their respective styles or chemistry didn't matter—the idea was to put them into a stressful situation and see who could stand the heat.

"It'll be fine," Hazel said, trying to sound reassuring. "As long as I don't get put with that Bella chick. I spoke to TikTok Benji for, like, two seconds yesterday, and she was contemplating homicide like a cartoon villain. What's her deal?"

Zoey stretched her hands above her head. She'd slept in a T-shirt with hearts on it. "You don't know? Bella's dad is rich, and she was on one of those daughters-of-the-housewives shows or something? She has two million followers on Insta."

"Lucky her." Hazel sat up. Is that what was needed to succeed? Some massive, preexisting social media presence? Hazel knew it was a help to some of the contestants, but she was counting on being one of those low-key ones who made an impression through the scale of her talent, not the number of her followers. The truth was, Hazel wasn't even on social media other than as a lurker so she could follow her favorite *Bridgerton* fan accounts and lull herself to sleep while scrolling TikTok. She'd never worked up the courage to post anything she'd sung, even though it was a great way to get discovered. Social media felt like a trap to her; an invitation to investigate who she was.

"It doesn't matter," Zoey said. "We got through the auditions, right? It's about what we do now that counts."

"Let's hope so." Hazel threw the covers off. "Ugh, I'm not sure what to wear today."

Zoey popped out of bed and reached for her toes. "I'm wearing red. Because it's intimidating and it makes my complexion glow. You should wear navy." Zoey stood and started to twist her body back and forth. "My mom taught me all about what to wear when I perform."

"That's great."

"Did you not have a stage mama?"

"Not really." Hazel reached for the remote and turned on the TV. It was tuned to *Extra*, which was doing a special on former child celebrities and where they were now. Hazel's neck started to prickle like it did right before it rained.

"Oh," Zoey said, completing her stretch and pointing at the TV. "Wasn't that the guy who was on that show . . . what's his name?" Zoey snapped her fingers. "Aaron Edwards! He was on that Disney show. You know the one, with that cute kid? The one who was always saying whoops-a-daisy?"

"Daisy Dawson."

"Yes! Wonder what happened to her?"

"Nothing good, I'm sure." Hazel felt slightly nauseated looking at Aaron's ravaged face. The years had not been kind. She snapped off the TV. "Should we get some breakfast?" Their stay included access to the unlimited breakfast buffet. Hazel had been looking forward to trading in Pop-Tarts for eggs and bacon and a mountain of fresh fruit, but now she mostly just wanted something else to talk about.

"I wanted to be her when I was a kid," Zoey said, ignoring Hazel's suggestion. "Not her, exactly, but famous, you know? I got the starring role in the Thanksgiving play and then I asked my teacher if she was going to send the video to a producer in Hollywood. Can you imagine?"

"That's a cute story." She walked over to Checkers's cage. He gave her that stare he had—like a sad, lonely child, which she supposed he was. Were bunnies social animals? She'd never wanted to know because if they were it would be too heartbreaking to keep him with her, alone.

"Ugh, I'm talking too much. Brooke says it's cringey, but I know she loves it. What about you? Child-star aspirations?"

Hazel stooped and started to clean out Checkers's cage. Anything to distract herself from the present conversation. "Oh, um . . . I was a ballet dancer—thought I'd go the whole *Swan Lake* route but turned out I like carbs too much. Realized I had singing talent in high school when I got cast in *Rent*. After that, I had the bug. Singing classes, private vocal coach, et cetera."

Hazel felt panicked. Where was this all coming from? If you're going to lie, you're supposed to keep it simple, and as close to the truth as possible. Instead, she'd invented an entire fake past. What if Zoey asked her to plié? What if she had to sing "Seasons of Love"? She couldn't even remember how many million minutes they were singing about in that song.

Zoey didn't seem to notice. "Guess we're both big dreamers. Benji's supertalented too. You saw that video he posted last night?"

Hazel had watched it when she couldn't get to sleep. He'd recorded a spontaneous jam on his hotel bed, shouting out to the judges and even Nick. Hazel wanted to hate him for the suck-up move, but the whole thing was adorable. His four million followers seemed to agree.

"He's good."

"I saw him flirting with Georgia yesterday before you got here," Zoey said, reaching for a red dress in the closet. "She was lapping it up. If we did that, we'd be suck-ups. Benji does it and it's totally fine."

"One hundred percent."

"Fuck the patriarchy." Zoey raised a fist in the air. "Even if he's cute."

Hazel laughed. "He seems like a big flirt."

"Could be fun?"

"Not really the time or place."

"We'll see—"

Their cell phones dinged simultaneously.

"Group auditions announced," Zoey said, but Hazel was one step ahead.

"You, me, Benji, and Bella."

"Sounds like a supergroup."

"Or a bad boy band?"

Zoey giggled. "Which one will it be?"

"Stay tuned to find out."

As they left their hotel room to go to their group practice session, Hazel slipped the DO NOT DISTURB sign onto the door handle.

"What's that for?" Zoey asked.

"Checkers."

Zoey wrinkled her nose. "Good idea."

Hazel thought she detected a bit of annoyance in Zoey's voice, but she didn't want to ask. Regardless, she couldn't keep housekeeping out forever. She was going to have to find a longer-term solution.

They rode the elevator down to the conference floor with a family in cloaks. Would Harry Potter fans want to adopt Checkers? She tried to think of whether there were magical bunnies in the books. None came to mind, but couldn't a rabbit be magical if you wanted it to?

The cloaked family got off on the ground floor. When the elevator reached the basement, Hazel and Zoey made their way to Conference Room C, their assigned practice room for the day. They'd have the morning to rehearse, then the performances were that afternoon. The judges could keep the whole group or only some of it. Twenty-five of the one hundred contestants would be cut. Hazel tried not to do the math on her chances. She knew from watching years of the show that one bad performance wasn't always enough to get you kicked off if you were someone they were hoping to keep around. The problem was, she had no idea whether she fit into that category or not.

Hazel shook out her hands to get rid of her nerves. One step at a time was all she could do. No sense in overthinking it now.

When they got to their practice room, Bella and Benji were already there, off in the corner having what looked like an intense conversation. Hazel wondered what they were talking about, but then shook that thought away too. She wasn't here to date—she was here to win.

"All right, you four, ready to start rehearsing?" That was Nick. Again.

Why was this guy suddenly everywhere? Today he was

wearing dark jeans, a chambray shirt, and a serious expression. She could admit he was attractive in a way Hazel appreciated. He reminded her of Max Irons, who Hazel had swooned over in *The White Queen* and when he'd played a spy in *Condor*. But why was he so serious all the time? You'd think *Nick* was a contestant, not someone with the power to influence the results.

Their eyes met, and for a second Hazel could've sworn he was smiling, but then he turned away.

"Hi, Nick. Are you going to accompany us?" Bella asked as she peeled herself away from Benji.

"That's the plan." Nick took a seat at the glossy black piano. His long fingers moved easily along the keys and settled into a C chord. "You all know how this works? I pick a song that you'll sing as a group. We rehearse, break for lunch, then into the auditorium for group scenes and performances."

"I thought we picked the song?" Hazel said.

Nick played another chord and met her gaze with a neutral expression. "That's for the audience at home. But we have tight parameters on what we have the rights to. I pick the song from an approved list based on what I think will challenge you and showcase your talents."

"Cool, cool," Benji said. "Are you open to suggestions? From the list, of course."

"What did you have in mind?"

"I've been getting a lot of engagement lately when I cover the Beatles or do a dance challenge to them. I was thinking we should do 'With a Little Help from My Friends'? You have those rights, yes? I checked and the Beatles have been covered on previous seasons."

"Yes, but . . . dance challenge? What?"

Hazel tried not to snicker. "It's this thing on TikTok where everyone dances to the same song."

Nick's hands fell from the keys as the camera crew walked in.

"Good time for us?" one of the cameramen asked.

"Sure, sure."

The crew set up quickly with a camera in the corner and one by the door, so they could get close-ups and wide angles.

"What does TikTok have to do with anything?" Nick asked Benji.

"It's not the medium. The Beatles are popular there, and that's our audience."

"Music from the sixties is popular?"

"It's iconic."

"And iconic is good?"

"Of course! Bruh, come on. It'll be epic."

Nick looked skeptical, but Hazel could tell he was wavering.

"How about this?" Hazel said. "What if we try it out and if it sounds good, we go with it, and if not, we go with your suggestion, which was . . . ?"

"Hmmm." Nick looked down at the keys. "How did you see it? In four voices or two?"

"Four," Benji said.

"Each of you needs a solo."

"Right." Benji pulled out his phone. "There are three verses, but also the pre-chorus. So, three of us could sing a verse and then one of us could sing the pre-chorus and then we all sing the chorus."

"That sounds lit, Benj," Bella said. "We're so lucky we're in a group with you."

Zoey rolled her eyes at Hazel dramatically, while Hazel kept her face blank, aware of the cameras and the boom mic hanging overhead. This was the kind of moment that made it on air—drama, tension. And, oh, Benji was a clever, clever boy. More screenworthy moments pressured the judges into letting a contestant through to the later rounds where the public voted.

"I think we should try it," Hazel said. "Zoey?"

"Sure!"

Hazel linked an arm through Zoey's and guided her toward Benji. He crooked his elbow to accept her left arm. Bella followed suit eagerly on the other side. The group turned as one to face Nick.

"You in, Nick?" Hazel said sweetly.

Nick clearly wanted to resist but he knew he was beat. "What the hell, why not?" He flexed his fingers and played the intro from memory. Hazel was impressed. Nick had skills. And really, was there anything hotter than a man who knew his way around a piano? "Hazel, you take the first verse."

Hazel was pleased. Going first was good for her in the competition, but there was something else too. Nick had a sly expression on his face, as if they'd done exactly what he wanted them to.

There were more than two of them playing this game.

Hazel knew what she and Benji were up to.

But what was Nick?

The auditorium smelled like fear and ambition.

Hazel's eyes tracked over the other groups. Some of them had dressed in costume, including one ill-conceived group that seemed to have taken the proximity to Harry Potter world too far.

OMG. Did their wands light up? There weren't songs in Harry Potter, were there?

"Should we have done costumes?" Zoey said anxiously.

"No. That's not how people make it through this round. You need to be a good group and give a solid individual performance, but gimmicks turn the judges off."

"How do you know so much?"

"I've watched more hours of this show than I can count. But don't worry, I'm happy to share my knowledge with you."

Until the individual rounds, that was. Then it was every woman for herself.

"Should we sit here?" Bella said, speaking to Benji.

Bella had been like this all day, moving herself so she was always next to Benji, his body a magnet. Hazel wasn't sure if it was nerves or strategy or if Bella was already that into Benji. If it was strategy, Hazel had to give Bella props. Benji was clearly going places in *The Sing Along*, and proximity to success was never a bad thing.

Hazel couldn't quite figure out if Benji was into Bella, though. He didn't seem to mind her clinginess, and his smiles seemed genuine. Then again, it sometimes felt like he was flirting with Hazel, but that could also be how he was with everyone. It was too early to tell.

"Cool," Benji said, a trace of nervousness in his voice.

Hazel was surprised to hear a crack in his surfer-cool

demeanor. He'd been so self-assured with Nick earlier, and Hazel was sure he had nothing to worry about. Based on their tech rehearsal, it was obvious Benji was going to get into the next round, just like the youngest person in the competition, Cole, a fourteen-year-old kid from the US Virgin Islands who had an angelic voice and played the guitar like a wizard. Bella was a maybe. Zoey, too, Hazel was sorry to say.

As for her? She had fight left in her yet.

Keshawn Jackson walked onto the stage in one of his trademark three-piece suits. "Hello, contestants! Are we excited?"

He held out his microphone to the crowd and everyone shouted and cheered.

"Fantastic." He turned to the large camera that was propped on a tripod in front of him. "All right, folks, here we are. The moment you've all been waiting for. The group auditions!"

More cheers, this time encouraged by an assistant who stood off to the side of the stage with a large sign that said APPLAUSE.

Keshawn turned back to the contestants. "Now, as you know, we shoot some things out of sequence. I'll be calling out your names in groups of four. Come up onstage and 'meet' your group when I say your name. For those of you in costume, I hope you brought a change of clothes? Now would be a good time to get back into your civvies."

There were a couple of chuckles from the crowd, and several groups scrambled to change right there in the auditorium.

The assistant wheeled a large plastic spinning ball onto the stage and Keshawn went through the pantomime of reaching in and calling out the groups they already knew they belonged to.

When Hazel's group was called, there were lots of catcalls and whistles when Benji whipped out his phone and live streamed the whole thing to TikTok. Keshawn shook his head in disapproval but you could tell he loved it. Once they were onstage, Bella photobombed his TikTok, and Benji wrapped his arm around her shoulders and pulled her in close to the screen. Hazel felt a flicker of jealousy. Like it or not, Benji's attention was something that was sure to help whoever he turned his spotlight on. But Hazel wasn't about to throw herself at Benji just for a thirty-second highlight on TikTok.

Instead, she linked arms with Zoey and did a little pirouette with her which drew applause from the other contestants and a headshake from Keshawn.

When all the groups had been announced, the director called a fifteen-minute break to reset the stage, and everyone went back to their places in the audience. Hazel sat down between Zoey and Bella to wait it out. Now that the cameras were off, Bella rubbed her hands nervously on her legs.

"We're going to be good," Benji said reassuringly.

"I still don't think I've nailed my verse. We could've used another run-through on the harmonies."

"You did great." Benji caught Hazel's eye. "We all did. Don't worry."

Hazel smiled at him as Bella clenched her hands into fists. "I hope you're right. I know everyone thinks I only got on this show because of my Insta or whatever, but I've been working toward this for years."

Hazel felt an edge of sympathy for Bella. She knew a thing or two about being judged by circumstances—more like ten or twenty things—and she'd done just that herself about Bella this morning. Bella *was* talented. Maybe her hyperfocus on Benji was simply a product of her nerves.

The assistant held up a sign calling for SILENCE.

Zoey grabbed Hazel's arm in a tight grip. "Ohmygod."

"What?"

"She's here!"

Georgia walked out from behind the curtain to the judges' stage. She was wearing a classic cowboy shirt with rhinestones and a jaunty pink cowboy hat that was cocked to the side.

Did she ever get tired of dressing like a twenty-five-year-old when she was well into her fifties? Hazel was already regretting making cowboy boots part of her signature look. They rubbed her heels in the worst way.

"How did you manage to audition in front of her?" Hazel asked.

Zoey shrugged. "I took a Xanax."

"Weren't you worried that would mess up your performance?"

"I take a Xanax before every performance."

"Oh, um . . ."

"It's no big deal."

"It's fine, Zo. Whatever you need to make it through."

Martin followed Georgia onto the stage wearing his a tweed jacket and dark slim chinos. And though they were inside, he was also wearing aviators, which reflected the contestants back at themselves. He bowed to the audience, then took his seat.

"All right, folks!" Keshawn said. "Here we go! What are you hoping to see tonight, judges?"

Martin pulled his mic toward him. "A bang-on performance where no one forgets the words."

"Don't forget the words, people!" Keshawn said to the audience. "Martin hates that!"

Martin scowled.

"And Georgia? What will sway you tonight?"

"You know I'm all about pitch."

Keshawn's teeth gleamed in the lights. "Stay on pitch! Don't forget the words! Great advice from our judges. Will it happen? Let's hope so!"

Keshawn walked to the spinning ball where the slips with the names of the groups had replaced the competitors' names. He reached in as Hazel's fingertips went numb. She'd never been able to tell from watching the show if the order was predetermined, but she knew it was good to go early or last. Early or last, she repeated in her mind. Early or—

"Group eight! Benji, Bella, Hazel, and Zoey, come on up! And, audience, don't forget to . . ."

". . . sing along if you know the words!" the room shouted back.

Zoey began to shake, while Benji gave Hazel a confident smile, his nerves back to being hidden. Bella seemed more confident, too, Benji's pep talk having had an effect.

"Ready, gang?" Benji asked.

"Ready!" They stood as one and walked to the aisle.

When they were in formation—Benji in front and Hazel bringing up the rear—Benji started a syncopated clap. All of them took up the beat as they marched up the aisle. The other contestants soon joined in, clapping them up to the stage. They climbed the steps and turned to face the audience, alternating clapping and slapping their thighs.

Hazel glanced over her shoulder at Nick, seated at the piano, who'd come up with the arrangement. They had eight beats to go, then he'd play the opening chords and it would be her turn to shine.

One and two and three and four and—

One and two and three and four and—

The clapping stopped, Nick played the familiar intro, and she started to sing about singing out of tune while trying desperately to stay on key.

Her verse ended on a perfect note, then they all sang the chorus, harmonizing well. There was a short interlude while they shuffled positions and now it was Zoey's turn. She flubbed a word but recovered quickly. Another harmonized chorus, and then Bella sang the pre-chorus, her voice lilting into the song and its plaintive request for needing somebody to love. Then it was Benji's turn, asking whether the audience believed in love at first sight, and eliciting more than a few excited giggles from some of the female contestants. He winked at Hazel, and they went seamlessly into the chorus together, a cappella this time, no music, just clapping in time.

Clap, clap, slap!

Clap, clap, slap!

Clap, clap, slap!

And . . . silence.

The room rose as one, whooping and cheering. Even the judges. Even Nick.

They'd done it!

They were safe and on to the next round.

Weren't they?

Chapter Four

"Howdy, partner," Benji said the next morning, tipping his surfer cap like it was a cowboy hat. He was staring down at her, brown eyes twinkling. "I hear you and I are duetting today."

Hazel looked up from her blueberry muffin. She and Zoey were sitting at a table in the breakfast room, where a massive buffet was set up every morning. Hazel had been so overwhelmed by the choices she'd ended up taking the muffin because it required the least amount of decision-making. "Howdy."

"You get some rest last night?"

"Eight perfect hours." That wasn't entirely true. She'd spent an hour tossing and turning, feeling like a fraud, until she'd finally fallen asleep, but Benji didn't need to know that.

Hazel and Zoey had skipped the celebratory dinner Benji and some of the other contestants had invited them to after they found out they'd made it to the next round. There'd be time enough to party once their place in the live shows was secured.

"Nice."

"You?"

"I wish. Dave stayed in my room last night because he's fighting with his roommate, and he snores like a drunken sailor."

"Oh, that's my partner," Zoey said. "Who is he again?"

Benji pointed to a white guy with sandy-brown hair piling his plate high at the buffet line.

"Can he sing?" Zoey asked. "I mean, like, for real?"

"I think he did all right in the group round yesterday? They were the ones with the light-up wands."

"Was that *his* idea? Martin was not amused."

Hazel remembered Dave now. His group had been disorganized and pitchy, and one of them, maybe Dave, had tripped on his robe. They were the last group to be put through, with Georgia arguing vigorously for them to get another chance because their musical track had cut out halfway through. Though Martin had argued that *all was fair between wizards*, he'd relented to the loud approval of the other contestants.

"I'm sure he won't be in costume today," Hazel said to Zoey. "You'll do great."

Zoey stared down at her egg-white omelet. "I wish they'd put *us* together. How come it's all boy-girl, anyway? JoJo Siwa got to dance with a girl on *Dancing with the Stars*."

"Good point," Bella said, sliding up to Benji. "You should say something to the producers."

41

"Maybe I will. Brooke's always telling me I should speak up more."

"Sing it, sister."

Zoey cringed at Bella's faux allyship, but Bella missed it.

"Morning, Bella," Hazel said in a friendly tone.

Bella's eyes tracked lazily to hers. "Oh, hi, Hazel. Missed you at dinner."

"I'm sure it was a blast."

"Maybe we should've gone?" Zoey said. She'd had a big case of FOMO the night before, texting Brooke, asking her if she thought they should socialize or rest. Brooke had been in the rest camp with Hazel, which Hazel was grateful for. She didn't need to deal with someone rolling in drunk at 2 a.m.

"Totally," Bella said. "Right, Benji?"

Benji gave her an easy smile. "You should both come next time."

"Maybe," Hazel said.

"Speaking of which," Bella said. "I got us on the list for Albert's tonight."

Albert's was a swanky club in Hollywood where celebrities went to party when they wanted to get photographed. Hazel hadn't been there in more than a decade, but she knew it had followed a typical Hollywood trajectory—making an initial splash, then sinking into obscurity, and rising like a phoenix when some of the latest crop of starlets decided it was hot again.

"Sounds great," Benji said. "Cool if Hazel and Zoey come too?"

Bella glanced at Hazel. "Yes, of course. The more the merrier."

"What do you think, Hazel?" Zoey asked nervously.

Zoey was obviously dying to go. When she wasn't texting Brooke she was obsessively checking TMZ and People.com for the latest celebrity comings and goings. Hazel got it. Until she came to L.A., Zoey had never seen a real celebrity—at least, not one who was known outside of country music. But Hazel was torn. She didn't want to go to Albert's but she didn't want to leave Zoey alone there either.

"Come on, Hazel," Zoey pleaded with her. "We have a day off tomorrow, right?"

"Yep, just the results in the morning," Benji said. "Plus, you only live once."

"True enough." Hazel relented. "Count us in."

Zoey clapped with an excitement that Hazel didn't feel, but she could worry about that later. Right now, it was time to go to work.

Their practice room was another conference room, with one long wooden table surrounded by standard-issue black office chairs. The cameras would show up at some point to record them practicing, but for now she and Benji were alone.

"What are you thinking for a song?" Benji asked, scrolling through his phone. They'd been emailed a list of approved selections earlier that morning.

"We could try 'Hallelujah,'" Hazel said. "I know a lot of people have covered it, but what if we did it on guitar? I think we could find a key that works well for both of us and make it fresh."

Benji cocked his head to the side. "Isn't that kind of sad? We don't want to go too depressing. Leave that to Lacey."

Lacey was a bald seventeen-year-old who'd finished her last round of chemo the day before she auditioned. She was sweet and talented, and Hazel was rooting for her even though she'd be stiff competition in the live rounds.

"The song is mostly about sex," Hazel said. "All that stuff about moving in you and drawing a hallelujah?"

"You're joking, right? I sang that song at my aunt Connie's funeral. That is all kinds of wrong."

"Don't worry. I bet you skipped the explicit verses. Everyone does. Unless Connie's friends were big Leonard Cohen fans they wouldn't have noticed."

"They're big bingo fans. Seriously. Like every time I visited her, she was playing bingo."

"Were you close?"

"Yeah, she was my dad's sister. We lost my dad when I was twelve. He was a musician too. Taught me guitar." His face lost all trace of the gloss it had when he was performing.

"That's hard. I'm sorry."

"I just wish he could see all this, you know? My dad wanted to perform full-time but he couldn't give up his day job because he had to take care of us. He'd be so happy to know I was doing this. I know it's cheesy, but I picture myself getting to the last round and dedicating my final performance to him."

"That's not cheesy, it's sweet."

"Thanks." He ran his hand through his hair. "Anyway, I think it's a good choice. Your voice is a lot like Julia Michaels's, and I can see her doing a kick-ass version of it."

Hazel felt a rush of warmth toward him. Julia Michaels was one of her favorite artists. "That's a really nice compliment."

"It's true. Let's give it a shot? I can pull up the lyrics on my—"

Someone knocked on the door.

"Come in," Hazel said.

Nick popped his head in, and Hazel felt her back straightening. She wasn't sure why, but Nick made her both nervous and like she had to have the best posture possible. Maybe it was because he walked around like he knew exactly how the show was going to go, which he probably did. Hazel guessed that he was keeping it to himself for sport.

"Hazel, Benji." Nick nodded hello as he entered. "Congrats on last night."

"Thanks, man. I'm glad it worked out."

"Your arrangement was great, Nick," Hazel said, meaning it. He might be a sourpuss, but he knew what he was doing musically.

"Thanks. We should talk about tonight's setup." He pulled a diagram from his back pocket and spread it on the conference table. "Gather round." He barely waited for Hazel and Benji to approach before he started tapping the diagram with a pencil. "This is where the key light will be coming from. I recommend you guys come onstage single file from stage left, and then spreading out, so the light can capture each of you before you reach your marks."

Hazel stood next to Nick so she could see where he was pointing. She could feel the heat from his body through the thin fabric of her dress. It was distracting, but Hazel did her best to focus. Nick's plan was good, but she had something else in mind. "I was thinking we should have two stagehands bring our guitars out and place them on individual stands. The mics and the stands could each be in a spot." Hazel pointed to the diagram to indicate where they'd be, her arm grazing Nick's in the process. "Then we step out of the darkness and into the spots. It'll create nice tension."

Nick cleared his throat. "I see."

"It would be pretty simple to execute. And I think it will be effective."

"Do you?"

"That's why I'm suggesting it."

"Perhaps." Nick jotted some notes on the diagram, then continued. "Now, the speakers are positioned to the right and left of the stage, angled to the audience. Make sure to avoid getting too close because of—"

"Feedback," Hazel said.

"I guess you don't need me."

"I'm sorry," Hazel said. But what was she apologizing for? Knowing something about their shared profession? "You were saying?"

"No, no, you seem to have this all in hand." As he rolled up the diagram, their arms came into contact again. Nick jolted away and then took a step away from Hazel for good measure. "You have two hours to rehearse. Another team needs the room by noon."

"Sure, no problem," Benji said smoothly. "Any tips?"

"Don't screw up." Nick walked out the door without so much as a good-bye or good luck.

"Weird energy, that dude," Benji said when the door clanged shut. "Glad he's gone."

"Agree," Hazel said, though she wasn't so sure. Inside, she was kicking herself for being such a know-it-all. Having Nick on her side would be an asset, but she seemed determined to put her worst foot forward every time she saw him. And then there was the way his skin felt touching hers . . . no, no, no. It had just been too long since she'd been with anyone. She needed to focus on repairing her professional relationship with Nick and forgetting that he smelled like a freshly made bed she wanted to crawl into.

She made a mental note to find a way to start over. But that would have to wait. If she and Benji didn't get this song right, there wouldn't be any need to apologize to anyone but herself.

Albert's was on Sunset in West Hollywood, and it was as swanky and exclusive as Hazel remembered, though the décor had changed completely since the last time she'd been there, as had, thankfully, the staff.

They were all still in their stage clothes and makeup, and when their Uber pulled up and they got out, several people in line started nudging each other and taking photographs of them on their phones. Not because they recognized them, not anyone but Benji and Bella, anyway, but because they *looked* like they must be someone with their perfect airbrushing and their glitzy outfits.

As they walked past the velvet rope of people waiting to get in, Hazel heard someone mention something about *Vanderpump*, while her friend disagreed and thought they must be some characters in the wide Kardashian orbit.

They were so far off that even Hazel found it funny, and she laughed when Zoey stopped and posed for photographs like she was on the red carpet.

"If you act it, you can make it happen," Zoey said.

"Fake it till you make it?" Hazel said.

"Precisely."

Hazel wondered about that—whether you could truly project your future and make it happen—but then the bouncer was asking for their names. After a moment's nervous searching, he found them on the list, and their foursome was swept past the velvet ropes then led to a roomy banquette where champagne and glasses sat waiting.

The club was large, loud, and full. Hazel did a quick inventory. A DJ was spinning Migos's "Modern Day" on a platform in the corner. Tall, pretty women flitted around in heels and trendy dresses, while men in tight suits vied for their attention. An A-list actress from a wildly popular Netflix show held court in the VIP section. Hazel had an odd sense of déjà vu but pushed it aside. She was living in the present now, and Zoey was right. If she acted like a winner, maybe she'd be one.

They settled in and the waitress popped the cork on the champagne, then poured them each a generous glass. Benji made a toast and they clinked, then Zoey drained hers quickly. She reached for the bottle and poured herself another before Hazel had even finished her first swallow. She downed that glass, too, then burst into tears, her red-carpet bravado gone in an instant.

"It wasn't that bad, Zoey," Hazel said, lying through her teeth as she rubbed Zoey's back, almost yelling over the thumping bass.

The truth was that Zoey and Dave's performance of Katy Perry's "Firework" had been abysmal. And while they were supposed to be judged individually, having a disastrous partner could sink you. Martin had told Zoey she was in "dangerous waters," and he'd nearly made Dave cry. Even Georgia had a hard time coming up with anything positive to say and had instead told Zoey that she was "beautiful."

"Besides, it was all Dave's fault," Hazel added. "They won't punish you for his mistakes."

"I'm going home, I know it."

"There's nothing you can do about it tonight. We have to wait to get the results tomorrow. So let's just try to have a good time, all right?"

"Oh-kkk-aay-aay."

Bella eyed Zoey unhappily across the table, then filled her glass from the bottle. She was dressed to kill in a white bandeau top, skinny jeans, and stilettos that Hazel wouldn't be able to walk three feet in without twisting an ankle. But Bella had sauntered around the stage with ease. Hazel couldn't blame Bella for her attitude. It was supposed to be a night of fun, not tears. And Bella and Cole had had a great performance of a classic Rolling Stones song, with Martin going so far as to say that they were "sailing through" this round. She had reason to celebrate.

"You just don't understand," Zoey almost wailed. "None of you do." She finished another glass and now the bottle of champagne was empty. Before Zoey's glass hit the table, a perky-breasted waitress in a skintight leather dress approached their table. "More drinks?"

"Yes," Zoey said through her tears. "Vodka shots. For all of us."

"And another bottle of champagne," Bella said. "The Cristal this time."

"Coming right up."

"I don't think shots are a good idea," Hazel said. And Cristal. That bottle was going to cost $1,000 at least. She didn't even want to think about how all of it was going to get paid for.

"I can't believe this is happening," Zoey said, slumped down with her elbows propping her up. "It's a nightmare."

"Come on, Zoey," Benji said, handing her a napkin. "I mean, it sucks that Dave forgot the words. And the cursing when he tripped on his dance move wasn't cool. I assume that'll all get bleeped out when it airs. But you sounded great. Even when he was shouting 'fuck' you were still harmonizing."

Zoey didn't seem reassured, just sad and drunk. But she'd finally stopped crying. "Thank you, Benji. You're smarter than you look." Zoey clasped a hand to her mouth. "Oh my god. I'm so sorry."

"It's fine."

Zoey stood up. "I'm going outside to call Brooke. Save my shot for me."

She bolted, and then it was just Bella, Benji, and Hazel left in the booth. In a short, swift move that Hazel had to admire, Bella sidled up to Benji, touching his arm while she complimented him on his performance.

It was a duet, Hazel wanted to say, but realized the danger of letting Bella know she was getting under Hazel's skin.

Their performance *was* spot-on. The judges loved the song choice, and Hazel and Benji had delivered a soulful, powerful performance that crackled with sexual energy.

Georgia fanned herself when it was over, and Keshawn had said they were "fire." Even Martin had complimented them effusively, and Nick had given her what she assumed was an approving head nod when she'd passed him backstage. No way they were getting cut.

"I was thinking about tomorrow," Bella purred. "We should totally go for a hike. Will Rogers Park is worth the hype if you've never been."

"No can do. A bunch of us are going to Harry Potter world with those tickets the prod co gave us. You're welcome to join. You, too, Hazel."

Hazel smiled to herself at Bella's disappointment. "Sure, why not? Zoey too?"

"Goes without saying."

"Bella?" A guy in his midthirties with short gelled hair approached their table. He was in a tight, expensive dark suit, and his shirt had one too many buttons open, revealing a tanned and waxed chest that was a total turnoff to Hazel.

Bella peeled herself away from Benji. "Oh, hey, bro. Benji, Hazel, this is my brother, Dan."

Hazel could see the resemblance. They both had the same calculating look about them.

"Come with me for a minute," Dan said. "There's a UTA guy I want you to meet."

Bella rose reluctantly, mouthing "I'll be back" to Benji, and then got swallowed up by the crowd.

A moment later, the waitress returned with four shots and a new bottle of champagne, but now there were only two of them. Hazel eyed the vodka, glistening in tall, skinny glasses. She hadn't done a shot in years, and vaguely remembered promising herself she'd never do one again. But one couldn't hurt, right?

Benji placed a glass in front of her. "Bottoms up." He clinked his glass against hers and waited for her to lift her shot in the air. When she did, he drained his, nodding to Hazel to do the same. Hazel followed suit, her face scrunched as she swallowed.

Damn, that hurt going down.

"You okay?" Benji moved closer. The salt-air smell he seemed to carry with him everywhere was mixed with a light cologne. It was seductive and inviting. Maybe this was why Bella had so much trouble keeping her distance.

Benji reached for a second shot, which he downed easily. Then he pulled Hazel toward him, so their faces were only inches away from one another.

Up close, his dark-brown eyes were unfocused, or maybe that was her.

"We were damn good today, Hazel." Benji traced the inside of her arm with his index finger, sending shivers down her spine.

"We were."

He leaned closer. They were an inch apart now. Hazel could feel his breath on her lips, warm and sweet. Part of her wanted to close the space between them, but something held her back. Instead of melting into the moment, her mind was racing through the reasons it was a bad idea. Like the competition, and Bella, who Hazel was pretty sure would *not* be happy about this turn of events. Like the fact that she'd lied about her age, and lots of other things too.

And Nick. She could see his disapproving gaze as clearly as if he was standing over them.

Hazel leaned away from Benji. This wasn't a decision she should be making when her mind was this crowded.

"I'm back," Bella announced loudly, her arms crossed. "What did I miss?"

Benji turned and smiled at Bella, then picked up the remaining shot, eyeing Hazel over the rim.

"We saved one for you," Benji said casually, handing it to Bella.

The moment was gone, and Hazel was safe.

Hallelujah, Hazel thought. *Hallelujah*.

Chapter Five

"Hazel?"

Hazel rolled over and groaned as she pressed her phone to her ear. Her head was pounding and she felt woozy. Shots. Fuck. Why had she agreed to that? She shouldn't be drinking at all, and she'd gone right to the atomic bomb of alcohol.

"Amber? Everything okay?"

"Girl, you cannot believe what Vern's been up to."

As Zoey moaned from her bed on the other side of the room, Hazel pulled a pillow over her head to block out the sunlight streaming through the shades they'd forgotten to close. She wasn't sure how either of them had gotten back from the bar. And did she almost kiss Benji? She was never doing shots again.

"Is he still a grade-one asshole?"

Amber snorted. Hazel could imagine her, sitting in the small plastic chair she kept outside her room, her sore feet propped up on the metal railing, a cigarette waiting to be lit. "You have no idea. He threw out all the stuff you got to make your room nice, just pitched it over the balcony and let it sit there on the concrete until garbage day. And now he's rented your place to some guy who puts on a *suit* to go to work."

All her stuff! Hazel knew she didn't have any right to expect that it wouldn't get thrown out after she left the way she did, but it still made her sad. She'd spent a lot of time rummaging through garage sales to find the perfect five-dollar lamp and that funky ten-dollar rug that only had one small, questionable stain on it. They'd made her depressing motel room home. And now they were trash.

"A man in a suit?" Hazel said. "What's he doing there?"

"Lord knows. I went right out and asked him if he had any idea what went on in the Motel California, and he got all snobby with me and said something about cheap rent."

"Takes all kinds."

"Don't I know it. You ain't upset about your stuff?"

"It's just stuff."

Zoey got up suddenly and rushed to the bathroom. Hazel could hear her retching through the partially closed door. Her own stomach lurched in response. She should probably go and see if Zoey was okay, but she couldn't make herself move.

"Vern sucks."

"He does."

"I covered you," Amber said with a long exhale of her cigarette.

"What?"

"I paid what you owed."

Hazel's throat felt tight. "You didn't have to do that."

"He was talking about filing a complaint. Like with the cops."

"Oh, fuck, really?"

"Yeah."

That would've been a disaster. "I'll pay you back. Just as soon as I can."

But how was she going to do that? They got a $150 per diem for the show, but that was it. She picked it up in an envelope from one of the assistants every morning. Whatever she'd managed to save over the last couple of days had evaporated last night. Today she was going to get an extra $450 for appearing in an episode that would air. She'd been planning on spending it on a new outfit. But she didn't need all that—or any of it—for clothes. She could wear something she already had. That meant she could give Amber six hundred and still have a bit left over. "How much was it?"

"Fifteen hundred."

"What? No."

"He said there were damages."

"But I gave a damage deposit. Five hundred dollars."

"I think Checkers may have chewed through some things?"

Ugh. He *was* always chewing on things. Just yesterday she'd had to pull him away from a dresser leg.

"Oh, Amber, I'm so sorry." Hazel didn't want to know how Amber had come up with the money. But she did know. "I hope it wasn't too awful."

"It was the dude who likes it when I dress like a nurse and pretend to check his prostate. I charged him double."

A laugh caught in her throat. "He was okay with that?"

"I told him I felt a lump and had probably saved his life."

She couldn't believe Amber had done that for her. "If I make it to the live rounds then I'll start making some real money. But I can give you six hundred."

"I'm so happy you made it onto the show."

"Thank you! They're paying me a bit now that I'm in the second round, so I can give that to you today."

"You sure, honey?"

"Absolutely. Can you get to Universal City? That's where we're staying. I've got something this morning but we're off this afternoon. Or I can drive to you. Though probably not a good idea for me to see Vern because I might commit a homicide."

"He wants to know where you are."

Like this day wasn't crap enough already. "What did you tell him?"

"Nothing, girl."

There was another particularly violent retch from the bathroom. "Okay, I've got to go. Text me later and I'll pay for your Uber, okay?"

"It'll be good to see you."

"I'm looking forward to it. And, Amber, thank you. Thank you so much for saving my ass."

"I'll shake my ass for you anytime, honey."

They hung up. Hazel rose and stood in her underwear and bra trying to figure out what to do. She looked out the window at the grounds below, swarming with witches and warlocks and harassed-looking parents. When she looked up, she caught some creep across the courtyard leering at her from his own window. She drew the curtains shut. She needed to stop and think for a minute.

Zoey retched again and Hazel gripped her stomach. "You okay, Zoey? You need help?"

"Maybe?"

"Coming!"

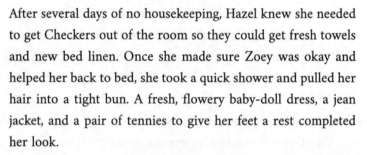

After several days of no housekeeping, Hazel knew she needed to get Checkers out of the room so they could get fresh towels and new bed linen. Once she made sure Zoey was okay and helped her back to bed, she took a quick shower and pulled her hair into a tight bun. A fresh, flowery baby-doll dress, a jean jacket, and a pair of tennies to give her feet a rest completed her look.

The jean jacket also worked as good camouflage for Checkers, who was excited at the prospect of getting out of the room. She hurried through the lobby and out to her car with him tucked against her chest. Palm leaves had gathered on its hood, giving it an abandoned look. She put Checkers in his cage, which she'd left on the backseat, cracked the windows, and swept the leaves off. The last thing she needed was some hotel cop on a power trip investigating her car too closely.

"I'll be back for you later, Checkers. Don't poop too much, okay?"

Checkers didn't respond. Most of the time she wasn't sure he even recognized his own name. But he did do the cutest double jump in his cage, which Hazel knew meant he was excited. Hazel's heart melted. If only the hotel allowed pets, this all would've been fine.

Maybe Amber would take him during the competition? She had a small house with a yard. But no, she'd done too much for Hazel already. She couldn't ask for anything more. She'd have to find another solution.

She locked her car and took a quick lap through the dining room, making sure to scoop up enough food to last her until dinner, then signed in for her per diem and extra payment. She felt guilty taking the cash knowing that she'd be spending it paying off her debts. But she hadn't signed anything promising to use it for the show. Paying back Amber was more important.

"Hey, Hazel, can I talk to you for a sec?"

Hazel looked up. Bella was standing in front of her, her usual confidence missing. "What's up?"

"I just wondered—is something going on with you and Benji?"

"You're asking because of last night?"

"Yeah."

"Not on my side."

Bella looked relieved. "You sure?"

Hazel checked herself. Did she want something with Benji? No. She'd pulled away even though he was attractive, and she'd had too much to drink. She liked Benji, but he was a flirt. Hazel had enough on her plate during the competition. She didn't need to get involved with the show's leading man. "I'm sure. But . . ."

"Yes?"

"Are you guys involved?"

Bella got that uncertain look about her again. "No, but, I

mean, we were hanging out a lot in the last couple of months at his TikTok house. When we both got on the show, it seemed like fate was putting us together."

Hazel couldn't believe she hadn't thought of this before. Bella and Benji already knew one another *before* the show. Bella had been harboring feelings for him for a while. That explained why she was so territorial about him so quickly. "I wouldn't want to stand in the way of fate."

Bella gave her a relieved smile. "I appreciate that."

"Good luck this morning."

"Thanks, you too."

She watched Bella walk away, thinking about the masks people wear. Before this conversation, she would've said that Bella was as cold as ice. But she was just as vulnerable as Hazel. The problem was, Hazel was nearly certain that Benji didn't want anything romantic with Bella. That, or he was a massive player. Either way, Bella was probably going to get her heart broken. But that wasn't Hazel's fault. *This* was why she wanted to keep it all business during the show. Even Bella's second-hand potential heartbreak was stressing her out.

Hazel checked the time, then left the breakfast area and walked toward the auditorium. She was early but she needed someplace where she could be alone with her thoughts. The day already felt chaotic, and the hangover didn't help.

As she got close, she could hear music. She opened the door as quietly as she could and was surprised to see Nick seated at the piano to the left of the stage. He was playing something she didn't recognize. She slipped into a seat to listen as his hands moved effortlessly across the keys. Then he started to sing.

"Which one of us ran?
What does it matter?
We flew in opposite directions,
That's all there is to say.

"Which one of us hurt the most?
You think you were sadder.
We had too much affection,
To ask the other to stay.

"But if I was courageous,
I would've run to you.
If I was brave,
I'd have ne-ver let you leave.

"And if I was courageous,
I would've run with you.
If I was a hero,
I'd have ne-ver let you go . . ."

Nick's singing was so intense Hazel found tears springing to her eyes. What was he doing as the musical director on this show? He should be a contestant. He should be a *star*.

He finished the song and she clapped wildly. Nick's head rose, startled that anyone was there. The tips of his ears turned pink as he stood quickly and walked toward Hazel. He was wearing a soft green sweater that matched his eyes, and the vulnerability on his face made him even more appealing. For once Hazel didn't feel like he had the upper hand.

"You're early," Nick said.

"And you're amazing. Did you write that?"

"It was on my first—and only—album."

"Who's it about? An ex, right? All good love songs are about exes."

"Not sure I agree with that."

"Okay, all good *sad* love songs." Hazel took out her phone. "What's it called? I'll download it immediately."

Nick winced. "You can't buy it. My album got shelved before it was released."

"What? Why?"

Nick glanced over her head as the doors clanged open loudly. "Sometimes dreams get snatched away right before they're about to become real."

"I get that."

Nick's eyes traced back to hers. She felt her heart quicken as their eyes locked, and an unfamiliar feeling spread through her. Something more than the idle flirtation with Benji. Something dangerous.

"Do you, Hazel?"

"I . . . I think . . ."

"Don't worry about it. I'll see you later, yes?" Before she could answer he walked away, passing Benji on his way up the stairs.

"This seat taken?" Benji said, smiling at her.

Hazel forced herself to smile in return, her mind still on Nick. "I saved it for you."

"Awesome." He plopped down next to her. "You look great."

She watched Nick over Benji's shoulder as he walked up the row of seats and left the room. She exhaled slowly. "I feel like crap. Whose idea was the shots?"

"Um, Zoey's I think?"

"I'll blame her for the first one but I'm definitely blaming you for the one after that."

"Fair enough."

The auditorium started to fill up and Hazel tried to concentrate. They were about to find out who was getting cut and who was staying. That should have her full attention. But what had Nick meant when he'd questioned whether she understood disappointment? And why had he looked at her like she was someone he knew too much about? Hazel couldn't be that blasé about a lost record, and she doubted Nick was either. What was he hiding?

Hazel was jostled into the present as Zoey and Bella joined them.

Zoey looked like Hazel felt, but now that Bella's confidence was back in place she seemed like she'd had a full eight hours of sleep and was as put together as if she had a personal glam team. And maybe she did. She'd pulled out a black Amex the night before to pay for the drinks, but Zoey had insisted they all contribute, which was easy for her to say because she came from money. Hazel would've been perfectly happy to take advantage of Bella's generosity, especially since the Amex had Bella's father's name on it.

When the auditorium was full and the cameras set up, Keshawn walked onto the stage and went through his hype routine. Applause, cheer, clap, smile. Hazel knew it was part of the package, but she wasn't feeling it today. Instead, she was extremely nervous that she was about to get cut.

But not as nervous as Zoey.

"Please don't send me home, please don't send me home,"

Zoey muttered under her breath, holding her fingers, arms, and legs crossed for good measure.

"Can I sit here?" Dave asked, pointing to the empty seat next to Hazel.

"No!" Hazel said, louder and more aggressively than she meant to, but honestly. That goofball was the reason Zoey was probably going home.

Dave held his hands up. "Okay, don't freak out."

"Don't trip trying to find a seat," Hazel said.

Bella snorted, and Benji cracked a smile, but Zoey just stared straight ahead.

"It'll be okay, Zo," Benji said.

"I just want them to announce it already. The waiting's killing me."

The judges arrived, waving for applause and settling into their seats. Then Keshawn started calling the contestants up in groups of five, asking some of them to take steps back or forward in a way that was intended to maximize the drama. Each minute felt like a thousand. Hazel's heart felt like it might explode.

When they were down to the last ten people, Hazel's phone started ringing insistently in her pocket. She snuck a peek. Shit. The name on the screen said "Jack."

"Who's Jack?" Benji asked, checking her screen.

Hazel turned her phone away. "No one." She sent the call to voice mail, but then it started ringing again. Hazel looked at the phone, knowing he'd keep calling until she answered.

"Hazel Fine!" Keshawn bellowed into his microphone.

"You can't take that call," Benji said with a note of panic. "You have to go up onstage."

Hazel looked at her phone again, the name staring back at her. She knew she should answer it, that it probably wouldn't matter if she was a few minutes late for her stage appearance because everything had already been decided, but she couldn't take that chance.

She sent the call to voice mail and tucked the phone away.

It was time to find out her future.

There'd be enough time later for the past.

Chapter Six

Hazel was out for a run in the lunchtime heat, grimacing as she pounded the streets of Universal City. She hadn't exercised in ages and while her lungs were angry with her, her legs fell into a familiar rhythm that propelled her forward.

After getting the word that she'd advanced to the next round, Hazel had returned to her room with the intention of taking a nap. But the excitement of making it to the live shows had made that impossible, hence the running. She'd been out for about twenty minutes when her cell phone dinged with a message from Zoey. She stopped and read it.

Where are you? Don't forget that we're going to Harry Potter world! Meet up in the lobby in an hour.

Harry Potter world? She had a faint memory of agreeing to it last night, but it wasn't how Hazel wanted to spend her afternoon off. She wanted to finish her run, have a shower, and then, after she gave Amber the money she owed her, she planned to watch old seasons of *The Sing Along* on her phone.

Please? Zoey texted before Hazel could answer. *It'll be fun! We need 2 celebrate!*

Hazel wiped the sweat from her brow. Zoey had made it through to the next round by some miracle. Hazel was glad she wasn't going home yet. They *should* celebrate with something fun. Plus, when was the next time she was going to have VIP passes to Harry Potter world? Never, that's when.

She tapped back, *Sure!* and received a *:)* in reply.

Change of plans . . . Hazel texted to Amber. *Can you meet me at Harry Potter world? I have your money. I'll email you a ticket and meet you by the entrance?*

They'd each been given two tickets by the production company so she might as well share the wealth. Amber needed a day at Harry Potter world way more than she did.

We're off to see the wizard . . . Amber wrote back. *C u there.*

Hazel ran back to the hotel, then mulled over what she'd wear as she quickly showered. She decided on jean shorts and a pink-and-white checkered shirt. Paired with white tennies, it was a cute look. She slicked on some lip gloss and twisted her hair into a side braid that curled over her left shoulder. She looked twenty, but that was the point. She stuck her tongue out at herself in the mirror and left.

Everyone was already gathered by the sliding exit doors by the time Hazel got there—Zoey, Benji, Bella, Lacey, and Cole, the fourteen-year-old guitar wunderkind. He was with his mother, a larger-than-life woman wearing a T-shirt that said "Cole's Mama."

Benji gave her a friendly wave as she walked up to the group.

Zoey grabbed her hand. "Benji specifically asked for you," she squealed in a pathetic attempt at a whisper that Benji and the others clearly overheard. "I told Brooke all about it. She checked him out on TikTok and totally ships you two."

Hazel sank in her shoes. She *never* should've told Zoey about the almost kiss with Benji. Especially not now that she'd expressly told Bella she wasn't interested in him. And was that Nick walking past them, smirking like he'd overheard Zoey?

Hazel tried desperately to catch Nick's eye but he just kept on walking.

"Um," she said, hopefully loud enough for him to hear, "there's nothing to—"

"Uh-huh," Zoey said with a wink. "Whatever you say, Hazel."

Hazel watched the back of Nick's head for the second time that day. She shouldn't care what he thought about her. Like Mr. Darcy, she was sure he never thought about her except to find fault, but it bothered her just the same.

"Oh," Zoey said, "by the way, speaking of Brooke. She was able to get time off from work so she's coming to see me tonight! You don't mind if she stays with us, do you?"

Hazel swallowed hard. The room barely fit her, Zoey, and Checkers.

"Not at all," she managed.

"Shall we?" Bella said, but it was more of an order. She was wearing a black jumpsuit that gave her an air of authority, and Hazel could tell that she relished being their de facto leader.

"Lead the way," Hazel said.

"Benji, sit with me on the bus. I want to tell you about—" She dropped her voice to a whisper.

Benji obeyed with a rueful glance at Hazel. Hazel shrugged like it didn't bother her, because it didn't, then fell into step with Zoey and Lacey, who were chatting about which rides they'd do first.

"How many times have you been to Harry Potter world?" Zoey asked Lacey.

"Twelve!" Lacey said proudly. "Make-A-Wish Foundation is the bomb. They sent me here so many times. I even went three times after I was in remission. They don't check," Lacey added, laughing.

Zoey's eyes widened. "That's, um . . ."

"Great, right? Even though I puked on the Forbidden Journey a bunch of times. Not sure if it was the chemo or the drop. Whatevs. Let's go!" She led them onto the bus, Hazel and Zoey exchanging wild glances behind her.

Hazel and Zoey found seats in the middle of the bus and sat down. Hazel was glad she'd come. A day of popcorn and fantasy sounded like the perfect recipe to distract her from the next step of the competition—their final solo number.

"Hang on," called a deep British voice as the engine idled. "One more for you."

They peered out the window as Martin approached the bus with Sarah Baines in tow. Sarah was a bluegrass singer with strawberry-blond hair and aqua eyes, and a voice that belied her petite build. But she also suffered from crippling nerves, which made her performances shaky. Everyone was surprised when she hadn't been cut after the duets because only Dave had screwed up worse.

"Excellent work this morning, Sarah," Martin said, patting her on the shoulder at the top of the stairs. "Have fun, children." He addressed the rest of them with a wave and got off the bus.

The driver closed the door and Sarah walked down the aisle to an empty seat.

"Sucking up much?" Cole called.

"Sucking something," Bella said from the back, and Hazel watched Sarah's face burn crimson.

The ride to Harry Potter was less than ten minutes, but Lacey insisted they sing, then broke into Britney Spears's "Circus," with the rest of them joining her one by one. The bus driver was not amused.

They drove up the hill to Universal Studios, passing a long line of palm trees that had lights strung around their trunks, then parked in the bus parking lot. They chatted happily as they went through the park entrance, past the massive silver globe that hung over a fountain, and made their way to the gates of Harry Potter world.

"Over here," said a familiar voice. "Hazel, it's me. By the butterbeer!"

"Um, Haze, someone's calling you," Zoey said, pointing.

Amber was standing next to an elderly man. She was holding a gigantic mug of the frozen drink, and Hazel almost didn't recognize her—she was dressed in pedal pushers and a tank top, and her hair was pulled back from her face and slicked into a ponytail. Six-year-old Theo was hiding behind her legs.

"I'll be right back." Hazel darted off to meet her friend. When Hazel got to her, Amber held up an index finger, signaling to Hazel she needed another minute with the old dude. Hazel hung back until she saw the man retreat. "Thanks for coming."

"No problem." Amber reached behind her and patted Theo on the head. "You remember Hazel, buddy?"

"I'm going to see Dumbledore!" he said, peeking around his mom and giving Hazel a wide grin. He was a towhead with bright-blue eyes. His two front teeth were missing.

"That's exciting!" Hazel said. "Who was that guy?"

Amber rolled her eyes. "A customer who recognized me even though I'm—" She motioned to herself. "Can you believe he wanted me to meet him later?"

"Ugh, I'm sorry."

"Girl, I'm used to it. Only, not usually around Theo."

Theo poked his head out again. "I'm going to get a wand!"

"You bet you are, buddy," Amber said.

Hazel smiled. "Here's your money. You're truly an angel." She handed over the wad of cash, which Amber slipped into her purse.

"Any time. Who's that cute Asian dude checking you out over there?"

Hazel checked over her shoulder. Benji was staring at them. Or more likely at Amber, who was breathtaking with all her usual makeup and pleather stripped away. "That's Benji. Very talented. But don't worry, I'll crush him."

"Not if he crushes you first. He's staring at your ass."

"He flirts with everyone. Hey, any chance you want to spend the day with us?" Hazel said. "It could be fun."

"We are here to have fun!" Theo announced.

"You sure you want me and my kid trailing along after you?"

"I'd like nothing better. Come on. It'll be great."

Amber agreed, and they walked back to the group together.

Hazel enjoyed the puzzled stares the others gave them as Hazel introduced Amber vaguely as an old friend. Let them wonder about how she knew Amber. No matter what they could be thinking, it wouldn't be anywhere close to the truth.

Four hours later, everyone's feet were aching. They'd had ice cream at Florean Fortescue's, bought overpriced wands at Ollivanders (except for Hazel), drunk way too much butterbeer, and ridden every ride at least three times (also except for Hazel, who was longtime scared of roller coasters, though she'd blamed a rumbly stomach).

Amber and Theo had left an hour earlier, after Theo threw up his second butterbeer.

"Time to pack it in, kids," Bella said. She made a remarkably good camp counselor, weaving them through the crowds and assigning them to groups when they needed to be. Hazel admired the way she took charge and how the others naturally listened to her. No one had ever listened to Hazel like that in her whole life.

It had been a good day, but Hazel was ready to leave. She was tired from the run, her hangover came and went in waves, and she'd developed a sunburn on the back of her calves.

But then Benji was beside her, grasping her wrist. "C'mon. One more ride with me before we go." He pointed to the roller coaster Hazel had been avoiding all day.

"I don't like roller coasters."

"Flight of the Hippogriff is a baby coaster." He laced his fingers through hers. "It doesn't even go upside down."

That didn't matter to Hazel; she was terrified of the drop. Online stories of faulty safety belts and riders getting scalped had made her swear off scary rides. And Bella's eyes were roving between Benji's and Hazel's hands in a way that made Hazel pull hers away. But if she said no, everyone would know she was afraid.

She could do this. "Okay, let's go!"

"I'm coming too!" Bella said. "One last ride will be fun."

Benji's grin was easy. "The more the merrier. Right, Hazel?"

She wasn't sure what he was suggesting, but Hazel was fine with Bella joining them. "That's my motto!" she said, trying to signal to Bella that she truly didn't care about being alone with Benji. Bella looked unsettled, so, for good measure, Hazel stepped ahead of them as they walked to the ride. Once there, they moved to the front of the line by flashing their VIP passes. The ride operator indicated for Hazel and Benji to take the first row, but Benji held Hazel back.

"She's a little nervous. Please put us somewhere safe."

The operator smirked, then nodded them toward the middle.

Bella tugged on Benji's arm. "Sit here, Benj, with me."

"Okay, Hazel?"

"Of course. I'll be fine." She turned and walked to the empty seat in the middle of the train. As Hazel lifted her leg to climb into the car, she lost her balance.

Someone grabbed her arm, steadying her. "Whoops-a-daisy!"

Hazel grimaced at Daisy's stupid catchphrase as she turned to the man who was holding her. It was Nick. He was wearing a blue madras short-sleeved shirt and khaki shorts, with his Wayfarers tucked into the vee of his shirt. The top two buttons were undone, and Hazel couldn't help but sneak a peek at his chest, which was tanned and had a sprinkling of dark hair across it.

"You okay?" he asked.

Hazel met his eyes, which glinted with amusement. "I'm fine." Hazel pulled her arm free of his and smoothed her hair back, then stopped herself. Why did she care if Nick saw her hot and sweaty? Even if he looked great and way more approachable in his day-off clothes. "What are you doing here?"

"Riding the hippogriff." He indicated that she should get in, and she did so more carefully this time. He sat down next to her, and his left leg touched her right one, skin on skin. He felt as warm as she did.

"You say so." She pulled the lap bar down tightly and closed her eyes to collect her thoughts. She was about to ride a roller coaster for the first time since she was a kid, and she had to do it with Nick. She didn't care if Benji saw her fright, but she didn't want to show that kind of weakness to Nick. But she couldn't help it.

"You afraid of roller coasters?"

She forced her eyes open. "Of course not. Only kids are afraid of roller coasters." She wished she sounded more convincing as the ride started its slow climb up the track.

"Don't worry," Nick said close to her ear. "I won't let anything happen to you."

She turned as his breath tickled her neck, their noses grazing. She pulled back, trying not to panic as the cranking noise increased around them.

They were halfway up the track, the park laid out before them, and her heart was pounding. She didn't care what Nick thought of her anymore, she couldn't watch. She squeezed her eyes shut. The drop was coming, the drop was coming, the drop was . . .

The world whooshed away, and she grabbed for something to hold on to. The nearest thing was Nick's hand, but again, she didn't care. She squeezed it tight as the car rocketed around the track, knocking her head back and forth as she counted to a hundred.

And then the ride was slowing, slowing, almost stopped.

Hazel opened her eyes and pulled her hand away from Nick's as the car entered the station. She was afraid to look at him.

The car rattled to a stop and the restraint bar lifted automatically. "Please exit to the left," the ride operator said.

Hazel was relieved. That meant she could get out without making eye contact. She stood and started to climb out. But before she could put her feet on the ground, Nick's amused voice was in her ear and his hands were on her elbow and back, helping guide her.

"Wouldn't want you to trip again."

She wished she could control the blush that was creeping up her neck. She stepped out quickly, almost running into Benji and Bella.

"What did you think?" Benji said, eyeing Nick behind her.

Nick patted her shoulder. "It was fun, right, Hazel?"

Hazel plastered on a smile and kept her eyes fixed on Benji. "Superfun."

It was after seven when they pulled up to the hotel.

Hazel was subdued on the ride back, thinking about what had happened with Nick and what he could possibly have been doing there. Maybe he simply loved Harry Potter world, but that didn't seem to track with what Hazel knew about him.

Zoey chatted excitedly about what a great time they'd had and how excited she was to see Brooke, who'd arrived safely at the hotel half an hour before. She was too wound up to notice Hazel's silence until they got back to the hotel.

"You okay, Haze?" Zoey asked as they were climbing off the bus. "You haven't said anything since we left the park."

"Yeah, I'm fine. Who's that waving to you over there?" Hazel pointed to a woman in her midtwenties with short blond hair who was wearing a flowery baby-doll dress and combat boots.

Zoey turned and squealed. "Brooke! Baby!" She ran to her and leaped into her arms.

Hazel watched their reunion with a smile on her face. Even if their hotel room would be crowded that night, it was worth it to see Zoey so happy.

"Hazel! Come meet Brooke!"

Hazel waved as her phone rang in her hand. It was Jack—again. What the hell? Three calls in one day? All of her instincts screamed at her to send it to voice mail, but what if it was an emergency?

"I've got to take this," Hazel called to Zoey, then answered the call.

"Did someone die?"

Her father clucked his tongue in disapproval. "This isn't

a game, my dear. I'm not interested in playing cat and mouse with you."

Hazel inched farther away from Zoey and Brooke, who were staring at her with curiosity. Hazel waved to them to go into the hotel and turned away. "Seriously, though, why are you calling?"

"You know why. You still haven't signed those papers."

"That's why?"

"Yes, of course."

"No 'Hi, how are you?' No 'How's your life going?'"

"Don't take that tone with me, young lady. It's very important that—"

Hazel ended the call then turned off her phone for good measure. She held it to her chest, her heart pounding, adrenaline coursing through her the way it always did when she had to talk to one of her parents. She hated that they still had this power over her.

She took a couple of slow breaths, then looked for Zoey and Brooke, but they were already gone. The bus had pulled away and everyone else had walked into the hotel.

Hazel went through the sliding doors, her heart still beating too quickly. She glanced around the lobby to make sure Zoey and Brooke hadn't waited for her. There was no sign of them, but the bar was open. Hazel decided she needed a stiff drink.

The bar was nearly empty, with one lone bartender and Kenny G on the sound system. She ordered a whiskey cocktail, charging it to her room using the twenty-dollar daily limit, then took a seat on a leather-covered stool and ran through the events of the day as she sipped her drink.

Amber. The money. Nick. The way his hand had felt when she'd clutched it, his breath on her neck. Her father. Before *The Sing Along*, her days had had a faded sameness to them. Wake up, work, go home exhausted, feed Checkers, sleep. Now each day was its own drama, with too many episodes to keep count.

She raised her hand to signal the bartender for another. This one would be on Zoey.

"Careful with those things, darlin'," said a slurred voice next to her. It was Georgia. Normally so composed, she was a wreck. Bloodshot eyes, lipstick smeared on her teeth, her cowboy hat askew.

"Are you okay?"

She ignored Hazel's question. "That gold stuff." She pointed at Hazel's freshened whiskey glass. "It's like honey going down. Down, down, down." She leaned in, steadying herself on the bar. Her breath was combustible. "Just watch yourself, doll. That honey can sting."

Hazel felt frozen, unsure of what to do. They were alone except for the bartender, but Hazel didn't want anyone to see Georgia like this. She was sure the woman would be mortified if she remembered this exchange in the morning. What could she do? Should she try to help Georgia to her room? No, they'd have to go to the lobby for that.

"Is there someone I can call, Georgia? To help you?"

"No one can help me."

A lump formed in Hazel's throat at the desperation in Georgia's voice. She tried to form a sentence that would convey her empathy, but before she had a chance, Georgia's assistant swept up with a determined expression on her face and took Georgia by the arm.

"Time to go," she said, giving Hazel a worried look.

"I won't say anything," Hazel said. "Don't worry."

The assistant thanked her as she maneuvered Georgia away from the bar. She slipped sunglasses onto Georgia's face and escorted her out of the hotel with a quiet efficiency that spoke of long practice.

Hazel turned back to her drink, feeling sad and thinking about how dangerous fame could be. She pushed the glass away.

It was time to shut this day down before she made any other mistakes.

Chapter Seven

Hazel woke up with a start, sitting bolt upright in bed. "Shit!"

"What?" Zoey said groggily. Brooke was snoring lightly beside her.

"I forgot Checkers in the car." Hazel jumped out of bed and slipped on a pair of flip-flops, not even bothering to change out of her pajamas. She was a terrible person. Who left their animal in the car overnight? People who ended up on the news with a dead child, that's who. Not that a dead bunny was newsworthy, but still.

Hazel hurried through the lobby, hoping she wouldn't run into anyone she knew. She made it out of the hotel and into the parking lot without incident. When she saw her car, she almost broke into a run. *Please, please, please let Checkers be okay!*

She yanked open the door and was hit with an awful smell.

Was Checkers dead? No, he'd just pooped up a storm out of anger over being abandoned.

"Oh, Checkers! I'm so, so sorry."

Checkers turned his listless head toward Hazel. She rubbed the fur behind his neck in the way she knew he liked, then reached into the front seat where she had a couple of water bottles stashed. She filled Checkers's bowl. He hobbled over to it.

"I forgot to bring anything for you to eat. Wait. Wait there."

Checkers wasn't going anywhere. He could barely drink the water in his bowl.

Hazel searched frantically for something she could feed him. Her eyes came to rest on the palm tree above. It was green. It must be okay, right? She'd flown out of the room without her phone, so she couldn't check. But the chances of it being poisonous were slim.

She jumped in the air, reaching for a leaf. She missed, then jumped higher, catching a large frond, and holding on for dear life.

Crack!

It came down, but so did the branch it was attached to, landing on her sad car and denting the hood.

"Dammit!"

"Can I be of assistance?" Martin said.

Hazel turned around slowly. Martin was smirking at her from a few feet away.

How long had he been watching her? And, crap, she was in her pajamas. She reached her hands up quickly and gathered her hair together, twisting it into a knot at the base of her neck. "I'm fine."

"Oh, I know you are." Martin gave her that same appraising

look from her audition. "But what, pray tell, are you doing?"

"Feeding my bunny?"

"Is that a euphemism?"

"No." She stepped aside so he could see Checkers lying pathetically in the backseat. "The hotel doesn't accept pets, so I had to keep him in my car, and I realized this morning that I forgot to feed him last night." Her words tumbled out. There was no point in lying. What else could she possibly say that would explain her presence in the parking lot at this hour and in this state?

"Ah."

"I'm not in trouble, am I?"

"It looks like your car might be."

"It's on its last legs anyway."

Martin smirked again, but it didn't seem to be connected to what Hazel had said. She wondered what he was doing in the far reaches of the parking lot this early in the morning.

"Can I give you a bit of advice, Hazel?"

"Yes, of course."

Martin took a step toward her. He was close enough that she could smell his cologne, too strong and sharp. She tried not to wrinkle her nose. At this distance she could see that he'd probably had as much Botox as Georgia; his face was unnaturally tight and shiny.

"You want to win *The Sing Along*, don't you?"

"Yes."

"You're talented. Of course, so many of you are."

"Thank you."

"Some contestants can benefit from a bit of extra coaching, though."

Hazel felt as if she was sinking into the ground. "Contestants like me?"

"Perhaps." He stroked his chin. "It's against the rules of course, so I'd need to be assured of your discretion."

What was he asking her? "I can keep a secret," Hazel said slowly.

"Yes, yes, I'm not surprised by that at *all*." He took another step toward her. "If you want my help, you only have to ask."

And now there was no ambiguity between them. Martin didn't want to help her get better; he wanted something from her. Hazel felt frozen. If she'd truly been twenty-two, she probably would've done something dramatic like vomit on his shoes. Her stomach was roiling, her aversion to him was so strong. But Hazel had been through a thing or two since her twenty-second birthday, and she didn't break so easily now.

"I'll keep that in mind," she said, trying to keep her voice neutral.

"Excellent." Martin squeezed her arm quickly then released it. "Good luck with your rabbit."

Hazel waited for Martin to get twenty feet away, then turned and grabbed the leaf from the top of her car. She shoved it at Checkers, her hands shaking, her mind like a race car. It had been a while since Hazel had been in a situation like this, but it wasn't the first time she'd been propositioned inappropriately by a powerful man in Hollywood.

The question was: What, if anything, was she going to do about it?

"Any thoughts on what you want to sing tonight, Hazel?" Nick asked later that morning in one of the smaller rehearsal spaces. Today's performance was the last of the audition rounds. Each of the remaining contestants would perform a song, solo, and then the judges would evaluate their overall performance and let them know individually whether they'd made it onto the live shows.

"I had thought of doing 'Lover' by Taylor Swift, but now ... I don't know."

Nick's face lit up. He was wearing his standard-issue black T-shirt and jeans, though he'd gotten some sun the day before at HPW, which pinked his cheeks and reddened the bridge of his nose. It suited him, Hazel thought. Made him more approachable somehow. "On the guitar?"

"Yes."

"I think that's a great choice for you."

"Really?"

"You'll be able to make something more of it that way. Maybe tighten up the rhythm in certain places. With your voice, it will be very seductive."

That's exactly what Hazel was worried about. Given her exchange with Martin in the parking lot, she didn't want to be singing about letting someone take her out and take her home, and cooing about how he was her lover. What had he meant about her and secrets? Did he know something, or was she being paranoid? Was that simply his usual pickup line? Either way, she didn't want to find out.

"Maybe I should do something else." Hazel walked to the credenza and picked up the list of approved songs that had been left there by an assistant. "What about an Olivia Rodrigo song?"

Nick's forehead creased. His usual brusque tone was gone, replaced by concern. "Half the contestants are doing something by her, including Bella."

"Is that a problem?"

"She's your biggest competition in terms of talent, but also genre. You should avoid covering the same artists if you can."

"Good advice."

"Why don't you want to do 'Lover'?" Nick asked, his tone softer. Kind.

"Not feeling it, I guess."

"Did something happen?"

Hazel glanced away from his penetrating gaze. Why was Nick the only person who could really see her in this whole competition? "No."

"Are you sure? You can tell me."

Hazel put the song list down. "It's nothing, Nick. I'll do the Taylor song."

Nick stayed silent, and Hazel could feel his eyes on her. Something about the intensity of his concern made her throat tighten. But no. No. She wasn't going to cry in front of Nick. This was ridiculous. *Nothing* had happened. Martin had made a pass at her. It wasn't the first time or the last time that was going to occur.

Hazel plastered on her best smile. "Should I do a run-through for you? I thought I might change the key."

Nick watched her, unsure about her swing of emotions. "That could work."

Hazel's face cracked so wide it was starting to hurt. "Why so serious? Do I need to take you back to Harry Potter world? Clutch your hand like a baby on another roller coaster?"

Nick laughed uneasily. "So, you admit you were scared."

"Never."

When Hazel got to the lunchroom after rehearsal, Benji beckoned her to his table with a wide smile. Hazel hesitated. She and Benji hadn't been alone since their almost kiss at the bar the other night, and Hazel still couldn't figure out what Benji's level of interest was. He'd taken her hand at Harry Potter world but had also seemed more than happy to spend much of the day with Bella. But she was hungry and she liked Benji. She dismissed her whirring brain, grabbed a prepared salad, and sat across from him.

"How's rehearsal going?" Benji asked.

"Pretty good, I think."

"What are you singing?"

"No way!"

"What?"

"You asked me to sit with you so you could get the scoop on what I was singing tonight?"

Benji held his hand to his heart. "I would never."

"Uh-huh. What are you singing, then?"

"Haven't decided yet."

"Look who's playing games now." Hazel opened the salad container and speared some lettuce with a fork. The salad was plain and boring, but after the pig-out the day before she needed something green.

"Just having a bit of fun."

"Gotcha."

Benji leaned back in his seat. "You're so calm."

"I am?"

"Seems that way to me."

"You should see the inside of my brain."

"Chaos?"

"Not sure if you saw me on that coaster, but it's a good approximation."

"I tried to." Benji's eyes were dancing with amusement. "But you wanted to sit with Nick."

"What? No. He was the last person I wanted to sit with."

"So, I didn't see you holding his hand?"

Hazel's face burned. Benji had seen that? "It was an involuntary response to fear. I was terrified. I grabbed the closest thing there was because I thought I was going to die. But honestly? I was so embarrassed. I mean, Nick? No. No, no, no."

Benji looked satisfied, but Hazel felt uncomfortable. Nick had been nice enough not to mention that moment during rehearsal earlier. And she'd had the feeling that if she'd told him about Martin, he would've tried to help. Why was she denying him so vehemently?

"I'm glad I don't have anything to worry about there," Benji said.

"Oh, I . . ."

Benji checked his watch. "Hey, I've got to go. But I'll see you at the performances tonight?"

"Of course."

"Promise you'll watch me?"

"Sure, but why?"

He gave a small shrug with his left shoulder. "I like knowing you're in the audience. That there's someone rooting for me."

"I'll be there," Hazel said gently.

"Good," Benji said. "Laters."

"Laters."

Hazel walked onto the stage with her guitar, planted her feet firmly, and avoided the heated stare Martin was giving her from the judges' platform.

The audience hushed, the lights turned low, while Hazel stood in the glow of the floodlights. She was wearing a simple red dress she'd borrowed from Zoey even if it wasn't her signature color. She could use all the power she could steal.

Hazel strummed the opening chords and a few of the other contestants clapped in appreciation. Benji nodded encouragingly from the front row. Behind him was a sea of faces. Sarah Baines, nervous and twitchy. Cole and his mother looking confident. Bella frowning, but maybe that was just the light. Only Nick was missing, but he was often busy backstage during the performances, making sure all the musical cues were set.

Hazel started to sing, and she knew immediately that it was going to be a good night. Her voice had the right throaty tone to it, and she turned the song into an anthem and a love song rolled into one. When she got to the part about leaving the Christmas lights up until January, green and red lights flashed behind her in the shape of a forest of trees and she could see the colors wend their way through the audience's faces.

She sang the next verse with confidence, getting lost in the song. When she came to the spoken verse, she let her guitar swing loose and addressed the audience, asking them to stand. They did and took up her clap, singing along when she resumed the chorus like it was her concert, and they were her fans.

When she was finished, they burst into applause. They'd loved it. Keshawn walked onto the stage, bowing to her, and Hazel laughed freely for the first time in days.

"Fantastic, Hazel," Keshawn said. "Fantastic. What say you, Georgia?"

Georgia blew Hazel a kiss from the judges' stand. She was doing her best to hide the hangover she must've been nursing, but Hazel could tell that she had a raging headache from the way she moved tenderly around her seat. "That was brilliant, Hazel, darlin'. Taylor would be proud. In fact, I'm going to send her your clip. Wouldn't be surprised if you heard from her."

Hazel's heart swelled. "Thank you, Georgia."

"Martin?"

Hazel turned to him nervously. He held his hands out to her and then gathered them together like he was praying. Probably for her to sleep with him, but in that moment she didn't care. She'd done it. She'd done her best. It was out of her hands now.

"What can I say, Hazel Fine?" Martin said. "That was your best performance yet, and one of the best performances of the competition." Martin sounded genuine, but Hazel knew better than to count on that. It didn't matter. He'd said what he said and that was all she could go on for now.

Hazel tripped off the stage feeling light and happy.

"You were amazing, Hazel!" Zoey said in the wings, where she was standing next to Brooke. She looked drawn in the blue lights, and terrified. "Tay Tay will *die* when she hears that."

"You'll be great, Zoey. Don't worry."

"You got this, Zo," Brooke said, giving her hand a squeeze.

"Zoey Johnson! Come to the stage, please."

Zoey gave one last terrified look to Hazel, then disappeared through the curtain to an explosion of applause. Zoey was popular in the competition, nice to everyone, and in a class of her own as the only female country singer left.

Hazel stood in the wings, watching Zoey as she made her way to the microphone. She looked adorable in a rhinestone-encrusted red number that was a tribute to Dolly. The dress, Hazel approved of. The song choice, not so much. Hazel had tried to talk Zoey out of attempting Dolly's version of "I Will Always Love You." It was a big song, even the way Dolly did it, and Zoey's voice, while sweet and pure, wasn't up to the task.

She cracked in the chorus, and it was all downhill from there. Hazel ached for her friend as she watched her suffer through the judges' comments ("oh, honey, this is not your night," and "disaster") and stood ready to console her when Zoey rushed off the stage into Brooke's arms.

But there was no consoling Zoey.

"It's okay, Zo," Brooke said, stroking her hair. "It's just a singing competition."

Hazel could tell that was the wrong thing to say. Brooke seemed as nice as Zoey, with her white-blond pixie cut and her almond-colored eyes, but she didn't get how Zoey felt about singing.

"You know they don't make their decisions based on one performance," Hazel said. "It's the whole package. And you have that, you do."

"Hear that, Zo? Listen to Hazel, okay? Please?"

Zoey sniffed. "Okay."

"Let's go get that dinner we talked about, all right?"

Zoey blew her nose. "You want to come, Hazel?"

They were supposed to stick around until the end of the taping, but sadly, Hazel didn't think anyone would care if Zoey left. "You guys go on ahead without me. Have fun. We'll hang tomorrow."

Brooke gave her a grateful smile, and she and Zoey left hand in hand by one of the emergency exits. Hazel couldn't walk back into auditorium while Cole was singing, so she walked to the green room.

The Sing Along had shot all ten seasons in this venue, and you could tell from the large windowless room. The couches were discarded from some earlier renovation, and one of the walls was full of signature scrawls from the famous and not-so-famous cast members. The opposite wall was covered with framed headshots of past winners.

Hazel sank onto a couch and closed her eyes. She was tired. The last few days were a lot to process. But she felt good about the night. If she made it through to the first live round, she was finally going to make some money. Enough to start paying off her credit card. But first, she needed to pay back the rest of what she owed Amber.

"Pleased with yourself, sweetheart?" Martin said, standing over her.

Hazel's eyes shot open. "How come you're not onstage?"

"They needed to reset."

Hazel stood. "I'll be getting back to the audience, then. Don't want to miss the other performances." She tried to walk past Martin but he gripped her arm, holding her back. "Please let me go."

"You never gave me an answer."

"What was the question?"

"Whether you were willing to do whatever it takes to make it on the show?"

Hazel looked him directly in the eyes, trying to mask her fear. "Yes, I am."

"Excellent. Shall we start rehearsals tonight—"

"Everything okay in here, Hazel?" Nick said. He was standing in the doorway with his arms crossed over his chambray shirt, anger radiating from him.

Martin dropped his hand. "Everything is fine, Nicholas. You're not needed here."

"That right? I'll wait to hear that from Hazel."

Hazel pulled away from Martin and walked over to Nick. "I'm fine, thank you." She shook her head imperceptibly as she talked, indicating that she wasn't okay.

Nick's face hardened, but he didn't seem surprised. "We're resuming taping in five. You should get back on set, Martin."

Martin clucked his tongue. "Yes, thank you, I do not need you to micromanage me." Martin walked to the door, but Nick was blocking his way out.

Hazel shook her head again slightly, willing Nick to understand that she didn't want this confrontation. Nick blinked twice, then moved aside.

"Cheers, then, Hazel," Martin said, a statement, not a question.

He left and Hazel released a long slow breath. "Thanks for that," she said to Nick.

"That man is a creep. Watch out for yourself around him, all right? He can be . . . vindictive if he doesn't get what he wants."

"Are you telling me to sleep with him?"

"Of course not."

Hazel put her hands on her hips. "What then?"

"I just thought—"

"I'll handle it."

Nick's expression went flat. "I'm sure you will." He turned on his heel and left.

Hazel wanted to call after him, to explain that she truly was grateful for his intervention, but he had to understand where she was coming from. What was the point of telling her that she was screwed if she didn't sleep with Martin? She could figure that out for herself. What she needed was a plan to avoid having to go through with it, but she couldn't come up with one. All her hope was draining away.

The lights flashed overhead, announcing that filming was about to resume. Hazel forced herself to leave the green room, turning abruptly as she left to get to the stage and smacking right into Bella.

"What the hell, Hazel?" Bella was wearing a pair of skin-tight leather pants and a crop top, her hair teased into an '80s style to go along with her fierce performance of Olivia Rodrigo's "Traitor." Hazel wondered if she was thinking of Benji when she sang it.

"I wasn't watching where I was going."

"Too distracted from flirting with Martin?"

Bella had heard that? Fantastic. "You're listening in on private conversations now? What are you even doing back here?"

Bella raised her chin. Her stage makeup made her blue eyes stand out in a way that was almost disconcerting. "I was looking for Benji."

"I don't know where he is."

"You had your hands full with other things, obviously."

"Oh, fuck off, Bella. You don't know what you're talking about."

Hazel didn't wait for an answer but regretted what she'd said as she stormed away. There wasn't any point in making an enemy out of Bella.

She had bigger problems to deal with.

Chapter Eight

Hazel watched the rest of the show with her stomach in knots. Whether someone did well or not barely registered. She just wanted it to be over so she could go back to her room and crawl into bed. She should've left with Zoey and Brooke, but she'd promised Benji earlier that she'd watch his performance, and so long as she was sitting in an audience full of people, she'd be safe from Martin.

The trick was getting out of the auditorium before he could approach her. Was he bold enough to come to her room? It wouldn't be hard for him to find out which one she was in, and at this point she wouldn't put it past him.

What had she done to deserve this? All she wanted to do was sing.

Benji took the stage with a ukulele and did a version of

"Rainbow Connection," which could've been cheesy as hell, but somehow wasn't. It was one of the best performances of the night, and Hazel clapped for him enthusiastically. There was no doubt that he was sailing through to the live rounds. Hazel quashed a moment of resentment that he didn't have to contemplate sleeping with Georgia to do it. It wasn't Benji's fault this was the way the world worked.

Before the lights went up, Hazel was up and out of her seat. She almost ran through the lobby, catching a look from one of the bellboys. When the elevator doors closed in front of her, she leaned back against the wall in relief. She just had to avoid Martin tonight. He might argue against her in the voting room tomorrow, but Georgia could outvote him—they were each allowed to put five people through on their own to eliminate ties. If she made it to the live rounds, Martin's influence was diminished. He could criticize her, but the audience at home were the ones who decided who made it and who didn't after this.

She got back to her room and peeled off her clothes. She stepped into the shower, hoping to wash the day away. When she got out, she fed Checkers and cleaned up after him. She'd smuggled him back into the room after her interaction with Martin under a bundle of clothes she'd pulled from a garbage bag in the back of her car.

She changed into a pair of comfortable cotton shorts and a ratty T-shirt. She was about to crawl into bed when there was a knock at her door.

Martin. He'd come to her room! What was she going to do now?

Wait. He didn't know she was in here. If she stayed silent maybe he'd go away.

"Hazel? It's Benji, you there?"

Hazel opened the door with gratitude. "Oh, hi. Sorry about that."

Benji grinned. He'd changed out of his stage clothes and was back in his surfer attire. "It's fine. Where'd you go?"

"Nowhere. I just wanted to freshen up. Long day."

"You were great."

"You too."

"We should celebrate."

"I don't know, I'm—" Hazel's phone dinged. "Give me a minute?"

"Sure."

Hazel went to check it. It was from an unknown number and said simply, *Bungalow 10, 30 minutes?*

Martin hadn't forgotten about her after all. She put her phone down and turned to Benji.

"What did you have in mind?"

When they got to Santa Monica Beach with their Whole Foods bags in tow, families were packing it in for the day and surfers were popping their boards into hard cases. People on light-blue cruiser bikes rolled along the concrete boardwalk and a few stragglers were doing pull-ups on one of the rusty metal structures that made up Muscle Beach.

The nearly white sand was sparkly in the dusky sunset and Hazel inhaled the salty air gratefully. The ocean always made her feel calmer; she didn't know why she kept forgetting that.

Hazel pointed to a flat area where they could set up a

picnic. She pulled out a makeshift picnic blanket that she'd swiped from her room and spread it over the pristine sand. As she breathed in the clean air, she couldn't help but think of Venice, just two miles down the beach. The homeless encampments that came and went like the tide. The grimy storefronts next to the fancy houses with beefed-up security systems. Hazel hadn't loved living there, but over the last year she'd gained respect for many of those who did.

"It's beautiful," Hazel said watching the waves crash into shore as the sun set slowly on the horizon.

"I love it here," Benji said, sitting next to her with a wide smile on his face.

"I'd love to live here someday. But that's probably a fantasy."

"You'll make it."

Hazel smiled at him. "Thank you. Not before you, though."

"Nah."

Two surfers walked by with their boards under their arms, sand clinging to their wet suits. One of them nodded to Benji in acknowledgment, and Benji gave him a thumbs-up.

"Looks like surfing is done for the day," Hazel said with some relief.

Hazel had never been on a surfboard, and she'd made up her mind when she agreed to come to the beach with Benji for a surf lesson and a picnic that she'd weasel her way out of the surf part and just watch him ride.

"For the day, yes. But surfing in the moonlight is a whole other experience."

"Food first?"

"You bet."

Benji pulled out the sushi they'd bought and emptied the

soy sauce packets into the lid. She'd picked two cucumber rolls and a seaweed salad. He'd chosen more adventurously—a pickled salmon skin and spicy avocado hand roll and two yellowfin jalapeño rolls. Hazel hadn't eaten raw fish in years. The places she could afford to eat weren't the kind of places where you wanted to experiment with food that wasn't fully cooked.

Benji had also grabbed a bottle of Chardonnay with a screw top that cost less than ten bucks. Now, that was something Hazel was very familiar with. It wasn't until they got to the beach that she realized they'd forgotten to buy cups.

"No glasses," Hazel said. "But I'm not above drinking this from the bottle."

"If you don't mind sharing with me."

"Of course."

Hazel cracked the top and took a swig. It was surprisingly good for grocery store wine, though that might've been the stress of the day talking. She still couldn't believe Martin had been bold enough to text her and suggest she come to his room.

It wasn't the come-on that shocked her; it was the paper trail.

Then again, what was she going to do about it? He was a billionaire music executive with a label she was trying to get a deal with. He knew it was safe to do whatever he wanted. That was probably part of the thrill.

She passed the bottle to Benji. "I'm going to love watching you surf in the moonlight from my comfy spot on the sand." Hazel patted the blanket. "I'll even film you for TikTok."

Benji's face darkened. "No video." He dunked a piece of yellowfin into his wasabi/soy sauce mixture and swirled it around. Then he lifted the chopsticks to Hazel's lips, which she quickly closed.

"Nope. I'm perfectly happy with my bacteria-free cucumber rolls."

"I'm going to get you to try *something* new tonight."

"We'll see." Hazel popped one of her rolls into her mouth, glad to have some calories in her. She couldn't remember the last time she'd eaten. "Why no surfing videos on TikTok? Talk about clickbait."

Benji lifted the wine bottle and took a long swig. "You ever heard of a TikTok house?"

"Yeah. You lived in one, right?"

He smiled faintly. "This was like a year ago. I was starting to build my brand, and this producer reached out to me and was like, hey, I have an opportunity for you. You can make a ton of money and get this huge following. Obviously, I was stoked. He said I'd move into a mansion in Malibu with a bunch of other TikTok stars and basically get paid to have fun and play my guitar."

"So far, sounds pretty great."

"Right? Anyway, I quit my day job as a surfing instructor. My mom was *not* psyched, but I did it anyway. Moved into the house. I got a million new followers superquickly, just like they'd promised. But within a week I realized I'd signed away my freedom. The producers made us perform twenty hours a day. Shameless product placement that made me feel like a clown. Zero privacy. And the contract I signed meant I had to give the producers fifty percent of any money I made from my posts and sponsorships. I was miserable. It's not like I think TikTok is this noble calling, but the house felt like a circus.

So when they wanted me to put up surfing videos, I refused. I needed something that belonged just to me."

"Why *The Sing Along*, then?"

Benji took another swig. "I still want to get a record deal. And I got a lawyer to read over the contract. He helped me break the deal with the TikTok house without too much damage."

"That's lucky."

"Totally." He watched the surf for a beat, then turned to Hazel. "What about you? I know you have a kick-ass voice and look cute in cowboy boots, but I want to know more."

"You also know that I'm scared of raw fish and roller coasters. That's a lot of information."

"Those are facts. I want to know *you*."

"I'm from Austin and—"

Benji held up the bottle. "There's my first question. You're from Texas but you don't have an accent. What's that about?"

Hazel hesitated. She didn't want to blab a bunch of nonsense about her past like she had to Zoey. She could answer this one honestly. "My parents were transplants from the Northeast. My dad kind of had it in for the Texas twang. I used to have to put a quarter in a jar every time I said y'all. Later, they hired me a diction coach. And, voilà, I sound like I'm from Connecticut."

"Interesting. What were your parents like growing up?"

Now it was Hazel's turn to gaze out at the ocean, a lump in her throat. "They pushed me very hard. Sometimes it felt like they couldn't separate my dreams from theirs. They had really high expectations. Kind of stop-at-nothing-to-accomplish-them sort of people." Hazel dug her fingers through the sand, feeling the grains accumulate under her nails.

"A lot of show business parents are like that. I mean, Cole's mom . . . she wears a T-shirt with his face on it every day."

"This was more than that. It's hard to explain, but . . . we're not close anymore. Like at all."

"I'm sure you have plenty of friends to count on. Like Jack? He called you during the results show?"

Hazel turned back to Benji. "Jack's not a friend." Benji was obviously expecting more, but Hazel wanted to change the subject. She'd already said too much about her parents. She pointed at a cresting wave. "No way I can go into that water without a wet suit. It must be freezing."

"Good thing I came prepared." Benji pulled a black wet suit from his backpack. He held it up to her shoulders. "That should fit nicely."

Benji's hand grazed her shoulders and Hazel pulled away. "Where did you get this?"

"I borrowed it from someone I know."

He meant a girl. Hazel could tell that Benji expected her to feel jealous, but she didn't. She did wonder, however, how long he'd been planning this. Had he brought it with him to the show along with a pack of condoms just in case? "Thank you."

"No worries. Let me grab the boards."

He popped up from the sand and loped to the parking lot, where he'd left his red pickup truck with the boards in the back.

Hazel watched the waves, trying to decide what she was doing there. This was clearly a date in Benji's eyes, and if she was being honest, she'd known that when she'd agreed to come. So why had she done it? Was it only to get away from Martin? She could've ignored his texts and hidden in her room. Zoey and Brooke would've come back from dinner eventually, and Martin wasn't going to break down her door.

Did she want something with Benji or was he simply a distraction? What if he was? Would it hurt to give in to him? It would be nice to have something fun and light for herself. This evening was the first time she'd truly relaxed in ages.

But as she stared at the waves crashing to the shore, Nick intruded into her thoughts. He'd been so angry at Martin earlier. Was it only because Martin was trying to take advantage of her, or because he thought she might give in? And what had he been doing in the green room in the first place? Then there was his concern for her during her rehearsal—was that tied to Martin? Ugh, enough. This kind of turmoil was exactly what she was trying to avoid. *This* is why she'd agreed to come to the beach with Benji—because he *didn't* make her head spin.

Benji strode back to the shoreline, a surfboard tucked under each arm. He'd changed into his wet suit at the truck, and it clung to his chiseled frame. "Ready?"

"Turn around," Hazel said, twirling her finger to indicate she needed privacy.

Benji did as she asked and Hazel stripped out of her shorts and tank top, folding them into a neat pile on the blanket. She slipped her underwear in between, grateful Benji wasn't seeing them. She bought them in bulk, and they were cheap and flimsy. She pulled on her bathing suit, then eased into the wet suit, which was a close fit, and whirled around.

"Zip me up," she said, and Benji came up behind her. His fingers tugged at the base of the zipper as he placed his other hand on her bare back. His touch was warm, and it had been too long since she'd felt like this. She didn't pull away this time.

She turned and faced Benji. "When I fall off, we stop. Deal?"

"Falling is part of learning. But I have confidence in you."

"That's one of us."

Benji laughed. "You're cute."

"And you're kind of hot." Oh boy. That was the wine talking. Probably not a good idea to drink before trying to learn how to surf. "I meant to say that in my head."

"I don't mind." Benji stared at her intently, his intentions clear.

Hazel dragged her eyes away. "We're learning to surf, right?"

"We are." He stepped away and put the two boards parallel to each other on the sand. "We start on our bellies."

So far, so good. Hazel could handle this. They lay down on the boards and went into cobra position, their heads and necks up and their hands propped in the sand.

"Okay, this is how you stand up on the board. Watch me." Benji got to his feet in a squat and twisted so that his body was perpendicular to the board. "Simple, yes?"

"Sure." Hazel mimicked his moves, except when she went to pivot to the side, her weight shifted and made the board tip to the right. She fell off and onto her back on the sand.

"Oh shit. You okay?" Benji crouched next to her.

"I'm fine." Hazel was embarrassed. How the hell had she managed to fall before they'd even put their boards in the water? Definitely the wine. She sat up. "Why don't we go for a swim? I'm covered in sand, and I'd love to rinse off."

"Sure." Benji reached out and pulled her up.

They walked into the water slowly, the cold waves lapping at their ankles and then climbing to their knees as they waded in farther. It was chilly, but the wet suit kept the worst of it at bay. Hazel counted down in her head from three, then glided into the water and took a few quick strokes.

Benji swam up next to her, then turned to float on his back. "Look at the moon," he said, pointing at the sky.

Hazel joined him on her back. The moon was a perfect crescent, bright and hanging low. She breathed in the salty scent of the ocean, feeling deeply relaxed. When was the last time she'd been in the water? She couldn't even remember.

"Are you cold?"

Hazel realized her teeth were chattering. "A little. You mind if we go in?"

"No problem."

A few quick strokes brought them back to shore. "We should probably call it a night," Hazel said as they strode out of the waves. "Big day coming up."

Tomorrow, they'd find out which of the contestants were advancing onto the live shows. They'd be winnowed down to ten men and ten women.

"You're in," Benji said.

"No, *you're* in. I'm a maybe."

"Not in my books."

"You're sweet."

They walked up the sand and Benji grabbed two towels they'd pilfered from the hotel and draped one over her shoulders. Hazel was collecting their trash and putting it into the empty Whole Foods bag when Benji stopped her.

"Let's chill a minute." He sat down on the blanket and motioned for her to sit next to him. "The night is too beautiful to rush back."

Hazel felt her resolve weakening. Benji's skin was glistening in the moonlight. She sat down next to him, and he turned to her.

"I've been thinking about you a lot," he said.

"Have you?" She flirted back on Autopilot. It was too hard to resist, with the sea air surrounding them, their silhouettes bathed in moonlight, the sweet taste of wine on their tongues.

"Let me show you." He pulled her close and pressed his lips to hers. His tongue slipped inside her mouth, exploring.

She kissed him back, first softly, then with more hunger. He pushed her back on the sand and kissed her jaw and then down her neck while his hand played with the wet suit's zipper. She closed her eyes and tried to give in, to let go, but something was holding her back. She pushed at his shoulders gently and sat up.

Benji's face was clouded. "Did I do something wrong?"

"No, no." She kissed him briefly, then pulled away and hugged her knees. "It's me. I . . . there's something I should tell you."

A searchlight cut across the sand.

"What the—?"

"Attention, beachgoers. You're in violation of L.A. County beach rules. Violators can face a thousand-dollar fine and a night in jail. I suggest you collect your belongings and leave the premises immediately."

The searchlight moved up and down the beach, lighting up their little picnic.

"Hurry!" Hazel said, desperately trying to collect her things in the harsh light.

"Let's make a run for it," he said. "I'll get the boards, you take the rest of our stuff."

They grabbed their things as quickly as they could, then sprinted to the parking lot as the searchlight crisscrossed their bodies and the sand. They reached the parking lot out of breath and laughing.

"What law do you think you think we were breaking?" Hazel said.

"Depends on whether the cops could see my thoughts."

"Probably pretty clear where they thought we were going."

"Can't fault a guy for trying."

"No," Hazel said. She kissed him quickly. "Thank you."

"What for?"

"Tonight. I needed this. I can't tell you how much."

Benji's dimple flashed in the moonlight. "Any time."

Chapter Nine

Given how upset Zoey had been after her performance, Hazel was glad to have somewhere else to sleep so Brooke and Zoey could have some time alone. The night before had been a bit awkward if Hazel was being honest. It was one thing to share a room with someone—quite another to share it with them and their romantic partner. Hazel had put in earplugs and put a pillow over her head, but some soft sighs of pleasure still made their way through. She'd had the most lurid dreams as a result about Max Irons, only he was dressed like Nick, in a tight black T-shirt and perfect jeans, and he said her name, *Hazel*, in this soft whisper that made her weak in the knees. She'd woken up embarrassed and confused.

It wasn't an experience she wanted to repeat. When they'd returned to the hotel, she'd asked Benji if he minded if she stayed in his room. Since Benji's roommate had been eliminated in the group rounds, they could sleep in separate beds. Benji had loaned her a T-shirt and a pair of shorts. He'd also made it clear that he wanted something more, but Hazel had suggested that they talk about it in the morning once their heads were clear. He'd agreed, kissed her gently, and had gone right to sleep. Hazel followed soon after, the long, complicated day wearing her out enough to make her night—thankfully—dreamless.

She was up now, though, butterflies in her stomach. Benji was in a deep sleep in his bed, his arms flung out, starfishing. He didn't snore and looked adorable, but Hazel was still glad that she'd stopped things before they got too serious. Not that she was above a random hookup, but Benji was a friend. She didn't want to treat him like that. And in the cold light of day, she knew she'd clung to Benji like a life raft last night to escape the *Titanic* that was Martin.

There was also the weight of the lies that she'd told since she entered *The Sing Along*. Whether or not Benji was looking for something casual or serious, Hazel didn't need to bring that kind of baggage into a relationship, no matter how brief.

Hazel checked the time. It was past eight. They were taping the results show later that morning, and she needed to get ready. She got up as quietly as she could and gathered her things. She watched Benji and made her decision. Later today, she'd tell Benji that this wasn't going anywhere. He'd understand. She doubted he was serious about her. Either way, this wasn't the place or the time to try to find out.

She gave him a last glance as she snuck through the room and slipped out.

"What. The. Fuck?"

Hazel came face-to-face with a very angry Bella. She hadn't put her makeup on yet, and her hair was loose around her shoulders. She looked young and vulnerable without her usual armor.

"Uh, hi, Bella."

"Benji's in there, I assume?" Bella pointed to the door that had just closed behind Hazel.

It wasn't possible to deny it. "Yes."

"How could you?"

"We didn't . . . it was nothing."

"Don't even." Bella crossed her arms. "You know what, Hazel? You pretend to be all friends with everybody, but you're bullshit. You don't care about anyone but yourself. I hope Zoey knows that."

"Zoey *is* my friend."

"Sure, right, whatever. You just take anything you want, regardless of who it belongs to."

"Benji doesn't belong to you."

"That's not the point."

"What is your point?"

"You *said* you weren't interested in him and you knew how I felt. But that didn't matter to you. Same goes for Martin. He and Sarah have a thing, but that didn't stop you from coming on to him to get ahead."

Hazel's anger rose at the mention of Martin. The idea that she'd ever hit on him to get somewhere in the competition was ridiculous. "You know what, Bella? You're just a jealous bitch."

She pushed past Bella and walked to the elevator, fighting to manage the feelings flooding through her. Hazel hadn't been this angry in a long time. She thought she'd gotten her rage under control. She'd had to. Nothing good happened when she acted emotionally. But here she was, letting Bella get under her skin.

"You're going to be sorry," Bella called after her.

Hazel glanced back at Bella. Her shoulders were slumped in defeat. Hazel felt terrible. She knew what it was like to want something and not get it. She might be about to find that out again.

"Believe it or not, I already am," Hazel said softly, but Bella had stormed away.

"Spill the tea," Zoey said, bouncing in her seat in the breakfast room. "What was it like?"

"What was *he* like?" Brooke added. She and Zoey were wearing matching T-shirts that said "No Justice, No Peace," and were holding hands on the table. Earlier, Brooke had been raving to Hazel about the vegan restaurant they'd gone to the night before, while Zoey made eyes at Hazel across the table, clearly signaling her not to mention the very unvegan bacon Zoey ate for breakfast most days.

"Nothing happened," Hazel said. "Not really. And that's it, okay? I'm not into sharing details."

"That is so disappointing," Zoey said. "Like completely."

Hazel played with her fork. They were trying to eat something before the big reveal of who was going to make it onto the live shows, but neither of them could get much down. "Sorry."

"I forgive you." Zoey turned to Brooke. "We'll get her drunk and get it out of her eventually."

"I love it when you're devious," Brooke said, laughing.

"That reminds me . . ." Hazel filled them in on her interaction with Bella. As she told them, she noticed that a few of the other contestants were giving her odd stares as they walked by to get their breakfasts from the buffet.

"What's gotten into Lacey?" Hazel asked in a whisper.

"She's really nice," Zoey said, giving Lacey a wave.

"She defrauded the Make-A-Wish Foundation."

Zoey flushed. "Yeah, okay, that's true. But she really loves Harry Potter world."

"She's giving me the death stare, what gives?"

Lacey was whispering with Cole's mom, her hand cupped around her face. Cole's mom's T-shirt was simply the word *Winner* over and over in a rainbow of colors. When they noticed Hazel watching them, they turned and walked away, giving her shocked glances over their shoulders.

"What the hell?"

"Is it true?" Benji asked, coming up to their table in a rush, his tone harsh, no smile in his eyes.

Hazel had never seen him angry before. What could've happened that would turn sunny Benji into a storm cloud? She'd left him sleeping peacefully only an hour ago.

"Is what true?"

"About you and Martin."

"Excuse me?" Hazel asked with a sinking feeling.

"You're sleeping with him."

"What?"

"It's all over the competition."

Zoey's slapped the table. "You take that back, Benji."

"I'm just telling Hazel what I heard."

"That's ridiculous. She's spent the whole competition with me, so when was this supposed to have happened?"

"I don't—"

"And Hazel slept in *your* room last night. Are you calling her a slut?"

"Zoey," Hazel implored. "Keep your voice down. Everyone's staring." She put a hand on Benji's arm. "Please sit down."

Benji reluctantly took a seat next to Hazel.

"Where did you hear this?"

"I got a text from Cole."

"Who heard it from Bella, I'll bet."

He frowned. "What's Bella got to do with it?"

"She hates me."

"She's not like that," Benji said stubbornly. "If you took the time to know her—"

"She overheard a conversation I had with Martin yesterday where he was propositioning me, only she thinks it's the other way around. Then she saw me come out of your room this morning. An hour later, suddenly there's a rumor I'm sleeping with him? Too many coincidences."

"Martin propositioned you?" Zoey and Benji said together.

Hazel motioned for them to lower their voices. "Yesterday, but Nick interrupted him. And then last night I was worried that he was going to come to my room."

"But instead, I did," Benji said.

Hazel hesitated. "Yes."

Zoey and Brooke exchanged glances. "I just realized I forgot something in the room I need for the taping," Zoey said, and she and Brooke rose and left.

"Is that why you came out with me?" Benji asked when they were gone.

"Partly, but . . ."

Benji put his hands on the table. "Honesty is really important to me."

Hazel's throat felt tight. "Okay. I get it."

"Is that why?"

"I wanted to get away. I needed a change of scene. But I had fun, Benji. You know I did."

His hands clenched into fists. "Why didn't you tell me about Martin?"

"What was there to tell? It happens all the time. I was dealing with it."

"I could've helped you."

"By what? Threatening to beat him up? That wouldn't have helped."

"It just makes me mad."

Hazel sighed. She knew Benji meant well, but she didn't want to have to manage *his* anger on top of her own. "Me too. He's going to vote against me. I'm probably going home."

"They'd be crazy to let you go."

"Crazier things have happened, believe me."

They sat in silence for a minute.

"Can I ask you something?" Hazel said. "Why was Bella coming to your room so early? Is something going on between you two?"

"Not on my end." Benji shrugged. "Maybe she has feelings."

"Which you knew, right? You were hanging out before *The Sing Along*? She told me."

"For a couple of months. But only as friends."

But Benji *had* flirted with Bella. Hazel had seen it. Was he someone who was careless with other people's feelings or was he just a flirt? Either way, Hazel was glad she hadn't let things go anywhere the night before.

"I'm not sure she knew that."

"Fair enough."

"And she is the one who started the rumor, I know it."

"Maybe it was Nick."

That had never even occurred to Hazel. But no, that was silly. "It wasn't Nick. He rescued me from Martin. He knows nothing happened."

"You sure? That guy has a crush on you."

"What? No. He's always so hard on me."

Benji lip curled. "You're cute."

"Ok-ay." Hazel willed herself to relax. But with what Benji had said about Nick spinning through her mind like a top, it was hard to do.

"I'm sorry I got mad," Benji said.

"It's all right."

"I had a lot of fun last night."

"Me too, but . . ."

"Not the right time?"

"I don't think so. There's already a lot of stress and pressure. You understand?"

"Of course."

"Let's go get our results?"

"Sounds like a plan."

"Benji Suzuki, come up to the stage," Keshawn said. Benji bounced up the steps with his usual enthusiasm. The audience, who'd dwindled significantly over the last hour as more and more contestants got eliminated, cheered him on.

Benji high-fived Keshawn.

"Benji, my man. How you feeling?"

"Good, man. Good. Surf's up, you know?"

Keshawn laughed. "Surf's up. Love that. And the judges loved your performance. You think you're through to the live rounds?"

"You tell me."

"Ha! Will do." Keshawn opened the envelope he was holding. "Benji, it looks like you're going to have some time to surf on your hands"—Benji's face fell, and the crowd started booing—"but not too much because we'll need you back here in two weeks!"

Benji shook his head with a grin. "You got me."

"I have to have my fun," Keshawn said, patting him on the back. "Congratulations."

"Thank you!" Benji turned to the judges and blew Georgia a kiss. He made eye contact with Hazel and smiled directly at her before walking off the stage.

Zoey gripped her hand tight. "The suspense is killing me."

Hazel felt the same. Eight women had been let through. There were two more spaces, but three women left: Zoey, Hazel, and Bella.

"Bella, come on up!"

Bella flounced up to the stage. Hazel started praying silently for Bella not to make it, but she knew deep down that wasn't going to happen. Because if Bella got eliminated then that meant Hazel and Zoey were automatically into the live rounds, and the show wouldn't get its dramatic moment.

As they watched Bella banter with Keshawn, Hazel wondered if Zoey had worked that out. She didn't ask, though, just watched the pantomime, and saw Bella's delight when it was announced that she was in the women's top ten.

"Zoey and Hazel!"

Zoey looked at her in panic. "Oh no."

"It's okay."

"I didn't want it to be between us."

"Me either. But it'll be all right, whatever happens."

They stood and walked up the aisle together hand in hand. As they climbed the steps to the stage, Hazel felt torn. If this was based purely on performance, she was in. She'd done well; Zoey had screwed up. But she also hadn't screwed Martin, and judging by the look he was giving her, that was going to be a factor.

"Hazel and Zoey," Keshawn said. "You two are roommates, right?"

"Yes," Hazel said. "And best friends in the competition." She squeezed Zoey's hand and shot Bella—who was standing in the wings, staring at them—a look.

"The best thing about *The Sing Along* has been meeting Hazel," Zoey added. "We're friends for life now."

Tears sprang to Hazel's eyes. Zoey truly was one of the nicest people she'd ever met.

"This competition has a way of pitting friends against each other," Keshawn said.

"That's okay," Hazel said. "We can take it."

He smiled at them and glanced at the teleprompter. Hazel could read what he was going to say. "Hazel, the judges loved your last performance, and your group round and duet hit the mark too. Zoey, things were a little rocky for you last night, but you've been a favorite of the judges since your audition. One of you is going home, and one of you is moving on."

Hazel gripped Zoey's hand more tightly and gazed out at the audience. Nick was standing in one of the fire exit doorways to the right of the stage, his face an unreadable mask. Did he have a crush on her? No, that was ridiculous. Bella probably started that rumor, too, to make it seem like Hazel had a leg up in the competition.

Keshawn pulled an envelope out of his pocket. "Zoey, Hazel, it's time."

He opened it. Hazel stared straight ahead, trying to tell herself that if she was the one going home it would be okay. She'd work it out. It wasn't the end of the world. She'd—

"Hazel, you're going through! Zoey, I'm sorry but it's the end of your journey with us."

Hazel stood rigid with shock. She'd made it. She'd made it. *Oh my god.*

Zoey grabbed her and held her tight. Hazel wrapped her arms around her. Zoey was crying, Hazel was crying—they were making great television.

"I'm sorry," she said into Zoey's ear. "I'm so sorry."

"No, I'm happy for you."

They broke apart and walked offstage while Keshawn called up the last two men. Benji grabbed her and gave her a hug as they congratulated one another, while Zoey collapsed into Brooke's arms. A crowd gathered around them, then broke apart, leaving Hazel in the wings, watching the others as they high-fived and backslapped and cried their disappointments away.

Hazel still couldn't believe it. She'd made it to the live rounds. She should savor this moment. It was happening. Finally, after everything, something good was in sight.

"You're pretty pleased with yourself, I bet," Bella hissed from behind her. "But I wouldn't get too comfortable, Hazel Fine. I'm onto you."

"Just leave me alone, Bella. You made it, why isn't that enough?"

"You're my competition now, aren't you?"

Hazel felt queasy as she turned around. Bella's beautiful face was twisted with rage and determination.

"I'm just a singer. Like you."

"But you aren't like me, are you? Your socials are nothing, you came from nowhere. Something's off about you, Hazel, and I'm going to find out what it is."

Hazel's hands turned to ice, but she couldn't show weakness. "Good luck to you, Bella."

Bella's face faltered, then reset. She stalked away as Benji approached.

"What was that about?" Benji asked, resting his hand on her back.

"Nothing good."

"Come on, we made it! Let's celebrate."

Hazel tried to smile, but the cloud that had loomed over her for what seemed like forever was growing, taking shape.

Hazel knew you couldn't control things like the weather.

You could only try to plan and hope for the best. It had been a long time since the best had happened for Hazel, though. Hope was a stranger. And Hazel knew it was only a matter of time before she was caught in a storm.

Chapter Ten

Sunlight flooded into Hazel's eyes, waking her way too early. She pulled the thick blanket she was using over her head, but it was no use. Once she woke up, that was it. There was no going back to sleep.

She sat up and moved her head back and forth slowly. She was in her car, parked on a side street in Venice, a few blocks away from the Motel California. Somehow, it always surprised Hazel to find herself sleeping in her car. Despite everything that had happened in her life, this felt like the lowest that she'd sunk.

And it was ridiculous, given that today was the start of the second part of *The Sing Along*. She was a contestant on one of the biggest singing competitions in the world and she didn't have a roof over her head. But there'd been a two-week break between when they'd found out they were in the live rounds and when taping began, and they weren't allowed to stay in the hotel until filming resumed. Zoey had gone back to Nashville, and the Motel California was out. No one was going to hire her for a two-week stint. Hazel had enough money from her time on the show to eat, but not enough for housing.

If the producers knew about this, they'd make a field day out of it, following her around as she tried to find a place to sleep, digging into her past to try to figure out how she'd ended up there. That was the last thing Hazel wanted. It might help her get the sympathy vote, but that wasn't how she wanted to win.

So when she was called in a week ago to tape background about her "journey" to the show, she'd blurted to the segment producers she was living with Benji at his former TikTok house. She knew it was a mistake the moment she said it, but she'd also watched their eyes light up with the knowledge that *The Sing Along* was finally going to have a showmance they could exploit.

All except Nick. He'd scowled at her answer and shaken his head like a sad parent, disappointed that she'd done exactly what he'd warned her against. Hazel had wanted to take it back, then, but the moment had passed. Besides, he didn't know what it was like, what Hazel had gone through. Maybe he'd lost his record deal, but he had a cushy job on *The Sing Along*, and there was no way he was sleeping in his car with a pooping rabbit.

Speaking of which . . .

Hazel peeked over the bucket seat into the front of the car where she'd put Checkers's cage. He was sleeping peacefully in a bed of straw, his little paws tucked under his chin. He was adorable as always, and she felt a burst of love for him.

"What am I going to do with you, Checkers?"

He opened his eyes slowly, giving her a sad-eyed stare. He didn't have any answers, and Hazel didn't either.

She'd never felt so far away from her dreams.

Hours later, Hazel pulled up to a modest bungalow in Los Feliz. It was a quiet street with palm trees and kids playing ball hockey in the road. The houses were small, but well kept, each stuccoed building a light-pastel shade that made the street feel happy and bright.

She got out of the car and put Checkers on his leash, an innovation borne out of necessity in the last two weeks. He was surprisingly okay with it, and Hazel mostly didn't mind the looks she got when she walked around with him. It wasn't even the tenth-weirdest thing she'd seen in Venice, particularly among the vanlord community. Some enterprising guy had parked a bunch of vans between Pacific and Abbot Kinney and was charging rent to the unhoused to get them off the beach. The guy in the van a block down from where Hazel parked was a snake charmer, and Hazel was worried Checkers would end up a python's lunch. Hence the leash.

Now he was straining against it to get to the neatly manicured lawn. Hazel wished she could let him run around at will, but the neighbor's barking dog stopped her. She walked to the palm tree in the center of the yard and looped the leash around it. Checkers would have a ten-foot circle to hop around in. That would have to do.

"Hey, girl," Amber said as she came out onto the porch. She was wearing a linen shift dress and her hair was pulled back, her face free of makeup. Once again, Hazel was struck by the contrast between work Amber and the real Amber. Which probably made her a terrible person. Of course Amber wouldn't dress like a sex worker if she wasn't, well, a sex worker.

"Hey, Amber. Good to see you."

"Rabbit!" Theo said, running out of the house in shorts, jellies, and no shirt. He rushed to where Checkers was hopping around, then stopped. "Can I pet him?"

"You can. His name is Checkers."

"Hi, Checkers!" He leaned down and petted the rabbit gingerly. "Mommy, Mommy, look, I'm petting a rabbit!"

"I see that, buddy. Good job."

Hazel walked up to the porch. She pulled a wad of cash out of her back pocket. She'd gotten her clothes budget for the first week the day before. She'd been tempted to stay a night in a hotel, but instead she'd put aside $500 for herself, which was more than enough for her to source outfits from some thrift stores and still repay Amber. She could stand showering one more time at the pay-as-you-go gym she'd used for the last two weeks. "This is for you."

"Thanks, hon." Amber tucked the money into her pocket.

"No, thank you. You saved me a world of trouble."

"Sure." Amber looked past her to the battered car on the street. "They going to let you back in the hotel?"

"Yes, thank god. Today."

"You could've stayed here."

"No, you gave me enough already. It was only two weeks. It was fine."

"Why not stay at that hottie's place, then?"

"Benji? We're not together."

"Why not?"

Hazel sighed. She'd stuck by her resolution not to let things go anywhere with Benji, and while she didn't regret it, it would've been so much easier if she'd just given in and accepted his invitation to stay at his former TikTok house. Benji hadn't seemed *that* disappointed when she'd said no. But then she'd gone and told the producers they were dating, and now that the show was starting again, they were going to have to pretend to be in some sort of relationship. Benji wasn't psyched when she'd told him about it, but he'd seen the value in the publicity it would get them. Hazel shuddered at the thought of how Bella was going to react when she found out. Her threats were probably idle, but Hazel didn't discount them entirely.

"We're together for the show, which is basically the same thing, right?"

Amber cracked a smile. "Does that mean you get laid 'for the show'?"

"Um, no."

"Bad deal then."

Hazel laughed. "It's complicated."

"Lone wolf, I get it."

"It's not that I *want* to be alone, I just am."

Amber frowned. "That's a choice, Hazel. Come on, now."

"I can find someone when I win."

"What if you don't win, though?" Amber put her hands on her hips. "You only have a five percent chance of winning, right?"

Theo stuck his head around the tree. "Mommy's real good at math!"

"I can see that."

"Sorry," Amber said.

"It's fine. I mean, it's not quite that simple—not all contestants are created equal."

"Still. What's the plan if things don't work out?"

"I just want to make a living with my music."

"And I just want to take care of my son. So, I'm okay with my choices. But, honey, you don't seem so okay with yours."

"You know my history." Amber was the only person Hazel had confided in about her past, her parents, all of it.

"I do. And you're always saying you want to leave all that behind. So do that."

"I'm trying."

"Good." Amber reached out and brought Hazel into a hug. After two weeks of isolation, Hazel felt emotional at another person's touch. She gave Amber a tight squeeze, then pulled away, wiping a tear off her cheek with a knuckle. "God, I'd better toughen up. I don't want to cry on national television."

Amber shook her head. "Would that be the worst thing in the world?"

"Kinda?"

"Hey, Mommy! Checkers likes me. Can I keep him, Mommy? Can I?"

Panic spread over Amber's face.

"Don't worry," Hazel said to Amber. Then to Theo, "Checkers is leaving with me."

"Thank you, hon. I love my kid, but I've cleaned up enough poop for a lifetime."

"Surprise!" Zoey said, throwing her arms out wide and embracing a shocked Hazel.

They were in one of the conference rooms in the hotel. It had been Bella's idea for them to gather and watch the last televised episode before the live shows started. Regardless of their personal problems, Hazel had to give it to Bella—she'd put together a nice party, with comfortable couches and a large-screen TV. There was even a bartender in the corner and a table full of food. The contestants were invited to bring friends or family, so the room was a mix of people Hazel knew and strangers, including Bella's brother, Dan, and a woman who must be Benji's mom.

"Are you here to watch with us?" Hazel asked.

"No! Lacey's cancer came back so she had to drop out. Isn't that great?"

"What?"

Zoey looked stricken. "I mean not great for her, obviously, but since I was the last runner-up, when she dropped out they called me."

"How come you didn't tell me?"

"Because I wanted to surprise you. Are you happy?"

"Of course I am. Only sad for Lacey, that's all. I hope she's okay."

"She's probably going to croak," Bella said, coming up to them with a glass of sparkling wine in her hand. "But you got a second chance, so who cares, right?"

"Seriously, Bella?" Hazel said. "Just walk away."

"This is *my* party."

"I thought it was *our* party," Benji said, walking up with a beer. "Hey, Hazel."

"Hey, Benji."

There was an awkward pause where Hazel could feel everyone's eyes on them. Clearly, the news about their relationship had spread through the competition like wildfire. Bella had probably lit the match.

"You want to meet my mom?" Benji asked casually.

"I'd love that."

"Where are your parents, Hazel?" Bella said. "Too busy to make the trip?"

"They're dead."

Benji's eyes met hers with a puzzled expression.

"It happened a long time ago," Hazel said quickly, feeling bad about the lie, and embarrassed for saying it in front of Benji. But she didn't want any sympathy from Bella.

"Bummer. Aren't you going to kiss for the cameras?" Bella pointed her glass to the cameraman in the corner. "That's what this is all about, right?"

Hazel wondered if Benji had told Bella what was really going on as she turned to where she was pointing. Nick was standing next to the cameraman with his arms crossed, his face set in his usual displeased/judgmental frown. Hazel met his gaze, then gave a small shrug and looked away. Then she deliberately turned her back to the camera while simultaneously checking that it was the only one in the room.

She stepped closer to Bella and lowered her voice. "Mean Girl isn't going to be a good look for you in the live rounds. It's not going to get anyone on your side. You're a talented singer, and you have a real shot at winning. You hate me, that's fine. But cut out this on-screen garbage. It's not going to end well for you, I promise."

"We'll see about that."

"I guess we will."

Hazel turned around slowly and plastered on a wide smile for the camera. Then she walked up to Benji and kissed him hard on the mouth. Several of the other contestants called whoops. while Zoey giggled, and Bella walked away wounded.

When they broke apart, Benji gave her a wink.

Hazel smiled back. They were on the same page, and that was good.

She scanned the room. Benji's mom smiled at her shyly and gave her a little wave. Hazel waved back, then caught Nick's eye again. The expression on his face was . . . that wasn't jealousy, was it? No, it was probably closer to contempt.

Surely he could see that this was all an act? And why did he care? It wasn't like she was sleeping with Martin.

But Hazel had a hard time turning away from Nick. Once again, something about the way he looked at her made her feel like he was the only person who saw the real Hazel, and that both scared and thrilled her.

"Hey, the show's starting!" Zoey said. "You don't want to miss it."

Hazel finally dragged her eyes away. Everyone had gathered around the TV except for Benji.

"Everything okay, Hazel?" he asked, speaking to her, but watching Nick.

Hazel gave him the biggest smile she could muster. "Of course. Why wouldn't it be?"

Chapter Eleven

"Well, well, well, if it isn't Hazel Fine," Martin drawled, a cigarette dangling from his lips as he stood outside the back entrance of the hotel. It was nearing ten o'clock and fully dark out. His cigarette butt glowed red in the night.

Hazel wasn't that surprised to see Martin. During her downtime in the last two weeks, she'd studied a map of the hotel. The private bungalows Martin had mentioned in his text to her were past the main building, behind a high hedge of bougainvillea that mostly covered the smell from the large dumpsters Martin was smoking next to. That probably explained why she kept running into him and Nick in this location—Nick, Martin, and Georgia must all be staying in the bungalows.

But just because she wasn't surprised he was there didn't mean that her heart didn't stutter in panic. She was once again smuggling Checkers into the hotel and had been in search of a laundry cart. She'd decided to do it under cover of darkness this time to have a better chance of avoiding detection, and to leave Zoey out of it, but that plan had clearly backfired.

"Martin." She tried as best she could to keep her voice professional, but it was hard to do with a bunny struggling under her arm. She just hoped that Checkers didn't start pooping.

"More rabbit issues, love?"

"I was giving him some fresh air."

"You wouldn't be bringing him into the hotel, now, would you? I understand they have a strict no-pets policy."

"I'm not a rule breaker."

"Oh no?" He took a long drag on his cigarette. "I'm staying in one of the bungalows *as you know*. Mine has a fenced-in courtyard. If you were inclined to rethink my offer, Checkers would be welcome."

Hazel worked hard to keep her features neutral. Did this monster really think she'd be willing to hop into his bed just to find a better place to keep her pet?

"Thank you for the offer, but—"

"She's not interested," Nick finished for her.

"Nicholas."

"Martin."

Nick stepped out of the shadows into the light cast by the spot outside the back entrance. He was dressed all in black. Did he have plans to burgle the hotel? No, no, that was silly. This was the way from the bungalows to the front entrance.

Hazel had spent too much time hanging out with people with bad intentions.

"You have a strange habit of showing up whenever Hazel is around," Martin said.

"I could say the same about you."

"Yes, well." Martin flicked his cigarette butt to the ground and crushed it with his heel. "The difference is, I don't have to answer to you." He nodded to Hazel. "Ms. Fine."

He stalked off toward the bungalows, the scent of his cigarette lingering in the air.

Hazel faced Nick, Checkers struggling in her grip. She was clutching him too hard and relaxed her arms slightly so he'd calm down.

"Looks like that rabbit wants to escape," Nick said, half amused.

"Can you blame him?"

Nick gave a small laugh. "No, I guess not. Where did you find him?"

"Oh, I . . . he's mine. His name is Checkers."

"You have a pet rabbit?"

"Yeah, I rescued him from this kid."

"Rescue seems to be the theme of the evening."

"*I* didn't need to be rescued."

"I know."

"And yet you did. Again."

Nick rubbed at the stubble on his chin. "I had to intervene. He's a terrible person."

"Why work for him, then?"

"You think it's so easy to walk away?"

"I didn't say that."

He took a step toward her. He smelled freshly laundered, like clothes just taken from a dryer. "You're not the only one whose choices are limited, Hazel."

"I didn't say—"

Nick put his hand on her shoulder. "I'll leave you to the wolves next time." He squeezed her shoulder gently, and before she could get a *thank you* out, he'd let go and started to walk away. She watched as he stopped at the edge of the pool of light and glanced over his shoulder. "Oh, and Hazel. You might want to try a different gambit than the whole bunny-in-the laundry-cart thing this time. A housekeeping cart wandering around the hotel at this time of day will stick out."

He disappeared into the darkness and Hazel was left standing there, holding Checkers, waiting for the moment when the choice to enter *The Sing Along* felt like the right one.

The next morning, Hazel stood in the hallway outside one of the conference rooms with a camera crew, feeling excited. She was wearing an outfit she'd found at a thrift store—a vintage wrap dress in a bright print that fit her better than something off the rack had any right to. Her hair was in a side braid, and she was wearing her signature cowboy boots, her guitar slung over her back.

She was waiting to make her entrance to meet her musical mentor. For this segment of *The Sing Along*, each of them would be assigned a mentor who'd already made it in the business and would help navigate them through the live rounds.

There was a lot of speculation among the contestants about

who they'd get. The fame level of each mentor varied from year to year, but they'd run the gamut from ex-contestants to huge pop stars like Bebe Rexha and, early on, Britney Spears. Hazel doubted it would be anyone of that caliber this time around, but Zoey had speculated during breakfast about who it might be, shouting random names out, like Carrie Underwood and Maren Morris.

Hazel didn't have the heart to tell her that it was more likely to be the fourth runner-up from season five. She wished she could feel Zoey's enthusiasm for the whole process, but her interaction with Martin the night before hung over her happiness like a net, keeping her heart from soaring the way it should.

But now that she was about to meet whoever it was, she felt the tension lifting. She wanted to enjoy her time on *The Sing Along* when she could, and meeting her musical mentor was one of the moments she'd most been looking forward to.

"Hey, Hazel," Benji said, ambling by her. They hadn't had a chance to discuss the whole kiss in front of his mom last night. They'd watched the show together, and his mother had been lovely, but then he'd had to drive her home and Hazel hadn't had the energy to track him down after what happened with Martin. Instead, she'd hidden Checkers under a bunch of towels and gotten him to her room without further incident.

"Hey, Benji, hold up a second."

He stopped. "What's up?"

Hazel walked closer to him and lowered her voice, checking that her mic was off. She didn't want the cameramen to overhear her. "I wanted to apologize for last night."

"What for?"

"Is your mic hot?"

Benji checked the mic pack on his belt. It was off. "What's going on?"

"All that stuff in front of the camera. The kiss, your mom. We didn't discuss how this was going to work."

Benji tossed his head in that practiced gesture he'd done the day they met. It made Hazel remember their initial connection—their shared ambition to succeed.

"We just pretend to be together for the cameras, right? Should be easy enough. Not like they're going to be checking our rooms for sleepovers."

"No, I know."

"So, easy peasy."

"And what about the other thing?"

"What's that?"

"What I said about my parents being dead. I know honesty's important to you."

Benji shrugged. "Sure. If we were dating, it would matter. But we're just friends, right? I'm sure you have a good reason for saying that."

"They're just not a part of my life, like I told you. I didn't want to have to explain that to Bella and everyone in front of the cameras."

"No worries." Benji rocked on his heels. "Anyway, I should jet. I'll be late to meet my mentor."

"Okay. Maybe we could grab lunch later?"

"Sure."

He walked away and Hazel felt more alone than ever. She didn't regret her decision to keep it platonic with Benji, but like a lot of things in her life, she hadn't thought the consequences through.

"You ready, Hazel?" the assistant said, popping her head out of the conference room. Her stomach lurched like it had when she was on the roller coaster at Harry Potter world. But there wasn't any time for nerves. She had a show to do. Hazel mustered an enthusiasm she did not feel. The competition felt like the only thing she had left. She couldn't screw that up too. "Ready!"

"Hazel, I'm so happy to meet you!" Kate Maple said.

Hazel raised her hands to the side of her face in a gesture she'd practiced in her mirror that morning, mimicking the usual reaction from contestants when they found out who their mentor was. The sudden movement didn't help her queasy belly, but Hazel *was* excited to see that it was Kate, one of her favorite contestants of all time.

Kate was in her early thirties and had won *The Sing Along* four years ago. She'd gone on to a platinum-selling album and a high-profile relationship with not one but two Oscar-nominated actors. She was currently rumored to be dating one of the stars of the Marvel Cinematic Universe, but that had never been confirmed.

"I'm huge fan," Hazel said. "I listened to your album on repeat for months when it came out."

Kate smiled. She had perfect small white teeth, and skin that belonged only to the very young or the very famous. Her blond hair was honey colored, and her arms and legs were tanned and toned. She had a cute button nose and deep-brown eyes that twinkled when she smiled, and was wearing a much more expensive sleeveless version of the dress that Hazel had on. "Don't you worry, you don't have to lie."

"I'm not!" Hazel's voice rose in a way that made it sound like that was exactly what she was doing. "I swear, I know all the words to 'Honeycomb.'"

Kate continued to look skeptical, which was one of the things Hazel had loved about her on the show. She didn't take herself too seriously, and, as far as Hazel could tell from the many interviews she'd watched since, that attitude had followed her into stardom.

Besides, what Hazel said was true, and she felt like she had to prove it to get off on the right foot with Kate. She steadied herself and threw her head back.

"I want to ru-un from you,
But my feet are planted to the ground.
I want to ge-et away,
But my voice won't make a sound.
You spoke in honeyed tones,
But you were only honeycomb."

There was a moment of silence when Hazel finished singing, then Kate broke into applause. "That was fantastic. You're the real deal, Hazel Fine, just like Nick said."

Hazel flushed with pleasure, then noticed the blinking light over Kate's shoulder. Was Kate only playing along for the cameras? Is that what Kate thought *she* was doing? Hazel couldn't blame Kate if she did, but all these questions were going to make her crazy. Hazel needed to get out of her own head.

"Thank you," Hazel said. "Honestly, I was so nervous before I walked in here."

"And now?"

"I'm excited."

"As you should be," Nick said, stepping out from behind a sound screen. He glanced at the cameraman. "You can cut."

The red camera light went out. Nick reached up and snapped off the key light, then addressed the crew. "All right, you can clear out. Come back in two hours when they've worked on some material."

The packed up quickly and stepped out of the room.

"That was great, Kate. You, too, Hazel." Nick said. He walked toward Kate with his hands out. "Thanks so much for doing this. I know your schedule's stacked."

Kate tossed her hair to the side. "Pretty sure it's in my contract, but you're welcome anyway."

Hazel's stomach sank, then flipped. Kate *was* playing a part. Hazel didn't know why she was surprised and disappointed.

"Oh no," Kate said, touching Hazel's arm lightly. "Don't look like that. I was just teasing Nick. He knows I was joking, don't you, Nick?"

"Kate loves her little jokes."

They laughed together, and Kate gave Nick a happy, possessive look that reminded Hazel of the way Bella looked at Benji. Only this time, it bothered her. What was happening? Hazel felt like she might throw up, and Nick was smiling with a genuineness that she'd never seen before.

"Are you okay, Hazel?" Nick asked. "You don't look so hot."

"Nick!" Kate slapped at his arm. "You can't say that to the

poor young thing. She looks like she's going to faint."

"Hazel? What? No, she's tougher than she—" Nick's face creased with concern. "Hazel. Kate's right. You don't look well. You should sit down." Then Nick was at her elbow holding her up. He led her to a couch in the corner of the room.

"I'm fine. I didn't each much this morning, that's all." She'd had a serving of eggs from the buffet, but they'd been sitting under the heat lamp for too long and had tasted off.

"You're not fine. Your eyes look glassy and—" He touched her forehead. His hand felt icy against her skin. "You're burning up. We need to take you to the doctor."

Hazel sank onto the couch, her legs giving out. What was wrong with her? "No, I—I don't have insurance."

Nick knelt in front of her. "Don't worry about that. The show will take care of it."

"Really, I'm fine. I just need to sit for a minute and eat something. I'll be okay, I promise." But at the thought of food, her stomach turned again.

"Hazel, be reasonable," Kate said. "Let Nick take you to the doctor."

Hazel clutched Nick's arm. "No, please. I don't want to lose my spot. I can power through this. It's the only thing I have left." Hazel hated how desperate she sounded, but it was true. She couldn't believe she'd said that out loud, though. She must be feverish.

"At least let me bring you something to eat. Orange juice? A croissant."

"Okay."

He gently pried her fingers off his arm. "Stay here. I'll be right back."

"Okay," Hazel said again.

He stood and left.

Hazel leaned back against the couch. The room was spinning. What could make her feel this way? She'd been fine when she woke up, hungry even. It had to be the eggs. Her stomach roiled at the thought of them, and she put her hand over her mouth, willing herself to take slow, deep breaths. The last thing she needed was to puke on Kate Maple.

At least the cameras were off.

Kate sat next to her. "You're sure you're okay?"

"I think I might have eaten something bad at breakfast. And it's been a rough couple of weeks. I haven't been sleeping." It was impossible to sleep more than a few hours at a time in the car. Last night she'd been too keyed up after the confrontation with Martin to fall asleep until past midnight.

"I've been there," Kate said. "You're lucky you have Nick looking out for you. I should've been so lucky."

Hazel breathed in and out slowly again. More air seemed to calm her stomach down. "He wasn't on the show then?"

Kate tucked a perfect lock of hair behind her left ear. She had on pretty star-shaped diamond earrings. "No, he was, but he was only the assistant to the musical director. This old-school guy called Donald who was a complete ass. But he gave Nick a chance, which was so great for him once his album was canceled. You know about that?" Kate glanced at her, and Hazel nodded slowly, trying to catch up. "He's so freaking talented but has terrible luck." Kate laughed bitterly. "Listen to me. I don't usually talk this much."

Hazel's head was spinning, and not just from whatever it was that was making her ill. "It's fine. I talk too much sometimes too."

Kate leaned toward her conspiratorially. "It's being around Nick again. Can you believe I had to agree to come on this show just so he'd spend time with me? He's so stubborn. But I know we can work it out if he gives us another chance."

Now Hazel was sure she was going to puke. "You and Nick?"

"The Beauty and the Beast, right?"

"Nick's not a beast."

Kate laughed. "He just plays one on TV."

Hazel forced a smile. "He's been supernice to me." That wasn't completely true, but Hazel felt the need to defend him.

"I'm glad to hear that. And your guy is quite the catch. Love his TikToks."

"Benji and I aren't—"

Kate pulled away as Nick walked back into the conference room with a large orange juice, a massive croissant, and a large coffee. "Nick, darling, you're a lifesaver."

Nick stopped in front of Hazel. "You take your coffee with two creams, right?"

"How did you . . . that's right, thank you. I think I might just need some air. The eggs I ate from the buffet aren't sitting right."

Nick made a face. "That buffet is a breeding ground for all kinds of bacteria. Feel free to eat in the producer's green room in the future. I'll let the attendant know."

"Thank you." Hazel gave Nick a wan smile. He smiled back as he handed her the coffee cup. Their fingers touched as she took it from him, and Hazel felt a flush creep up the back of her neck that had nothing to do with a fever. Hazel could feel Kate's gaze bearing down on her. She wished she could tell

Kate that she had nothing to worry about, that Nick was likely an idiot who'd soon see the error of his ways. But that was hard to do when Nick was staring at her so intently, looking like she was about to break.

Chapter Twelve

"Kate Maple!" Zoey said, stretching out on her bed. "You're so lucky."

"I know, right?"

Hazel wasn't feeling very lucky, but she wanted to recapture the enthusiasm she'd felt when she'd first seen Kate that morning. They'd had a good day working together once Hazel felt better, but it was still awkward between them. Plus, Nick was acting oddly, being superchatty and acting like he couldn't sit down. Hazel couldn't help but think that Kate wasn't going to have much trouble getting him back.

Which was fine. *Fine.* Hazel was fine with it. It was right there in her name.

"You've got a good mentor too," Hazel said.

Zoey flipped her hand dismissively. "I guess. I mean, he

made it to the top ten, right? So that's good. I'm sure he'll have all kinds of valuable advice."

Zoey had gotten paired with Dwayne Rogers, the only other Black country singer who'd ever been on the show. Hazel wished she could believe that this was some sort of coincidence, that the producers hadn't been so obvious as to simply see their race and genre and decide that that was enough, but since this was a competition that employed Martin, she didn't have much faith. The truth was that Dwayne hadn't gone anywhere after *The Sing Along*, and Zoey needed all the help she could get. Hazel felt bad for her friend.

"How did it go today in rehearsals?" Hazel asked.

"Pretty good. I'm going to do a Maren Morris song."

"That's a good choice for you."

"Yeah, that producer, Jen, wanted me to do 'Old Town Road,' but I put my foot down."

"What the hell?"

"Right?" Zoey twisted her hair around her finger. "That's what I said, and she actually listened. Anyway, what are you singing?"

"Julia Michaels's 'Issues.'"

"Ooh, I love that song."

"Me too."

"You totally sound like her."

"I wish."

There was a knock at the door. Hazel went to open it reluctantly. There were murmurs of a floor party floating around, but she just wanted to sleep.

It was Benji, with a guilty look on his face and a camera crew behind him.

"What's all this?" Hazel asked as her hand went to her head. Her hair was wrapped in a towel, and she was wearing a robe. She'd spent twenty minutes under a hot shower scrubbing the day away.

"I heard you weren't feeling well earlier, and I wanted to check on you."

"Bad breakfast buffet," Hazel said, rubbing her stomach. "I'm better now."

"That's good news."

Benji pulled her into a hug while the cameraman hovered behind him, rolling. Hazel buried her face in Benji's shoulder. He smelled like the ocean, and Hazel flashed back to their night on the beach.

"Sorry about this," he said, whispering in her ear.

She squeezed him, then pulled away. "It's fine. Thank you for checking on me."

Benji spoke to the cameraman. "A little privacy? You got your shot, right?"

"Sure, man, no problem." The camera fell from his shoulder, and he walked away.

"You want to come in?" Hazel said.

Benji followed her into the room, then sat down on the edge of Hazel's bed. He seemed tired, defeated.

"Hey, Benj. Good day?" Zoey asked.

"I've had better."

"I feel you." Zoey stood up. "I'll give you two some privacy."

"Thanks, Zo."

Zoey grabbed her phone and room key and left.

"Everything okay?" Hazel asked when the door shut. "Who did you get as your mentor?"

"You didn't hear? It's Brian Watanabe."

Of course it was. Only, unlike Zoey's mentor, Brian was a massive star, possibly the biggest one to come out of *The Sing Along* since it started. Hazel had long thought that the choice of mentor was a signal the producers gave to the public about who they thought should win. Kate was a positive choice, but getting Brian was more than a seal of approval. It was like saying *This is our winner right here* on a bright, blinking sign.

"That's fantastic, Benji."

"Yeah, he's all right."

"All right? Come *on*. You're a total shoo-in for the final now."

Benji nodded but it was joyless.

Hazel sat next to him. "So what's up?"

"It's just all this. Lying to the public. I thought I was okay with it, but I'm not."

"You're the one who brought the camera crew."

"Yeah, I know. I was in Cole's room, and he told me you were sick, and the crew was already there, so they insisted they come with me."

"You don't have to explain."

"But I want to."

"What changed from this morning?"

He sighed. "I had this whole conversation with Brian. He's so authentic, you know? And it reminded me that that's how I want to be. Because if you can't be yourself, then what's the point?"

Benji wanted to be authentic. Unlike Hazel, he was suggesting. Hazel the faker. Hazel the liar. "I get it," Hazel said. "We can break up."

"Not that we dated."

"No. We just had a bit of fun, right?"

"Yeah, we did." But Benji looked sad.

He didn't have real feelings for her, did he? No, that was crazy. They'd only hung out together that one time. Besides, she was too old for him. Not that he knew that.

It was funny. If she'd been twenty-two, she might've taken this hard. But everything that had happened since then had dulled her senses. Now she just felt a bit of regret. "How do you want to do it?"

"I don't think we can."

"Why not?"

"I saw it all the time in the TikTok house. There was always blowback on someone when there was a breakup."

"We can make it my fault."

"I don't want that."

"What do we do, then?"

Benji raised his shoulder. "Keep pretending, I guess."

"Okay."

"Let's try to keep those fake moments to a minimum, though, right?"

Hazel smiled to show him it was okay. "I certainly don't want to be in a towel on camera on a regular basis."

"I get it."

"I guess Bella will keep on hating me."

"I don't think—"

Hazel stopped him. "Let's not fight about it, okay?"

"Sure."

"Though . . ."

"What?"

"If we have to pretend that we're dating, maybe there's a way to use that to our advantage."

Benji sighed heavily. "What did you have in mind?"

J

The next day at breakfast, Hazel deliberately took a seat at the table next to where Bella was sitting. She then proceeded to discuss how ill she'd felt the day before in a loud voice with Zoey, knowing Bella was listening and couldn't resist jumping in with some sarcastic comment.

And then, right on cue: "You should go pee on a stick or something," Bella said. She had a plate of fruit in front of her, which was all she tended to eat in the mornings, or potentially at all. Bella had lost a few pounds between the first round and this one. Not that she needed to. If they were friends, Hazel might be worried about her.

"Excuse me?" Hazel said.

"You were sick yesterday? You've been going at it like bunnies with Benji. Sounds like you might be preggers."

"That's ridiculous."

"You say so."

"Mind your own business."

Bella gritted her teeth. "I'm trying to. You're the one who sat next to me when this whole place is practically empty."

Zoey crumpled up her napkin and stood. "I'm going to go to the bathroom." Part of the plan was that Zoey would leave for the next part. She wasn't the best at hiding her emotions or keeping secrets. Which was a good trait, but not very useful at that moment.

"Still digging for dirt, Bella?" Hazel said, knowing she was headed for dangerous territory. But you had to take some risks to get a reward.

"Just pointing out the glaringly obvious."

"And what's that?"

"That'll you do anything to get ahead. Including trapping poor Benji with a baby."

"Don't be ridiculous. I haven't even been with Benji since..." Hazel let her face fall. "Oh, you weren't supposed to know that."

"What?"

Hazel slumped in her chair, letting tears gather in her eyes. She'd always been able to cry on cue. "We're not together. I don't even think he likes me. He didn't call after we spent the night together. You know that time you caught me leaving his room?"

Bella's features narrowed in suspicion. "I find that hard to believe."

"It's true."

"Why the kiss the other night in front of the cameras?"

"You know how they are. Anything for ratings. They're making us do that."

"Why don't you just say no?"

Hazel wiped at her eyes, then lowered her voice. "I tried, but they didn't listen to me. Instead, everyone thinks I'm dating him, and he'll only talk to me when a camera's around."

"That's . . . is that true?"

"He even showed up at my room last night to film some stupid scene while I was in a *towel*. No warning." Hazel's lip started to quiver, and a few tears escaped. "It's so humiliating."

Hazel was crying in earnest now, putting her back into her performance. She slumped over the table, resting her forehead on her arms, hoping it wasn't too much.

Hazel felt a hand on her shoulder, patting her awkwardly.

"Hey, don't cry," Bella said tentatively. "You'll ruin your makeup."

Hazel lifted her head, tears streaking her cheeks. She dabbed at them with a napkin. "Sorry to lose it like that. I just can't believe I was so stupid."

"Men. They're all the same."

"Yeah. And you were totally right. I knew you were into him, and I should've stayed away. Stupid Hazel, stupid, stupid."

Bella handed her another napkin. "Don't be so hard on yourself. He's very flirty. I fell for it too."

"At least you didn't sleep with him."

"I'm sure I would have."

Benji walked into the breakfast room right on cue. He raised a hand in greeting, but then saw Hazel's smudged face and Bella's glare and backed out of the room slowly. Hazel had to hand it to him. If she didn't know better, she would've believed every gesture of that performance.

"The nerve of that guy," Bella said.

"It's fine. He has to eat."

"Not while you're here."

"I just don't know what to do. I can't stand having to pretend that we're together all the time. It's so fake. It just reminds me of the worst mistake I've ever made in my life."

Bella patted her on the arm again. "Let me take care of that."

"How?"

"My brother's friends with one of the producers. I'll drop him a word about what's really going on with you two and they'll stop focusing on you."

That was an unforeseen bonus. "Are you sure? I don't want to cause any trouble. For Benji either."

"Oh, he'll be fine. Men always are. We women have to stick together."

Hazel grinned at Bella. "You're right, we do. And I'm so sorry. I hope . . . I hope we can be friends?"

Bella paused. "We *are* still in competition with one another."

"I know. But so is Zoey and I swear, I would be happy if she won."

"Probably not going to happen, though."

Hazel wanted to agree with her, to cement her new bond with Bella, but there was only so far she could go. Bella was speaking the truth, but it wasn't one Hazel wanted to acknowledge.

"I think once the voting starts, anything can happen," Hazel said. "Behind the scenes, I'd like to root for all of us."

"Even Benji?"

"Even him."

Bella smiled as Zoey returned to the table.

Please don't ask why Zoey took so long in the bathroom, please don't ask why Zoey took so long in the—

"Wait, you guys are talking?" Zoey said with an incredulity that wasn't necessarily faked. She hadn't thought the plan was going to work, which was one more reason why Hazel had sent her to the bathroom with instructions to set a timer for ten minutes.

"Bella's been great. I told her about, well, you know—"

"Benji the bastard," Bella said.

Zoey stared at Bella. "You don't like him anymore?"

"I never *really* did. I kind of saw through him."

"Uh—"

"Of course you did." Hazel interrupted Zoey. "You're much more perceptive than me."

"I should've warned you," Bella said.

"I should've warned myself."

Bella smiled with satisfaction as she rose from the table. She'd eaten maybe three blueberries. Hazel didn't know how she had the energy to get through the day.

"I should go and call Dan, let him know about all this."

"Thank you so much for doing that."

"Not a problem. Maybe we can all have dinner later?"

Hazel worked hard to keep her face in check. "Definitely."

"Buck up, Hazel. You'll be okay. Bella's on the case."

Bella gave Hazel a last look of pity and walked away with a determined step. One thing Hazel knew about Bella: if you gave her a situation to manage, she'd be all over it.

"What did you do to her?" Zoey asked when Bella was thankfully out of earshot.

"I cried."

"That's all it took?"

"That and a lot of sucking up. Ugh. I just hope it was worth it."

"Maybe now Bella will stop trying to, you know, destroy you or whatever."

"Here's hoping."

Hazel pulled her phone out to check her makeup, but when she flipped the camera's view to selfie mode, she found more than her wrecked face. Nick was sitting two tables away, and he'd seen the whole thing.

She turned slowly to face him. He raised his hands deliberately, then started slow clapping.

"Performance of the whole competition, right there," he said as she sank in her seat.

Chapter Thirteen

"Hazel Fine!" Keshawn drawled into his microphone. "Come on up!"

Hazel left her seat and walked up to the stage. It was the first live results show, where they'd be winnowed down from twenty to sixteen. Two people had already been eliminated, but Benji, Zoey, and Bella were through, as was Cole.

Hazel was feeling increasingly nervous as the show went on, even though she'd been happy with her performance. She'd done a mix of an a cappella version of "Issues" and a rocking swing version. Her voice was in fine form, and she'd drawn praise from Georgia and Martin, though his had been a bit grudging.

The one thing that hadn't gone according to plan was Julia Michaels herself being that week's guest judge. She'd been very complimentary of Hazel's performance, but Martin had made a sly suggestion that Hazel had found out, somehow, who the judge was going to be and had catered her song choice accordingly. Georgia leaped to her defense, but you never could tell how those types of comments would influence the audience at home, who were now in charge of deciding who stayed and who didn't.

"How are you feeling about your performance last night?" Keshawn asked.

"Better thirty minutes ago."

"Ha!" Keshawn laughed and the audience laughed along with him.

Half the audience was contestants who'd been eliminated earlier in the season and the current contestants' families. She was the only one who didn't have anyone in her reserved seats.

She'd invited Amber and Theo, but Amber had to work. She promised she'd come next week if Hazel made it through. "I voted for you, though," Amber said on the phone. "Five times."

"You going to make me wait all night?" Hazel said to Keshawn in a teasing voice.

This was the sort of stuff the audience at home loved. You had to be likeable and approachable but show some grit too. At least, that's what Hazel had put together through her continued analysis of the show. If you didn't have a gimmick like Cole and his mama with her supportive T-shirts, then you had to pick a lane most people could easily understand.

"A girl who knows what she wants. Love it."

Hazel smiled even as she saw Martin frowning from the judges' stage. "You know it."

"And what about Benji Suzuki?"

"What about Benji?"

"You want him, too, I heard."

Hazel cringed but hid it behind a wide smile. "Oh, so you think *I'm* the pursuer, huh?"

"No?"

"The only thing I'm here to pursue is a win."

"Go for it, girlfriend."

"I am."

Keshawn laughed again, *just delighted.* "Before we get to these results"—Keshawn tapped the envelope in his hand against his palm—"let's get your mentor out here to hear what she has to say. Kate?"

Kate walked on from stage left as the audience roared its approval. During her season, Kate had mastered her rapport with the audience and had won with her positivity and easy laugh, though at almost thirty, she was one of the oldest female contestants the show had ever had. Knowing Kate the way she did now, it was easy to understand why she'd been so successful. Kate was a sunny person, instantly likeable, and supertalented too.

She waved to the audience and gave Hazel a hug.

"Glad to have you back, Kate," Keshawn said.

"I'm so happy to be here. I couldn't be prouder of my girl." She put her arm around Hazel's shoulders. "She nailed it."

"Nailed it!" Keshawn sang in a slightly reedy voice. "Agreed."

"Now show us those results," Kate said with a cheerful laugh.

"Yes, ma'am. You ready, Hazel?"

"Ready!"

Keshawn grinned, then tore open the envelope. "Hazel, I hope you like this hotel because you'll be living here for another week. You're through to the next round!"

A wave of happiness broke over Hazel. She'd done it. She'd made it to the round of sixteen. She felt stunned and happy all at once.

Kate grabbed her and they jumped up and down as Keshawn cut to commercial.

"You did it," Kate said in her ear. "Now let's take the whole thing."

Later that night, the cast and crew were in a bar a few blocks from the hotel that had been rented out for them for the night. It was the only way to ensure that no outsiders got in while they let off a bit of steam before starting the whole machine again the next week.

Kate had come with her for the first part of the evening, and they'd shared a cocktail, then strategized about the rest of the competition. Kate had all kinds of plans for Hazel, and talking to her made Hazel feel like she really had a shot at winning *The Sing Along*.

While they talked, Kate kept checking her phone and eventually confessed that Nick was supposed to join them. But he'd been caught up in something at work, so when they finished their drink, Kate apologized for cutting the evening short and left.

Hazel wasn't sure whether she should be reassured that you

could be that successful and *still* be that insecure about a guy, or depressed. She opted for getting another drink and joining Zoey at the bar with Brooke, who was back in town for the week.

Cole was sitting with Dave to the left of Hazel. Hazel gave them a polite nod. Even though Zoey had made it back on the show, it was no thanks to Dave. Hazel couldn't even understand how Dave was still *on* the show, as he continued to be a lowlight week after week.

Hazel worked through her drink slowly, watching a bit of drama unfold when Cole's mother caught him drinking a light beer. She took it away from him and shook her fist at the bartender while Cole flushed with embarrassment.

Hazel gave him a sympathetic smile as he scowled into the Diet Coke the bartender placed in front of him instead.

Zoey and Brooke were tied up with each other, so Hazel picked up her glass and turned in her stool to watch the party. The music was loud and full of bass, and the bar was dark with a smoky effect that made everyone a bit blurry. Hazel knew she should finish her drink and go back to the hotel, but the people watching was too interesting to give up.

For example, Bella had pressed Benji into a corner and was talking to him with animated hand gestures. Luckily, there weren't any cameras around, because as far as the show and the audience at home knew, Hazel and Benji were still together.

Whatever Bella had said to her brother Dan, *if* she had, hadn't changed a thing. An assistant had told her and Benji to walk into the bar hand in hand through the swarm of paparazzi outside. He'd dropped her hand the moment they were through the door. He was clearly pissed that they had to keep up this ruse, and Hazel couldn't blame him.

But really, was it so terrible to act like he liked her for a few minutes a day?

Nick walked up to the bar, squeezing between her and Zoey. "Can I get a Heineken?"

Hazel spun his way. Her bare leg swept against his arm, and she felt a shiver of something she wasn't sure she wanted to explore.

"Make that two," Hazel said, pushing her empty cocktail glass away.

The bartender reached down into the fridge, emerging with two green bottles. He popped off the caps. "Glass or bottle?"

"It comes in a glass," Nick said, and Hazel laughed.

"Cheers," Nick said, tilting his bottle in her direction after the bartender handed them the beers.

They clinked, then each took a swig. The beer felt cool slipping down her throat.

"Good job yesterday," Nick said.

"Thank you. Kate's a good coach."

"She is." He'd traded in his T-shirt for a dark-green long-sleeved button-down, which he'd rolled up to the elbows. It was a good color on him, and Hazel appreciated how good he looked and smelled. In a different world, he was the guy in this bar she'd be drawn to, but in *The Sing Along*, it was hard to pin him down. Sometimes he was nicer than she expected, and others he was worse. But there *was* something between them. Hazel just wasn't sure what.

"You missed her," Hazel said. "She went home."

"She texted."

"Were you avoiding her?"

He put his beer down slowly. "What makes you say that?"

"Just . . . what work could there be tonight?"

"If you must know, I was prepping song selections for next week. I had some last-minute negotiations with one of the publishers to get some songs I thought we could use."

"Oh, sorry."

"It's fine." Nick picked up his beer and drained half of it. "How's the rabbit?"

"Surviving."

"You took a risk bringing him to the hotel."

"I know. But he's important to me, and I couldn't just leave him behind. You're not going to rat me out, are you?"

"No, but I can't say the same for Martin." Nick played with his bar napkin. "No family you could leave him with?"

"No." Hazel was about to launch into the my-parents-are-dead spiel then stopped herself. She didn't need to lie about that to Nick.

"Fair enough."

"Kate's pretty into you."

He took a beat. "She tell you that?"

"In a manner of speaking." Hazel felt embarrassed that she'd blurted that out. She didn't need to tell on Kate. "I mean, it's kind of obvious."

"You think so?"

"If you hang out with you guys, then yes. I think it's great. You make a cute couple." Hazel was speaking in a way that felt slightly manic. She picked up her beer to stop herself.

"We're not together."

"But you might be again, right? I mean, why not?"

Nick didn't say anything, just kept his gaze leveled at her.

Hazel felt a flush rising. He always seemed so calm when he looked at Hazel like that, while Hazel felt anything but.

"Is that song I heard you sing a couple of weeks ago about her?"

"I make it a policy not to discuss song inspirations."

"I'll take that as a yes." Hazel gulped for breath, her mind going *rat-tat-tat*. "It's a great song. I wish your album had worked out, but you know you don't need a label to put out music. You could upload it yourself to SoundCloud or iTunes or Spotify."

Shut up, Hazel. Just shut up.

"I know that."

"Then why don't you?"

He finished his beer. "Because I don't want to make it that way. Hustling that hard. I was souring on the business before my album went south. I love music, don't get me wrong, but what you have to do to make it, what Kate has to do . . . it's not for me."

"You don't want to put yourself out there."

"I want to be able to control which parts of me I share and which I don't. But that's not how the business works anymore. Doling out your traumas at least once an album is required. I'm not into it."

"Not everyone has to do that—"

But Nick was on a roll. "Take this whole thing with you and Benji."

"What whole thing?"

"You know what I mean. Your made-for-the-cameras relationship. It's a perfect example of what I'm talking about. They take something innocent and blow it up to create drama."

"If we both don't care, what's the harm?"

"Do you both not care, though?"

Nick hadn't looked away. Hazel wanted to, but that would feel like defeat. "We'll be fine."

"I'm sure you will." Nick smiled slowly. "That was quite the number you did on Bella the other day."

"Shh! No one can know about that." Hazel twisted her head around, worried Bella might be within earshot, but she was still deep in conversation with Benji across the room.

Cole was sitting a few seats away, though, drinking what looked like a gin and tonic, his mama nowhere in sight. He raised his glass to her, and she returned the gesture. He didn't seem to have heard what Nick said or have understood it if he had. Phew.

She returned her attention to Nick, who righted himself and stepped closer to Hazel. He was standing between her legs now, the inside of her knees touching his jeans. She could feel the heat of his body through them, and an answering heat in herself.

"I won't spill your secrets, Hazel Fine." His tone was low and intimate.

"No?"

He leaned closer so he was speaking almost into her ear. "No."

His breath tickled her neck and started a beat between her legs. She could feel his lips hovering above her exposed skin and she wanted to reach up and cradle his face, to meet his lips with hers and find out what he tasted like.

"Hazel?"

The touch of his voice made her freeze. What was he doing? What was *she* doing?

Hazel pulled her body back. "Is that what happened to you and Kate?"

"Excuse me?" He straightened, the moment disappearing fast.

"She wanted to share, you didn't?"

"Where is this coming from?"

"'Honeycomb.' Those lyrics. They're about you, right?"

He grimaced. "Absolutely not."

"Sorry, did I hit a nerve?"

"It's fine. I should get going."

"Okay."

"Congratulations again. Keep up the good work."

Hazel reached out and caught the edge of his sleeve. "Wait, Nick."

"Yes?"

"What . . . what were you doing at Harry Potter world?"

"What?"

"A few weeks ago, on the roller coaster. Why were you there?"

He raised his shoulder. "Sometimes a roller coaster is just a roller coaster."

"Is that a metaphor?"

"It's just a fact. Night, Hazel."

She started to watch him walk away then spun her chair around to stop herself. She didn't need to be watching Nick like he was some important person in her life, and this was some big dramatic moment full of meaning. There was an attraction, sure, but that's all it was and all it could be.

"What can I get you?" the bartender asked. "You want to stick with the beer?"

"She wants champagne!" Bella said, slapping her on the back. "Right, Hazel!" Bella was drunk, slurring her words.

"I was thinking about leaving."

"Oh, poo. Don't be a spoilsport. Come on." She tapped Brooke's shoulder until she and Zoey broke apart. "You guys want champagne, right?"

"Yes, please," Brooke said while Zoey nodded enthusiastically.

"A bottle of champagne, and four glasses."

"Champagne's not on the menu tonight," the bartender said.

Bella took her black card out and slipped it across the bar. "It is now."

"Bollinger okay?"

"That'll do. Right, Hazel?"

"Sure, sounds great."

The bartender left to fetch the bottle.

"I'm so happy!" Bella said, sitting next to Hazel and turning her stool around in a circle and then again with her arms in the air.

Hazel couldn't help but laugh. What had gotten into Bella?

"You did great, Bella," Zoey said. "Congratulations."

"We all did! Right, Hazel? We kicked some ass."

"Everything okay?" Hazel said.

"Everything is great. Why wouldn't it be! We're on *The Sing Along*!" She said it so loudly others in the bar heard them. A cheer rose up as the bartender brought the champagne and glasses out. He popped the cork.

"That's a happy sound!" Bella said. "Let's pour it."

"What happened with you and Benji over there?" Zoey asked. "I thought he was the enemy?"

Bella smiled like a cat. "Don't you worry about him. I'm taking care of it."

"Bella." Hazel's voice was a warning.

"Don't worry. A little revenge never hurt anyone."

"I think it does, actually."

"I'm just giving him a taste of his own medicine."

Hazel's heart sank. People didn't change. Certainly not Bella. "He's not a bad guy . . ."

"Enough. Who cares about him? We're celebrating us!" Bella picked up a glass and pushed the others toward Hazel, Zoey, and Brooke. "To the women of the show. My soul sisters."

Zoey's faced clouded and Brooke looked like she was going to break into a lecture about cultural appropriation.

"It's a nice sentiment, right, girls?" Hazel said, given them both a warning with her eyes. Now was not the time. She picked up two champagne glasses and handed them to them. "What should we toast to?"

"To us," Bella said. "The belles of the ball!"

"To us!" they all said together, and clinked their glasses.

Hazel brought the champagne to her lips, and as the first bubbles slid down, she felt buoyed. She was always too serious about everything. She was in the top sixteen!

Bella was right. It was time to celebrate.

Chapter Fourteen

When Hazel's phone shattered her sleep the next morning, she was glad she'd stopped at one glass of Bella's champagne. It was the start of a new week, and she was going to have to learn not just one song, but two. There was also a group number with choreography, never her strong suit. She needed all her faculties, and then some.

She'd never truly appreciated when she watched all those seasons of *The Sing Along* how hard the contestants had to work. Not that she was complaining. This was her dream, and she was prepared to work as hard as necessary to win. Plus, they were finally getting paid more than a per diem, and she was socking away as much of it as she could so that she'd have a cushion if this didn't work out.

The show also uploaded their performances to iTunes and

Spotify each week, and they got a small cut of the royalties, though it was shocking how many streams it took to get any real money. Hazel was both pleased and amazed to see that two of her performances already had over a million streams. Someone outside the bar the night before had even asked for her autograph.

It had been a long time since Hazel had felt like the center of anyone's attention, and she could admit she liked it. It also created danger signs, a tickle at the back of her neck that was a warning that something ominous was coming.

She should've paid more attention to that feeling.

Because the call she was about to miss wasn't from Amber or Benji or even Vern.

It was from her mom.

She stared at the phone vibrating on the nightstand with that accusatory word lighting up the screen: *Mom*. Before the brief conversation with her father after Harry Potter world, she hadn't talked to her parents in over a year, after their last blowout fight when Hazel had made it clear that she was leaving Austin for good and going to L.A. Her parents thought she should walk away from the industry, that she should do something safe and boring like teach music or work in a library. Mostly, they just wanted her to live with them so they could go back to controlling everything about her.

But Hazel had had enough of their control and manipulation. If she made mistakes in the future, she wanted them to be her own mistakes, not theirs.

The phone stopped buzzing and the call went to voice mail. Hazel breathed a sigh of relief. But then her mother called back.

"You going to get that?" Zoey said groggily from her bed as Brooke groaned quietly beside her. They'd helped Bella finish the bottle of champagne and the next one. Hazel had had to help them back to the room and had vowed to ask Zoey to get a separate room the next time Brooke was in town.

"Getting it," she said. She picked up the phone. "Hold on one second."

"Hello?" Her mother's shrill voice set her teeth on edge.

"Just wait a second."

Hazel slipped on a pair of shoes and grabbed her room key while holding the phone against her chest. Brooke was spooned around Zoey in their bed. They looked so adorable. Hazel wished she could have that. She saw a flash of her and Nick curled into one another, then dismissed it. Nick wasn't the solution to her problems, even if he wanted something with her, which she doubted despite the way he was acting last night. Besides, all this sentiment was clearly a prereaction to speaking to her mother, which she couldn't put off any longer.

She opened the door and went into the hall. She leaned against the wall and raised the phone to her ear. "I'm here."

"Jack! She's on the line. Jack!"

"Mom, can you just talk to me? I can talk to Dad after."

"Jack? Are you picking up? She answered!"

Hazel sank down the wall to the carpet. It was scratchy and smelled faintly of chemicals. Hazel wanted to hang up but she knew that now that her parents had it in their minds that they were going to talk to her there was no escaping it. They'd call and call until she changed her number.

"Hello?"

"Hi, Dad."

"Where are you?"

"How are you, Dad?"

"What's that? Oh, I'm fine, I'm fine. Your mother is fine too."

"That's good."

"You never called me back about those documents."

"I told you I'm not signing those. So you can stop asking."

"Yes, well—"

"What's all this about you being on a television program?" her mother said, interrupting her father the way she'd done all of Hazel's life.

Hazel could imagine her, sitting in the kitchen, clinging to the beige wall phone they'd insisted on bringing with them from their old house like it was a lifeline. Her father was probably in his office, a dark, oak room that the decorator had promised was *very* masculine. The shelves were lined with books he'd never read. They'd used a service, he'd told her proudly, that purchased used books to fill library shelves *for design purposes.*

"It's a singing competition."

"A singing competition?"

Hazel closed her eyes. Her parents lived in a weird world where the only television they watched was PBS. If it wasn't on "the PBS" then it didn't exist. Her parents had been older when they'd had her, in their early forties, and Hazel had felt that multigenerational gap most of her life. "Mom, come on. You know what a singing competition is. We used to watch *American Idol* together."

"Oh, yes, I remember. Is that what you're on?"

"No, it's called *The Sing Along.* You can look it up online. Dad can show you."

"Do you think that's wise?" her father said, his gravelly voice like breaking rocks.

"Wise to look it up for Mom?"

"That was not what I meant, young lady."

Deep breaths, Hazel told herself. *Serenity now, insanity later.* "How did you know I was on the show if you aren't watching it?"

"I saw an advertisement on the television. I almost didn't recognize you—my own daughter!—and why are they saying your name is Hazel Fine?" her father asked.

Hazel felt a sense of satisfaction that even her parents had trouble recognizing her. "You know that's my name now."

"I don't appreciate it. And why didn't you tell us you were doing the show?"

"Because you would've told me not to do it."

"We would have," her father agreed. "Because this is a terrible idea."

"It's my life."

"That's not entirely true. I can't believe you're courting publicity in this way. What if—"

"No one knows about that."

"And if they find out? What will you do then?"

Hazel stared at her toes. Her manicure was chipped, and the tops of her feet were bruised from the heels she'd been wearing the night before. "I don't know, Dad. Weather the storm, I guess, just like I have everything else."

"And what about us?"

"What about *you*?"

"This reflects badly on us," her father said, like he was talking to a child. He'd never stopped talking to Hazel like that, not in her whole life, even though she'd been the most adult person in the house since she was twelve. "You don't know what your mother has suffered all these years. And now you want to go and drag it all up again."

"I'm not dragging anything up. God. This isn't about *you*."

"There's no need to shout. Or take the lord's name in vain."

Hazel clutched the phone. She had been shouting, but she couldn't help it. She and her parents had been at loggerheads from the moment Hazel could talk, even though to the outside world they were a perfect little unit. But people should know better. It's the nicest families that are often rotten to the core.

This was about more than that, though. Her parents had used her and betrayed her in a way Hazel didn't think she could come back from. And the worst part was they'd never even expressed one grain of regret or remorse. How were you supposed to forgive people who didn't even think they had to ask for it?

"Sorry," Hazel said.

"It's all right, dear," her mother said. "You just go and quit that competition and then you can come back here, and we can get you into that program we talked about."

"The teaching program?"

"That's right. You could teach music to kids. Wouldn't you like that?"

Hazel dropped her head into her hands. That was the most frustrating thing about her parents. They understood enough about her to zero in on something that was adjacent to something she'd like. As a child, they'd supported her interest in music and singing and gotten involved. Overinvolved. But they never truly understood her. Hazel didn't want to teach music to kids, she wanted to *play*, to *write*, to *perform*. She wanted to make a living off the high she got onstage. And she could explain that to them until she was blue in the face, but they'd never get it.

"I don't want to do that. I've told you and told you."

One of the doors down the hall opened and Cole and his mother tripped out. Her daily T-shirt was a screen print of Cole singing that looked like a Warhol painting. It was cute, but she was the last person Hazel wanted to see right now. Overinvolved stage mothers were something she had strong opinions about, especially when they were giving her judgmental looks like Cole's mom was.

"I have to go," Hazel said, her voice a whisper.

"What's that, dear?"

"I have to go. It's time for breakfast."

"You never told us where you were staying."

"I'm in a hotel. The competition puts us up."

"That's better than—"

"I have to go. Thanks for calling."

Hazel hung up as her parents continued to talk. She didn't need to hear the rest of this conversation. She knew where it was going. They'd insist that Hazel come home, and it would end in tears and yelling, and Hazel couldn't take that right now.

She was twenty-eight years old. Wasn't there a statute of limitations on when your parents' opinions didn't reduce you to childhood?

"Everything okay, Hazel?" Benji said, coming down the hall. His hair was wet, his face sun-kissed.

"Out for a morning surf?"

"Yep. You should join me sometime."

Hazel looked around for a camera, but they were alone in the hallway. "I'd like that. Maybe not the surfing part, but the swim was nice."

Benji held his hand out and Hazel took it, letting him hoist her up.

"You're crying," Benji said.

"Am I?" Hazel lifted her T-shirt to wipe her tears away. "Sorry."

"What are you apologizing for?"

"I don't know."

"Who were you talking to?"

Hazel lowered her voice. "My parents."

"Ah."

"We don't have to talk about this."

"No, it's fine." Benji ran his hand through his hair. "Parents can be tough."

"We just don't . . . we're so different."

"Is that why you said they were dead?"

"No, I—it's hard for me to explain. I can't have them in my life. I knew that the show liked to make the families a big part of the picture, all those *Hazel goes home*, et cetera, segments. So I thought it would be easier."

"To lie."

"Yes."

Benji didn't say anything, but Hazel could feel his judgment. Maybe if he knew everything that had happened, he'd feel differently about her. But then again, probably not. It wasn't a pretty story, and part of the whole reason she'd lied about her age and kept her parents out of it was to move on from that ugliness.

"Dodged a bullet, huh?" Hazel said lightly.

"I didn't want to dodge you."

Hazel felt the weight of his gaze and thought, briefly, of doing something about it. Everything would be so much easier if they were together. Benji was the kind of guy who'd be behind you, encouraging you, loyal. Maybe not forever, but while you were together that's how it would be. She knew enough about him to know that.

But it was no use. There was a wedge between them now made up of her lies, and he didn't even know the half of it.

"Well, it's good you did," Hazel said. "I'm a mess."

"Can I help?"

"You have. You are."

The door to Bella's room opened and she stepped out. She stopped when she saw Hazel and Benji together, a sliver of doubt crossing her face.

Hazel took a step back. She didn't want Bella to think there was anything going on with her and Benji. And Hazel wasn't fooled by Bella's professions of sisterhood at the bar. She still had a thing for him, and if Benji was into it, then what did it matter to Hazel?

Besides, if Benji "cheated" on Hazel with Bella, that would make Hazel the victim, and she might get some sympathy votes.

Ugh. Hazel hated how her brain worked sometimes.

"Hi, Bella," Hazel said. "Ready for today?"

"Think so."

"I'm supernervous. Had a little breakdown out here in the hall and Benji found me."

Benji raised an eyebrow. *Always with the lies*, Hazel could see him thinking.

"You're nervous?" Bella asked.

"Everyone gets nervous."

"I didn't think you did."

"Today's a big deal. Top sixteen. This shit is getting real." Hazel gave Bella an anxious smile that was only partly an act. She *was* worried about this week. Anything could happen at this point, including her going home. Or, in her case, back to her car. "You're nervous, too, right Benj?"

He shrugged. "I caught some nice waves this morning. It chills me out."

"Surfing stresses me out." Hazel caught a look from Benji and moved on quickly. "I should ask Zoey for a Xanax."

Bella's head twitched. "Zoey has Xanax?"

Why couldn't she keep her mouth shut? Hazel needed to get out of this hallway. It was time to take Checkers for a walk anyway, and maybe then let him spend a night in the car as a break for Brooke and Zoey.

"I was joking."

"You sure are acting weird," Bella said.

"I woke up on the wrong side of the bed. I'm going to go take a shower and shake those cobwebs out then report for duty, and I'm sure I'll be as right as rain soon."

Bella started to laugh. "As right as rain? You sound a million years old."

"It's something my dad used to say. And he was approximately a million years old, yes." Hazel turned and put her key against the keypad before this scene got any weirder. "I'll see you two later?"

"Sure, Hazel."

"Thanks for scraping me up off the floor, Benji."

"Any time."

Hazel slipped back into her room as her phone buzzed. It was a text from her father, which shocked her because she didn't know he knew how to text.

I did not appreciate how you ended that conversation. Your mother is very upset.

Hazel threw her phone down on her bed.

There was a lot of things she didn't appreciate about her parents, but the worst of it was how easily they could get to her. For once, though, Hazel was going to keep that thought to herself instead of writing back to him angrily. She needed to find the strength to do that more often.

A resolution more easily made than kept.

Chapter Fifteen

The day after the call with her parents, Hazel was in an Uber weaving through traffic in West Hollywood, on her way to meet Kate for lunch. They were meeting at the San Vicente Bungalows, a private club Hazel had heard about but never dreamed of attending.

"It's there," the driver said, pointing to a white building that didn't look fancy enough to be a club full of all the hottest celebrities. But there was a valet outside, a small velvet rope, and several tall men in black T-shirts with earpieces in their ears—all the trappings of potential celebrity sightings. That was the odd thing about Los Angeles: you never knew what was going to take off and why, or what was inside a faded facade.

Hazel walked up the steps and went to the check-in

station. She told the ultrathin woman behind the counter, who was wearing four-inch heels and a tight black dress, that she was there to meet Kate.

"There's no photography inside."

"No problem."

The woman handed her a plastic strip with two green stickers on it, the larger of which read "San Vincente Bungalows" in a fancy script. "What are these for?"

"To cover the cameras on your phone."

"You can't be serious?"

"We are. Please take out your phone."

Hazel pulled it out and put it on the counter. Its case was cracked and dingy, and the whole device needed to be replaced. "Put the stickers here and here." The woman pointed to the camera on the back and then the front.

Hazel followed her directions. "Everyone does this?"

"Our members value their privacy."

"So, they come to a place to be seen but they don't want to be photographed?"

"Indeed. Robert will show you to your table."

An older man in a waistcoat appeared at Hazel's elbow and walked her through the main restaurant, which looked like an old greenhouse with small bistro tables littered around a koi pond, to an oak-paneled "library."

"Here we are, miss."

"Thank you."

Hazel took a seat on a red leather banquette and glanced around. There was another woman in the room, sitting at a large round table, drinking a cocktail and working on her laptop. There was no sticker across the laptop camera, Hazel noticed, a breach in security that seemed like a sloppy mistake. Also, what was stopping her from taking the stickers off her phone? Nothing, that's what.

Hazel turned and looked back into the greenhouse. There were several people who seemed familiar, but none Hazel could place. They were likely celebrity adjacent, agents and screenwriters, and the real celebrities were probably escorted to the private bungalows at the back.

"Can I bring you some water, miss?" a waiter asked.

Hazel's stomach rumbled. "Do you have a menu?"

"I can't serve you any food until your member arrives. I can bring you a drink, though."

Hazel sighed inside. This was exactly the kind of rule that drove her mad. She could get shitfaced before Kate got there but god forbid she eat a morsel of food.

"Can I get a glass of prosecco?"

"Yes, miss, right away."

He put a small card with the lunch offerings down on the table then beetled away. Hazel read it. The menu was surprising, full of fried items that were very un-Hollywood but sounded delicious. She pushed it away. Reading it only made her hungrier.

"Here you are!" Kate said, swanning up to the table with a drink in her hand, wearing a white linen jumpsuit and a wide-brim hat that would look ridiculous on Hazel but suited Kate perfectly. "I was just talking to Shawn."

"Shawn?"

"Mendes. He's so cute. He has a bungalow for the day."

She'd been right about the real celebrities being tucked away somewhere else. "No problem."

The waiter brought her glass of prosecco on a small tray.

Kate sat across from her. "Oh, you got a drink, great. And the fried zucchini is delicious. We'll have an order of that. And some of that saganaki cheese. I at least want to watch you while you eat it."

Hazel laughed, but she knew it wasn't a joke. Kate was thin, on the border of being too thin—that scale where you could tip from everyone telling you that you looked ah-mazing to people asking if you were okay.

"You have to try at least one," Hazel said. "I insist."

"Don't worry, I will. I've been saving my calories for this." Kate made a face and took another sip of her vodka and soda. Real tonic was too much sugar. "So, you're probably wondering why I dragged you all the way out here."

"I was. Not that I'm not grateful to see this place. It's a trip."

Kate laughed. "It's old-fashioned and fusty. My manager insisted I join. Did they make you do that silly thing to your phone?"

"They did."

"Keep the stickers. They're a status symbol now." She flashed her phone at Hazel, the back of which was littered with green Bungalows stickers.

"The things we do . . ."

"Exactly. Which is what I wanted to discuss. I really like you, Hazel, and I agree with Nick that you're one of the most talented people on the show this year."

Hazel flushed as she took a sip of her drink. The bubbles tickled her nose. "Thank you."

"He didn't tell you that, did he?"

"No."

Kate tapped the straw in her drink up and down. "That man. He's so infuriating sometimes."

"That I can agree with."

"It's hopeless between us, you know."

"Why do you say that?"

"Because I'm too much for him. This"—she flashed her hand around the room—"is too much for him. And as much as I profess to hate it, I really kind of don't, you know? I mean, my life is pretty fabulous."

"I'm glad you're happy. That's refreshing."

"I am. I'm not saying there aren't bad parts, but maybe because I was older when it happened, I can appreciate it. I didn't have to grow up in the public eye. I feel sorry for those who did."

"Me too," Hazel said with more feeling than she meant to.

"I think it could happen for you, too, Hazel, but we need a gimmick. Something to make you stand out and get people to root for you. The Benji thing is good—everyone likes a showmance—but it's not enough."

Hazel took a sip of her drink. "We aren't even together, to be honest."

"Really? Huh. Does the show know?"

"They do, but they don't seem to care."

"That figures," Kate said. "That's going to be tough to keep up. No chance of reconciliation there?"

"I don't think so. We weren't ever together. We just went on one date, but that was enough for the show."

"What happened?"

"Would you believe I'm not into him?"

Kate laughed. "Is it the truth?"

"It is. He's great, don't get me wrong, but we don't have that spark."

"Fair enough. Hmmm. What about your childhood? I noticed your parents aren't around. Anything we can mine there?"

Hazel tried not to wince. "I'd rather not."

"Okay, I get it. There has to be something." She tapped her perfect nails on the table.

The waiter arrived with their food, a delicious *mezze* of fried items and Greek condiments. Hazel didn't care if she didn't fit into her outfit for this week's show. No way was she going to be able to resist this spread. She picked up a piece of fried zucchini and nearly groaned when she bit into it.

"That good?" Kate asked.

"You have to have one."

Kate eyed the plate with trepidation as one of her songs came on over the sound system. It was an early track, full of hope about her new life.

Hazel wondered if they did it on purpose, played their member's tunes when they were in the house. The last two songs had been by Shawn Mendes.

"What about trying an original song?" Hazel said.

"That you wrote? Are you good? That's superrisky."

"I do write, but I was thinking more of Nick's songs, maybe? The ones on his album that were never released. I heard one of them, and, man."

Kate picked up a piece of zucchini. "He played you one of his songs?"

So much for Kate being over him. "I walked in on him

in the auditorium when he thought he was alone. Something about people running from one another. Was it about you?"

Kate popped the zucchini into her mouth. She closed her eyes in appreciation. "I wish. All those songs are about his college girlfriend. 'The one that got away,' though you know what, we ran into her once and she was a total bitch."

Hazel burst out laughing. "Dudes love bitches."

"I know. What is up with that?"

"No idea."

"Hmmm. It's a good idea, doing something original. Not the songs on his album necessarily, but maybe you could write something together. He's a great collaborator."

"You've written together?"

Kate picked up a piece of bread and dunked it in the tzatziki. Hazel felt guilty for being her gateway to unhealthy eating.

"My last album. 'Honeycomb,' some of the other singles."

"Is *that* about Nick?" Hazel couldn't resist asking, especially because of Nick's reaction when she'd asked the other night.

Kate dropped the piece of bread. "What? No."

"Oh, sorry, I just assumed—"

"What is *he* doing here?"

Hazel turned around. It was Martin, and he was directing Sarah Baines to a table in the greenhouse. He nodded briefly to Kate and ignored Hazel.

Like Dave, Sarah was still, improbably, in the competition, though everyone said she *had* to get cut this round. There was no way enough people at home were going to vote for her regardless of the amount of praise Martin heaped on her each week after her mediocre performances.

"That poor girl," Kate said.

"I guess she knows what she's doing."

"I doubt that. You should stay away from him."

"I already got that memo, unfortunately."

Kate leaned forward. "You didn't give in, did you?"

"No. Absolutely not."

"Good." Kate drained her glass and made a sign to the waiter to bring her another one. Then she picked up the bread she'd dropped and put it in her mouth. "That asshole."

"Did he . . ."

Kate wouldn't meet her eyes. "'Honeycomb.' It's about him."

"I'm so sorry."

"Yeah, well, I don't know what I was thinking. Nick was the one who saved me. I thought he was going to kill Martin, he was so mad."

"Why is he allowed to get away with it?"

"Because he's Martin. Full stop. He makes the big bucks, so they look the other way. And it's not like it isn't all 'consensual.' I mean, not really, because of the power dynamics, but just enough so the higher-ups can shake their heads and talk about the appeal of powerful men."

"That's screwed up."

"It is." Kate's hands were shaking. "I knew coming back on the show was a mistake."

"Are you okay?"

"I'll be fine. You turned him down?"

"I did."

"Did he say that he'd tank you if you didn't comply?"

"Not in so many words, but that was definitely the subtext."

Kate picked up her fresh drink from Robert's tray before

he could put it down. "Good for you." She took a long sip. "Okay, we're doing this. We're going to start writing songs for you. One an episode. That's going to be your thing. You up for the challenge?"

Hazel raised the remainder of her glass. "To prove Martin wrong?"

"You got it."

"I'm in."

"Okay, Hazel," Nick said, sitting at the piano in their rehearsal room the next day. His T-shirt was sage green instead of black, and it brought out the green in his eyes. "What do you want to write about?"

They were alone. Kate was supposed to join them later, but for now, it was just the two of them. Hazel had found herself taking more care than she usually did with her appearance when it was only a rehearsal, and she'd forgone her usual age-reducing braids. Instead, she'd straightened her hair and let it hang loose against her shoulders, and paired it with a pair of worn jeans and a boyfriend T-shirt that felt comfortable and sexy at the same time. Nick had smiled at her in appreciation when she'd walked in, and she'd savored the moment despite her nerves at having to write a whole new song.

"Can't I do one of your songs?" Hazel asked. "What about the one I heard you singing a couple of weeks ago? That was beautiful."

"If we're going to say it's an original song, it has to be new and original to you. Otherwise it's just a cover of a song no one's ever heard."

"I'm not feeling that inspired these days."

"This was your idea."

"Kate's actually." Hazel sat down at the conference room table. Maybe it was the setting that was problematic. The beige-and-pink wallpaper wasn't particularly inspiring and the chairs felt too plush for songwriting. It was funny how quickly you could get used to luxury, even when you'd been living in your car.

Nick considered her from the piano. Hazel wanted to sit on the bench next to him, but that felt too forward. "When you wrote in the past, what did you write about?"

"Depended. It felt like the words just came to me most of the time. Not divine intervention, but like my subconscious was working on stuff without me thinking about it."

"Sure, I get it. Those kinds of songs can be great. But if you want to be a real songwriter, then you need to be able to write even when you're not feeling it."

"Like a job?"

"It is a job." Nick started playing a chord progression in halftones on an offbeat.

"That's pretty."

"Anything coming to you?"

"Keep playing." Nick repeated the chords a few more times, but it was no use. "What were *you* thinking about when you wrote that?"

Nick dropped his hands from the keys. "You can't use my life to inspire your songs. You have to dig into your own stuff. Get real with yourself, even if you code it in the lyrics."

Hazel understood what he was saying. Be honest. Which felt like what Benji was always saying to her too.

Despite the evidence to the contrary, Hazel didn't think she was a dishonest person before *The Sing Along*. Besides, she'd only lied about her age, which people did all the time. Well, and about her background. And okay, her parents being dead. And that whole story she'd told Zoey about ballet and theater and whatever other nonsense she'd spouted. And fake dating Benji . . .

So she was. She was a liar. Was that her defining characteristic now?

"Okay, I get it. It's just been a minute since I've written anything."

"Why don't you play me the last thing you wrote? Maybe it's a starting point."

Hazel agreed and went to get her guitar out of its case, thinking about the last song she'd written, almost a year ago. When she'd first come to L.A. she'd been writing a lot. She'd had a lot to process. But then the mundane aspects of her life had taken over and she felt the creativity flowing out of her. Writing songs was like that. The muscle could get rusty and eventually waste away.

She sat on a chair and played a few chords to make sure her guitar was in tune. "This is called 'Fresh Start.'"

She strummed the opening chords, feeling nervous. She'd sung in front of Nick a bunch of times, and in front of millions of people last week on the live show. But this felt different. Intimate. She was exposing herself.

"New day, fresh start,
Too many scars on my heart.

New day, fresh start,
But I'm falling apart.

"Never thought I'd get so low,
No idea where to go.
If everyone can see my scars,
I won't get far."

Hazel kept singing all the way through to the end. Her voice was wavering, and she was right back in her feelings, how alone and sad she'd felt when she'd written this song while the car alarms and sirens of Venice wailed in the background.

She got to the final note, held it, then stopped.

She looked at Nick nervously. He had a slow smile on his face. "You wrote that?"

"I did."

"And then, what, just tucked it away in your guitar case?"

"What else was I supposed to do with it?"

Nick smirked. "I seem to recall an ambitious young lady telling me I shouldn't just wait for another deal, that I should put out my own music."

"Ha."

"Well?"

"I wrote it for me."

"I can tell."

"What's that supposed to mean?"

He put his hands out in front of him. "Don't get me wrong, it's great. But it's way too confessional for a pop song. Or this show."

Hazel felt defeated. It was always how she wrote songs.

And it was always why she never did anything with them. Because her whole self was exposed.

"That doesn't mean we can't work with it," Nick said. "The melody is great. And the theme. We just need to make it a little less obvious that you went through hell, okay?"

"Is that what you helped Kate do for 'Honeycomb'?"

Nick frowned. "She tell you that at lunch?"

"Martin was there."

"Is she okay?"

Hazel finally understood the full force of his anger. All the details had spilled out after Kate had her third vodka soda. How Martin had offered to help her after the auditions, just like he'd done with Hazel. Kate hadn't been naïve, but she was flattered and thought she could handle it. By the time the competition had started in earnest, she'd felt trapped. Martin made it clear that if she didn't stay with him she'd never make it through to the end. It had been Nick who'd helped her find the courage to break up with him the minute the show was over.

"She was shook up, that's for sure."

Nick ran his hand through his hair. "She told me she'd be okay if she came back this season. I should've known."

"I just don't get it," Hazel said.

"What?"

"How you keep working with him. Knowing what he did. How he hurt someone you cared about. How he's still doing it."

"What do you expect me to do about it?"

"Tell on him."

"To who? It's his production company that runs this whole thing."

"So, it's about your job?"

"It's not just that. And it's not my decision. Kate didn't want to come forward. Do you?"

Hazel felt panicked at the thought of having to tell anyone official about what had happened to her. "I . . ."

"Right, I didn't think so." Nick expelled a long breath. "Look, I get it. It's maddening. I fucking hate that guy. Working with him makes me sick. But at least if I'm around I can head him off at the pass most of the time."

"What about Sarah Baines?"

"I can't save everyone."

"She was there with him. At the San Vicente Bungalows. He's not even trying to hide it."

Nick sighed. "I did warn her, but she didn't want to hear it. Unfortunately, some people see the advantage of sleeping with him as something to be endured."

"That's terrible."

"It is terrible. Honestly, I hate this business, but I'm not good at anything else."

"Is that why you won't be with Kate?"

"She tell you that too?" He shook his head. "How many drinks did you have at this lunch?"

"Me? One."

"And Kate?"

"I stopped counting."

He smiled briefly. "She must like you."

"I like her."

"She's great."

"But not for you?" Hazel wasn't sure why she was probing so hard. Did she care if Nick dated Kate? There was a strange pit at the bottom of her stomach that told her that maybe she did.

"We're very different people. She was grateful that I was there for her, and yeah, we dated for a bit. Things ended, and that's the way they've stayed. No drama."

"You don't think she came back on the show for you?"

"Did she say that?"

"Maybe?"

He laughed. "She came back on the show because she was contractually obligated to do at least two seasons. I asked her to make this one of them."

"Why?"

A shy expression crept across Nick's face. "I thought you could use the help. She's a great coach."

"She is. Thank you for doing that."

"Sure. Now, that song is not going to write itself." Nick put his hands back on the piano keys. "Let's make it less personal."

"How?"

"What's the core emotion you were going for? What was the song about?"

Hazel's stomach fluttered with nerves. "Like, actually about?"

"Thematically."

"Moving on, I guess. Leaving the past behind."

"Good. Let's start with that."

The next night, Hazel sat in a pool of light on a simple stool, holding on to her guitar for dear life. She'd never felt so exposed. The theater was full and Hazel felt like she could hear everything and everyone in it. The lights around her were low, leaving the audience in shadows. It made it easier to ignore them, and to do what Nick had suggested: look directly into the camera.

Hazel started to strum. They'd turned "Fresh Start" from a slow expression of pain into an upbeat pop number that made Hazel want to tap her toes. But the words still had meaning, and that was the trick of pulling off the song. Hazel alternated between syncopated chords and slapping the side of her guitar.

"Fresh start,
Beats of my heart.
We pull apart,
I think I'm so smart.

"But I'll be okay,
I'll be fine.
I'm moving on,
I'm on the run."

Hazel started clapping in a syncopated way. Clap, clap-clap, clap. Clap, clap-clap, clap. The audience joined in as she went into the second verse.

"Fresh start,
I did depart.
Wisdom imparts,
Fight from a rampart.
"But I'll be okay,
I'll be just fine.
I'll settle down,
I'll have some fun.

"Yeah, I'll be okay,
I'll be so fine.
I'll come around,
I'll be all mine."

She finished singing, and there was a long pause from the audience during which Hazel felt like she might die. Then the applause started, slow at first, then building into a crescendo. She was getting a—yes, it was a standing ovation.

"Hazel, Hazel, Hazel," Keshawn said as he walked toward her. "You're making me feel things."

"I'm sorry?" Hazel said, and the audience erupted in laughter.

"Just don't do it again."

"No, sir."

Hazel put her guitar on its stand, her hands shaking. She searched the crowd for Nick, but she couldn't find him. Then, there he was, sitting next to Kate. They were both looking at her like proud parents. Not that Hazel had ever seen that expression on her own parents' faces. Hazel was happy, but she wasn't sure she wanted Nick thinking of her as a kid.

"All right, Hazel, we know the audience loved your performance, now let's hear from the judges. Georgia, what did you think?"

Georgia's face was glowing. She'd been in a great mood all night, effusive in her praise and enjoying an easy repartee with Keshawn. Hazel couldn't help but wonder if she had something more than water in the cup she kept sipping on.

"Hazel, darlin', what can I say? That performance was outstanding, and we need to talk about me covering that song. Bravo, honey. You're on your way."

"Thank you, Georgia."

"I'm being honest here. That song had me in my feelings."

"Me too."

"Ha! I thought so," Keshawn said. "Confessional time? Who's the song about? Another one of the contestants, perhaps?"

"I'll never tell," Hazel said, winking at the camera.

Keshawn shook his head, *oh that Hazel*, and it felt to Hazel as if she could feel people picking up their phones and texting their votes to the number that was below her on their screens.

"Now, Martin, we haven't forgotten about you. What did you think of Hazel's song?"

Hazel looked at Martin for the first time. She'd been avoiding him, not wanting to remind him of her existence if that was possible. But she was in the spotlight now, literally and figuratively, and there was no changing that.

"It was a bold choice," Martin said, striking a pose of contemplation. "But ultimately a failure. The song was maudlin and contrived. Sorry, love, but it's true."

The audience started to boo, which made Hazel feel a bit better, but not enough. Martin's comments were devastating, and Hazel knew that when he said things like that it had an impact. He was the show's tastemaker, and if he didn't think her song was good, it wasn't. It was his record label she was trying to get a deal with after all.

"Don't boo, vote!" Keshawn said, with a glint of something in his eye. Clearly, she wasn't the only one displeased with Martin.

Then Kate stood up and started clapping while chanting "Ha-zel. Ha-zel." The audience took it up and Hazel felt buoyed.

Martin's face creased in anger, then released. He even forced a smile as the chant rounded the room and embraced Hazel.

She'd have an anxious day waiting until tomorrow to find out if she had the votes to get to the round of twelve, but right now she felt safe.

She should've known better than to trust that feeling.

Chapter Sixteen

They were down to twelve.

Bella, Benji, Hazel, Zoey, Cole, Dave, and Martin's protégé, Sarah, were all through.

Despite her rocky start, and the fact that she was a replacement for cancer-stricken Lacey, Zoey had started to shine. Her mentor was a bit useless, but Georgia had taken her under her wing, giving her extra pointers off camera even though she wasn't supposed to.

"And then she told me that Darius Rucker hit on her once, can you believe it?" Zoey said, as they walked Checkers on his leash in a nearby park. "I would've died."

"Who is that again?"

Zoey tipped her black cowboy hat back on her head. "Seriously, Hazel? How are we even friends?"

"We can't be friends because I don't know everything about country music?"

"I'm not saying that. But honestly, it's like you have these huge gaps in your understanding of the culture. You grew up in Texas and wear cowboy boots. How did you miss country music?"

Hazel watched Checkers hop around on the grass. She couldn't quite believe they'd managed to keep him hidden for so long, alternating between putting him in the car overnight and the room. Zoey had fallen in love with him, but Brooke had shot him a look of disgust as she finally decamped, claiming that she had to go back to work.

"Busy doing other things, I guess."

"Ballet, right?"

"What? Oh, yes, that's right. And music lessons. My parents had me taking piano from when I was three."

That part was true. Her parents had been obsessed with laying down a classical foundation for her, with lessons five days a week under a severe woman who didn't understand why a child didn't want to practice two hours a day. When Hazel had taken up the guitar at twelve and insisted on quitting the piano they'd been devastated and had threatened to ground her. They'd made her keep at her piano lessons as a compromise, which she'd done for years even though she mostly hated it.

"I didn't know you could play piano," Zoey said. "Why don't you incorporate that into your performances? Like Taylor or Gaga?"

That was a good question. A piano performance was something that would elevate her performances, make her more than just the girl with the cowboy boots and the guitar. But Hazel resisted the thought. The piano was too linked to her parents.

"Maybe."

A large black Lab came into the park and made a beeline for Checkers. Hazel stooped down and scooped him up before he got attacked. Checkers's whole body was shaking, and Hazel was pretty sure she was about to get pooped on. "We should go back to the hotel."

"Sure, sure, I should call Brooke anyway. I hope she got home all right."

"I'm sure she got home fine."

Zoey gave her a lazy grin. "I wish you had someone like her in your life."

"That would be nice."

"What about Nick?"

Hazel blushed. Nick tended to cross her mind at the oddest moments. Their interaction at the bar, the way her skin had felt when his hand grazed her leg. How intimate it had felt when they wrote that song together. She'd even had an X-rated dream about him the night before, waking up worried that she'd been groaning in her sleep.

"What about him?"

"Now that you're not with Benji anymore . . . you're *not* with him, right?"

"We were never together, Zo, I told you."

"I know. He's just so cute and he's clearly into you. That segment you guys did yesterday was adorable."

Hazel turned away. *The Sing Along* had the cast doing commercials, and she and Benji had to do one for some new, disgusting caffeine drink. The commercial's director had them gazing into one another's eyes as they sipped the terrible stuff. It had taken all of Hazel's acting prowess to make it believable, and the drink had left her feeling wired for hours. "Let's drop it, okay?"

"Sure, sure. But Nick—"

"Nick is too old for me. Isn't he like thirtysomething?"

"Whatever. He's into you. Go for it. Even Georgia thinks that."

"What?"

Zoey twirled a curl around her finger. "Yeah, she was saying the other day that he's great and that the last time she saw him this excited about a contestant was Kate. They dated, right?"

"I think so."

"She really hates Martin."

"Kate does?"

"No, Georgia."

They left the park. It was a few blocks from the hotel, and since Checkers had stopped shaking, she put him back down on the ground to let him hop along the sidewalk for a while before he got locked in her car for the day.

"She told you that?"

"No, it's obvious, though. She told me to watch out for him. Said I was his type."

"I think anyone he can coerce is his type. Look at poor Sarah."

Zoey shrugged. "She's a grown-up. Like, if that's how she wants to get an advantage in the competition, more power to her."

Hazel stopped. "You don't really think that, do you?"

"Yeah, why not?"

"He's in charge of the competition. It's not an equal power dynamic."

"Oh, come on. He's not her boss. She's twenty-five years old. If she wants to sleep with some old gross guy, then she can. It's her choice."

"But it's not a real choice. She wouldn't be doing it if he wasn't who he is."

"You don't know that. And she's getting something out of it too."

Hazel couldn't believe what she was hearing. "Weren't you the one who was saying we had to fight the patriarchy?"

"Yeah, we do. And if they're stupid enough to be governed by their dumbsticks, then why shouldn't women take advantage?"

"Maybe we should talk about something else."

Zoey jutted out her chin. "I'm allowed to disagree with you."

"I know."

"You don't even know Sarah."

"You're right, I don't."

"Maybe he's actually into her."

Hazel clamped her jaw shut. Zoey knew Martin had propositioned her but not any of the details. Zoey had asked after that day at breakfast when she'd told Benji, Zoey, and Brooke, but Hazel had deflected and downplayed how bad it was because she was trying not to make a big deal about it. She hadn't told Zoey that he'd renewed his offer in the parking lot.

She wasn't sure why she didn't feel like she could talk about it with Zoey, only confiding didn't come naturally to her. And though Zoey thought they were the same age, Hazel often felt the age difference between them, the life difference.

"Anything is possible," Hazel said.

"Wonder why Georgia hates him, though?"

"Maybe he hit on her?"

Zoey started to laugh. "Girl, no. One thing we can agree on is that Martin wouldn't be seen dead with a woman who isn't at least twenty years younger than him."

"That doesn't piss you off?"

Zoey shrugged again. "He's rich and powerful. If he can date young, hot women, why not?"

Hazel had a million reasons why not. "Does Brooke know?"

"Does Brooke know what?"

"That you're going to throw her over for a younger model just as soon as you get your record deal."

Zoey had a shocked moment, then burst out laughing. "You know Brooke would bust a gut if you told her that."

"Don't worry, I was only joking."

"I trust you. Brooke can be a little hard-core sometimes, but I love her."

"I know, Zo."

Brooke would also bust a gut if she heard Zoey's take on Martin and Sarah, Hazel was sure. But it wasn't her job to police Zoey's opinions.

"So, if not Nick, who, then?" Zoey said. "Maybe Dave?"

Hazel yoked her arm around Zoey's neck. "Now, there's an idea. Maybe he can let me know his secret to remaining in the competition when you don't have any talent."

The next day, Hazel, Kate, and Nick were in a rehearsal room working on Hazel's upcoming performance.

Hazel had taken one thing to heart from her conversation with Zoey, and she was seated at the piano, working on a stripped-down version of "Honeycomb." She was having trouble finding the right approach. Her fingers felt awkward on the keys since it had been so long since she'd played. And after her conversation with Zoey, the topic hit too close to the bone.

"That was better," Nick said. "Maybe do the third verse a cappella?"

"That's a good idea."

Hazel started the run before the third verse. She hit a wrong note and slammed the lid of the piano shut. "Damn it!"

"It's not that bad."

"I suck."

Kate cocked her head to the side. Her hair was in an intricate braid with a piece of silk wound through it, a trend that had taken off on TikTok. "You don't. It's just a harder song than it looks."

"Here," Nick said. "Let me show you."

He sat down next to her on the bench, his left leg touching her right one. Even though they were both wearing jeans, Hazel felt that same warmth as she had at the bar when he'd stepped between her legs and leaned in close. She tried to steady herself with a deep breath, catching his scent—that fresh laundry smell that was oddly calming.

Nick cleared his throat. "It's A minor, then C, then D." He played the chords, his fingers intertwining through hers. "It would be easier if you moved your hands."

"Oh, sorry." Hazel dropped her hands into her lap.

"It's fine," Nick said, and Hazel realized that he had a twinkle in his eye. He repeated the chord progression, adding a pretty flourish at the end. "And then you go into the verse. Now you try."

Hazel concentrated on the keys, trying to repeat Nick's graceful movements.

"That was better," Nick said, patting her leg under the piano.

Was it just her, or had his hand lingered on her thigh a bit longer than it needed to? Hazel shifted, and Nick's hand was gone. "Thank you."

"No problem. Just do it another ten times and you should get it." Nick stood and looked at his phone.

"Maybe we should pick something else?" Hazel said, losing confidence once he stepped away. "Something for guitar where I won't make so many mistakes."

"No, this is the right song for you. It will complement the song we wrote and showcase another side of you." He tucked his phone away. "I've got to go. Kate, you got this?"

"Of course."

He squeezed Hazel's shoulder gently, then left. Hazel felt herself blushing but felt awkward in front of Kate. She lowered her head and tried the chord progression again. It was better, but still not perfect.

"What's wrong?" Kate asked.

"I'm having trouble connecting to it."

"Why?"

"Because I know what it's about. How am I supposed to sing that with Martin watching? Does he know it's about him?"

"Are you kidding? That would require him to be self-aware."

"I feel bad for Sarah."

Kate rubbed her hands together. Her nails were a perfectly manufactured high-gloss pink. "I know, me too."

"My roommate, Zoey, it doesn't concern her. She's like, Sarah's getting something out of it, so is he, what's the big deal?"

"That's not the first time I've heard that."

"I wish there was something we could do."

"There isn't though."

Hazel spun her legs over the piano bench. "But it still affects you, right? What happened?"

"Yes," Kate said quietly. "It does."

"And yet you can sing that song all the time."

"That's the job. Take your pain, filter it into an ambiguous song lyric, and sing it every night like it was the first time. After a while, the song takes on another meaning and it doesn't hurt so much."

"That's good."

Kate considered her. "What's really bothering you? It can't just be Martin."

"I don't know. I guess I've faced a lot of unfairness in my life, and it bothers me when the wrong person gets punished."

"Who's the wrong person in this scenario?"

"Sarah. She doesn't deserve to have this happen to her. And Martin shouldn't keep on getting away with it."

"Are you scared of him?"

"Yeah, I am. You saw what he tried to do to me onstage last week. If Keshawn hadn't stepped in, he would've sunk me."

Kate smiled. "That was nice of Keshawn to do that."

"So nice, but it's not the point. Martin shouldn't have that power."

"It's his show."

"More powerful men than him have been taken down."

"That's true."

Hazel turned back to the piano and played a minor chord. It come out flat and ominous. "What if we *did* tell on him?"

"How?"

"What about the network? Or something online? Like on Twitter."

"You want to tweet about Martin?"

Hazel thought about it. Before the show, she'd only been on Twitter as a voyeur under a pseudonym, following a few celebrities and news outlets. The show had made her set up an account, and now she suddenly had hundreds of thousands of followers. But she was already terrified to tweet anything other than the prepackaged announcements about the show's airdate and when her songs dropped on iTunes. No way she could take this on.

"I can't tweet as myself. But maybe anonymously? Like a blind item where everyone knows who you're talking about?"

Kate's mouth twisted. "Would anyone even notice?"

"Maybe if *you* tweeted it."

"I'm not sure I'm ready to do that."

"I get it. I don't want to force you."

Kate nodded slowly. "I've wanted to tell on him so many times. Back when it happened, and every time there's a groundswell about someone new. I just haven't been able to."

"What's stopping you?"

"My management would kill me, for one."

"They don't have to know. Not if we set up an anonymous account."

"Can't that be traced back to us?"

"Not if we're smart. Not if we're careful."

"But if it's an anonymous account then no one will take it seriously."

That was true, though other women had come forward against powerful men through anonymous accounts, and those posts had taken off. How had they done that? "Do you have a connect at TMZ?"

"Of course."

"Just like that?"

Kate shrugged. "It comes with the territory, unfortunately."

"Do you trust this guy?"

"He's never blown my cover. He knows if he does then his source dries up."

"Would that make it easier? If you knew it couldn't be traced back to you? I totally get it if you don't want to be in the spotlight for something like this. If you just want to forget it."

Kate sighed. "I *haven't* been able to forget it, though. I wish I could."

"We wouldn't have to make it about you, precisely. It could be more about his pattern of behavior. We know he's done this a bunch of times. That he's doing it right now."

"There's comfort in numbers."

"And anonymity."

Kate smiled. "What did you have in mind?"

"You up for causing some trouble?"

"For Martin?"

Hazel played that same ominous chord again. "Yes."

"Count me in."

Chapter Seventeen

"Holy shit," Zoey said. "What did you do?"

Hazel pried her eyes open. She'd had a terrible night's sleep, full of memories banging through her brain. She'd lurched awake at three, sweaty and scared, and had trouble falling back asleep. She'd eventually broken into the minibar, using her twenty-dollar per diem and Zoey's to down several mini bottles of vodka. And now her head felt like it was splitting open. She would've been better off just toughing it out. "What are you talking about?"

"This," Zoey said, holding her phone in front of Hazel's face.

Hazel took a moment to focus as she took the phone from Zoey's hand.

It was a tweet from an anonymous account that read:

Martin Taylor offers "private lessons" to contestants who want to get a leg up in The Sing Along. *He's been doing it for years. Everyone knows and says nothing. #MeToo.*

It had been posted at eight the night before and had been liked and retweeted thousands of times in the hours since.

Hazel's heart thumped with excitement and nerves. "How did you find this?"

"It's all over the media. There's an Insta account, too, same thing. TMZ covered it."

Hazel propped herself up. She ought to have known Zoey would be the first person to find out about the account. She was always surfing People.com and TMZ, like a nervous tic.

"Is that all?" Hazel said. "One anonymous tweet?"

"No, look. There's lots of people saying stuff in the comments."

Hazel scrolled down below the original tweet. There were hundreds of comments, from men accusing the tweeter of being a host of gross misogynistic things, to people saying *well, duh,* and all kinds of terrible memes about horrible men past. Interspersed were tweets from former contestants saying simply #MeToo. One even offered details, writing that Martin had propositioned her repeatedly and that she was sure she'd been kicked off because she'd turned him down. Hazel recognized the name from season three. A beautiful girl with a sometimes shaky voice who'd been eliminated in the early rounds.

"Are you behind this?" Zoey asked. Hazel let the phone fall to the bed. She'd never seen Zoey angry. Happy, nervous, drunk, silly, confident, giddy, frustrated, yes. But Zoey was angry now. Her fists were clenched and her jaw was tight, and Hazel was a little afraid of her. "Did you tweet that?"

"No." That was technically true. Though she'd helped write the tweet, it was Kate's anonymous Twitter account, set up using an encrypted email service.

As they'd worked out the details of their plan yesterday, they'd done everything they could to protect Kate's privacy, but it had to be Kate to tweet. That was the only way her TMZ connection would agree to amplify it.

Hazel had been relieved. Even though it was her idea, the thought of putting her neck out like that left her shaky and nervous. But after her initial resistance, Kate was determined. She'd finished her three-record contract for Martin's label and had signed with a new label six months ago. She was established enough that she ought to be relatively protected if it ever came out that it was her.

"I don't believe you," Zoey said. "It's too much of a coincidence. We were just talking about this *yesterday*. And you were so mad. You've hated Martin since the beginning."

"That's not true."

Zoey snorted. "Please. I know you think you're smarter than me, or whatever, but I notice things."

"I never thought you weren't smart."

Zoey crossed her arms over her chest, her eyes boring into Hazel's.

Hazel turned away and pulled herself out of bed. She felt queasy, and not only because of the alcohol. "I didn't tweet that."

"But you know who did."

"Maybe."

"Who?"

"It's anonymous, Zo. Clearly for a reason."

"I think it's bullshit."

"You think she's making it up?"

"If it was true, why not come forward when it happened? Why do it anonymously on Twitter and let the mob cancel him?"

Hazel reached for a pair of shorts. She wanted to take a shower and wash the terrible night off her, but she couldn't walk out on this conversation. She just didn't feel like having it in her underwear.

"You can't actually be that naïve, can you?" Hazel said, feeling some anger herself now. "Why are you taking Martin's side? Did you read those comments? People are calling that woman horrible things and threatening her. That's just the beginning of what happens when you come out against a powerful man."

"People shouldn't have to answer anonymous allegations. And cancel culture is bullshit."

"In a perfect world, I agree with you. But the world is far from perfect."

"I think you wrote the post."

"I didn't. Why won't you believe me?"

"Because you lie all the time, Hazel. I didn't really care when it was just about Benji, because that didn't matter. You wanted to get ahead in the competition. I respected that. But this is different. This could destroy *The Sing Along*. Everything I've been working for, and you too. Is that what you want?"

Hazel was shaking. Zoey's assessment of her was devastating, and worse, it was mostly true. "No."

"Then why post this now?"

That was a good question that Hazel didn't have an answer

for. There was no reason for them to unmask Martin now. They could've waited until after the season was over. But that would have left her vulnerable to further harassment, and Sarah too.

"Because of Martin. He keeps coming on to me. He wanted me to come to his room that night I went out with Benji. He even invited me and Checkers to move into his bungalow. And because I keep saying no, he keeps trying to sabotage me."

Zoey's face softened for a moment, then her shell was back. "But you didn't get cut."

"So? He cornered me in the green room. It was awful. Nick had to save me. The second time too. And you heard what he said about my song. He wants me gone because I won't give in to him."

"How do I know any of this is true and not just some scheme to get Martin to stop criticizing you so you can win?"

"You think I'd do that?"

"I don't know, Hazel. Is it so different than pretending to be in a fake relationship to get a bunch of attention?"

Hazel felt like the wind had been knocked out of her. "Ask Nick, then. And Bella too. She overheard part of it. That's why she started that rumor about me. And I have the texts. The texts from Martin." A wave of nausea was rising. She had to get to the bathroom.

She pushed past Zoey then paused in the doorway. "Not for nothing, but this is why women don't come forward."

She launched herself into the bathroom and got to the toilet just in time.

When her body had finished heaving, she sat on the cool tile floor with her back against the wall and remembered how, two days ago, she'd felt like everything was finally falling into place. How she was stupid enough to think that things were finally going her way.

How many times could one person be fooled about their own life, Hazel wondered, before they gave up and just walked away?

One thing that Zoey was right about—the timing of the disclosure was terrible. *The Sing Along* descended into chaos and divided into two camps: those for and those against Martin.

The divisions were a little surprising. Besides Zoey, Cole and Dave were publicly pro-Martin, tweeting hashtags like #noanonymousaccusers and #proveyourallegations.

Everyone else was too scared to say anything out loud, though many had privately shown support for the accuser in a series of whispered conversations that always stopped abruptly whenever someone else entered the room.

Amber was on Hazel's side, though. Hazel had always been able to confide in her, so when the chaos swirled, she called Amber and let her know what was going on.

"Girl, good," Amber said, her voice laced with smoke. "Men have been getting away with that shit for way too long."

"Right?"

"It's criminal."

"I don't think the police will get involved."

"They never do." Amber sighed. "You okay, though? You got enough support there?"

"I'll be okay."

"What about Benji? He on your side?"

"He is, but . . ."

"You ain't together? Sure looks like it on TV."

"That's acting."

"That's too bad. What's this Martin asshole say, anyway?"

Martin had issued a terse denial, and the contestants waited anxiously for something more to happen. More women to come forward, Sarah to say something, an investigation to be announced, anything to break the tension. But none of that happened. Instead, Zoey moved out of their room, shifting her alliance to Sarah, with whom she had several tearful conversations in the break room, sitting in a corner, nodding fiercely.

The move-out had happened the day after the story broke, when its effects were still being felt like an earthquake. That day's rumor was that *The Sing Along* was going to be shut down, at least for the season, while they waited for the dust to settle.

"I told you so," Zoey had said as she'd thrown her clothes into her suitcase. "You've ruined everything."

Hazel hadn't bothered to deny it that time. Whether she'd sent the tweet or not was a semantic difference. She hadn't thought through the consequences of her actions, and not for the first time. She'd been so mad at Martin that she hadn't thought past what would happen if he was exposed.

"I'm sorry," she'd said.

"You think you get more than one shot in life, Hazel? This was *mine*. And when I got cut, I thought it was over. But then Lacey got sick, and I got the call." Zoey stopped and gulped back her tears. "Everything I was praying for was happening. I'm doing well. People like me, despite who I am. I have *fans*.

And now it's all going to go away. We'll all be tainted. If anyone remembers us, it will just be because they think we were the one who slept with Martin."

"You'll get another shot, Zoey. Come on, you're great—"

"No. You don't know what it's like for me. A queer Black woman in country music? Can you name one? Do you have any idea what someone like Lil Nas X has to deal with on a daily basis?"

"You know I don't follow country." Hazel had been trying to lighten the mood, but it had backfired, just like everything else she'd done.

"But you've heard of the big names. The *white* names."

"Yes."

"Exactly. This is why I needed this. I needed this so much more than you."

"How can you say that?"

Zoey had rubbed the backs of her palms against her eyes. "Because you were willing to throw it away just to make a point."

Zoey had zipped up her suitcase and left, and since then they'd avoided each other.

To make matters worse, from what she'd heard from others, Sarah was saying that *she* was the one who'd approached Martin, not the other way around, and she was seriously thinking of dropping out because now everyone thought she was just trying to sleep her way to the top. Hazel didn't believe that for a minute. Martin had obviously gotten to her as soon as the story broke with threats or promises or both. Either way, Sarah was walking around like she was about to crack wide open, and her performance had been pitchy and off.

Zoey on the other hand had a fantastic night, but when Hazel went to congratulate her, she'd turned her back and walked away.

Now it was the day after their performances, and Hazel, Bella, Benji, and Cole were sitting in the hotel restaurant, trying to eat something before the results were announced that night.

Four more people would be eliminated, and they'd be down to eight.

Despite her inner turmoil, Hazel felt good about her chances. Given everything that was going on, they switched out "Honeycomb" for her audition song because Hazel knew she could nail it.

She'd done it at the piano, and the band had covered over her nervous fingers. Georgia had loved the performance but Martin had pointedly noted that she'd done the song before, saying that he'd "expected more from her." Hazel didn't have to look at him to know that he was certain she was behind the revelations. Even if the idea hadn't occurred to him, she was sure Zoey was spreading that poison via Sarah.

"This sucks," Bella said.

Hazel laughed. "Probably the understatement of the year."

Cole was fiddling with his fork, tapping it nervously against the table like he was sending a message in Morse code. "My mom says Bella and Benji are through. Sarah's out. Zoey's in. You're on the bubble, Hazel."

"Thanks, Cole."

He looked at her, then away. "Sorry."

"Not your fault that your mom's predictions are devastatingly accurate," Hazel said gently.

She was pretty sure his mama was behind his Twitter support for Martin. She was cunning and determined that Cole was going to win. Come to think of it, she probably didn't even let Cole control his own Twitter account.

"She's called every winner since the show started," Cole said proudly.

Benji held up a hand. "Please don't tell us who she's picked for this year."

Benji had been particularly nice to Hazel this week, given that he knew what she'd gone through with Martin. He'd even tried to talk to Zoey, but she'd pushed him aside like she'd done with Hazel.

Cole grinned. "Me, of course."

"Might be a bit of bias there," Bella said.

"She's been right so far."

That silenced them. Not that they believed that Cole's mother had any true insight into the competition, but it was possible that she did. She *had* said that Zoey was going to make it through to the live rounds, and when she didn't, Hazel had taken it as a sign of her fallibility. But there Zoey was, glaring at her from across the room, still going strong.

Tap, tap, tap.

"Can you please stop that, Cole?" Hazel snapped.

Cole's fork stopped moving.

"Hazel," Benji warned.

"Sorry. I'm just on edge."

Cole nodded but Hazel could tell he was pissed. Cole was a sweet kid but he was very spoiled. He'd clearly never been told no in his life. Hazel was familiar with the type, and might have even been like that herself when she was younger.

"Cole understands that, right, Cole?" Benji said.

"Sure, sure. I'll see you in the auditorium?" Cole didn't wait for their response, just got up and left the table.

"Hazel Fine, making enemies wherever she goes," Hazel said.

"Cole's a brat," Bella said. Bella was one of the ones who spoke viciously against Martin in private. She said she didn't believe anyone should *get special attention* with total certainty and zero personal insight. "Ignore him."

"I know, but it just feels like we're all fighting now."

"That's not your fault," Bella said.

Hazel and Benji shared a glance.

"It's good that woman came forward," Benji said. "It had to happen. Even if it makes things difficult for us."

"One hundred percent," Bella said. "Look how he propositioned Hazel. Disgusting."

Hazel bit the inside of her cheek. When that had happened, Bella was all too happy to believe that Hazel had been into it and to spread a rumor that she was sleeping with Martin. That had been because she was jealous and wanted Benji for herself, but still. Even though she professed to be on Hazel's side now, it was hard to trust her. But Hazel wanted to keep Bella on her side, so she kept that thought to herself.

"Who do you think SubtleSinger is?" Bella asked.

"I have no idea," Hazel said.

Benji nodded but didn't say anything. He'd never asked Hazel if she'd sent the tweet, but she was certain he assumed it was her. Hazel didn't bother to try to correct his impression. She was just grateful he was still talking to her.

"I think it's Sarah," Bella said.

"What? Why?"

"Look at what a mess she is." Hazel followed Bella's gaze to where Sarah was sitting across the room. She was crying again, and seemed miserable.

"You think she's going to drop out?"

"I guess we'll see tonight if Cole's mama is right."

"Right."

Bella stood. "I'm going to get ready for the taping."

"See you there."

Bella walked away and Hazel slumped in her seat. "This is a nightmare."

"It will blow over," Benji said.

"Will it?"

"Sarah will go home this week and since no one else is coming forward, it'll go away."

"And Martin rides off into the sunset."

"I guess."

"I don't even want a record contract with that guy."

"Hey, hey," Benji said, reaching out and lifting her chin with his fingers. "Don't talk like that. If you win, you don't have to take the deal with him. You can sign with anyone."

"That's true."

"Don't let Martin win, right? That's what's important."

"I just wish we felt comfortable taking a public position against him." She and Benji had discussed it, but it seemed too risky. They'd kept silent, along with the majority of the contestants.

"What does Nick say?"

Hazel sat up. Nick had been avoiding her since the tweet,

working with her and Kate in rehearsals, but then leaving as soon as their session was done. Added to that, she'd walked in on an intense conversation between Kate and Nick just the day before. Hazel had wanted to ask what they were discussing, but for once she'd kept her thoughts to herself.

"Nick?"

"The musical director of the show." Benji raised his hand above his head. "About this tall? Looks like a Hemsworth brother but with fewer smiles?"

"He hasn't said anything about it."

"Interesting. Did he at least tell you you were safe tonight?"

"What are you talking about?"

"The results. Nick gets them beforehand."

"How do you know that?"

Benji flipped his hair. "I thought it was common knowledge."

"Has he been telling *you* the results before the shows?"

"'Course not. I just thought—"

"He doesn't have a crush on me."

"Okay."

"He doesn't."

Benji gave her his no-worries smile. "Hazel, if there's one thing I know, it's that you're terrible at telling when someone's interested in you."

"What's that supposed to mean?"

Benji stood to leave. "You figure it out."

Hazel watched him walk away, letting his words sink in. Was he really saying that his interest in her had been more than a passing thing? And Nick. Did Benji know what he was talking about where he was concerned? Was she too stupid to understand what was going on in own her life?

One thing she did know: everyone was holding up a mirror to her, and she didn't like what she saw.

Chapter Eighteen

A few hours later, Hazel was in a familiar position, standing on the stage, facing the judges, waiting to learn her fate.

Dave, Benji, Bella, and Zoey had all been put through. Sarah was out in a flood of tears, and now it was down to her and Cole. They'd been called up onstage together, and were standing, as protocol demanded, with their hands intertwined. Cole's hand was cold and clammy, and he was staring at his mom in the front row, who was wearing one of her signature T-shirts and holding a big sign with his face on it.

Cole's performance had been great, if a little uninspired, but he was clearly nervous. Hazel was nervous, too, but she was always nervous these days.

Keshawn went through his usual spiel, but when he got to the judges, things started to go awry. Georgia had been increasingly boisterous all night, and Hazel had seen her topple on her heels during a commercial, when she'd taken a bathroom break. She'd barely made it back to her seat on time and had tripped into Martin's lap. Where she would normally have laughed it off, this time Georgia took a swat at him and then a phalanx of assistants swept in. When they parted, Georgia was back in her seat, a steaming cup of hot coffee in front of her.

Hazel felt sorry for Georgia, but she was low on Hazel's order of priorities. Besides, she was Zoey's mentor, and probably not on Hazel's side now, though her comments about Hazel's performance had been positive. Hazel kicked herself. Not everyone was like Martin, taking things out on other people when they didn't get what they wanted.

"Hazel, Cole, are you ready?" Keshawn said. Even he looked discomfited by the turn of events, though his suit was perfectly pressed as always.

Hazel squeezed Cole's hand. She could go out with dignity. "Ready."

Keshawn ripped open the envelope and read the contents. His eyebrows rose in surprise. "Folks, this is something I've never seen before. Cole, Hazel, you both got an equal number of votes. So you're both through to the next round. Congratulations!"

Hazel's heart skipped a beat, and she reached to hug Cole. "We made it," she said into his ear. "Congratulations."

"Mama's never wrong."

"You're right. She isn't."

"We shouldn't have the same number of votes," Cole said in a petulant tone.

Hazel pulled away. The audience was still applauding and

probably no one heard Cole's comment, but she didn't want to take the risk. She raised her hand to the audience, took Cole by the elbow and almost dragged him off the stage.

"Hey, what are you doing?" he said.

Hazel got him into the wings and disconnected his mic from the mic pack. "You're still mic'd up. You don't want to say something like that onstage."

He pouted. "It's true."

"Look, your mom is great, but she's not magical. She couldn't have known what the exact vote count would be. You're still here. What's the problem?"

Cole jutted out his chin. "Don't talk shit about my mom."

"I wasn't."

"She knows things. She's always right."

"She's human. Mistakes happen. You should be celebrating."

"Nuh-uh. We were tied. That means I'm in trouble. One vote either way, and I was going home."

"Same stands for me."

"Yeah, but . . ."

". . . you're supposed to win." Hazel completed the thought for him.

"Yes."

"That might not happen, Cole."

Cole's mouth dropped open. "Why would you say that to me?"

"It's the truth."

"You're not so big on that."

"What?"

He gave her a contemptuous look. "I heard you. I heard you at the bar, that whole thing you did to get Bella on your side."

Hazel raised her hand and patted the air. "Keep your voice down."

"Whatever. You're probably behind the whole MeToo thing too."

"Cole, come on. What possible advantage would that be to me?"

"Sarah. She's a nice girl, but she's your competition, right? Same kind of music, similar vibe. And now she's out."

"I didn't make Sarah take up with Martin. And it's not my fault she gave a bad performance."

"Take what up with Martin?" Martin said, stepping out from behind the side curtain.

"Where did you come from?" Hazel said, her voice shaking. She should know better than to think it was possible to have any conversation in private backstage.

Martin didn't answer, just stared at Hazel while Cole took the cue and spun away into the darkness.

"What's up, love?" Martin drawled. "Have you been playing around where you don't belong?"

"I don't have to talk to you."

"You think that's true?"

"Just leave me alone."

Martin reached out and caught Hazel's wrist. She couldn't believe he was touching her like that, in full view, after everything that had happened. But no one was coming to her rescue this time. She pulled her arm away, but he held firm. "Let go."

"Or?"

"I'll scream. I'll scream and then everyone will know it's true."

He scowled at her. His eyes were almost black in the

backstage light. "What's true, *Hazel*? That I enjoy the company of willing and beautiful young women? I make no secret of that. But you turned me down and that was your decision. You seem to be doing just *fine* without me."

Hazel swallowed back her words. What Martin was saying was so close to Zoey's opinion it was almost as if they'd rehearsed it. But that was crazy. Zoey wasn't in bed with Martin, she was just reflecting the reason powerful men had gotten away with this shit for generations.

"I'd like to leave now," Hazel said.

Martin released her. "You were always free to go. Good night, Hazel. And good luck."

Hazel pushed past his threat to the side stage. Georgia was standing there, swaying in her cowboy boots, her eyes unfocused. She'd seen the whole thing.

"Good for you, girl," Georgia said. "Goods for you."

"Are you okay, Georgia?"

"Am. I. Okay?" Georgia cocked her head to the side and Hazel thought she might keel over. "That's an intershting question, Hazel. Intereshting."

Hazel searched around desperately for someone to help her, but the usual hustle and bustle of backstage seemed to have scattered. The only people left were Zoey, who was on the other side of the stage, and one of the stagehands.

"Zoey," Hazel called to her.

She didn't answer. She was frowning at her phone, and the show's theme music was still blaring through the speakers.

"Stay right here," Hazel said to Georgia, then rushed across the stage.

She put her hand on Zoey's arm to get her attention and

was met with a nasty expression. "What do you want?"

"I know you're not talking to me, but Georgia needs your help." Hazel lowered her voice. "She's drunk and making a scene. She needs someone to get her out of here."

Zoey's hand flew to her mouth, and she followed Hazel back to Georgia's side.

"I've got you, Georgia," Zoey said. "Okay?"

"What's that?"

"Let me take you back to your bungalow. It'll be better there."

"Martin?"

"No, Martin won't be there." Zoey's eyes flew to Hazel's. "We'll get you into bed. Or a bath, wouldn't that be nice?"

"Sounds nice."

"It will be nice."

Zoey pulled Georgia closer to her. "What happened?"

"Martin. Georgia saw him harassing me."

Zoey looked like she might be sick as Georgia swayed in her boots. "I've got to get her to her room. Come on, Georgia, let's go." Zoey took Georgia by the hand and led her out of the backstage area.

Hazel watched them go, her heart sinking. Everything and everyone was falling apart, and it was her fault. She didn't know what to do. She hadn't meant to start this rock rolling downhill, and now it was a rockslide that she couldn't get out of the way of. All her life she'd never thought through the consequences of her actions. Most of the time she only ended up hurting herself, but now she was hurting other people she cared about. She was pushing them away, and she might never get them back.

She turned away from the scene and walked down the stairs to the back hallway.

Nick was standing there, his arms crossed, a scowl on his face. And even though Hazel had seen this expression before, too many times, it pierced her in a way she didn't expect.

"You happy now?" he said.

Hazel's heart started to hammer in her chest as her throat went dry. "Excuse me?"

"This place is a shit show."

"You think that's my fault?"

Nick didn't say anything, and the rage built inside Hazel, replacing the sadness and regret. Even though she'd just been blaming herself, for that very thing, she didn't need Nick confirming her worst fears. Hazel wasn't the perpetrator; she was just the whistleblower. She hadn't done anything wrong—she'd only tried to protect herself and others, too, even if they didn't want that protection. She shouldn't feel this guilty. She should be proud of what she'd done, and Nick should too. Nick, who knew what Martin was but hadn't had the courage to speak out.

"You know what, Nick?"

"What?"

"I'm not the one—" Hazel stopped. She wanted to scream and yell and throw a fit, but she couldn't find the words. She didn't know how to express all the swirling emotions in her head, her heart. She was fuming but she also wanted to throw herself into Nick's arms and let it all go. But she couldn't do that. She couldn't lose it right now, and certainly not in front of Nick. Not with the way he was looking at her, like she was a disappointment, like she'd let him down after he'd asked her not to.

"What did you want to say, Hazel?"

"Forget it," she managed to squeak out, then she turned and ran.

Chapter Nineteen

"Hazel, I'm sorry. Please let me in."

Hazel had flung herself on her bed, pity enveloping her, as Nick rapped on the door to her room. She wanted him to go away, to leave her alone in her misery. Come to think of it, she should leave. Pack her things and fade into the night without telling anyone. Maybe that would fix things. Maybe that would put everything back to the way it was. Because all she did was spread misery wherever she went. Maybe she wasn't as bad as Martin—okay, she knew she wasn't—but she seemed to have made way more people unhappy.

"Go away, Nick."

"No, I'm not going away. Just let me in. Come on."

"Why?"

"Because I want to apologize but I don't want to do it through a hotel room door."

Apologize? Hazel almost laughed. Nick wasn't someone who apologized. She hadn't known him that long, but she was sure about that. Only, he sounded sincere, and Hazel could use someone who cared about how they treated people right now.

She pulled herself from the bed and checked her face in the mirror. She looked terrible, but what did it matter? She opened the door.

Nick was standing there, his shoulders hanging low. "Can I come in?"

Hazel stepped aside then closed the door behind him. She directed him to Zoey's bed, now abandoned, and sat on the edge of her own bed, facing him.

He looked around the room, his eyes coming to rest on Checkers's cage, where he was sleeping. "The famous rabbit."

"His name is Checkers." Hazel's voice was clipped.

"I'm sorry," Nick said. "What I said backstage. That was uncalled for."

"You so sure? Seems to be the prevailing sentiment around here."

"Yeah . . . I was mad. I've been angry."

"At me?"

"Mostly at Martin. Some at Kate." He was staring at his hands, which were folded in his lap.

"Why?"

"I know she was the one who tweeted about Martin. She told me about it. And that you encouraged her."

"So you are mad at me."

"It's complicated." He rubbed his hands over his face. "Look, I'm glad she came out about it. I am. I tried to get her to do that when it happened, but she wasn't ready."

"I didn't know that."

"Yeah. Anyway, everything is a mess. The studio is freaking out and there was talk of canceling the whole season, but they seemed to have backed off that now."

So the rumors had been true. "Was that a real possibility?"

Some of the edge crept back into Nick's voice. "It's Martin's show, Hazel. It's his production company, he owns the rights, all of it. There is no *The Sing Along* without Martin, not unless he sells his stake, and he's not going to do that."

"I didn't know that."

"Right, I figured."

"You could've lost your job."

"Yes. We all could've."

Hazel's shoulders slumped. "I'm so sorry. I didn't think it through. He wouldn't stop and I just wanted to stop him. It was stupid to try to do anything."

"No!" Nick said with passion and anger. He stood up and moved toward Hazel, crouching in front of her. "No," he said more quietly. "It wasn't stupid. It was brave."

"I didn't do it, though. Kate did."

"She never would've said anything without you. And Martin knows that. Or thinks he does."

Hazel's shoulders slumped. "He said as much earlier."

"He threatened you?"

Hazel explained the scene between her and Martin backstage briefly.

Anger flashed across Nick's face. "I truly hate that man."

"Welcome to the club."

"Oh, I started that club a long time ago."

Hazel grimaced. "What do we do?"

"Right now? Nothing. This isn't over, but a period of calm is probably a good idea."

Hazel smiled briefly. "No more tweets?"

"I wouldn't."

"What about Georgia?" Hazel asked. "She's a wreck."

"That's a long-standing problem."

"Do you think it's connected?"

"I don't know. There were rumors about them years ago." Nick rose and sat next to Hazel, his weight dipping the bed so that she tilted toward him. "This business."

"It has its problems."

He gave a small laugh. "That's an understatement."

"Not everyone's like Martin."

"No, but enough of them are." He sighed. "This is why I was kind of okay with my deal falling through. My album getting shelved."

"Because of Martin?"

"Because of all the shit that comes with putting music out. All the terrible people, and the parts of you that you have to give up. The parts you have to hide. I know it's what you want, Hazel, and I hope it works out for you, I really do. But it comes with so many pitfalls."

"I know that."

Nick turned and their faces were inches apart. "And you still want it? Despite everything?"

Hazel felt like she was looking at him for the first time. His green eyes had brown flecks in them, and his nose was slightly crooked, as if it had been broken once in a fight. "I do."

"It's a tough road to choose."

"I might not look like it right now, but I'm tough. I've been through a lot."

"I can see that."

"You can?"

Nick shook his head gently, then leaned his forehead so it was resting against hers. Hazel was surprised by the contact, but it felt good. Righter than with Benji. Like they fit.

Hazel put her hand on Nick's, covering the back of it. She felt that warmth spread through her again, stronger, urgent. Her breath quickened as she tilted her face toward his.

"This is probably a bad idea," Nick said softly.

"Probably."

"I can go."

"I don't want you to."

Nick brought his hands to her shoulders and rested them there. Hazel could feel his breath on her lips and smell the spice of his aftershave. A flood of images played through her mind as she breathed him in: Benji, Kate, her disapproving parents, Martin. But she didn't want them there. She wanted to forget them all. To be present in this moment.

Hazel moved her face forward until her lips met Nick's. His mouth was soft and firm, and she felt an instant connection, that feeling when a kiss is right, when your tastes line up and you're kissing someone familiar, even if they're a stranger. And he was responding to her, his lips moving in tandem with hers, a small groan escaping his throat when she sucked gently on his bottom lip.

She reached for his waist while his hands cupped her face.

His kisses were assured, the kisses of a man rather than those of a boy, and she opened herself to him, meeting his passion with hers. She leaned forward, wanting to feel his body against hers. She pressed against his chest as his arms encircled her, pulling her closer until there was no space between them. She could feel her heart beating against his chest, and his heart beneath it, their rhythms matching.

"Are you sure?" Nick asked, his breath ragged against her teeth.

"God, yes."

He laughed, then tipped her back onto the bed. She pulled him on top of her, wanting to feel his weight, to get lost in his hands, which were traveling over her body in a slow and deliberate way.

He ran his tongue along her jawline and then down to the crevice in her throat. She moaned as she reached for the buttons on his shirt, undoing them slowly, deliberately. He shrugged free of it, and she ran her hands along his skin. He was strong, lean, with a light triangle of hair on his chest. She pushed him onto his back, then kissed his shoulders, his chest, traveling down to his navel. She pulled her shirt over her head, straddling him, feeling how ready he was and how ready she was too.

He sat up and took her breast in his mouth, first one, then the other. She held him against her, her fingers in his hair, while he sucked her nipple gently and pushed up against her. She was wet and a pulse beat between her legs.

"You're wearing too many clothes," Hazel said.

"That right?"

"Definitely."

He rolled her off him gently, resting her on the bed. He

stood and quickly removed his pants and underwear, then took off the rest of Hazel's clothes. She watched him, admiring his flat stomach as he lowered himself next to her. He lay on his side, his lips against her ear and his hand trailing down her belly to between her legs.

"I didn't come here for this," he said, his breath heavy.

"No?"

"No."

"Regrets?"

She felt his smile against her earlobe. "No. You?"

"Only that you're not inside me right now."

He slipped his fingers inside her as her back arched. His thumb rubbed her as he moved his fingers in and out slowly. She could feel the pressure mounting, as she reached down and stroked him. He was hard, ready.

"Do you have something?" she asked.

"No, I . . . I didn't think . . ."

She smiled against his lips. "Good thing the show hands out condoms like candy." She pointed to a gift bag in the corner. "In there."

Nick rose and riffled through the bag that had been in Hazel's room when she arrived.

"Is Checkers going to watch us?" Nick said, amused.

Hazel rolled over. Checkers was awake now, munching on his food. "Here, drape this over him." Hazel threw Nick's T-shirt to him. He caught it in a deft move and used it to cover the front of the cage. Hazel laughed and patted the bed next to her. "You don't want an audience?"

"I'm more of a behind-the-scenes guy, as you know."

Nick came back to the bed and kissed along her jaw as he

positioned himself over her. Their eyes locked and she guided him inside of her. He moved in and out slowly, rocking his hips while he continued to stoke her. She wrapped her legs around him, pulling him in closer as she felt herself close to coming. He rocked into her a few more times, then released a moment before she did, groaning in her ear, and relaxing on top of her.

Out of breath, he kissed her gently, tracing circles in her back.

"Can you come to my room 'not for that' every night?" Hazel said when she caught her breath.

"If you like."

Hazel smiled. "I do."

The next morning, Hazel woke up wondering if she was dreaming. It was a good dream—the best—full of Nick's smell and their melding together, but that couldn't be right. Yesterday had been a nightmare, not a fantasy.

But when she turned over, there Nick was in the bed next to her. Her dream was real—all the gentle touches and tender words. That had happened, and he was still there. He hadn't tried to sneak out in the middle of the night or left before she woke up. Instead, he was curled on his side, breathing gently, completely at peace.

Surprisingly, so was Hazel. Maybe it was a postcoital haze, but Hazel felt purely happy for the first time in as long as she could remember. Being in *The Sing Along* was supposed to be a good thing, but it came with so much anxiety that the good got drowned out by the bad. But this—this just felt right.

"Good morning," Nick said, his voice deep and sexy.

Hazel rolled toward him. "Hi."

"How are you?"

"I'm good, you?"

Nick smiled. "Very formal this morning, I see."

Hazel snuggled closer. "Feeling a bit shy, maybe."

"And regrets?"

"No. You?"

"No."

"But?" Hazel tried to hide her disappointment.

"But it's complicated."

"Naturally."

Nick tucked the pillow under this head. "I mean, you *are* dating another man."

"What?"

"Benji?"

Hazel laughed. "Oh, ha. God, I forgot all about that. No, no. That's all fake. You know that. Right?"

Nick smiled. "I do."

Hazel wrapped her arms around his waist. "It was nothing but a kiss."

"Oh really?"

Hazel poked him in the stomach. "Are you jealous?"

"Nope."

"It was on a moonlit beach . . ."

Nick held up his hand. "Okay, maybe I'm a little jealous."

Hazel kissed him. "There's no need to be."

"I know. I even double-checked with Benji."

Hazel pulled back. "What?"

"I asked him if you guys were dating. Just to make sure."

"When was this?"

"Couple of weeks ago?"

Hazel tried to imagine the scene. She couldn't. "That explains it."

"What?"

"Benji's been convinced you had a crush on me for a while."

Nick grinned. "Ah. I guess I wasn't as subtle as I thought."

"I was half convinced that you hated me, so . . ."

Nick bent and nuzzled down into her neck. "And now?"

"I guess Benji was right."

"Um-hum."

Hazel dipped her head and met his mouth. They had a long, slow, lazy kiss before breaking apart. "So, what do we do?"

"About what?"

"Everyone thinking I'm dating Benji?"

Nick arched an eyebrow. "Probably best to leave that alone. There's enough drama on set."

"Because of me."

"Because of He Who Will Not Be Named."

Hazel sighed. "No nightly repeat, then."

"Oh no, I'm holding you to that." Nick pulled her closer. "But for right this minute, I thought a shower then room service?"

"That sounds great. Twenty-dollar limit on the room service, though."

"Isn't Zoey gone?"

"Would it be wrong to use her contribution?"

"In the grand scheme of things, I think it's fine."

"Okay, but tonight we stay in your room."

He laughed. "Why?"

"Because I have a feeling that your bungalow has zero limit on the spend and access to a much nicer menu."

He grinned. "That's possible."

"We on, then?"

"Definitely. Join me in the shower?"

"I thought you'd never ask."

Hazel wanted to hide out with Nick in her room for the rest of the day, but that wasn't in the cards. They had a rehearsal with Kate at ten, so after they'd lingered in the shower, then eaten forty dollars' worth of fruit and yoghurt, they'd gotten dressed.

Hazel left the room first, making sure there was no one in the hall before Nick left. No one was going to believe she was dating Benji if Nick was seen leaving her room in the early morning. They both agreed they had to keep this on the down-low for right now, though Nick insisted he had to tell Kate. Hazel felt nervous about that, but Nick said she wouldn't be surprised. "She knew the minute she met you why I'd asked her to come back to the show," he said. "She knows me well enough for that."

"She said she came on the show this season to try to get back together with you."

Nick laughed. "She was messing with you. Testing you, to see if you liked me."

"She was?" Hazel couldn't believe she'd been fooled like

that. Though, come to think of it, was it so different than what she'd done to Bella?

"She's protective of me. Plus, she's been seeing someone for over a year. He's not in the business, so they keep it quiet."

"That's possible?"

"It can be, if you never talk about it and occasionally go out with other people so no one starts asking too many questions."

"You could have done that."

Nick shook his head. "No. We don't work. I . . . maybe someday I'll tell you all about it, okay? But for now, trust me, Kate will be fine with it."

But Hazel was still nervous as she stood outside the rehearsal space while Nick was inside with Kate. Everything Hazel did lately turned out badly, and the fact that she was still in *The Sing Along* felt like a miracle.

Had sleeping with Nick been a mistake? Clearly, yes. But she did like him, more than she'd admitted to herself until now, and she didn't regret it. She just hoped it wasn't going to turn on her like everything else in her life seemed to.

The door opened and Nick popped his head out. "Hazel, can you come in?"

"Everything okay?"

Nick nodded but he his face was clouded. "Close the door."

Hazel did as he asked, then searched out Kate. She was lovely and poised, her blond hair blown out and pulled back, wearing an effortless summer dress that looked like you should've been able to buy it at Forever 21, but which probably cost thousands of dollars. She seemed concerned, but not upset.

"What's going on? Is this about—" She searched Nick's

face, wondering if this was it. If he was going to dump her right there in front of Kate before they even got going.

"It's not that."

"What then?"

Nick hesitated. "Are you . . . you're not pregnant, are you?"

"What?"

Nick relaxed slightly. "Any idea why someone might say you are?"

"Who's saying that?"

"Kate heard it in the green room."

"From who? Martin?"

"It was Georgia, actually," Kate said. "She was nursing a bad hangover, but she was lucid."

Hazel's heart was pounding so hard it felt like she might be having a heart attack. "It's just dumb gossip."

"It's more than that. My guy at TMZ called to confirm the story a few minutes ago. It's dropping soon."

Hazel felt dizzy. Why would anyone think that she was pregnant? Last night was the first time she'd had sex in . . . she wasn't even sure how long it had been.

"Any idea what could've prompted this?" Nick asked.

Hazel's mind was spinning. There must be an explanation. "Is this because . . . because of what happened at rehearsal a couple of weeks ago? When I was sick?"

"They have that part of the story, but there are other details. Something about you and Benji on the beach?"

Hazel flushed. "They think it's Benji's?"

"Given your showmance, and then there's photos of you drinking. It looks like you're being highly irresponsible."

"That's ridiculous. I'm not pregnant. We'll just tell them I'm not and that will be the end of it."

"Come on, Hazel, I know you're not that naïve." Kate's phone beeped. She checked it. "Story's out. And . . . oh dear, that's unfortunate."

"What?"

Kate held her phone out. SINGING FOR TWO? the headline read. Below it was a picture of Hazel cradling her stomach and looking pale. Then there was another photo of her looking fat in an outfit she didn't even remember wearing, and one of her doing shots with Benji when they'd been at Albert's. The narrative it told was obvious. She'd gotten drunk with Benji and had irresponsible sex, and now she was paying the price.

"Where did they even get these photos?"

Kate put her phone away. "Everyone's always snapping everything on their phones. And the show has roaming photographers, you know that, following the contestants around for candids."

"For show publicity, not to tank my career."

"Agreed," Nick said. "It's a problem."

"Even if it's not true?"

"That doesn't matter. It's the kiss of death. Remember season two? What happened to Cath?"

Hazel did remember. It had come out that Cath was pregnant, and even though she was married, the audience had turned against her. She'd gone from front-runner to eliminated so quickly it made your head spin.

"This is going to hurt Benji too," Hazel said.

"Maybe," Kate said. "Hard to predict that one. It might

help him. Depending on how people take it. Whether they think you're trying to trap him or if people buy into your 'love story.'"

Something about that phrase triggered something in Hazel's memory. Someone had accused her of that very possibility not that long ago. *Bella.*

"Who hates you this much?" Nick asked.

"A few weeks ago, I would've said Bella, but I patched that up, I thought. It must be Martin. Retaliation for the MeToo stuff."

"That's what I think," Nick said. "He certainly has access to all the material he needs to make this happen, and the connections."

Hazel sank into a chair. "I'm done."

"What?" Kate said. "No. No way. We can fight back."

"How?"

"We'll show them you're not pregnant."

"How do we do that?"

Kate smiled in a way that was a little frightening. "I've got some ideas. Let's get to work."

Chapter Twenty

Hazel was standing in the wings, watching Benji perform, waiting for her turn to go on. It had been a tense week on the show, with the rumors about her and Benji swirling. She'd issued a formal denial, and the producers had even wanted her to take a pregnancy test, but she'd refused. She didn't know who to trust, and just taking the test could be viewed as confirmation that she thought she might be pregnant, which was almost like admitting that she was.

Instead, she'd followed Kate's plan to a T, working out daily with Kate's trainer, with a special focus on her abs, eating no carbs or salt to prevent bloating, and being seen running up the hill to Universal Studios in the hardest workout she'd ever done.

Benji had agreed to do the workouts with her, so they

were presenting a united front. If people thought they'd broken up, everyone would assume it was because of the pregnancy, which would reflect badly on him. Instead, they decided to keep up the ruse, and made sure to look happy and unconcerned whenever there were cameras around.

Benji tried to make the workouts fun, and he had strict instructions from Kate to never make it look like he was coddling Hazel or checking that she was okay. It was insane how many rules there were, but Hazel was down five pounds, which was ridiculous and not sustainable. According to Kate, all she had to do was last through her performance to make this stick.

"Don't touch your stomach," Nick almost growled in her ear.

"I'm hungry."

"You can eat after the show. You look great by the way."

Hazel's outfit was something she couldn't believe she was wearing. It was a dress Kate had procured for her, a tight, figure-hugging number with a cutout that exposed most of her stomach. There was no missing the message it sent: Hazel was *not pregnant*.

To put a definitive point on it, Hazel was going to be singing "Fight Song," a rocking number that required her to execute some dance moves that were harder than anything she'd done in a long, long time.

She could deny all the rumors she wanted, but unless she *showed* the audience she wasn't pregnant, she was going home. It was stupid and antiquated, and part of her wished she could be the one to change it. But she'd caused enough trouble with her attempt to take out Martin, and there were only so many battles one woman could fight.

"Thanks, Nick," Hazel said.

"Maybe later, I can come to your room and . . ." He got closer to her ear and suggested something that made her knees quiver.

Despite his promises after their first night together, they hadn't been spending every night since then on repeat. Given the scrutiny Hazel was facing, they agreed it would be best for them to put their relationship on hold. That didn't mean he couldn't send her suggestive texts, which he did at the most unexpected moments.

"I'd like that very much," Hazel said. "But only after I eat a hamburger—or two."

"Hazel, you're on after commercial break," one of back-stage hands said as he gave her a once-over. If she did get kicked off, it wasn't going to be for lack of trying.

"Ready, Hazel?" Nick asked as the in-between-commercial music started up.

"Ready."

Benji walked offstage and did a double take. "Whoa. You look fantastic."

"Thanks, Benji. You did a great job out there, as always."

"Thanks. Listen, Hazel—" Benji eyed Nick, who stepped away to give them a moment. "For the record, I don't agree with what's been happening to you."

"Thanks, Benji. I didn't think you did."

"I know, but it's important to say it sometimes." He leaned in and kissed her cheek. "Blow them away out there."

"I'll do my best."

He smiled and started to walk away.

"Wait." Hazel reached for him. Despite all the time they'd

spent together in the last week, they hadn't had a chance to talk. "Do you know who it is? Who told on me to the tabloids?"

His face went blank. "I don't like to get involved in that kind of stuff."

"I get it, Benji. I do. But we're talking about someone trying to destroy my career—and yours, too, come to think of it."

"On in thirty seconds, Hazel."

"Benji, please, I have a right to know."

"You sure you haven't figured it out?"

"It's Martin?"

"No." Benji's eyes traveled to where Zoey was standing in the wings, getting final touches to her makeup. She was on right after Hazel.

"Zoey?"

Benji nodded slightly. "I think so. I'm sorry, Hazel."

Zoey. *Zoey* had betrayed her?

It was one thing that they weren't speaking. That hurt enough. Hazel had thought after what happened with Georgia that Zoey might back down from her position. But then the pregnancy news had dropped, and she hadn't had a chance to talk to her. Had Zoey kept her distance because she was the one behind it? Sweet Zoey had made up an entire story about Hazel to the tabloids? She'd actively tried to get Hazel kicked off all because she'd told the truth about Martin?

"You ready, Hazel?"

"What? Yes, yes, I'm ready."

Hazel shot Zoey one last look as she walked onto the stage and slapped on a smile.

The band kicked in and Hazel took a deep breath. She

found Amber in the audience, waving enthusiastically, and started to relax. Regardless of everything, she had people in her corner. She tried to clear her mind, to wipe away all the machinations and worries and fears. The only thing she could control was her voice. It was the one thing that had been with her through all of it.

This was *her* fight song. And she was in it for the win.

"You were great, Hazel!" Amber said, pulling her into a hug. She'd agreed to meet up with Hazel at the club where they were holding the cast party. "You didn't look pregnant at all."

"Shhh!" Hazel glanced around to make sure no one could hear them over the thumping music. No one seemed to have noticed them. Hazel pulled Amber to a booth in the corner. "I hate having to be this paranoid all the time."

Amber took a seat in the booth and tapped her acrylic nails against the table. "Comes with the territory. Someone's always going to be after your spot or want to take you down a peg."

"How come you didn't tell me that before I got myself into all of this?"

"Girl, please. You already knew all about it."

"Okay, okay." Hazel reached out across the table to Amber and squeezed her hand. "Thanks for being on my side, no matter what."

"'Course. Now, where is this Nick dude you chose over Benji?"

"We're keeping things quiet for now given the whole . . ."

Hazel motioned to herself. She was wearing a crop top and tight pants. She was basically going to have to show her stomach for the rest of her life it felt like. "But I am supposed to meet up with him later."

"Get it!"

"I will."

"And then . . ."

Hazel's attention pulled away from Amber as she saw Zoey out of the corner of her eye. She watched her walk to the back of the club, where the bathrooms were. "Hold on a minute, will you?"

"What are you—"

But Hazel didn't stop to listen to the rest of what Amber was saying. Instead, she darted through the sweaty crowd until she got to the bathroom.

Zoey was checking herself in the bathroom mirror.

"I can't believe you'd do that to me," Hazel said.

"What are you talking about?" Zoey applied lip gloss. The music from the club was a loud thump in the background. Zoey seemed unfazed, though, by both the environment and Hazel's presence. Hazel had always thought of Zoey as innocent, but she'd taken on a harder edge in the last couple of weeks. Grown up, Hazel supposed, but not for any of the right reasons. Or maybe her earlier naïveté had been the act. Hazel didn't have a lock on playing someone you weren't.

"You made up a story that I was pregnant and sold it to TMZ."

Zoey lowered her lip gloss slowly. "I didn't do that."

"Why would Benji say that you did, then?"

Zoey's face fell and Hazel caught a glimpse of the woman

she knew. "I guess he overheard me and Bella talking the other day . . ."

"Go on."

"I can understand how he could think it meant I'd done it. I was—I was pretty angry and was saying you were getting what you deserved."

"Why did you think that?"

She turned to Hazel. "Because of what you did to *The Sing Along*. It's supposed to be a singing competition. It's supposed to be fun! And then it's all serious conversations about MeToo and consent and it was like all those rallies Brooke makes me go to."

"I didn't think it through—I just wanted Martin to stop. I'm sorry, Zoey. Truly."

"Yeah, MeToo." She made her fingers into a hashtag symbol and rolled her eyes.

Hazel couldn't help but laugh. It wasn't something to make fun of, obviously, but they needed a lighter moment. "It really wasn't you?"

Zoey's eyes brimmed with tears. "I would never do that, Hazel. I was mad, but I didn't want that to happen to you." She hiccupped a cry. "I've been really sad that we don't hang out anymore. Ever since that night with Georgia, I've wanted to say something. I just didn't have the words. I've missed you."

"I missed you too."

"For real?"

"Yeah. It's sucked. You're my best friend here."

Zoey wiped at her tears. "I thought you were all friends with Bella now."

"I'm glad that Bella has calmed down and isn't trying to

kill me with her eyes all the time, but I'm never going to be close to her like I was with you."

"Was?"

"Am, I hope." Hazel pulled Zoey close. "Even Checkers missed you."

"He did?"

"He's barely looking at me these days."

Zoey laughed. "I'm not missing Checkers that much, to be honest."

"I don't blame you."

"But I do want to room again, if you do."

Hazel hesitated.

"Or not," Zoey said. "It's fine if you don't trust me anymore."

"No, it's not that . . . hold on." Hazel crouched down and made sure no one else was in the bathroom. She couldn't rely on whether she could see feet given what she was about to disclose. She put her head under one stall whose door wouldn't open. But they were alone.

"What's this all about?" Zoey said.

"You can never be too careful."

"Why?"

"It's Nick."

"Wait, what? Nick? Grumpy Nick?"

Hazel smiled. "Not that grumpy."

"I'm shocked," Zoey said.

"Weren't *you* the one who was telling me he had a crush?"

Zoey made a face. "Yeah, but I didn't think you'd do anything about it."

"What's the big deal?"

"Weren't *you* the one saying that it wasn't okay for

Sarah to be with Martin because he's, like, in charge of the competition?"

"Nick isn't Martin."

"He's the musical director. And he paired you with a great mentor. When we did the group audition, he gave you the best part."

"But I wasn't sleeping with him to get those things."

"He had a crush, though."

Hazel felt stunned into silence. Was Zoey right? Was there no difference between her and Nick, and Sarah and Martin?

No, no. Martin had pursued Hazel and threatened her and made her feel uncomfortable. Nick had saved Hazel from Martin. He'd protected her. He didn't do it because he expected her to sleep with him. He hadn't made it a precondition. And Hazel wasn't some young, naïve girl. Nick was only a couple of years older than she was. Not that he knew that.

"I don't know what to say."

Zoey grimaced. "Not so easy to judge after all."

Hazel clamped her jaw shut. She'd only just reconciled with Zoey. She didn't need to restart the fight. Besides, Zoey was raising good questions, ones Hazel wasn't entirely satisfied with her own answers for. "I guess not."

"I could use a drink."

"Same," Hazel said. "Amber's here. Come join us for a round."

"Should you? In your condition and all?"

Hazel laughed, but it came out more like a sigh. "I think the fake baby can take it."

Chapter Twenty-one

And now it was down to six of them: Bella, Benji, Zoey, Hazel, Cole and, improbably, Dave. No one paid him much attention, but somehow he was still around.

The tension on set had dissipated around Hazel after she put the pregnancy rumors to bed with her performance. The Martin story was yesterday's news. Everything was now focused on the final six, and that night's show was a two-hour extravaganza. Hazel had two solo performances and a group performance to do—an encore of the number Bella, Benji, Hazel, and Zoey had done in the early rounds. That meant constant rehearsals, diva moments, fittings, dance rehearsals, and no time to eat.

Hazel hadn't been this exhausted since she was a kid. She kept telling herself she wanted this, and when she was onstage, in the moment, feeling the music flow through her and watching the audience react with joy, that made it all worth it. But offstage, there were tensions and almost fights, tears, and silences. Things with her and Zoey were better, but tentative, and any time that she spoke to Nick she felt Zoey's questions hanging over her head.

She and Nick were keeping their distance, catching small, stolen moments when no one was around. It made it hard for Hazel to know what was going on with them, but she couldn't blame Nick for that. Even if Zoey hadn't made Hazel doubt his intentions, she didn't have time to conduct both a fake romance with Benji and a real romance with Nick.

It occurred to her that in the beginning, she'd told herself she wasn't going to mix that kind of complication with *The Sing Along*, and then she'd gone right ahead and done so. Hazel knew life was like that sometimes—things you didn't know you wanted showed up unexpectedly. But she also knew that she tended to self-sabotage, and it was hard for her to tell if that was what she was doing. Hazel used to think she had good instincts, but she couldn't maintain that illusion with herself now.

Regardless, the reality was that there were only two weeks left and then she could say good-bye to Benji and figure out what she was doing with Nick outside the chaos of the show.

But all that meant that Hazel was frazzled, and she wasn't the only one.

It all came to a head a couple of hours before they were set to go onstage. Hazel was doing a final rehearsal of her solo number with Kate and Nick in their rehearsal space. Hazel was back at the piano, working through the chords of a song she and Nick had written that week. Though it was coded, it was full of the tension between them. Hazel hadn't been able to help herself from writing about them, their future, why they were together in the first place.

"I can't help but wonder,
Was I your choice.
Was it my voice,
You say fate of course . . ."

"Better, Hazel," Nick said. "But your vibrato's off on the word *fate*, and it should be a C diminished chord."

Hazel's hands dropped into her lap. "We should just do the backup song."

"No," Kate said. "This is what's going to get you into the finals. Keep trying, it's good." Kate's phone rang and she stepped into the hall to answer it.

Hazel tried the song again and made the same mistake. She stood and walked away from the piano in frustration. "I'm not going to win anything if I screw up the performance. The song's not ready."

Nick spoke to her gently. "It is. You just have to deliver it. Lean into it."

"I know, Nick."

"Hey. Hey." He walked to her and put his hands on her shoulders, rubbing at the tension. "It's going to be okay."

She pushed him off. "Not here."

"Right, sorry."

"Why do you care so much anyway?"

Nick's mouth turned down. "What do you mean?"

"Why do you care if I make it through to the finals? You're

not my mentor, Kate is. Aren't you supposed to be helping everyone?"

"Where is this coming from?" Nick asked, his voice low.

"I'm just not sure why I get so much special attention, that's all."

"What are you accusing me of?"

"Nothing."

"Hazel, come on. Something's been bugging you all week."

"It's something Zoey said."

He put his fingers on her chin and lifted her face so she was looking at him. His eyes were dark green, the color they got when he was upset or confused. "What?"

"That you've been helping me because you had feelings for me. That basically, we're no better than Martin and Sarah."

Nick's jaw tightened. "Excuse me?"

"It's not what I said."

"But you're telling me. So you must think there's some truth to it."

Hazel kicked her toe at the ground. "Isn't there? Why did you give me the best part in the group number? Why don't you help the other contestants the way you help me? And you got Kate to come back for me, you admitted that, and you've been helping me write songs . . . and we are sleeping together. I mean we did. Was that what this was about?"

Nick sat down slowly on a nearby chair, like the wind had been knocked out of him. And maybe it had. The Hazel had certainly been knocked out of him. Hazel was pretty sure about that.

"This is what you think of me? That I was helping you to get you into bed?"

"Were you?"

Nick's face was a mask. "If I say no, are you going to believe me?"

"Yes, of course."

"I wasn't."

"Then why all the extra help? What was that about?"

"Isn't it possible I think you're talented and deserve a break?"

"That applies to everyone here."

"No, you're special, Hazel. Everyone else is good, some are even great, but there's only one special contestant each year, and this year, it's you."

Hazel felt a shiver go through her. She wanted to believe what he was saying, to rush into his arms and tell him she was sorry, that she was stupid for even doubting him, but she didn't. Something held her back. "How did you know it was me?"

"I just did. I've been doing this long enough."

Hazel bit the inside of her cheek. "And in Kate's year it was her?"

"It was."

"And you ended up with her as well."

Nick's eyes turned darker. "What are you implying?"

"I'm just trying to figure out what's going on."

"You and Kate. That's it. Two contestants I've been with in ten years. But you're right, it's probably something I shouldn't do. I didn't plan on it, though. Not with her and not with you."

"I'm sorry."

"The last thing I want is for you to feel like you have to be with me to succeed."

"I didn't say that."

"That's what this is, right?" Nick put his hands up. "So let's just take that off the table, okay?"

Hazel's spirits sank. This wasn't what she wanted. "You're mad."

"I'm upset; there's a difference. We have a show in two hours and there are other things, other contestants, I need to check on."

"Nick, I—"

Kate walked back into the room. "What's going on?"

"Nothing," Nick said, standing up and picking his phone up off the piano. "I have to go. Hazel, play through the song two more times, then leave it. You'll be great, I promise." Nick rushed out of the room without saying another word.

Kate watched him go, then turned to Hazel. "What was that about?"

"That was me, claiming my crown as the queen of self-sabotage."

Two hours later, Hazel's first number had gone well—a cover of Billie Eilish's "Everything I Wanted" that she'd done at the piano, wearing a long flowing ballet-pink dress that Kate had once again sourced for her. She was lucky the chord progression was simple and the song wasn't that vocally challenging. But with this song, it was the performance that was important, and she channeled all her angst and fear about Nick and their argument into the lyrics while a single spot shone down on her. The stage behind her glittered with colored fairy lights.

It had been beautiful when she'd done the tech rehearsal, and it was even more so in front of a live audience with the lights down low.

When she hit the last chord, she held it for as long as she could, and the audience went perfectly still before erupting in applause. Keshawn blew her a kiss while she took a bow, and she avoided eye contact with Martin. She scanned the crowd for any sign of Nick, but he was nowhere to be found. She had to put any thought of him aside. She just had to make it through tonight, and then she could fix things with him. She could fix things with everyone.

She left the stage and went to the quick-change area to get ready for her group number. Zoey was already there, slipping into the black shirt and pants they'd decided to add to the number. They were all going to wear miners' caps with lights that would syncopate with the clapping they'd done the first time around.

"Where's Bella?" Hazel said.

Zoey shrugged and adjusted her cap. "What do you think?"

"I think we look silly, but it will be effective."

The costumes had been Benji's idea. The teams who'd dressed up in the group auditions hadn't succeeded but that was then, and this was now. When they'd done a run-through and Hazel had watched the playback on a monitor, she'd known he was right to insist on it. Nick had agreed. Hazel had wondered, then, if that was still part of him helping her, because even though the group number didn't count toward your individual performances, every minute you were onstage was important, and Hazel had the best part in the song.

"We should get in place," Zoey said.

"Right."

Zoey was walking away from her prep area when her phone flashed on the desk. "It's Brooke, let me just check it real quick."

"Okay, but we don't want to miss our cue."

Zoey picked up her phone. Hazel knew in an instant that something was wrong. Zoey's eyes went wild, and her hands started to shake.

"Is Brooke okay?"

Zoey stared at her. "Is it true?"

"Is what true?"

Zoey's eyes tracked to her phone then back to Hazel. "Are you her?" She held up her phone, turning it toward Hazel. On it was an image of a young girl, about eight years old, striking a jazz hand pose. "Are you Daisy Dawson?"

Hazel felt like she was floating, like she might rise right up out of her shoes and leave the earth behind. But the past, *her* past, was tethering her to the ground. It had been an anvil around her neck ever since she'd agreed to go on that show when she was seven.

No, that wasn't fair. She'd begged her parents to let her be Daisy Dawson, America's little sister. She'd begged and begged, and they'd relented. Her life had been a disaster ever since.

"You are?"

All Hazel could do was nod.

"Hazel, Zoey, what are you doing here? Onstage, now," Nick said, pulling the curtain aside without even checking to make sure they were dressed.

Zoey put her phone down and walked past Hazel in a daze.

"You coming, Hazel?" Nick asked, a tinge of annoyance in his voice, which Hazel couldn't blame him for.

"Right behind you."

Hazel followed Nick to their staging area outside the fire doors. They were going to start the song in the audience, just like in the group rounds.

Bella was up ahead of her. She shot Hazel a nasty glare over her shoulder and Hazel knew, right then and there, who'd done this to her. It was Bella. Bella all along who'd been plotting against her. Their détente had been a fake out, or if it had been real, then something had happened to set her against Hazel again. She was the one who'd leaked that stupid pregnancy story, and somehow, she'd found out about Hazel's past.

"Ready, Hazel?" Bella said sweetly. "Careful out there. You wouldn't want to do a 'whoops-a-daisy.'"

Hazel closed her eyes as the lights dimmed.

Her secret was out.

Her secret was out.

The fake pregnancy was going to be a cakewalk compared to this.

But she couldn't do anything about that right now. All she could do was sing.

Chapter Twenty-two

Hazel was sitting in her hotel room, feeling caught in a time loop.

There it was, her whole life, spilling out before her on the TV. It was all coming out now, reminding everyone of every lowlight she'd ever faced back when she was known professionally as Harper Fuller. Harper, the name her parents still called her, though she'd gone by her middle name, Hazel, ever since she was fourteen.

From ages seven to twelve, Harper had been America's little sister on *The Dawsons*, with her winning smile and her cute catchphrase. Then the show had been canceled, and she'd had a wild two years, during which she'd ruled the clubs, after which she'd been dragged back to Austin by her parents and stuck in a superstrict Catholic school even though she was half Jewish. They'd threatened her with rehab if she didn't go, even though she'd never had a problem with alcohol, and never did drugs. She'd wanted to run away, but she'd been fourteen and hadn't had access to her own money. She'd put on her school uniform, introduced herself as Hazel, and tried to blend in.

Eventually, she'd disappeared into her new role of model student, the girl who never got in trouble.

By the time she'd graduated from high school, she was unrecognizable. She'd let her hair go back to its natural dark brown. She'd grown up and filled out—eating consistently instead of when your child handler let you did that. When she went to college, she'd also started using her mother's maiden name, Fine, to go along with Hazel. She'd gone to a state school in the Midwest where no one cared about Hollywood, and majored in music.

When she graduated four years later, she tried to get an album deal in New York. She'd told people then that she was Harper Fuller because she knew that was the most likely path to success, but every time she'd walk into a room, she could see their disappointment. Where had that cute kid gone? Who was this angsty singer who'd replaced her? They wanted a pop princess they could mold and exploit, but that wasn't who Hazel was anymore.

She'd gone back to Austin with her tail between her legs.

At least all the money she'd made was waiting in trust for her, she'd reasoned. She hadn't touched any of it, and it would be a good cushion until she figured out what she wanted to do with her life. Only, there hadn't been any money. It turned out that the house in Austin, with its wide lawn and oak-paneled study, had been paid for by Hazel. Ditto the cars and her parents' condo in the California desert.

All Hazel had left were the small residual checks that came in every six months, which were not enough to live on. Hazel consulted a lawyer who told her that she could sue her parents for all of it. She could take everything they had. She could go public and humiliate them. But Hazel didn't want to go there. She'd seen other families blow up and she didn't want to be back in the headlines as the victim of parental fraud. So instead, she'd negotiated an agreement. They sold their condo in Palm Springs and gave her half the proceeds. She'd get the other half when she signed the papers absolving them of all liability.

She'd never signed, though, just gotten in the shitty car she'd purchased with the first half of the money and left. She had enough to last a couple of years in L.A. if she was frugal, or so she'd thought. She could take one last chance to make it, on her own this time, without her parents touching any of it.

But L.A. was more expensive than she planned on. She couldn't afford a nice apartment if she wanted to give herself the time she needed. And she'd have to get a job to help make ends meet. She found the Motel California and the waitressing job at the café. She played every open mic night she could. She never told anyone who she was. The only person she confided in was Amber. When she'd finally gotten the invite to *The Sing Along*, she was two months away from having to leave town.

The tabloids didn't know most of that story. All they did was focus on the fact that she'd lied about who she was to get on *The Sing Along*. The truth didn't matter. She was that day's villain on Twitter, and that was enough. She was done. She was over. If America didn't cancel her, the show most certainly would.

"Hazel, come on, let me in." Zoey was outside the hotel room door, banging on it. Hazel had put the security chain on so Zoey couldn't get in. It was a dick move, but Hazel needed to be alone right now.

"Go away, Zoey."

"No."

Hazel turned over on her side and pulled the covers up over her head. She wanted to shut out the world forever, but mostly she wanted one more night of sleep in a comfortable bed before she was relegated back to her car or worse.

She hugged her knees to her chest as she heard the mechanical lock click open and the chain slide off its track. Hazel lowered the blanket. Zoey stood in the doorway.

What the hell? "How did you get in here?"

"I saw this thing on YouTube about how to remove a security chain," Zoey said, now inside the room. Hazel could feel her presence looming over her. "Come on, Hazel, talk to me."

Hazel pulled the covers back up. "Just go away. I want to be alone."

"No, I'm not abandoning you."

"You must hate me even more now."

"I never hated you. Just talk to me."

Hazel sighed. It was hot under the blankets, and hard to breathe. But it was hard to breathe out there in reality too.

Hazel sat up. Zoey was standing over her, her features larger than life in her stage makeup and glitter falling off her bedazzled dress. Hazel was still wearing her last costume for the night. She'd been in a daze, but she'd sung the song she'd written with Nick, tears streaming down her face by the end.

She could feel the streaks in the makeup; her misery, dried in place.

"Should I call you Harper?" Zoey said.

Hazel grimaced. She supposed she deserved that. "I always hated that name. I've gone by Hazel for a long time now. It's my middle name. Fine too."

"I'm glad something's real."

Hazel sat up as she felt that punch to the gut. "Okay, that was deserved."

"Has anything else you've told me been true? Or is that the truth?" Zoey pointed to the television that was on without sound.

Hazel had turned it on when she'd gotten back to the room because she had to see it. She had to know what they were saying about her, even though there were no surprises in anything they unearthed. Hours later, she was still the main story, as if she was some sort of natural disaster. She didn't need the sound on to know what they were saying. *Fraud, liar.* All those titles applied. Would she get a special logo?

"I don't know how to explain it."

Zoey sat on the edge of the bed. "Just tell me."

"I wanted a fresh start. I deserved it."

"But why lie about who you were?"

Hazel pushed her hair out of her face. "That's such a hard question to answer."

"Try."

"There's stuff that's not on there. On the TV. When my

show got canceled, I tried to book something else. But nothing stuck. By then, I was the sole breadwinner for my family. That's not how it should be when you're twelve. But eventually, we decided—they decided—to go back to Austin. We had enough to live on comfortably, I guess. I could try again in a couple of years if I wanted to. Eventually, I realized I didn't want that life. Being on sets all day. Having everyone control everything you eat and wear and do. It's no place for a kid.

"Anyway, I guess my parents resented me for that? When they realized I wasn't going to go back to it? My parents . . . they took everything I had. It's not an original story."

"It's a sad story," Zoey said. She wrapped her arms around her body, like she was giving herself a hug. "Go on."

"I sound like a whiny baby."

"No, you're not whining. All of that sounds like a lot."

"It was. I guess the only thing I felt like I could control was my identity. I wanted to be something that was separate from them. Something they couldn't touch."

"I can't believe they did that."

"My parents were looking out for themselves. The way they always did." Hazel wiped away her tears with her arm. "Anyway, I decided I wanted to give my career one more shot. So I moved into this long-stay motel in Venice. I got a job in a coffee shop. I did open mic nights. No one ever guessed who I was. No one even said I looked like Harper anymore—I look so different from when I was a kid."

"So you thought you could get away with it."

"Obviously."

"But you lied about your age. You're twenty-eight."

"I did."

"Why?"

"I needed to cover my tracks. To project an image that was as different from Harper as possible. Younger, innocent, cowboy boots."

Zoey bit her lip. "It almost worked."

"If not for Bella."

"We don't know that it was her."

"Who else could it be? I just don't know why. We were getting along."

"It was because of Cole," Zoey said.

"What?"

"He heard you, that night at the bar. When you were talking with Nick about how you'd gotten Bella on our side. And he was pissed that you guys were tied in that round a couple of weeks ago. So he told her. I heard them talking, when we weren't talking."

"That little shit."

"He's ambitious, that's for sure."

Hazel touched Zoey's knee. "Do you hate me?"

"No."

"Can you forgive me?"

"I'm working on that."

"Okay, I get it. What's everyone else saying?"

"I think the producers are trying to decide what to do if you make it through on votes. I heard someone say something about a morals clause?"

Hazel wasn't surprised. It was what she expected. The contracts they'd signed had a built-in out for the production company. If they discovered something about you that made you an undesirable contestant, they could kick you out without repercussions. "It lets them decide who's in and who's out if you screw up in your personal life."

"Hmmm." Zoey got a glint in her eye and took out her phone.

"What are you doing?"

"You'll see." She tapped at her phone for a minute, then showed it to Hazel. It was open to Twitter, where Zoey had written a thread.

@ThisisZoey Hazel made some mistakes but she deserves to be here. She got where she is on talent and deserves a second chance. @ItsBellaBitch was probably the one who exposed her so she could win the @SingAlongIfYouKnowTheWords.

@ThisisZoey I'm #TeamHazel and you should be too. #VoteforHazel #HazelShouldStay #HazelisFine.

In the minute since she'd written the tweets they'd already been liked and retweeted a hundred times. It updated while Hazel was reading it. Two hundred. Three hundred. It was going viral. "Holy shit."

"I'm going to ask Kate to retweet it. That'll help a lot."

"Look, she already did."

Kate retweeted it, then she quote tweeted it and added: *Hazel Fine is the best singer in @SingAlongIfYouKnowTheWords. Dirty tactics shouldn't take this away from her. #TeamHazel #KeepHazel #HazelisFine.*

"That was nice of her," Hazel said. "It's just Twitter, though."

Zoey slapped at her knee. "Are you kidding? Twitter is where it's at for these things. If the Twitterverse decides you should stay, then you're staying."

"Didn't work for Martin."

"But that wasn't a public decision. There wasn't any way to vote *him* off. It's different for you. Especially if we get everyone in the competition to retweet it." Zoey stood. "I'll go speak to Benji. He'll marshal the troops."

"You so sure about that?"

"He'll do the right thing."

"Is it the right thing, though? I did lie. Maybe I should go."

"No. No way. If you lose, fine. But not because of this."

Zoey looked so fierce that Hazel couldn't help but smile. "Thank you, Zoey. You're more than I deserve."

Zoey nodded. "Probably. Get some sleep if you can. Tomorrow we go to war."

Hazel stripped off her dress, washed off her makeup, and took a long, hot shower.

When she got back into bed, she texted Nick the only words she could think of.

I'm sorry.

It wasn't enough, and he didn't answer, but she didn't expect him to.

As she was putting her phone down, her mother called, but she declined it and sent it to voice mail. God knows what she must be thinking right now, and her father . . . Hazel could only imagine. Not that she actually had to. *We told you so.* That's what her father would say, while her mother wailed about how everyone would be talking about her at the club.

She should turn off her phone and try to go to sleep. But now Hazel couldn't help herself. Instead of turning off her phone, Hazel checked Twitter. #TeamHazel was trending, but so was #TeamBella. She dipped into the comments on Kate's post, but quickly logged off when she realized it was a mix of death threats and bizarre memes she didn't understand, and she was afraid to google.

Hazel put her phone down on the nightstand, then played her life on a slow tape in her mind, rewinding and replaying the worst parts over and over until she finally fell into a fitful sleep.

She woke to the sounds of scratching. She assumed it was Checkers, but after a minute, she realized it was someone rapping on her door quietly. She glanced at the clock. It was just after seven in the morning. Her call time wasn't until ten. She wanted to tell whoever it was to go away, but it was time to stop hiding.

She opened the door. Benji was standing there, his hair still wet from his morning surf.

"Hey, Benji."

"Hazel." His jaw was set in a firm line. "I guess I was right."

"About?"

"You."

Hazel hadn't expected Benji to be happy with her, but this hurt. "What does that mean?"

"More lies. You know how I feel about that."

Hazel stiffened her back. "Yeah, I do. But I'm not your girlfriend, so I don't know what it is to you."

"I thought we were friends."

"We are."

"Friends don't lie to one another."

"Come on, Benji."

He stepped back. "You're saying *I* lied to *you*?"

"Didn't you?"

"How?"

"Playing me and Bella from the beginning? You knew she was into you, and you didn't care. You didn't tell her she didn't have a chance. You let her think she might, even when you knew her jealousy was a problem. And what were you doing with me, anyway? Just another conquest. Someone you tried to do because you thought you could."

He shook his head slowly. "That isn't what happened."

"Isn't it? Could've fooled me."

"I liked you."

"Okay."

"I was honest with you."

"Sure." Hazel crossed her arms over her chest. "What did you come here to say? How disappointed you are in me? Was that it? Get in line."

Benji rested his hand against the doorframe. "I wanted to explain why I'm not supporting you staying on *The Sing Along*, because I thought you deserved to hear that from me directly, given that we were friends."

Hazel felt sick. "You're not supporting me?"

"No. I told the producers you should be out."

"Because I lied about my age? What does that have to do with anything?"

"Because you lied about everything." Benji's voice was hard as bullets.

"Sure. I did. I lied about my past. Do you think I would've even been allowed in this competition if they knew who I was? That they would've judged me on my talent?"

Benji expelled a slow breath. "You don't know. They might have. You didn't even try to find out."

Anger rose inside Hazel even though Benji was right. "I didn't. Because I know exactly how people are. I've been judged since I was seven years old. Too fat, too thin, too many smiles, not smiling enough. Dance, monkey, dance."

"Yet you entered a singing competition to get judged again?"

"Yeah, I did. Just like you did after your experience with the TikTok house. To do it on my terms. So I could have control of my own narrative for once. So I could get my career back and do what I love." Hazel's voice was shaking. Her body was too. "You told me once about how you felt in that house. How you felt like you'd sold out, like you couldn't have anything for yourself, that they even tried to take surfing away from you. That's what my life was like times a thousand. No freedom. Losing every cent I'd made. My parents getting away scot-free. So yeah, damn right I lied. Damn right I hid my past. I'm not going to apologize for that."

"See, Benji," Bella said, poking her head around the door. "I told you."

"Go away, Bella," Hazel said.

"Or what?"

"I'm not going to punch you if that's what you want."

"Why would I want that?"

Hazel threw her hands up. "Oh jeez, I don't know. Because it would ensure that I get kicked out. Because maybe they can overlook my lies, but not physical violence against another contestant no matter how provoked."

Bella pursed her lips, and Hazel knew she'd made an accurate guess.

"I never did anything to you, Bella, you know that, right?"

Bella raised one shoulder slowly. "I never did anything to *you*."

"What's all this, then? You're saying that you're not the one who told the world who I was?"

"How was I supposed to know about that?"

Bella raised a good point, but Hazel was too worked up to consider it. "You listening to this, Benji? You think I'm the one with the problem? You're on *her* side. You two deserve each other." Hazel started to close the door but Benji put his foot in the way.

"We're not done here."

"Yes, we are." Hazel put more force on the door and Benji stepped back. "Good luck tonight."

Benji's face clouded with confusion. "I didn't mean . . ."

"It's fine. Enough. Go."

Hazel closed the door and leaned against it, feeling lost and tired.

She should quit right now and leave. She could go somewhere and start over. Again. She wasn't sure where exactly, because now she was recognizable as Hazel, so that might not be a possibility.

But she'd changed her look, her name, her life, once before. She could do it again.

A wave of exhaustion and anger hit her. Why did she have to, though? She'd gotten where she was because she deserved it as much as anyone else in *The Sing Along*. Why did she have to walk away?

No. This was bullshit.

Hazel pulled herself up and stepped into the bathroom.

She avoided herself in the mirror because she could only imagine the ravages of a bad night's sleep on her face.

She took a quick shower, then blew out her hair and applied her makeup as carefully as she could. She chose something from her wardrobe that was simple and understated—a black jumpsuit she'd bought at a thrift store as a potential outfit for the show. She paired it with a jean jacket and put on flats instead of her cowboy boots. Only then did she inspect herself in the full-length mirror. Her cheeks were hollowed out from the dieting she'd done to quell the pregnancy rumor and the stress of the last few days.

Despite that, she looked more like herself. Like the self she wanted to be.

There was a knock at her door. It was after eight now, but still. Why couldn't people leave her alone?

She opened it. It was Nick, a solemn expression on his face. By the dark circles under his eyes, Hazel guessed he'd had almost as bad a night as she had.

"Good, you're ready," Nick said.

"For what?"

"You're meeting with the producers. You didn't get my text?"

Hazel hadn't checked her phone that morning. "No, I . . . right now?"

"Right now, Hazel."

"Okay, I'm ready."

Nick gave her a brief smile. "Play to Georgia."

"What's that supposed to mean?"

"You'll see."

Chapter Twenty-three

Twenty minutes later, Hazel was in one of the bungalows standing in front of the show's executive producers—Martin, Georgia, and two serious-looking men in suits Hazel had seen hanging around the live shows, but with whom she'd otherwise had zero contact.

Nick was there, too, and Keshawn, but it was Martin who was in charge.

"Hazel Fine, what have you got to say for yourself?" Martin said. He was lounging on a steel-gray couch, his right leg crossed over the other. Georgia sat in a wing chair on the other side of the couch, the suited men standing between them. Nick hovered behind Georgia.

Hazel wasn't sure what to say, but it couldn't hurt to start with a mea culpa. "I want to apologize for misleading you about my past."

"Is that all?"

"I think I should stay. If I get the votes, that is. I earned my place here. My performances weren't a lie. We should let the people decide."

"Let the people decide," Martin drawled. "What an interesting concept you Americans have. You think voting makes you democratic. But everything can be manipulated."

"I know that."

His eyes bored into Hazel's. "Do you, Hazel? Do you understand how much goes into casting this show, how we choose each of you carefully and craft your narrative, and that your 'performances' as you put it are only a small detail?"

Hazel bit back a sarcastic response. She wasn't a moron. She knew the show had its favorites, its shiny pennies that it put under the lights. She knew Nick had helped her and Kate too. But in the end, she was the one who had to deliver. If she didn't perform, then the audience would send her home. There had been upsets in the past, obvious first choices who hadn't been able to take the pressure, and oddballs the public had fallen in love with who'd made it all the way to the end.

"I think I do, yes."

"Then you shouldn't be so naïve as to think this is simply about what the people want."

"I'm not. I was just trying to say that you should wait to see the result of the vote. That they should factor in to your decision."

Martin checked his manicure. "Ah, yes. Your little Twitter campaign."

"It isn't mine."

"No? I'm disappointed, Hazel. But then again, you've let me down in many ways."

Hazel knew what he meant. She'd let him down because she hadn't slept with him. She couldn't believe he'd be so brazen as to say it in front of everyone. She couldn't be the only one who understood.

She caught Nick's eye and she knew she wasn't. He looked like he wanted to throttle Martin with his bare hands.

"Enough of that, Martin," Georgia said, her voice steady and sober. "I agree with Hazel. We should let her stay. If the audience decides to keep her, then that's what they want. And we should give the people what they want."

Hazel turned to Georgia gratefully. She was clear-eyed, her hair and makeup perfect. "Thank you, Georgia."

"Of course, darlin'. You know I've been rooting for you since the beginning."

"That means a lot to me."

"You have talent. And moxie. I like it."

"Yes, yes," Martin said. "Hazel has moxie. Hazel has talent. But should Hazel be on our show?"

"The audience thinks so," Nick said.

"Thank you, Nicholas, I am aware."

"I say she stays," Keshawn said. He'd been silent the entire meeting, standing in the background, his usual megawatt smile dimmed by the surroundings. There were tensions and loyalties in this room Hazel didn't understand, but she appreciated any show of support. "Think about the ratings," he added. "Tonight's episode is going to be lit."

Martin's head perked up. Now they were talking his language.

"Keshawn's right," one of the men in suits said. "Our ratings have been down this season. When we lost that girl with cancer . . ."

"Excuse me," Hazel said. "You mean Lacey?"

"Yes, that's right. She was a ratings bonanza."

"Steven," Georgia said. "Honestly. She's very ill. She may not make it."

"Is that true?" Hazel asked.

Georgia smiled sadly. "Yes, I'm sorry to report. I saw her yesterday at the hospital and things are not looking good."

"That's terrible."

"It is."

"It's also beside the point," Martin said. "That singing show in costumes is nipping at our heels. Perhaps Keshawn is right. We should wait and see what happens tonight and then assess tomorrow once we have the overnights." Martin's gaze paused on Hazel. "This Twitter campaign, you should be actively pursuing that. If you want to stay."

"I'll do my best."

"All right." Martin checked his watch. "Voting ends at five. We'll put out a statement saying that we are, as you put it, 'letting the people decide.' If the ratings come in and you get the votes, then we'll let you go on to the final."

That didn't sound as if it was entirely decided to Hazel, but Nick patted her shoulder quickly, and she knew what she had to say. "Thank you."

"Don't thank me yet," Martin said, giving her a quick once-over. Each time his eyes rested on her Hazel felt like she needed a shower. "You should make yourself visible."

"Pardon?"

"Go forth into the world. Don't hide. If you want to stay around, that is."

"I do."

"Then go."

Hazel didn't have to be told twice. She walked out of the bungalow feeling as if she was escaping a scolding from her parents.

Outside, the air was heavy with humidity, and encircled her like a weighted blanket. But she was still there, still on the show she'd put so much on the line for. If she could get the votes, they'd have to keep her. It would be too much of scandal not to.

But first she had to get the votes.

She knew just what to do.

J

"Are you sure this is a good idea?" Zoey asked, biting her nails nervously. She was wearing an old-fashioned cowboy shirt tucked into tight, dark jeans.

"It's the only way I can think of to get votes."

"You might attract the wrong kind of attention too."

"I know. I can handle it."

"Okay, sit in that chair, then."

Hazel went to the corner of her hotel room where there was a wing chair near the window, with a light above it. She sat and checked herself on her phone. Her makeup was good, her hair was smooth, and she looked much calmer than she felt.

Zoey was mounting her phone on a ring light that she'd

finagled off one of the assistants, and had cued up Instagram. "Ready to go live?"

"Ready."

Zoey clicked a button on the remote and held up her fingers, counting down to three, two, one.

"Hi, everyone, Hazel Fine here. First, I wanted to thank Zoey for her support and for letting me squat on her Insta. Some of you know that I'm not really on social media other than the socials I put out for the show, and probably wondered about that. If you asked, I would've spun some bullshit about it being a distraction and toxic, but the truth is that even in the competition, I wanted to keep a low profile.

"Anyway, I guess everyone knows who I am now. Or you think you do. Maybe you think I'm Daisy Dawson, a girl who was always tripping over her own feet and saying cute catchphrases. Maybe you think I'm a liar and not a very nice person. And you'd be right in some ways. A lot of that is true and those are things I've been at some point in my life."

Hazel paused to take a breath. The camera was close enough that she could see that thousands of people were watching her. Comments were scrolling by too fast to read. She saw a lot of multicolored hearts, but also devil emojis and other symbols she didn't even understand.

"But it's not everything there is to know about me. It's just points on a map in my life. Public things you can point to and say, 'I know that girl.' To put me in a box, to categorize me, to decide how you're going to feel about me.

"It's one of the problems with being in the public eye. How much do you share? How much do you reveal? Do you know that at the start of your career they sit you down and ask you to fill out a questionnaire about every bad thing that happened in your life so they can decide when to deal out the details? Which movie or album or whatever they'll work best for? Only when you're a child star, that's not how it happens. All those mistakes you hear celebrities talking about when they're promoting something—you make all of those with everyone watching."

There were tens of thousands of people watching the live feed now. More hearts, more harsh words flashing by.

Hazel Suxs.

Daisy forever.

Whoops-a-daisy.

#TeamBella

Lock her up!

Hazel dragged her eyes away from the feed. "I'm not complaining. I know no one wants to hear anything about how difficult it is to grow up in the spotlight. But whatever you think you know about me, it isn't the whole story, and it wasn't a story I wanted to tell. It's my story, my life. I wanted to keep something for myself."

Hazel paused. There were fifty thousand people watching now, a number that was both unbelievable and unsurprising. Everyone likes a train wreck. She'd been counting on that.

"And I also wanted to sing. That's what I started out trying to do when I was a kid. I got the chance to be Daisy, and I took it because I thought it would get me there. Music was always what drove me, what consoled me, but no one would take me seriously. If I wanted to be a manufactured pop princess, I could put out a record. But record my own stuff? Show my personality? No, thank you, Hazel, we want Harper.

"Problem was, Harper was an invention. And I didn't want to keep pretending. So I turned away from it for a long time. It gave me time to think and reset, to become a different person—Hazel, who'd had a normal childhood, gone to college, had real friends. It gave me an opportunity to fall back in love with music. To find my voice."

Kick her off!

Hazel deserves to stay!

This bitch talks a lot.

"I knew no one was going to let me sing, though. Not Harper. But maybe Hazel might have a chance. I didn't want to be Harper anymore, if I ever was her. So I lied. I hid my past. That's not *The Sing Along*'s fault, it's mine and I own it. But what you've seen from me in this competition, that's the truth. Me singing. Me writing those songs."

Screw Bella!

Bella should go.

I'm going to fuck that bitch up.

Hazel paused. Whatever Bella had done, she didn't deserve threats. And maybe she wasn't the one who'd told on Hazel. She'd denied it, even if she was gloating about it.

"One more thing—if it was Bella who told on me, it's not her fault. This competition pits people against each other, and I did some things wrong too. If I'd been a better friend to her, a better ally, she wouldn't have done it. So I forgive you, Bella, and I'm sorry."

Zoey made a face behind the phone, but Hazel felt genuine in the moment. She'd disregarded Bella's feelings and manipulated her to get what she wanted. Whether Bella deserved it or not was beside the point.

"And for everyone else I care about who I've hurt, I'm sorry too." She paused, wanting to say Nick's name and Benji's. Were they watching? Nick would barely look at her in that meeting with the suits. She should put any thoughts about him away.

She cleared her throat and continued. "All of which leaves *you* with a choice. The producers have said that if I get the votes, I can stay. They're going to let you, the viewers, decide. So, it's in your hands. If you want me to be in the finals, vote for me. And if you don't, that's all right. I get it. Every single person still in the competition is supertalented and everyone deserves to be here. Including me.

"I believe that now, and that's a gift I won't forget. Thank you for listening."

Hazel nodded to Zoey, and she turned off the feed.

"You think you did enough?" Zoey asked.

"I guess we'll see tonight."

The afternoon was a mess of nerves, none of them eating, all of them avoiding each other except Zoey and Hazel. The hotel was under siege by journalists, so they holed up in Hazel's room, playing with Checkers and telling each other that it was all going to be fine.

But it wasn't, because only one woman and one man were going through to the final round. It could be any one of them, but everything that had happened had taken the focus off Zoey. Hazel felt bad about that. Zoey deserved as much attention as anyone. If Hazel didn't make it, she wanted Zoey to get in.

Around five, they separated to get ready, then went through the motions onstage. They each had individual performances and then a group number. Hazel floated through them like she was having an out-of-body experience. And now it was ten minutes to the end of the show and Keshawn had gathered them all onstage. Hazel linked her hand through Zoey's and squeezed tight.

Keshawn flashed a smile at the audience and tapped the envelopes against his hand. Hazel wondered whether he knew the results. He was too good of an actor for her to tell.

"The moment you've all been waiting for, tweeting for, hashtagging for."

The audience laughed.

"But first, let's do the men, shall we?"

The audience groaned. Hazel's heart felt like it might explode.

"Benji, Cole, Dave—please step forward."

The men advanced in a line but they didn't hold hands like the women usually did. Cole was self-assured, Benji was nervous, and Dave was his usual inscrutable self, like he wasn't quite sure how he'd gotten this far. He'd sung like it, too, and if there was any connection between talent and success, he should be one of the ones going home. But between Benji and Cole, it wasn't clear who the favorite was. They'd both sung their hearts out, and they both had their fan bases.

Hazel wanted Benji to stay. She understood why he was mad at her, and she couldn't blame him. He'd made it clear since the beginning that honesty was important to him, and all she'd done was lie. If she'd told him the truth that moonlit night on the beach, and opened up to him fully, would things be different now? Was that even what she wanted?

No. She found Nick in the wings and smiled at him. He'd kept his distance, too, but it had a different quality to it. Hazel couldn't explain why, but his silence didn't feel hostile, only cautious. Besides, she'd screwed things up there before any of her secrets had come out.

As if to confirm her thoughts, Nick smiled back before turning away and answering a question from one of the crew.

"Dave, you sang an Elvis medley. Martin thought it was off balance, and Georgia said it was 'just okay.' Cole, you sang John Mayer's 'Gravity,' and Martin called it transcendent, but Georgia simply fanned herself. Benji, you sang 'Tangled Up in Blue' and Martin said that Dylan would be envious, and Georgia gave you a one-minute standing ovation. Two of you are going home."

Keshawn opened the envelope and then paused. "Dave, this is the end of your journey on the show."

The audience erupted in applause. It wasn't entirely clear if they were applauding Dave leaving or if they were congratulating him on his journey. Dave took it as the latter, smiling through his montage, then taking a bow before leaving the stage. Benji and Cole moved closer together. Benji towered over Cole, who hadn't finished growing.

"We love you, Cole!" someone in the audience shouted, likely his mama.

"We love you, Benji!" screamed three girls together, and the audience laughed and applauded.

"Benji, Cole, lot of love for you out there. You both have

an assured future in this business. But one of you is going home tonight." He tapped the card, hiding the answer he was about to reveal. "Cole, I'm sorry, but it's the end of the line for you."

Hazel let out the breath she was holding. So, it was Benji. If she made it, she was going to have to go up against him. That felt fitting.

There was some booing from the crowd, again mostly from Cole's camp, and then a retrospective of Cole's time on the show started to play. Hazel watched the screen, Zoey's hand shaking in hers, Bella unnaturally still next to her. When Cole's film ended, he took a bow, then rushed off the stage in tears.

Benji waved to a room full of applause, then followed him.

"All right, ladies, your turn," Keshawn said, a fresh envelope in his hand.

Hazel and Zoey stepped forward, but Bella was rooted to the spot. Hazel reached back and extended her hand to Bella. Bella looked incredulous, then took it and stepped forward. A cheer rose from the crowd.

"That's nice to see," Keshawn said. "Truly."

Hazel smiled at him, and he gave her a brief nod. Was he telegraphing something to her?

"Hazel!" someone in the crowd screamed.

"Maybe!" Keshawn answered, chuckling at his own joke.

Hazel closed her eyes as he went through his usual spiel summarizing their performances and reminding them of the judges' comments.

"Zoey," Hazel heard him say, and for a moment Hazel thought it was over. But then she realized he was saying that

Zoey was going home, and it was down to her and Bella. The perfect moment for the show.

Hazel hugged Zoey as hard as she could, then held on to her as Zoey's montage played, her arm around Zoey's shaking shoulder. It wasn't the place to talk, but she hoped Zoey would be okay. Thankfully, Brooke had arrived late in the day to be her support system.

The montage was over, and Zoey left. Hazel stepped toward Bella, their hands linked. Whatever happened, she had to be okay with it. Whatever happened, she was okay with it. Whatever happened—

"Hazel, Bella, your competition has been one for the ages. And by only fifty votes, Bella . . . you're going home tonight."

Hazel felt like she might pass out. She'd done it! She'd made it into the final. She started shaking, letting out the emotion she'd been holding in. She felt the tears fall as Bella pulled her into a hug.

"I'm sorry," Bella said, and Hazel hugged her tighter.

"Me too," Hazel said. "Me too."

Chapter Twenty-four

The next morning, Hazel woke early and clearheaded.

Her mind was full of the same mantra as the night before. She'd done it. She'd made it. She was in the final two. It was down to her and Benji now. How had this even happened? Hazel hadn't had the energy to think about it the night before. She'd just begged off the after-party and gone to her room, diving into her bed like she was diving for pearls.

But now the sun was streaming in the windows because she'd forgotten to close the blackout blinds, and Checkers was hopping around and scratching, and her heart was racing.

She was terrified.

She could admit that now. All the feelings she'd pushed aside, the things she hadn't thought through. How she was never going to remain anonymous if she made it to the end. Someone, somewhere, would've dredged up her past and exposed it. If she was being honest, she never thought she'd get here. And if she did, then she supposed she would've had some insulation. In the moments she'd let herself think about it, she'd assumed that if it happened after her success, then it wouldn't be that bad. That she might even find a way to tell the story herself, like a controlled explosion used to bring down a building before it fell on its own.

What was she supposed to do now? The building was down and she was standing in the rubble. It hadn't taken her out, but she was wounded. She still had enemies. People who wished her harm. When it came down to it, were they going to let her win?

Or had she already won? Coming in second was still a potential path to fulfilling her dreams, and that scared her too. Did that happen nowadays, though? She couldn't think of the last runner-up on *The Sing Along*, or any other singing competition, who'd gone on to make it big. It happened back in the heyday of *American Idol*, but that was when the whole concept was new and fresh. Now the attention and prize money went to the winner, and then the next season started up and everyone moved on.

To assure her future, she needed to win. For now, there was nothing she could do but wait it out. The final show was in two days, but today was an off-day before the final preparations began tomorrow. She needed to get out of the hotel. Do something normal, something for herself that would take her mind off everything.

She rose and fed Checkers, then cleaned out his cage. Then she dressed in running clothes, shoved her hair into a baseball hat, and grabbed her phone and the earbuds that had been in the favor bags for the special guests a couple of weeks ago.

She left her room as she slipped the earbuds into her ears, feeling the luxury of something she couldn't afford. She couldn't believe the things they gave away to the special guests. Rich people didn't need favors, and that's why they left them behind week after week. The contestants were allowed to take them once the show was over, hence the perfect sonic quality that was now in her ears.

She cued up "Heat Wave" by the Glass Animals and loped out the back way that she used to get Checkers in and out of the hotel. She ran a few blocks and felt free. Her feet on the pavement, the song repeating in her ears. This was what she needed.

And then she saw them. A huddle of cars up the road with telephoto lenses hanging out the windows. Vultures. She wasn't surprised that she hadn't evaded them, but she was resentful. Couldn't she just go for a run in peace? She was only trying to get some peace.

"Hey, get in." It was Nick, driving a black SUV. He reached across the passenger's seat and opened the door.

Hazel looked up the street, then back at Nick. This would get caught on camera, too, but who cared? No one knew who Nick was, sad to say. Hazel jumped into the car and closed the door. Nick did a U-turn, then sped down a side street, glancing back over his shoulder. "They don't seem to be following."

"I'm not Britney."

"And you never want to be."

"Amen."

They drove in silence, Hazel aware of the fact that she was sweating on his expensive leather seats. "Where are we going?"

"My place isn't far from here. If that's okay?"

"Sure."

They drove into Studio City. Hazel hadn't been in that area of town for a long time, and she admired the bungalows flashing past. She'd love to own her own home someday, but one of these places seemed out of reach.

"Sorry to get you involved in all this," she said.

"It's fine."

She watched his hands on the wheel. They were gripping it tightly. "Is it, though? You've barely spoken to me in days."

Nick glanced at her, then back to the road. "Things have been hectic."

"Sure, but . . ."

"And you did accuse me of helping you to sleep with you."

Hazel sank in her seat. "Okay, true."

"But?"

"I didn't mean it. Someone was putting ideas in my head."

He slowed to a stop at a red light. "What does that mean?"

"I wasn't thinking straight. I'm sorry."

"You had a lot on your plate."

Hazel wished he'd look at her for more than a second. "You weren't mad?"

"I wouldn't go that far."

"Okay." That was it then. She'd screwed this up too.

The light changed and Nick stepped on the gas. "But anger passes."

"Does it?"

Now, finally, he was looking at her. "It does." He smiled at her in a way she recognized from their night together. "I went to your room this morning."

"Oh?"

"You weren't there."

"I was running."

"So Benji told me. I guess he saw you leave."

Hazel hadn't noticed Benji when she'd left, but that didn't surprise her. She was so up in her head, she doubted she would've noticed an elephant in the hall. "What were you there to tell me?"

He smiled at her again. "That I wasn't mad anymore."

She smiled back. "Good. Don't hit that guy, though."

Nick dragged his eyes back to the road, slowing the car before it hit the one in front of them. "I'll just concentrate on driving for a bit."

"Sure." Hazel hugged herself, feeling happy. She opened the window and put her arms on the sill. Hazel couldn't remember the last time she'd been a passenger in someone else's car. There was a feeling of freedom about it that she'd missed. Her car was always in danger of falling apart, and she only drove it when she absolutely had to. It was never happy and carefree. But this was different. They could go anywhere; they only had to decide.

Nick maneuvered onto a side street full of desert-appropriate lawns and palm trees, then slowed the car and turned up a driveway. The house was a midsized white adobe bungalow with a red tile roof. Traditional California architecture if you had a million or so to spare. Maybe two.

Hazel wondered how Nick could afford the place, then

kicked herself. She had no idea how much he got paid, or if he had points in the show, or if he was otherwise wealthy. She shouldn't make assumptions either way. "It's really nice," she said.

"Thanks. I'll be paying for it till I die."

Hazel laughed and they got out of the car. Nick led her up the front walkway. The front door was an old piece of driftwood, and inside the walls were white and the doorways were arched. More driftwood on the floor, with large clean windows looking at a trio of palm trees in the yard.

"It's great, Nick."

"Thank you. It was a mess when I got it, but it turned out all right."

Hazel snorted. "You should see where I've been living."

"A five-star hotel?"

"No, dummy, before that."

His features softened. "You want to take a shower?"

"Um, what?"

"I meant, do you want to get out of those running clothes and rinse off? There's towels in the bathroom and I can probably scrounge up some clothes for you."

"That'd be great, thanks."

"It's through there."

Hazel followed his directions down a short hall to the master bedroom. It wasn't big, but it had a queen bed with a wood headboard, crisp white sheets, and a matching dresser. The bathroom was behind it, a spacious room with a large walk-in shower and a window that was frosted in strategic places. The whole house felt light and happy, and it had been so long since Hazel had been in a real home that she almost felt like weeping.

"There's a robe on the back of the door," Nick yelled from the other room.

"Thank you!"

Hazel turned on the water and stepped into the warm spray. She let herself rinse off for a few minutes, then used Nick's shampoo. It smelled spicy and rich, the way she remembered him smelling during their night together. It felt surprising to be here, in this shower, with him so close by. That night felt like it had taken place a million years ago, when she could count the days on her fingers. Too much had happened since then, things she couldn't change or take back.

She didn't regret it. Only the way she'd handled it afterward.

She turned off the shower and stepped out. She wound a towel around her head and slipped on Nick's robe. It was big and loose, and she cinched it tight. Then she found a comb on the counter and used it to untangle her hair. The room was foggy, and she wiped a streak off the glass to get a look at herself. Her face was clear of makeup, her eyes tired, and her skin pale. She'd have to do.

She walked into the bedroom. There was a simple white tennis dress on the bed that looked like it would fit. There was also a pair of undershorts that would do for underwear, and on inspection, the dress had a bra built in. She dressed quickly and put her hair in a braid.

When she checked herself again in the mirror, she looked ready for Wimbledon.

She walked into the living room. Nick was off to the side, in the kitchen.

"You want a smoothie?" he asked, holding up a blender full of a thick liquid.

"Sure, that would be nice."

He grinned. "You look cute in that."

"Is it Kate's?"

"What? No, it's my sister's."

"You have a sister?"

"I do."

"I didn't know that." Nick handed her a glass. The liquid inside was bright green in color and smelled like grass. "I guess we sort of skipped over the usual get-to-know-you stuff."

A cloud passed across his face and Hazel regretted her words. "We did," he said. "I'm sorry about that."

"You're not the one who has to apologize."

"No, I do."

Hazel took a sip of the concoction. It tasted like grass, too, but it made her feel extremely healthy, drinking it, which she supposed was the point. "Why?"

He ran his hand through his hair. "I never should've agreed to this."

"To what?"

"All of it."

"Nick. Just tell me."

He sighed out the words. "I knew."

The glass was sweating in her hand. She was worried she might drop it. "Excuse me?"

"I knew who you were. We all did."

Hazel thought her life was all out of surprises. She should've known better. But this, this, she never saw this coming.

"You knew who I was? The whole time?"

Nick's head hung low. "Yes."

"What? How? Why?"

"Let me explain."

Hazel put the glass of grass down on the counter carefully. Really, she wanted to throw it and mar the white walls. "I think I should go."

"Please, Hazel. Stay. At least long enough for me to explain."

Hazel considered her options. She wanted to leave, but she wanted to understand her life too. And clearly, she didn't. "Only because I have no other way to get back to the hotel."

"Fair enough."

Nick walked out from behind the counter and led her into the living room. He sat on a midcentury modern couch covered in a buttery, dark leather. Hazel sat in one of the matching lighter-tone chairs across from it, wishing she knew where to put her hands, her feet, her thoughts.

He knew. They *knew*. They knew the whole time.

"The scout recognized you," Nick said. "At that open mic."

"He did? How?"

"He's very good at faces."

Hazel thought back to the brief conversation she'd had months ago with the guy in his midthirties who'd praised her performance and handed her a card. It had felt like validation, like divine intervention, because she'd been thinking of applying to *The Sing Along* for months, but something had been holding her back. And then there he was, a real scout, inviting her to participate after she'd given her all onstage. But even that was a sham. It didn't have anything to do with her performance, and the universe wasn't looking out for her. Instead, someone had seen an opportunity to profit off her once again.

"I was asked to audition for the show because he knew I was Harper?"

Nick rested his hands flat on his knees. "I wouldn't say that exactly. He was curious. He said you were fantastic, and he was also shocked at where you were."

Hazel's throat felt tight. "You had this conversation?"

"We did."

"And what did you think?"

"I didn't know what to think. I wasn't sure it was you. And people the scouts invite don't always end up submitting tapes."

"I did submit a tape, though."

"You did. And you were great, just like he said."

Hazel had worked on that tape for a week, take after take in her hotel room at night after her shifts, every minute of every day off, until she got it right. Then she'd waited weeks after that to hear anything, convinced it wasn't going to happen. When she'd gotten the call with the invitation to the general auditions, she'd been relieved and disappointed. But she still had a shot, she reasoned. Contestants made it out of the general auditions all the time.

"Once you got my tape, you knew it was me?"

"We investigated." Nick raised his shoulders. "I don't know how, but they confirmed that you were Harper."

"So you knew it was me," Hazel said again. "And you put me in the cattle call. Not right through to the audition room like Benji or Bella."

"We did."

"Why?"

Nicks fingers tapped at his knees like was playing the piano. "Because the decision we made—the decision *I* made— was *not* to expose who you were. If we'd put you through to the auditions, we would've called too much attention to you.

You know we always do those special video montages about where you come from for those contestants."

And there was no special montage for Hazel. "I remember."

"That would've been a problem. We had a contingency plan in case it came out, but I wanted to see how you could do without the baggage of your name or your past."

"*You* made the decision."

"I did." Nick leaned forward. His eyes were clear, focused. "Remember when I told you that every year there was someone special, one contestant who stood out from the beginning? You were that person, Hazel. I told you that. I could see it in your audition tape, but I knew that if your identity was revealed then your time on the show would become only about that. So I convinced the powers that be to hide it."

Hazel worked it through in her mind. "Martin knew?"

"He did."

"I'm shocked he didn't threaten to reveal it in order to get me into bed with him."

Nick spoke through gritted teeth. "I would've killed him if he did that. But he knew better than to use your secret like that. That could've blown back on all of us."

Hazel remembered all the times Martin had touched her with his eyes. All the innuendos he'd made, how she'd felt trapped around him. "What he did was bad enough."

"Agreed." Nick put up his hand. "I know, I know. This is my last year on the show."

"What?"

"I've been in talks with *The Voice*. Their musical director is moving on. It's going to be announced in a couple of weeks."

"That's great."

"Thanks."

Hazel flexed her hands. She felt an odd mix of emotions. Anger, sadness, disappointment, and . . . relief. "I can't believe you knew."

"I'm sorry, Hazel. I should've told you."

"No, I—I think I'm glad you didn't."

"Why?"

"I wouldn't have done the show if being Harper was part of it."

"Why not?"

"Because I didn't want to drag all that up again. Look, I'm not naïve, okay? I knew it was a risk that it would come out. But that's different from a certainty. I was willing to take the risk but not to put it out there myself. If you'd told me you knew and that it was going to be part of the show, I would've bowed out."

"Okay, but I shouldn't have lied."

"Well, yeah. If I've learned one thing it's that."

Nick sighed. "You're not mad?"

"I don't know. I'm tired."

"You want me to take you back to the hotel?"

Hazel thought about it. This was difficult and complicated, but that was her life everywhere she went. "Honestly?"

"Of course."

"I'd rather stay here, if you don't mind."

He gave her a slow smile. "I don't mind. There's a pool if you like?"

That sounded appealing, but what she needed was a nap. "Do you have a guest room?"

"I do, in fact."

"Do you mind if I take a rest? I haven't been sleeping and I'm worn-out."

"Of course." Nick stood and Hazel followed him back down the hall. He opened one of the doors. There was a comfortable guest room behind it, with a large bed, guitars on the walls, and a series of black-and-white photographs above the headboard.

"Is this your sister's room?"

"Yeah, when she's here."

"Thank you."

"My pleasure." He put his hands on her shoulders, first one and then the other. Their eyes locked, and Hazel thought he was going to kiss her, but then he let go and left. Hazel wanted to call after him, to bring him back to her side, to ask him to help fill the ache inside her, but she was so tired right now she couldn't take any more emotions.

Instead, Hazel took off the tennis dress and slipped between the sheets. The bed was soft, the sheets cool. Hazel released the tension from her body and closed her eyes.

If she tried hard enough, maybe she could sleep until tomorrow.

When Hazel woke up the sun was setting.

She lay on her back listening to the unfamiliar sounds around her. Nick in the kitchen, washing up. Someone coughing in the distance. Birds she couldn't identify in the trees outside.

She still felt tired, her brain fuzzy. She turned over on her side and tried to go back to sleep, but after a few minutes, she realized it was no use. She might have a reserve of missed sleep to tap into but napping most of the day had exhausted it. She was also ravenous. She got up and went into the guest bath. There was a fresh toothbrush there, which she used, then she put the tennis dress back on and arranged her hair as best she could.

She ventured out of the room feeling shy. "Nick?"

"In here," he called. She followed his voice to the kitchen. He was standing at the counter, frowning at his phone. There were pots on the stove and a rich tomato aroma filled the room.

Nick put his phone down and smiled at her. "You hungry?"

"God, yes."

"Dinner will be ready shortly. Glass of wine?"

"Sure, thank you."

He reached into the sleek fridge and pulled out a bottle that Hazel knew from the label was four times as much as the wine she usually bought. He poured her a glass and handed it to her. It was rich and buttery and when she took a sip it brought back memories of her old life.

"That is very good, thank you."

"Sure."

"What's for dinner?"

"Rigatoni and meatballs."

"Yum."

"Probably not on Kate's you're-not-pregnant diet."

"I say this with the utmost respect for her and her diet but screw that. For this meal at least."

Nick laughed. "Good girl. My sentiments exactly."

Hazel took another sip of wine, then put the glass down. She had to be careful. On her empty stomach, too much wine would go right to her head. "Not sure I'm younger enough than you for you to use that expression."

"Real Hazel or Fake Hazel?"

"Hey!"

He dipped his head. "Couldn't resist."

"I see how it is," Hazel said. Their eyes met and held before they both looked away. Was this the way it was always going to be between them now? Long looks and things left unsaid?

"Why don't you let me finish this up," Nick said, gesturing to the pot simmering on the stove. "You can sit in the living room if you like?"

Hazel felt like she was being dismissed. "Sure."

She picked up her glass and took it to the living room. Nick's taste was simple and sparse. The walls were creamy, and he had a black grand piano, and another row of guitars on the wall. There were a few framed pictures of what Hazel assumed were his family, but everything still smelled new, like he'd only moved in a few weeks ago.

Hazel wished she had a home like this. Well, not exactly like this one, though it was gorgeous, but something truly her own that she could decorate to her taste. Not like the soulless McMansion her parents had bought with her money, but something small and cozy that felt like an escape rather than an obligation.

Hazel pushed those thoughts aside as she heard a phone buzz. It was hers, sitting on the coffee table. She picked it up. She'd missed three texts from Zoey.

The last one read: *Where are you? I'm worried.*

Hazel walked into the backyard through the sliding glass doors. There was bright-green turf on the ground, and it was enclosed by a cement wall with purple-flowered vines growing along it. A rectangular cement pool glistened in the fading sunlight.

Sorry, I had to bail. I'm at Nick's.

A moment of wait, then: *Oh?*

Not like that. He rescued me from the paparazzi.

Your hero!

I'm not a princess.

True.

Can you look after Checkers? Hazel sat down on a teak lounger that was covered in a dark-beige cushion and stared at the glistening water. This is where she should've spent her day, not hiding in a dark bedroom.

Of course! I'm sure Brooke won't mind.

Hazel smiled. She was glad Brooke had stayed even though Zoey wasn't in the finals. Zoey was still in town because they'd be doing several group numbers during the final show.

You still have your key? Hazel asked.

I do!

Thank you so much. Pretty sure Checkers prefers you to me.

He's grown on me.

Hazel smiled. *Right? He's so cute.*

So cute. Just like Nick.

Nick looks like Checkers?

Ha-ha. You know what I mean.

I do. Hazel took another sip of her wine. *His house is nice.*

That's great.

I'll be back in a few hours.

Feel free to stay out all night!

Hazel frowned. What had gotten into Zoey? They might've reconciled but as far as she knew, Zoey hadn't changed her opinion about Nick. *I thought you were against me being with Nick?*

Brooke said I was being a jerk.

Ah.

You think so?

You made some good points. Anyway, it doesn't matter. There is no me and Nick.

You so sure about that?

It's complicated.

No shit, girl.

Hazel sent back a devil emoji and put her phone down.

"What are you grinning at?"

Hazel started. Nick was standing above her, his hand shading his eyes as he looked down.

"Oh, Zoey's being funny."

"She okay?"

"She'll survive."

"She's talented."

"I know."

Nick sat on the lounger next to her. "I could make some calls if you like. Set up some meetings for her."

Hazel felt a rush of warmth toward him. "That would be great."

"Consider it done. Dinner's ready."

"Maybe we could eat out here?"

"Sounds good. You want another glass of wine?"

"Not sure. I've got to keep my wits about me."

Nick's mouth twisted. "How come?"

"I'm in the enemies' camp."

"I'm the enemy now?"

"I'm teasing."

Nick stood. "Can you help me bring the stuff out?"

"Of course." Hazel got up, then took a step toward him, almost tripping on the edge of the chair leg.

Nick reached out and caught hold of her. "Whoopsie—"

"Oh no, don't you dare." Hazel put her hands on his chest and gave him a push that wasn't hard, but that he wasn't expecting.

He tripped backward over his feet and tumbled into the pool. He landed on his back, splashing out a big arc of water behind him. Hazel's hand flew to her mouth as he flailed in the water for a minute, but Nick was fine. He wasn't going to drown in the shallow end of his own pool.

He regained his footing, spluttering then wiping his eyes as his sodden clothes hung down around him. "Did I deserve that?" He was half mad, half laughing.

"I think so."

"All right, fair enough."

He pushed his hair back as Hazel admired the way the water glistened on his skin. The way it darkened his hair. How his T-shirt clung to his . . .

No. Stop.

This wasn't a good idea. It was easy, yes. She felt at ease with Nick. But all they'd done since they'd met was lie to one another. Hazel didn't blame Nick—she'd been lying, too— but it wasn't a solid foundation for a relationship. Hazel's instinct was to put that aside and jump in the pool to join him, but her instincts had led her down every wrong path, forever. She needed to use her rational mind if she could still find it. And Rational Hazel was telling her to park her feelings and keep things professional. Which was what Rational Hazel had advised way back in the beginning, and she'd been right.

"Hey," Nick said. "Where did you go?"

"Nowhere."

"Hazel."

She forced a smile. "It's fine. Come on, get out of the pool. Let's eat."

Nick looked unsure, then hauled himself up. Hazel couldn't help but watch him, how his pants clung to his body, and her memory of what lay underneath. How good they'd felt together. He caught her staring, and she turned away.

"It's fine," he said.

"What is?"

"If you don't want to. If you don't want me."

"It's not that."

"It's something. Come on, tell me."

Hazel couldn't meet his eyes. Instead, she focused past him on the glimmering pool. "You and me. It's not a good idea."

"Why not?"

"Because you don't want to go where I want to go."

"Fame?"

Hazel turned back to him. "Yeah."

"Is that the only reason?"

"We haven't been truthful with one another for one minute that we've known each other."

Nick caught her hand. "Hey, now, wait, that's not fair."

"Isn't it, though? I lied, you lied, you knew I was lying. It's a mess."

"My feelings are real."

"How can you even know?"

"I do." He spoke softly, almost a caress, and Hazel wanted to give in. She wanted to believe that what was between them was real, that it wasn't all twisted by the lies they'd told one another. But it was, it *was*, and there was no getting past it.

"I don't," Hazel said. "I'm sorry."

"I get it." Nick let go and took a step back. "I'll get changed and then we can eat."

He walked away and Hazel wanted to be dramatic and ask him to stay, the way they did in the movies, even though he'd be back in a minute. But instead, she let him go. She turned and watched the sun set, the sky turning into a streak of orange and pink, the light dimming.

If this was the end of her and Nick, at least it was pretty.

Chapter Twenty-five

The next morning, Hazel hid in the backseat of Nick's car once they got closer to the hotel, not wanting to repeat yesterday's frenzy with the press.

After everything, they'd had a nice dinner full of tension and things unsaid, then gone to their separate bedrooms. Hazel had trouble sleeping because of the day of napping, but eventually she'd drifted off, letting the sunlight wake her in the morning.

She felt at peace with her decision about Nick. Tomorrow, the show would be over. Win or lose, she was going to have to move on from this idyll. Even though it had been full of conflict and strife, it had been a respite from her real life. She wasn't sure what that was going to look like now, but she'd figure it out.

Nick turned off the car engine and she sat up. They were in the parking garage, a concrete structure at the back of the hotel with slats of sunlight running through it.

"Thanks for this," Hazel said. "For yesterday. For everything."

Nick turned in his seat. "Of course."

"I'm sorry it's all such a mess."

"That's both our faults."

"I'm sorry just the same."

"Me too."

Hazel got out of the car before she said anything else. The garage smelled of gasoline and exhaust, and it made Hazel feel claustrophobic. She walked away quickly.

"Hazel?" Nick called after her.

"I'll see you later, Nick." She didn't turn around, just rushed through the bowels of the hotel until she got to the elevator. When the doors closed, she leaned back against the wall, feeling relief as it raised her out of the earth and toward sunlight. She'd feel better when she was in her room. Things would feel normal then. Whatever normal meant.

But when got to her floor and left the elevator, her key in hand, there was a surprise waiting for her—her mother and father were standing outside her door, pacing anxiously.

Hazel felt frozen, trapped, and all she wanted to do was flee. But she couldn't do that.

It was time to face the music.

Ugh.

She walked down the hall with as much dignity as she could while wearing yesterday's running clothes, having clearly not spent the night in her hotel room.

"Harper!"

"Mother."

Her mother's mouth turned down. She'd let her hair go gray since the last time Hazel had seen her and she was wearing it in a bob. But she was also wearing a version of the same slacks and blazer that she'd worn all of Hazel's life. Paired with a jewel-toned silk shirt, it was her "look" and it didn't matter if they were in the heat of Texas or a cold New York winter. She only dressed up, never down, and Hazel had never seen her in shorts or jeans.

"You know I hate it when you call me that."

"The feeling's mutual." Hazel turned to her father. He'd gone more casual, though his salt-and-pepper hair was in the same short, '50s-style haircut he'd worn all his life. He was in a pair of dark chinos and a kelly green polo shirt with a golf logo on it. "Father."

"Hazel, please," her mother said.

That was all it took for years of rage to come flooding back, even if her mother had finally gotten her name right. "Please what? What are you even doing here?"

"We've come to support you," her father said.

"Support me? Right. Now that I've got a fifty percent chance of winning the grand prize and getting a record deal? You're not my managers anymore. You're not getting your cut."

Her mother raised her hands to her chest. "How could you think that about us?"

"Hmmm. Let me count the ways." Over her parents' shoulders Hazel saw Bella poke her head out of her room, but she didn't care. She ticked the list off on her fingers. "You tried to control everything I ever did. You lived off my success, and then you stole all my money."

Her father coughed nervously. "That's water under the bridge."

"Under *whose* bridge?"

"It's in the past. We need to deal with your present."

"I'm dealing."

He gestured to the hall around them as more heads popped out of doors. "It doesn't appear as if you are."

Hazel gritted her teeth, embarrassed that this was playing out in public. "That's not your concern anymore."

"It's *our* family," her mother said.

"We haven't been a family for a very long time."

"She told people you were dead," Bella said from down the hall.

Her mother paled. "Is that true, Hazel?"

Hazel shot Bella a look. Bella shrugged and mouthed "You did."

"So what if it is?"

"How could you do that?"

"Because it was easier than explaining the truth."

"That's exactly what's wrong with you, young lady," her father said. "You never want to face the truth."

Hazel hated it the most when her father was insightful. "At least I've had to pay for my mistakes. I live with the consequences. You and Mom got away scot-free."

Hazel was almost shouting now, her words biting and angry.

Her father shrank under them. "That's enough, Hazel."

"Is it? Is it?"

Her father took her mother's elbow. "We're going to go check into our room and let you have a chance to calm down."

Hazel bit back that there wasn't enough time in the world for that to happen. She just wanted her parents to go, and if this is what it took, then so be it. They walked past her, and she swiped her key card and stepped into her room. Before the door was closed, tears started to fall.

"You okay, Hazel?" Zoey and Brooke were sitting on one of the beds with guilty expressions on their faces.

"My parents are here."

"I thought your . . . oh. Right."

"I'm sorry."

Zoey frowned. "It's okay. But—"

Hazel wiped her tears away. "What's going on?"

"Um, remember how you asked us to watch Checkers?"

Hazel's eyes darted around the room. Checkers's makeshift cage was there but it was empty. "Where is he? Is he okay?"

"We don't know. He's missing."

"How do you put out an APB for a bunny you're not even supposed to have in the hotel?" Hazel asked Nick an hour later.

They were in their rehearsal space waiting for Georgia to show up. Hazel had to sing a duet with her in the finale, and they needed a run-through or six, especially since it was a deep-country song that Hazel wasn't comfortable with, and she'd never sung with Georgia before.

"An excellent question," Nick said. He was sitting at the

piano, fiddling around with a score for something pretty that he kept playing small snippets of. He'd traded in his usual black T-shirt for a soft green sweater that matched his eyes.

"That's not helpful."

Nick rearranged his features. "No, I know, I'm sorry. I'm sure he'll turn up eventually."

"One of the Harry Potter kids probably took him."

"Would that be a bad thing?"

"I love Checkers!"

"Then we'll find him." Nick picked up his pencil and wrote something on the paper score in front of him. "I told the desk manager to be on the lookout."

"You did?" Hazel felt a beat of hope. "What did he say?"

"He was too busy spiriting away the hundred I slipped him not to say anything but yes, sir."

Hazel rushed to the piano and hugged Nick from behind. "Thank you." She let go and stepped back. Was this all her resolve took? A nice gesture?

Nick turned around slowly. "You're welcome."

"Look, Nick—"

The door banged open and there was Georgia. She was well put together, but Hazel could smell the fumes from whatever she'd been drinking across the room.

"Shit," Nick said under his breath. He stood and walked to Georgia. "Georgia, so glad you could make it."

"Am I late?"

"Not at all. In fact, Hazel and I were just saying we should get some coffee. Does that sound good? I'll have some sent in?"

"Sure, sure." Georgia wove over to the piano and sat on the

bench. She adjusted her cowboy hat to an even more rakish angle. "Shall we do shomething on the piano?"

"If you like," Hazel said. "Maybe—"

"What about 'On My Own'? That's always a crowd-pleaser."

"I thought we were doing one of your songs?"

Georgia rolled her eyes toward Hazel. "Honey, none of them are my songs."

"Oh, I . . ."

"S'all right. You get used to it. You make . . . compromises . . ." Georgia started plucking out a tune that was both discordant and poignant. "You learn to look the other way. You find coping—what are those things called?"

"Coping mechanisms?"

Georgia pointed a wobbly finger at her. "That's the one."

Hazel's heart sank. What more could go wrong today? "Are you okay, Georgia? We can do this another time."

"Another time? Hmmm. No, I think this is the right time."

Hazel and Nick exchanged panicked expressions. They'd both seen Georgia after she'd had too much to drink, but this was something else.

"Did something happen, Georgia?" Nick asked.

Georgia swiveled her head around. "I saw a bunny in the hallway. Or I thought I did. Maybe I'm hallucinating."

"No, I don't think you are." Nick mouthed "Stay here" to Hazel and left.

Hazel didn't know what to do. Georgia looked like she might fall over, and Hazel was embarrassed for her. Is this what she was striving so hard to get to? Being blind drunk at ten in the morning on a Tuesday?

"Where did Nick go?"

"I think he went to see about the rabbit."

Georgia cocked her head to the side. "Now, there, I was not expecting you to say that."

"I'm going to order that coffee." Hazel went to the credenza in the corner where there was a hotel phone. She made the order quickly, telling them to make it extrastrong, then came back to the piano. Georgia was now slumped on her arms, an off-key note sounding from beneath her as she moved around.

"Georgia, do you want to maybe go back to your room?"

"No."

"Okay."

Georgia lifted her head. "I know I'm a mess."

"I'm sorry."

"What are you apologizing for? You didn't do this to me."

"I know, but—"

"It was Martin."

"Martin?"

"That's right, love." Her impersonation of his Britishism was devastatingly accurate despite the alcohol.

"He gave you alcohol?"

Georgia tucked her head to the side. "Did he? It's possible. There was a big basket of alcohol in my room when I checked in. And it keeps. On. Coming. Maybe Martin sent it?"

Hazel felt sick. Who would deliver alcohol to an alcoholic? "Why would he do that?"

"Because he knows me, and he wants me to be quiet." She raised her finger to her mouth. *"Shhh."*

"Why?"

"He doesn't want anyone to listen to me."

"About what?"

"About him."

Oh god, not Georgia too. "What about him?"

"He's a bad, bad man."

"He is."

"No one even knows how bad."

"Do you mean what . . . what they were tweeting about?"

"Tip of the iceberg." She pointed at her chest. "I'ms the iceberg."

"Are you sure you want to be telling me this?"

"What's it matter, anyhow? It's alls coming out now."

"What do you mean?"

Georgia paused as if she was trying to recall what she meant. "Ah yes. Talked to someone about it."

"You did? Who?"

"One of those guys who were looking for you. Big camera."

"The paparazzi? You told a paparazzo?"

"Yes."

"What did you tell them, Georgia?"

The door opened and Nick walked back in. "What's going on?"

"Georgia spoke to a pap."

"About?"

"*Martin.*"

Nick crouched in front of Georgia. "Who did you speak to?"

Georgia waved her hand dismissively. "His number's in my phone."

"What did you say exactly?"

"I told him. I told him that everything about Martin was the truth, and that there was so much more if he just did a little digging." She gestured like she was shoveling dirt. "A little excavation and it would alls come out into the light."

"I see."

"You understand, don't you, Nick?" She patted his chest.

"Yes."

"I couldn't keep it in anymore. It was killing me."

Nick took her hand and folded it in his. "I understand, and I'm here for you. But I need to know who you spoke to so I can make sure you're protected."

Georgia reached into the pocket of her rhinestone jeans and took out her phone. "He's in here."

"Thank you."

Nick stood and Hazel followed him to the door. "What are you going to do?"

"I'm going to find out whatever it was that she told this guy and go from there."

"Okay. I'm sorry."

"What about?"

"I'm the reason all this is happening."

"No, Hazel. You aren't. Martin is."

"Right."

"You should believe that."

"But this could bring down *The Sing Along*. Everyone who works here, everyone is going to be affected. Even Georgia."

Nick looked at Georgia's phone. "Maybe that's a good thing."

"You really think that?"

"Let me go make this call, okay?"

"Yes. Oh wait, I guess you didn't find Checkers?"

"No, I'm sorry."

Hazel was worried. How long could Checkers survive without her or the protection humans provided? He was an inside bunny, and even Universal City had predators. "Okay, thanks."

"Zoey and Brooke said they were looking for him."

"Maybe he'll turn up, then."

Nick squeezed her hand then released it. "Get some coffee in her. Then rehearse if you can. I'll be back when I find out what kind of fire we're facing."

"Path of destruction."

"What's that?"

"The title of the song we should be singing."

Nick gave her a brief smile. "Maybe this place needs to be burned down so something better can grow in its place."

"Like what?"

"I haven't gotten that far yet."

"Better put out the fire first."

"You're right." Nick gave her one last look, then walked out.

Hazel knew better than to ask, but she couldn't help wondering if this day was going to get better or worse.

Two hours later, Georgia had finally sobered up enough to rehearse, and Nick had returned with a serious expression on his face, but no more details. He'd simply said that he'd gotten the story held, and that was that.

The run-through was shaky, but Nick promised to get Georgia a sober companion and clear out the booze from her bungalow. He assured Hazel that it would be enough for Georgia to turn in her usual clean performance at the finals.

Hazel hoped he was right.

Nick took Georgia back to her room and asked Hazel to stay back, saying he'd return in a few minutes. Hazel had a tech rehearsal that night, and she wanted to take a bath and stave off the growing headache between her eyes. Zoey and Brooke had been texting her updates on the Checkers search. There had apparently been a sighting in the garden, but that turned out to be a raccoon whose presence was just as puzzling to the desk staff as a potentially missing rabbit.

But first, she needed to decide what song she was going to sing tomorrow night.

Hazel sat at the piano and flipped through the music Nick had left behind. She got to the piece he was working on earlier, and though she knew she should leave it, she couldn't help checking it out. It was untitled and the words were fragmentary, but the music was mostly there. She plucked out the notes, warming up her fingers as she ran through it to the end. Then she went back to the beginning and played it again.

"That's lovely," Kate said as she came into the room. She was wearing a black jumpsuit with cute ankle booties, her blond hair swept back in a ponytail. She was effortlessly gorgeous, and Hazel had a hard time believing in that moment that Nick could be interested in her when he'd been with someone who looked like Kate.

Hazel let her fingers rest on the keys. "Nick wrote it."

"It sounds like him."

"It is true you're dating a normie?" Hazel asked.

"What's that?"

"Nick said you were dating someone not in the business?"

Kate was bemused. "That's right."

"Why tell me otherwise, then?"

"I never tell anyone about him."

"Sure, but you said you were into Nick."

Kate patted her on the shoulder. "I'm sorry, honey, I just couldn't resist. You were so obviously into each other, and I knew Nick would never make a move, not after me, so I gave you a little push. I'm glad it worked."

"We're not together."

"I thought Nick said . . . ?"

"We were. But not now. It's complicated."

"When is it not?"

Hazel smiled. "Thank you for tweeting for me, by the way. That was supernice of you."

"I'm glad it worked out. You deserve to be here."

"I'm not going to win, though."

"Why not?"

"Georgia's a mess, and we still haven't settled on my final song. And Benji's doing a duet with Colin Fort."

Technically, a performance with Georgia shouldn't count in the voting, but since voting would be open during the live show and the votes would be announced at the end of the hour, anything could happen. Especially since Benji was getting to perform with the prior year's winner, a guy who'd gone on to have a streaming hit that broke records. "It feels like the show isn't playing fair."

"What song did Benji get?" Kate meant the final song that each contestant had to sing. *The Sing Along* offered a short roster of original songs to choose from and they were rarely any good.

"That's the only thing that's potentially in my favor. His song is forgettable." If they were on better terms, Hazel would've asked him why he didn't just sing one of his own songs, but they weren't, so she didn't. "But my options aren't any good either. Honestly, I hate all of them."

"What about writing something?"

"There isn't enough time." For the other shows they'd had a week to prepare. But now there was only a couple of days. "I'm screwed."

"What's that?" Nick said as he came back into the rehearsal space.

Kate smiled at him. "Hazel's feeling a tiny bit sorry for herself."

"I'll get over it," Hazel said. "How's Georgia?"

"She's fine." Nick glanced at the music in front of Hazel. "That's not ready."

"Sorry." Hazel stood and walked away from the piano.

"You settle on your final song?" Nick asked, shuffling the sheet music behind the other pages on the piano.

"We were just talking about that," Kate said.

"We could try to write something," Nick suggested. "There's still time."

"No, I—I'm too tired, honestly. I think I'll go back to my room and listen to the selections again. I'll pick one and let you know later, okay?"

"Sure.

Hazel waved good-bye to Kate and walked toward the door.

Nick caught up to her. "Are you sure you're okay?"

"Just tired. I'll be all right."

"I'll check in on you later."

"You don't have to."

"I want to."

Hazel sighed and turned away. She felt a wave of sadness and loss. She needed to get a hold of herself or she was going to be a complete mess, and it wouldn't matter what song she was singing.

She was going to lose.

Chapter Twenty-six

Hazel stumbled out of the rehearsal space without any direction in mind. The hotel was full of land mines—paparazzi, her parents, Nick, Benji. Being in her room would only remind her that Checkers was missing, but she needed to lie down and gather herself.

She was making her way through the lobby when someone called her name. It was Bella, standing there with an expression Hazel couldn't identify on her face.

"I'm really tired, Bella. Can we talk later?"

"Okay, I just wanted to . . . apologize."

"For ratting me out?"

"No. I didn't do that. I told you."

"For what, then?"

"For giving you reason to think I'd do that. I—" Bella glanced around. "Could we sit?"

"Okay."

They walked to one of the bistro tables in front of the coffee cart. Hazel took a seat, glancing around nervously. There wasn't anyone who was an obvious pap, but that didn't mean they weren't listening, blending in like tourists.

"How are you?" Bella asked.

"I'm . . . I'm tired, I told you."

"I slept twelve hours last night. The competition takes a toll on you. I didn't realize until I basically collapsed."

"Is that what you wanted to say?"

She made a face. "You don't have to be so hostile."

Hazel sighed. "You're right. But I don't have time for this."

"I can go."

"You really didn't tell on me?"

"No. I didn't know who you were. No one did."

But that wasn't entirely true. Some people knew. Nick. The production company. The other producers. But Nick had dismissed that. They didn't want it to come out, especially not after everything with Martin. "I just wish I knew who did it."

"Why?" Bella asked.

"Because it's weird, knowing there's someone out there who wants to bring you down."

"Do you have a lot of enemies?"

"I didn't think so. Though . . . oh my god, it didn't even occur to me until now, but it could've been my parents."

"Why did you lie about them being dead? And why would they want to blow your cover?"

Hazel's stomach churned. "They aren't good people."

"Do they hate you?"

That was a good question. Did her parents hate her? They were disappointed in her for sure. And they had a totally warped sense of who owed what to whom. But hate? Did she even hate them?

"I don't know. There's a lot of terrible stuff between us, and they certainly didn't want me on this show."

"But what would be in it for them if you got kicked off?"

"I'd have nowhere to go but home."

"Oh," Bella said. She reached across the table and squeezed Hazel's hand. "I'm sorry."

"It's all right."

"Families are complicated. My dad . . . he's not a nice person. They only thing he can give me is money. So I take it, but I feel guilty, you know? Like, if I wasn't related to him, I'd never even talk to the dude."

Hazel looked at Bella in a new light. Not that it should be a surprise to her that not everything was what it seemed, but still. Hazel had assumed Bella had it easy. That hadn't been fair of her. "I get that. What's next for you?"

"Not sure. I've gotten calls from agents and I have some meetings next week."

"That's great. You *are* very talented."

"You really think so?"

"Of course." Hazel played with a fork on the table. "That's probably why I felt so threatened by you."

"You were threatened by me?"

"Well, yeah. And then . . . have you spoken to Benji? Does he hate me forever now?"

"He'll get over it."

"He wasn't that into me. Maybe there's a chance for you guys."

Bella smiled briefly. "Nah. I chased after him for six months and he was never interested. He liked the attention, sure, but . . . no. I deserve better than that."

"We all do."

"We do." She smiled. "What are you going to sing tomorrow?"

"I'm supposed to be figuring that out right now."

"I'll let you go, then."

"Thanks, Bella. And keep in touch, okay?"

"I'd like that."

After her conversation with Bella, Hazel barely had time to wolf down some food and change before it was time for tech rehearsal.

A quick check of her phone let her know that Checkers was still missing. She wanted to search for him herself, but every place she went in the hotel was a land mine that might expose someone or something from her past. Hazel knew she'd done this to herself, that each decision she'd made along the way had brought her to this moment. What she didn't understand or appreciate was how all *her* bad decisions seemed to have consequences when people like Martin traipsed through the world without any repercussions.

And Benji? Benji wouldn't look her in the eye even though they were supposed to sing a duet together. She'd balked when Nick had told her that he'd picked "If the World Was Ending" by JP Saxe and Julia Michaels. She loved the song, but it was overdone. Nick had pointed out that the female part was much more challenging, and in her key, and that she'd be at an advantage over Benji, and Hazel had eventually agreed. That didn't mean she was looking forward to the performance.

"I think we should start on opposite sides of the stage," Benji said when Hazel joined him in the auditorium, "then walk toward one another slowly as the song culminates."

"Didn't JP and Julia do that when they performed at the *Voice* finale a couple of years ago?"

Benji's face fell. "So?"

"We should be original."

"How?"

Hazel thought about it. "Why don't we start the opposite way? With our backs to one another and then walking away. Like we've just broken up when the earthquake happens and we're farther away from each other by the time the song ends."

"You don't want to sing the song to each other at all?"

"I think it might be more powerful. Like we're thinking of each other because of the earthquake, but we're not together and we aren't going to be."

Benji frowned. "You sure you want to do it that way?"

"It's the truth, isn't it? It will make the performance stronger."

"All right. We can do a run-through and see."

"Great."

"What were you thinking for costume and lighting?" Benji said.

"Maybe black and white?"

Benji raised his eyebrows. "With you in white?"

"You want to be in white?"

"What are you playing at, Hazel?"

"Nothing. I'm just trying to put on the best show we can."

"Uh-huh. Sure." Benji turned away from Hazel. "Hey, Nick?"

Nick popped his head out from behind the curtain. "What's up?"

"I'm going to switch out my final song for one of my originals."

"What?" Hazel said. "I thought you were doing the song the show gave you."

Benji glanced at her. "Just trying to give the audience the best show possible, right?"

Nick nodded. "Of course. What are you singing?"

"'Catch Me If You Can.'"

Hazel's throat felt tight. It was one of Benji's original songs that had propelled him to fame on TikTok. "That's a great song."

"Thanks," Benji said casually, but Hazel saw the calculating look in his eye. "Should we do this thing?"

Hazel threw her shoulders back, trying to project confidence. "Sure, right. Let's go."

An hour later, Hazel was feeling panicky. The rehearsal with Benji had gone well—the imagery she'd suggested had worked and it told a powerful story. But then Benji had sung his song and he'd crushed it. When it was Hazel's turn, she fell back on the first song she and Nick had written because she hadn't had time to review the other song choices, and she muffed at least one line and went off-key in the second chorus.

Nick told her that she'd nail it the next day, she just

needed to get some rest, but Hazel wasn't so sure. The only thing she felt confident about was her number with Benji, and that wasn't going to be enough to get her the win.

Hazel stepped down from the stage as Georgia walked into the auditorium with her assistant. Thankfully, she was much more put together than she'd been that morning.

"Everything okay, Georgia?"

"What's that, honey?"

Hazel lowered her voice. "You feeling better?"

"Yes, yes." Georgia rolled her eyes to Hazel's. "I've sobered up if that's what you're worried about."

"No, I just meant—"

"It's fine, darlin'. I get it. I see you." Georgia poked Hazel lightly in the chest. "Don't you worry about tomorrow. I'll show up. I always do."

"I wasn't worried."

"Darlin', of course you were. And I don't blame you. But I've got a reputation to protect, too, and when this all breaks . . . let's just say I want to put my best foot forward."

"When what all breaks?"

"About Martin."

"I thought Nick had headed that off?"

Georgia smiled. "No, no. He only delayed it. That's all you can do with the inevitable."

"You sure you want to do this?"

"I am. I've been under that man's thumb for too many years." Her expression was steely now.

"But Martin—"

"Someone asking for me?" Martin said, strolling up to them as if he didn't have a care in the world.

Did Martin have a superpower that let him walk into any conversation where his name was mentioned? Like invoke the devil, and he appeared?

"I don't think so, no," Georgia said through gritted teeth.

"What are you plotting with Hazel here, loves?" Martin drawled, unconcerned.

"We were discussing our performance tomorrow, if you must know."

"That right, Hazel?"

Hazel smiled sweetly. "What else would be discussing, Martin?"

Martin tapped her twice on the shoulder. "I've heard a rumor that someone's been tattling to the press again."

"About you?"

"You think I give an arse about anyone else?"

"No, I don't."

Martin smirked. "We understand each other, then."

"I didn't have anything to do with any rumor you might've heard about."

"I don't believe you."

"I can't do anything about that." Hazel tried to move past him but he stopped her.

"You should know—win or lose, you aren't getting a record contract with me." His breath was hot on her face and smelled of stale cigarettes.

Hazel's heart hammered, being so close to him. But she was safe, surrounded by people. "Okay."

"That's all you have to say?" Martin asked, his voice full of surprise. "Okay?"

"What else is there to say?"

"No," Georgia said.

"What's that, Georgia? Isn't it time for a cocktail?"

"You're not getting away with this."

Martin cocked an eyebrow. "Getting away with what?"

"You know exactly what, mister." Georgia lifted a finger and pointed it at him, her face rigid with anger. "And tomorrow, everyone else will too."

"What are you talking about, you daft girl?"

"You're going to read all about it, and then you're going to be canceled."

Martin stepped away from Hazel and leaned into Georgia's face. "What did you do?"

"You'll just have to wait and see, won't you?"

Hazel was briefly worried that Martin might do something violent, but then he took a step back, realizing that they were in a room full of people. He gave Georgia a hard stare, then turned and left.

Georgia held herself erect until he was out of the auditorium, then swayed against Hazel.

"I've got you."

"Thank you, honey."

"No, thank you. Thank you for your courage. For standing up for me and every other woman who was going to come on this show and get harassed by that monster."

Georgia straightened her cowboy hat. "I'm not going to have a job after this."

"You and me both."

"I'm sorry about that."

"It's fine," Hazel said. And maybe it was. Maybe it was.

Georgia put her arm around Hazel's shoulder and gave

her a squeeze. "You go out there tomorrow and you win this thing, all right?"

"I'll try."

"No, honey. You do it. You believe it. You can make it happen." She pulled Hazel into a hug. "You win this. You win this for all of us."

Hazel sank into her bath with a sigh. Finally, *finally*, this day was almost over, and she could soak it away and hopefully get some sleep. She'd poured one mini bottle of scotch into a glass and half the bottle of bubble bath that came with the room into the tub, and made the water as hot as she could stand it. When she was fully in it, she almost disappeared.

If only someone wasn't knocking insistently at her door.

Go away, she shouted in her mind, but that didn't stop the knocking.

Hazel pulled herself from the tub. She wrapped herself in her robe and went to the door.

"Nick! What are you doing here? Is it Checkers?"

Nick ran his hand over his face. His eyes were tired, and his shoulders drooped. "No, I'm sorry, he's still missing."

Hazel slumped against the doorframe. "We're never going to find him."

"Don't give up."

"Hard not to."

"I get it. Can I come in?"

"I'm not sure that's a good idea."

"It's not for that. I wanted to . . . just let me in, all right?

I don't want to talk about this in the hall." Nick was nervous. Hazel wasn't sure about what.

She stepped back and let him in. He closed the door and followed her past the bathroom, glancing in as he walked past the door.

"That looks perfect."

"It *was*."

Nick grimaced. "Sorry to interrupt—it's just, I finished it, and I thought you could sing it tomorrow night."

"Finished what?"

"The song I was working on. The one you were looking at earlier." He reached into his pocket and pulled out a folded piece of sheet music. "You don't have to use it."

"I'm sure it's great." Hazel took the paper. "I'm sorry to be rude. It's . . . it's been a day."

"It has."

"Did Georgia tell you—"

"That she's going ahead with the story?" Nick nodded. "Yes."

Hazel moved to her bed, sitting down on the end, and pulling her robe tighter around her. "That's it, then?"

Nick leaned against the TV console, facing her. "We'll see. Martin's a snake. Maybe he'll slither away from all of this."

"He said he wasn't giving me a record deal even if I won."

"Do you want a deal with him?"

"Of course not. But what's the point of all this, then?" Hazel tapped the piece of sheet music against her hand.

"If you win, you'll have other opportunities."

"You sure?"

"I am." He sighed. "Anyway, I wrote out the chords for

guitar if you're more comfortable that way. And like I said, you don't have to sing it. If you don't like it, I mean."

"Nick, come on. You know I'm going to love it."

Their eyes met as Hazel said the word *love* and it lingered there in the air, like it had been written. Hazel felt heated, but that might've been the lingering effects of the bath. She was too tired to tell.

"I really appreciate you doing this for me," Hazel said. "Truly."

"Sure." Nick pushed himself off the console. "I'll let you get back to your bath."

"Okay."

"You'll be great tomorrow. Get some sleep and it will all work out."

"I hope so."

Nick smiled briefly. "I have faith."

The stared at one another. Hazel was certain Nick wanted to say something else. Maybe she did, also, but in the end, she said nothing, and Nick said, "Night, Hazel."

"Good night."

He left the room and Hazel swelled with regret. Nick was a good man—maybe not perfect, but who was? Not her, certainly. Hazel wished there was a way to know what it might've been like between them if they'd met in different circumstances. Would anything have happened? Or was it simply the crucible of the competition that had thrown them together? She was never going to know, and all the lies that lay between them were still there, a wall she didn't know how to scale.

That made her sad and disappointed. She didn't want to be alone. She didn't want to have to restrict her life to random hookups on terrible dating apps. She didn't want her parents' life, but something stable, something where she could be herself without having to hide her flaws—that she did want.

She hadn't been acting like that, though. Instead, she careened off one thing to the next, never stopping to think about what she truly wanted or how to get it. Never asking herself whether it was safe or right to want it at all. She should've done better with the choices presented to her. She *had* to do better in the future if she ever wanted to break this pattern with herself.

But for now, all that was left was *The Sing Along*. One more day, a few more songs, and then she'd know. Had she done her best? Had it all been worth it?

She unfolded the paper Nick had given her. The song was called "Opportunities." Her eyes scanned the words as her heart expanded.

This is my chance,
This stage, these keys,
All I see are opportunities.

This is my shot,
These words, this verse,
So full of possibilities.

So, I'll play these chords,
I'll sing it out,
I'll do as I please.

I've learned it by heart,

There's no doubt,
I've got a future to seize.

Because this is my shot,
This is my life,
I want all the opportunities.

So, I'll play these chords,
I'll sing it out,
I'll do as I please.

I've learned it by heart,
There's no doubt,
I've got a future to seize,

And I deserve all these opportunities.

This was it. This was what she'd been searching for all those weeks of writing songs together, the words she could never get down, the emotion. She could see it now, her at the piano, the soft glow of the spot, the way her voice would ache, the way her heart did. She had a chance now to win this whole thing, and Nick had given it to her. Just like he'd given her a shot in the competition in the first place.

She wanted to go after him, to yank open her hotel room door and call to him down the hall, to run after him like the end of a romantic comedy, but her life was more complicated than that, and she'd just told him to go.

So instead, she simply said, "Thank you, Nick," to the empty room and brought the paper to her lips.

Chapter Twenty-seven

It was the last morning.

Hazel felt tired but energized, the way she always used to feel before a taping of *The Dawsons*. It was weird reconnecting to those feelings, another piece of her that she'd thought she'd left behind.

It was early and the hotel was quiet. Hazel appreciated the absence of noise, so different from the Motel California. But that was probably where she was going to end back up, at least in the short term. There or somewhere like it. She had enough money saved from the show to keep her in L.A. for a few months. Enough time to find a job or make a deal if she was lucky. The time past that was a dark blur that scared her. After all of this, to end up alone, back where she started? No.

The money was enough time for her to get back on her feet. To figure out what she wanted.

Who she wanted to be.

Her phone beeped. It was a message from Zoey.

Checkers sighting! Meet me at my room in ten!

Finally, some good news.

Only it wasn't. When Hazel knocked on Zoey's door, and Zoey opened it with a guilty expression, Hazel knew there was something wrong. What she didn't expect was her parents to be sitting in the room, watching the scene unfold expectantly.

"No Checkers?"

"Sorry, Hazel." Zoey glanced back at her parents. "They just seemed so pathetic sitting there at breakfast."

"They have a way of doing that."

"Maybe you should talk to them," Zoey said quietly.

"We talked yesterday."

"I heard, but . . . they're your parents, Hazel."

"Tell *them* that."

"You don't think they know?"

"I've often wondered."

"Would it hurt to hear them out?"

Zoey was so innocent and optimistic. She didn't know what it was like. "It might. It might hurt a lot."

That penetrated. "I can ask them to leave."

Hazel looked at her parents again. They seemed pathetic, defeated, and Hazel felt some pity for them. They'd come to say something to her; maybe she should hear them out.

"No, it's all right."

"Do you want me to stay?"

"I'll be fine."

Zoey hugged her impulsively. "I'll be outside. If you don't come out in thirty minutes, I'll come in and get you, okay?"

"Thank you."

"You bet."

Zoey left. Her parents hadn't spoken this whole time, just sat holding hands on the bed, like it was a lifeboat and they might fall off if a wave hit them. And maybe that was right. Maybe Hazel was the wave if she wanted to be.

"What do you want?" Hazel said, trying to keep her voice neutral, but the rage was just below the surface, bubbling.

"We want to talk to you, honey," her mother said. "That's all we've been trying to do for years."

"That's why the only thing you call me about is legal papers?"

"That's not what this is about," her mother said. "You don't have to sign."

"I know I don't."

"Hazel," her father said.

Her throat went dry. She hadn't had to correct him to get him to call her by her name. "Yes, Jack," she said because she couldn't help it. It always drove him nuts when she called him anything but dad or father.

But he didn't react. Instead, he said, "We want to start over. We want to find a way to move forward with you in our lives. You're our daughter and we love you. We know we made mistakes. There's a lot we'd change if we could."

"Start over?"

"Yes," her father said. "We can't change the past, but maybe we can find a new future together."

"How do we do that?"

"We let it go."

"Like the song?"

"I don't know that song," he said. "Did you write it?"

"No, I . . . what are you talking about?"

Her mother patted his hand. "I think what your father means is we should try to leave the past in the past."

"Just forget everything that happened? All the ways you disappointed me?"

"Yes," her mother said gently. "And we'd do the same."

Hazel wanted to scream. They'd let *her* offenses go? Did they mean being a child star? Setting them up for life? Being the victim of their financial fraud?

"You just want me to forget everything?"

"No, you don't have to forget. We did a terrible thing. That money, it was yours. Even if it felt like ours because of everything we'd sacrificed to get it, that was wrong."

"Everything *you* sacrificed?"

"Our careers, our friends."

Hazel shook her head. "We didn't have to go to Hollywood."

"Oh, Hazel. Maybe you don't remember, but you wanted to go so badly. When those casting agents found you, it was all you'd talk about."

"I was *seven*."

Her mother looked down. "Yes, I know. I see what you mean now. But then, we just wanted you to be happy. We thought it was a good opportunity, for you, for all of us. But it was never anything we sought out. And then, when it all fell apart, you were so sad, so lost. We were worried you were going to make some irrevocable decision that you'd never recover from. So we brought you home. And here you are. You're healthy. You didn't end up in rehab or worse."

Hazel's mind was a jumble. Everything her mother was saying was the antithesis of the way she viewed the key moments of her life. But there was also the possibility that she was wrong. What did she actually remember from when she was seven? And it wasn't like all her time on the show had been torture. It was after the fact that it felt like a loss. Maybe she'd been in more trouble than she realized.

But that didn't answer all of her accusations. There were so many other things her parents had done to her, more recently, as an adult, when her memory was clear as a bell.

"That's not how I remember it. And I don't know if I can forgive all of that—how would that even work?"

"We love you, Hazel," her mother said, tears in her eyes. "Maybe we haven't shown that in the way that we should, but we do. We always did. And we're so sorry for everything that went wrong between us. We want you in our life. Not like before, but the way it always should have been."

Hazel couldn't remember the last time she'd seen her mother cry, or get emotional, and it touched her in a way that the words hadn't. Her mother had also apologized, something Hazel never thought she'd hear. And though that didn't erase the past, it did smooth it out, if only a little. She didn't think she could do what her parents were asking, just forget, forgive, and move on. It couldn't be that simple. But sometimes it felt like she'd lived her whole life as a reaction to them. If they said jump, she sat down. And look where that had gotten her. She needed to try something, anything, different or her life was going to get away from her again.

Hazel let out a long, slow sigh. "Okay."

"Okay?" her mother said, and her voice was so full of hope it nearly crushed Hazel.

"Okay."

"Oh, honey." Her mother stood up and pulled Hazel into a hug. She smelled like Hazel's childhood, like Chanel No. 5 and expensive soap and the sandalwood from her closet, which preserved the clothes Hazel's labor had bought. "Thank you."

Hazel tried to keep her emotions in check, but it was too hard. She was so tired of being alone, of being on her own. She hugged her mother back, then wiped her tears away.

"I have to go to rehearsal."

Her mother pulled a tissue out of her sleeve and dabbed at her eyes. "'Course you do, honey. We can't wait to see the show tonight."

"I'll make sure you get some good seats."

"Thank you."

Her father rose and patted her on the shoulder, as close as he got to hugging. "Thank you, Hazel. This means a lot to us."

"Okay, Dad."

"You should come home after everything. It would do you some good. It would do us some good."

Would visiting her parents be better than living in her car? Rational Hazel said yes, but Hazel-Hazel was still pushing back. "I'll think about it."

"We'd like that."

Hazel nodded, then watched them walk out of the room. Her legs gave way as they exited, and she fell against the wall, her head in her hands.

"Hazel," Zoey said. "Are you okay?"

Hazel raised her shoulders up and down.

"You need a moment?" Brooke asked.

"No, no, I'm okay. I'll be okay."

Zoey crouched in front of her. "Did we do the right thing?"

"Yes, it's fine."

"Doesn't look like you're fine."

"But I am. I'm Hazel Fine. I'm always A-okay."

Zoey let out a belly laugh. "How long have you been holding that one in check?"

"Would you believe me if I told you I just made that up on the spot?"

"Not one bit."

Hazel was laugh-sobbing. "We have to find Checkers, guys."

"We're on it," Brooke said. "It's going to be okay."

"Everyone keeps saying that."

"Then it must be true."

"Right," Hazel said. "What next?"

"Now you go dry your tears and get ready to win this competition."

They searched for an hour but they didn't find Checkers.

When they gave up, Hazel got some breakfast and left Brooke and Zoey in charge of the search. Then she went to her rehearsal space and spent several hours learning Nick's song by heart.

It was perfect for her, showcasing her talents, hiding her flaws, and hitting all the right emotional notes. She decided to do it alone on the piano, with no accompaniment from the show's musicians. It was a risk, especially since she knew from the tech rehearsal that Benji was doing a full production on his song, but it felt right.

She'd find out soon enough.

When it was finally late afternoon, Hazel forced herself to eat and tried to keep from biting her nails while she sat in hair and makeup. Then it was time to get dressed, go backstage, and get mic'd up. The theater filled with people, their low chatter a hum that mixed with the nervous energy of the stagehands and former contestants getting ready for their last performance.

Hazel went to her mark behind the main curtain. Keshawn was off to the right, reading through his prompter scroll, learning it by heart. Hazel was wearing tight leather pants, and her hair was teased high. Benji was next to her in a leather jacket, his hair greased back. They were leading a cheesy group number with all the old contestants of a song from *Grease*. Zoey was on her other side wearing a saddle skirt and shoes, and Bella was to the left of Benji in a pink silk jacket.

The four of them, together again, back where they'd started.

Benji gave her a cold stare, and Hazel tried to think about what it would look like to the audience as they sang "You're the One That I Want" to each other. Would they buy that their chills were multiplying? The part that Hazel was playing, that they all were?

Only if they sold it.

She grabbed Zoey's hand and Benji's, too, and plastered a big smile on her face as the music started and the curtain rose.

Hazel's eyes searched the audience as they whooped and

cheered. There her parents were in the second row, sitting next to Brooke. Her father even had a proud look on his face. Her mother was beaming, too, and clapping enthusiastically. Amber was there, waving with Theo. Kate sat with a man Hazel didn't recognize, who was also clapping enthusiastically. On the judging dais, Georgia raised her soda water in a gesture of approval, and Martin scowled, his arms crossed over his chest.

The only person she couldn't find was Nick, but she knew he was backstage, somewhere, rooting for her, even if they couldn't be together. Hazel's heart was full. She didn't know how to process what was happening; she only knew that it was time to give it her all.

And then Checkers hopped onto the stage.

Pandemonium.

Checkers bounded between the contestants as they tried to sing the group number and execute their dance moves. Hazel wanted to scoop him up, but she was at the front, and this was the finals. She tried to signal to Zoey to get him, but she couldn't catch Zoey's eye. Hazel had no choice but to grin and bear it as the audience laughed and pointed whenever Checkers popped into view.

Finally, the number was over. The curtain closed and Hazel scurried around, madly trying to find Checkers.

"I've got him," Nick said.

Hazel stood up. "Thank you." She held out her arms.

Nick patted Checkers on the head. "I'll put him somewhere safe. Go get ready for your next performance."

"Are you sure?"

"Of course."

"I'm sorry he ruined the number."

Nick laughed as Checkers struggled against him. "Are you kidding? It's blowing up. This episode is going to be—what would Benji call it?"

"Iconic?"

"That's it."

"Was I okay? It was hard to concentrate."

"You were great."

Someone bumped into Hazel as they rushed to get in their places for another group number to fill out the time before Benji and Hazel had to perform again. Nick put out his hand to keep her from tipping over.

"Don't you say it."

"I wouldn't dare."

They smiled at one another as a bell chimed. Two minutes to the next number. "I have to go."

"I'll see you after. Break a leg."

"Thank you," Hazel said. "He probably needs to eat."

"What?"

"Checkers."

"Okay, I'll find something for him. Now go."

Hazel reached forward and kissed Checkers on the head. "Be good, Checkers!" Then she rushed to her quick-change area without looking back.

"That was fantastic," Hazel said to Benji when he came off the stage half an hour later.

They'd done their duet in the third segment, and it was a

hit. The costuming Hazel had suggested had highlighted them both perfectly and there had been enthusiastic applause when they'd finished.

But Benji's performance of his own song, "Catch Me If You Can," had brought tears to her eyes as she watched side-stage, and she wasn't the only one. When she'd first heard his song on TikTok she'd assumed it was a lighthearted surfer tale that played well on social. But knowing more about Benji's life and listening to the way he was singing it, Hazel knew it was about more than that. It was an ode to all the dreams he'd thought he'd make come true, how they'd been washed away. But he could catch them again, just like the next wave.

Benji tossed his hair in his signature move. "Thanks."

Hazel put her hand on his arm to keep him from walking away. "You should win."

"You don't really think that."

"I do. You're the only one left who didn't do something wrong to get here. It should be you."

Benji's features softened. "Thank you for saying that."

"I know integrity is important to you."

"It is."

"And you've got it. You did it the right way, Benji. Congratulations."

"Thanks, Hazel. You're going to do great out there."

"Hope so."

They hugged and Hazel relaxed into it. She was glad she'd said something. She hoped this meant that she and Benji could find a way back to being friends, that they could get past all the things that had been holding them apart. He was a good guy, and Hazel needed more people like him in her life.

They broke apart.

"Friends?" Hazel said.

"I'd like that."

"Even after everything I did?"

"If you own it, I can get past it. Forgiveness, you know? It's a thing."

Hazel smiled as Nick flashed before her. Forgiveness. That hadn't been a big feature in her life, but hadn't she just agreed to do that with her parents? To leave the past behind and move forward? Was that something she could do with Nick? Had she been too quick to assume that they'd never work?

It wasn't only up to her, though. Nick was part of the equation. He hadn't fought for her, hadn't disagreed when she'd said that they should leave it alone. Then again, he'd protected her. Over and over again he'd helped her. Even after she said they couldn't be together, he'd been there for her. That meant something.

And the song she was about to sing. He'd written that song for her.

Was *he* her opportunity?

"Everything all right, Hazel?" Benji asked.

"Yes, I just need to find someone."

"Aren't you performing in a few minutes?"

"I have time." Hazel left him and searched the backstage area. There were so many people wandering around dressed all in black she didn't see him at first. But then she found him by one of the monitors, frowning at it like he always did. Her heart swelled at his familiar expression because it meant he cared. His resting face was concern. For her, for the others, for all of it.

"Nick."

He stared at her in alarm. "You need to be onstage."

"I know. I just . . . who did you write that song for? The one I'm singing tonight."

"You know."

"I need to hear you say it."

He took a step toward her and spoke quietly. "I wrote it for you, Hazel."

"Thank you."

Keshawn's voice vibrated through the auditorium. "We've got one more performance tonight. Please put your hands together for Hazel Fine!"

"Go, Hazel," Nick said. "Don't miss your chance."

Hazel turned on her heel and ran. She stopped herself before she got to the side curtain, took a deep breath, and walked out on the stage and waved to the audience as they cheered. This was it. One more moment.

The piano was sitting in a spotlight. She walked over to it, sat down, and put her fingers on the keys. She looked out at the audience, half in darkness but still visible. She could feel their expectations. Would she do it? Would she be able to best Benji? Did she have it in her to do what it took to win?

She thought about the words Nick had written, not about some old lost love, but about her. How she might have a chance if she'd let herself be happy. If she took this opportunity.

Hazel Fine wasn't playing a part anymore.

She was herself, alone and vulnerable on the stage. That scared her but it thrilled her too.

So even though she hated it when singers did that, she closed her eyes and sang as if her life depended on it.

Because it did.

Chapter Twenty-eight

When Hazel came off stage, it was in a glow of happiness. She'd given it her all, and it was in the audience's hands now. They were in a commercial break, and then the other contestants were going to do a group number without Hazel and Benji, so they could reset and come out when they announced the winner.

"Pretty pleased with yourself, aren't you, love?" Martin drawled from the darkness.

Hazel closed her eyes. One more hour and then she could be free of this man forever. "Leave me alone, Martin."

"Like you left me alone?" Martin stepped out and caught her arm in a tight grip. "Always scheming, always plotting. First with Kate, then with Georgia. Why can't you just *go away?*"

Hazel's breath caught as she made eye contact with him. She

wasn't scared, exactly, but there was a new menace to his voice. She tried to pull away but he held steady on her arm. Why was there never anyone around when he was being his worst?

But that wasn't true. Nick was usually around. And he would have been this time if she hadn't pushed him away like the idiot she was.

"Let me go, Martin."

"No."

They stared at one another as their previous interactions cycled through her mind. And then it hit her. It was *Martin*. Martin was the one who knew who she was and told the press about it. Martin, who was in the glare of the spotlight until the story about her had emerged, shifting the narrative and the focus away from him. Because he'd tried every other way to get her off the show, and nothing had worked.

"It was you."

"What?"

"*You* went to the press about me."

His eyes narrowed in the dim light. "What if I did?"

"You tried to destroy me."

"Right back at you."

"I didn't do anything like you did."

"It's all a matter of perspective, love." His face was close to hers now, his breath hot. "You've got your way of looking at things, and I've got mine."

Hazel pulled back. "It's over for you, though. When Georgia's story comes out tomorrow. Some young women no one cares about? That was just the dent. But when she tells them that you've been sexually harassing her for years? That you sent her alcohol when you knew she was an alcoholic to keep her quiet? She's Georgia *Hayes*. I'd pack if I were you, and head right out of town."

Martin released her arm and took a step back. He looked uncertain for the first time since Hazel had known him. And maybe she was wrong. Maybe he was going to get through this unscathed, but she doubted it. So, whether she won *The Sing Along* or not, she'd done something good.

"Hazel Fine to the stage, please! Hazel Fine!"

The commercial break was over and Hazel needed to get into position.

"You should be on set, Martin."

He glared at her one last time, then turned on his heel and stalked off. Hazel breathed a sigh of relief. She'd done it. She'd gotten through an interaction with Martin without help or a savior. She'd saved herself.

And that was enough.

Much later, Hazel found Nick in the hotel bar. She'd searched for him everywhere backstage after they'd announced the results, but he'd been nowhere to be seen.

She stood apart from him, watching him nurse a drink. The TV above the bar was on, the nightly news playing. From behind her she could hear the after-show celebration. There was confetti in her hair from when Keshawn had pointed at the sky and let it rain down on her and Benji. The cheers had swelled around them, embracing them, and then they'd embraced, both happy with the result.

It was over. Months of working, striving, loss, and laughter came down to a vote. The winner had been announced, and it was set down in history, maybe for the last time. *The Sing Along* might be over for good—that remained to be seen—but this year's show was definitely over.

What now?

"Nick?"

He glanced back over his shoulder, then away. Not the welcome she was hoping for. Should she leave? Forget this?

No. That's what she always did. Run away from things when they got hard. The show was the only thing she'd stuck with when it got hard for a very long time. She needed to learn to stick to other things too.

Other people.

Hazel stepped forward. She was still in her final dress, a flowing light-pink number that was something she could've have worn to the Oscars. Her feet kept getting caught in the hem, but she was determined not to make an ass of herself.

"Why are you hiding in here?" Hazel said, stepping up the bar.

"Seemed like as good as place as any."

"I looked for you after they announced the results."

Nick rolled his head toward her. His cheeks were pink from the alcohol. "And now you've found me."

"Are you drunk?"

"Might be."

"Why?"

"We lost." He picked up his glass and drained it. Then signaled to the bartender to bring him another.

"You mean, I lost." That's what Keshawn had announced when he'd opened the gold-embossed envelope. The audience had chosen Benji, not her. But Hazel had meant what she'd said to Benji backstage. She'd wanted him to win. He deserved it. It was nice to know that sometimes the right person still ended up on top.

Nick nodded.

"*I* should be drinking then."

"Suit yourself."

Hazel sat on the stool next to him, gathering her skirt around her, and asked the bartender for her own drink. When it came she clinked her glass against Nick's. "To us, then."

"Us, huh?"

"I wouldn't have gotten here without you. Thank you."

"You're welcome."

"You're really drunk because I lost?"

Nick turned toward her. "Why are you surprised?"

"I didn't expect you to be more upset than I am."

"You're not upset?"

"I mean, I guess so? I haven't processed it."

Nick's face softened, his scowl turning into a soft smile. "I'm sorry, Hazel."

"For what?"

"I should've managed this better for you."

Hazel tapped him on the shoulder. "You did great."

"You say so."

"You did. And guess what, I figured out who ratted me out to the tabloids."

His raised his eyebrows. "Who?"

"Martin."

"That fucker."

"Yep. But it's going to backfire on him."

"How?"

"It's all going to come out when Georgia's piece drops tomorrow. He's toast."

Nick nodded his head slowly. "That's something at least."

Hazel felt like laughing. "Nick?"

"Yeah?"

"Aren't you supposed to be consoling *me*?"

"Ah, shit, Hazel, I'm sorry." He pushed his glass away and sat up straighter. Then he repositioned his stool so his legs were framing hers. Like that night at the bar, she could feel the heat of his skin through two layers of fabric. She wanted more of it. She wanted more of him.

"You deserved to win," Nick said.

"Thank you."

"Now, why aren't you upset?"

"I wasn't going to get a record deal with Martin anyway. Not that I wanted one. And Kate introduced me to her agent and a label rep right after the show, and they want to sit and talk about a deal."

His eyes lit up. "Kate did that?"

"She did."

"Good on her."

"I thought so."

"Plus, we found Checkers."

Nick glanced up at the TV above the bar. It had flipped to coverage of that night's episode. There Checkers was, jumping across the stage as former contestants in *Grease* costumes fled out of the way like he was a rat.

Nick smiled at her sloppily. "Everything is working out for you, then."

"Not everything."

"Oh?"

Hazel picked up her drink and tasted it. The scotch was rich and powerful as it slid down her throat. She felt its warmth spread through her, giving her courage. She eyed Nick over the rim of the glass. "Didn't get you."

"You sure about that?"

Hazel put the glass down. "I screwed us up."

"Pretty sure that was me."

"We both did it." Hazel leaned closer to Nick. She breathed in his scent, scotch and spice. "But you wrote me that song."

"I did."

"I've blown so many opportunities."

He leaned his head forward so it was almost touching her forehead. "Me too."

"We should stop."

Nick put his hands on her bare shoulders. They were warm, and his skin on hers was almost too much. "You want me to stop?"

"I meant missing things. Not this."

"You sure?"

"Nick."

"Yeah?"

"Are you going to kiss me or what?"

Nick brought his mouth to hers swiftly. She sighed into his kiss and closed her eyes. Her hands found his waist and she pulled him toward her. He tasted of the drink they'd both been drinking, and all Hazel could think of was how far away her hotel room was.

"Hey, hey, hey. We're not that kind of bar."

They broke apart. The bartender was shaking his head at them disapprovingly. Hazel was out of breath but also happy. Nick looked happy too. But Hazel knew better than to trust her first, second, or last impression.

"He thinks we should get a room," Hazel said to Nick.

"You have a room."

"So do you."

"Yours is closer."

"Well, then." Hazel hopped off her stool. "Can I get a bottle of champagne?" she said to the bartender. He nodded and bent to get one out of the fridge. "Least the production company could do for me, right?"

Nick nodded slowly, not sure where she was going with this.

"Oh, I forgot," Hazel said.

"What's that?"

"Kate's label wants to talk to you."

"What about?"

"Your album."

"*My* album?"

"They want to put it out. Maybe add a few of the new numbers."

Nick shook his head. "You're amazing, you know that?"

"Sometimes."

The bartender handed her the bottle and two glasses. "You can charge that to my room," Hazel said. She gave him the number, then started to walk away.

She stopped and glanced over her shoulder at Nick. He had that same expression he'd had when they met. Somewhere between amused and annoyed. But Hazel knew it for what it was now: Nick trying to make sure everything was all right, that he wasn't going to screw things up for the people he cared about.

That he wasn't going to lose her.

"You coming?" Hazel said, and Nick's face broke into a wide smile that filled her heart with possibilities.

Epilogue

THREE MONTHS LATER

"Hey, Hazel, that's great," Peter, the sound engineer, said. "You need a break?"

Hazel pulled her headphones off her ears. They squeezed her head, and she had the beginnings of a headache. "Yeah, I could use thirty?"

"No problem."

Hazel sat on the simple wooden stool behind her and closed her eyes. It was weird being in a studio all day—or all night, as the case may be. There were no windows, and with all the soundproofing, it felt like being enveloped in a big muffled hug.

She thought back to the song she'd just finished the vocals for. She was proud of it, and she was tired but satisfied. The album was coming together. It felt like her life was too.

Two hands placed themselves gently on her shoulders, as breath tickled her ear. "Hey," Nick said. "You're doing great."

"Thank you." She leaned back against Nick's solid chest and his arms wound around her waist. He nuzzled into her, sending shivers down the back of neck. "I'm not going to be able to concentrate if you keep doing that."

"That is the idea."

She turned and met his lips, soft and warm with just the right firmness behind them. She wasn't sure if Peter had left the booth, but she didn't care. Nick's tongue nudged into her mouth, entwining with hers as she moved her hands to his face, then his neck, playing with his hair. Now that they were together for real, it was always like this between them. She'd never been one for public displays of affection, but they couldn't seem to keep their hands off each other for long whenever they were near each other.

Nick turned her around on the stool so she faced him, and she wrapped her legs around his. He held her tightly against his chest as the kiss deepened. Then, just as Hazel thought that they might truly embarrass themselves in front of a relative stranger, he pulled back.

"Hi," he said, looking directly into her eyes. She loved how he did that, how he wasn't afraid to be vulnerable in front of her.

"Hello."

"I have some news."

"Oh?"

He nudged his nose against hers. "My album's dropping next month."

"So soon?"

"Yeah, they thought it was ready, so . . ."

Hazel grinned from ear to ear. "That's fantastic, Nick. I'm so happy for you."

"There's more."

She dropped her hands to his shoulders. "Tell me."

"The results of the investigation into Martin are in."

Hazel's heart skipped a beat. "And?"

"He's out."

Hazel breathed out in relief. "Good. Though maybe not so good for *The Sing Along*."

"No, that's the best part. They're bringing in Kate to replace him."

"Oh, that's delicious."

"You're delicious."

"Ha!" Hazel put her hands on Nick's chest. She could feel his heart beating in time with her own. She glanced into the booth. Peter *was* there, grinning at them. "Sorry for the show, Pete."

His voice crackled over the PA system. "No worries."

Nick laughed as Hazel turned back to him. "So, album drop, that means tour, yes? What about *The Voice*? Did you tell them you weren't taking the gig?"

"Hmmm. I wanted to talk to you about that."

Hazel felt a moment of panic. Nick's label had promised a major splash behind his album. Was he about to tell her that he was going on tour for months? It wasn't that she didn't think their relationship could survive the separation, but she didn't really want to find out. "When do you leave?"

"When do *we* leave, you mean?"

"You want me to go on tour with you?"

"No," Nick said. "I want you to tour *with* me."

"Oh." Hazel looked down at the floor. Did she want to be Nick's opening act? It made sense. He was the more seasoned artist, and after all his years on *The Sing Along*, he had so many guest stars on his album Hazel felt like it was the only thing people were talking about on Twitter and TikTok. She was just finding her footing. Her album wouldn't be out until next year, but she had hopes that she'd get the kind of support Nick was getting. That she'd be sent out on her own tour.

"Hazel?"

"Yeah?"

Nick put his hand under her chin and raised her face so they were looking at each other again. "It's not what you think," he said.

"What do I think?"

"That I'm asking you to open for me. It's written all over your face."

"Aren't you?"

"That's what the label suggested, but I countered."

"You did?"

He nodded. "I did."

"With what?"

"Co-headliner. Alternating nights in the first position, and a half set of us together in the middle."

Hazel's mouth fell open in shock. "No way they went for that."

"They did."

"For real?"

"It took a moment of convincing, but once I laid it out for them, they saw the potential."

"But my album's not even out."

"You've got half an album already on the streamers from the show. Plus our songs. You'll do some covers and a few originals from these sessions. It's enough."

Hazel shook her head. "You're already stage directing me?"

"Suggestions only." Nick smiled nervously. "What do you say?"

"You didn't have to use your bargaining power on me."

"I wanted to."

"Why?"

"Because I didn't want to be on tour without you. Hazel—" Nick glanced at the booth, then leaned down and unplugged Hazel's microphone.

"What are you doing?"

"Pete doesn't need to hear this."

"What?"

Nick righted himself and put his hands on Hazel's shoulders. "I love you."

Hazel's breath caught. It was hard to describe how she was feeling, how unprepared she was for this moment, even though she'd hoped for it. "You sure about that?"

Nick laughed. "I've loved you since I saw the adorable expression you made when I tuned your guitar on the first day of the competition."

"That was so annoying!"

"It was patently obvious that you felt that way." Nick looked away, breaking eye contact.

"Hey, Nick?"

"Yeah?"

Hazel tucked her thumb under his chin and brought his face back to hers. "I love you too."

Nick didn't say anything, just brought his smiling lips to hers and kissed her fiercely. She pressed herself against him, clasping her hands behind his back. She didn't know if she could ever get close enough to him, but certainly not in this studio. Hazel felt a strange sensation flood through her and she wasn't sure what it was at first, but then she knew.

She was happy, without any fears or regrets, probably for the first time in her life.

They broke apart. "So," Nick said. "You coming on tour with me or what?"

"Yes," Hazel said. "Yes."

Acknowledgments

This book began as something else, as books sometimes do, and I'm so grateful to my friend, Elyssa, for her generous support and encouragement to me to finish it anyway. I couldn't have done it without you.

To my mom—for reading all my drafts and letting me borrow her maiden name for this adventure.

To my agent, Stephanie Kip Rostan—thank you for helping make my dream of having Hazel out there in the world come true.

To my editor, Deanna McFadden—it's such a pleasure to be working with you again after all the years! Life comes full circle sometimes in the best way.

To the entire team at W by Wattpad Books—thank you for finding my mistakes, the gorgeous cover, and the amazing marketing support.

And to the readers on Wattpad and everywhere—thank you for embracing Hazel. Writing is a dream come true that only exists because of you.

About the Author

Katie Wicks was born and raised in Montreal, Canada, where she now lives and writes full-time. An amateur guitar and tennis player, Katie has been obsessed with reality TV singing competitions since *American Idol* debuted twenty years ago, but has never worked up the courage to audition herself. *Hazel Fine Sings Along* is Katie's debut novel.

Hazel Fine Sings Along

PLAYLIST

Lights Camera Action
Analogue Revolution

Titanium
David Guetta, Sia

1 step forward, 3 steps back
Olivia Rodrigo

Break In
Halestorm

With A Little Help From My Friends
The Beatles

Help!
The Beatles

Two Of Us
The Beatles

Hallelujah
Jeff Buckly

Love Song
Sara Bareilles

Run, Baby, Run
Sheryl Crow

ROLLERCOASTER
The Lumineers

Lover
Taylor Swift

Don't Look for Me
Jeffrey Foucault

Rainbow Connection
Kermit

Rumors
Lizzo, Cardi B

Fresh Start
Bailey Bryan

Don't Let Me Down
The Chainsmokers, Daya

Hazel Fine Sings Along

DISCUSSION QUESTIONS

1. Hazel ultimately seizes the chance to "let herself be happy" and not play a part anymore. What can we learn from Hazel's journey to be her true self?

2. The book explores many dual identities, from Hazel vs. Harper to Benji vs. his TikTok persona. What does the book suggest about presenting different versions of ourselves? What role do social media and other forms of media like reality TV play in this?

3. Nick makes a case that it wasn't his place to expose Martin. Was that the right or the wrong decision? What responsibility do we have, if any, to "see something, say something"?

4. Is it Sarah's choice to date Martin? Is it Hazel's choice to date Nick? What is the book cautioning about relationships with people in positions of power?

5. Through Bella and Hazel what does the book insinuate about female competition and friendship? What can we learn from their forgiveness of each other?

6. The book refers to Amber as a sex worker. What does her character add to the story? How does the portrayal of Amber challenge our perceptions of women in the sex worker industry?

7. How does Zoey's experience in the competition shed light on how people of color and those in the LGBTQ+ community are treated?

8. Take a closer look at the lyrics throughout the book. They touch on loss and longing. How do these songs reflect the characters' journeys?

9. Hazel loses the competition. What would be different had she won?

10. Hazel learns to face her past, present, and future head-on instead of running from them. What can Hazel teach us about acceptance and facing our fears?

Turn the page for a preview of
Katie Wick's upcoming novel,

Chloe Baker's Lost Date

Coming Summer 2024

Chapter One

He was late. Late for our date.

Five minutes, seven, ten.

I sat at a table covered with a checkered tablecloth in the brunch place on Columbus Avenue where we'd agreed to meet, clutching my phone, waiting for an explanation for his tardiness.

Twelve minutes, sixteen, twenty.

I sipped slowly at the freshly squeezed orange juice I'd ordered and read the pun-filled menu for the tenth time, full of items like *You're bacon me crazy* and *I like you a waffle lot*. I smiled nervously at the waitress, a pretty Black woman who looked like she was in her early twenties and whose name tag said JANIE. She was starting to look at me with pity. How many times had she seen someone stood up by a blind date?

Judging from her expression, I wasn't the first.

What was the reasonable cutoff time for me to leave? Half an hour, right? Any longer would be ridiculous.

I crossed my legs nervously under the table, tapping my light-gray Vans against the tiled floor. My faded-wash jeans felt too tight, and I was regretting the thin blue shirt I'd chosen last night. It matched my eyes, but I was worried it was see-through in the sunlight that poured through the window.

This is why I hate dating. It turns me into a questioning mess.

It was my best friend, Kit, who'd insisted I go on a date with Jack Dunne, the tech guy from her office.

"You need to go out with him, Chloe Baker," Kit had said, her thick black hair swinging around her face as she moved her hands for emphasis. "And get back out there. Your dry season has gone on way too long."

"No need to be so smug, Katherine Wang. Not all of us were lucky enough to be set up with the perfect guy by our *mother*."

Kit made a face, but it was true. Her mother, Lian—who refuses to call Kit by the nickname I gave her in third grade—had set Kit up with John the Vet after he'd treated her sadly cancerous Maltipoo.

"When was the last date you went on?"

"In Ohio or New York?"

"Have you been on a date in New York?"

"Maybe?"

Kit shook her head. "Feels like something you'd know."

"I haven't met anyone yet."

"How could you have? It's only been a *year* since you moved here."

"I'm settling in."

The truth was, New York guys intimidated me. Every time I dipped a toe into one of those dating sites it felt like I was bombarded by dick pics and guys who just wanted to hook up. I'd never been into hook-up culture, and I'd yet to meet a girl who was happy to receive an unsolicited dick pic. But my office was 100 percent female. Hence the dry spell.

"Will you think about it, at least?" Kit had asked, texting me Jack's number and a screenshot of his picture from their company directory, in which he did, admittedly, look hot. Dark curly hair, a slim build, and eyes that could be brown or hazel. Kit promised he was twenty-eight, stable, and interested in a relationship. He was the New York equivalent of a unicorn.

Twenty-three minutes, twenty-seven, thirty.

There was no way he was coming, but I couldn't face the humiliation of walking to the door alone, convinced that everyone in the restaurant knew exactly what had happened.

I opened our short text thread. He preferred to meet in person, he'd said, rather than text, and that was the first thing I liked about him. Texting with a stranger made me sweat. The silences and pauses provided too many chances to worry about what I'd written or how it was being perceived. In person, I had facial expressions to gauge. In person I was funny. In person was definitely better. Theoretically, anyway. If the guy actually showed.

Are you on your way? I wrote, feeling stupid. He was obviously not on his way. If he was running late, he'd have let me know.

I waited for his bubble of reply, but nothing.

He's thirty minutes late! I texted Kit. *I ducking knew this would happen.* Kit and I never bothered to correct our phones when they censored us. We'd met at age seven and had been friends for twenty years. We knew what the other meant.

Oh shot, Kit wrote. *Maybe he's stuck at work? The company's server is down.*

BLACK HUNK DOWN, I wrote reflexively. Kit and I had this thing where we turned random words or phrases into porny movie titles.

Not your best work.

I know. I sighed. *I never should've agreed to this. I blame you!*

She sent me a kiss-off emoji and I put down my phone. It was partly Kit's fault, but I had myself to blame too. I hated blind dates, but when I found myself desperately trying to find an Amazon rep to talk to about my missing vibrator shipment, I had a moment of clarity. Kit was right. I'd texted Jack and we'd agreed to meet.

But I'd been waiting for thirty-five minutes now, and that was enough. It didn't matter what the restaurant patrons thought. The Upper West Side wasn't even my neighborhood. I'd never see any of these people again. I'd only agreed to meet him here because Jack said the eggs Benny were amazing. I didn't need amazing eggs Benny, though. My replacement vibrator had finally shown, and the coffee shop down the street from my apartment in Bushwick sold great breakfast sandwiches. I just had to signal the waitress and get the duck out of here.

I lifted my hand to get Janie's attention and my body flooded with relief. Jack was walking through the door. He seemed troubled and stressed, his eyes darting around nervously, but it was definitely him. I waved enthusiastically, getting his attention. He walked toward me after a moment's hesitation.

I stood as he approached the table. "You made it, finally," I said in a voice that was too loud. "You got the servers working again?"

Before he could say anything, I drew him into a friendly hug. "Just go with it, okay?" I said into his ear. "Think of it as your punishment."

He pulled away with a nervous laugh. "My *what?*"

"For almost standing me up," I said in a low voice. "For being thirty-five minutes late for our blind date and making everyone in the restaurant think I'm a loser."

"Ah." Jack nodded. "I was stuck in the subway. I'm so sorry," he said, his voice booming, then pulled me back into the hug. "That do the trick?"

His breath tickled my ear and sent a shiver down my neck. "It was perfect."

"I'm glad you made it," I said ten minutes later, after we'd both gotten coffee and put in our orders. *Friends with eggs Benedict* for me and *I hope our paths croissant again* for him. "I was about to give up."

"I'm sorry," Jack said, fiddling with his fork. Up close, he was different from his photo. Not in a bad way, but his face was broader, his hair shorter, and he had ten pounds more of muscle. His eyes were definitely hazel, and there were a few flecks of early gray in his dark-brown hair. This was common, though. In my experience, only about 10 percent of people had profile pictures that accurately reflected what they looked like

IRL. Mine, on the other hand, was devastatingly accurate, right down to the curl in my strawberry blond hair that I could never get straight no matter how expensive the flat iron.

"What happened? Were the servers at work down?"

Jack gave me a crooked smile. "Do you mind trying something with me?" His voice was clear and deep over the restaurant clatter. Our original meeting time had been for ten. It was close to eleven now and the place was full, a line forming outside and trailing along the sidewalk.

"What's that?"

"Let's not talk about work. You know, all that usual conversation—*what do you do? and where are you from?*"

"Small talk?"

He pointed his fork at me. "Exactly. Small talk. Let's not do that."

"What should we talk about?"

"Hmm." He rested his hand on his chin. He was wearing a forest green checked shirt that made his eyes pop, and had an almost beard. I liked the look of him. "I've put us in a box, haven't I?"

"I like boxes."

"You do? Why?"

"That would violate the whole we-can't-talk-about-work rule."

He smiled as Janie arrived with our food. As she put my eggs down, she mouthed, *He's cute.* I blushed and glanced at my plate. She put the rest of our things on the table and left us alone.

"She thinks I'm cute, huh?"

I met Jack's eyes with a challenge. "Guess so. You want to get her number?"

"Nope, I'm good." He reached for his croissant, which was flaky and too dark. "Your eggs look fantastic."

"Right?" I cut a bite and put it into my mouth. The sauce was thick and the egg was cooked perfectly. "Thanks for the recommendation."

He bit into his croissant and made a face.

"Not good?"

"A bit stale." He reached toward my plate. "You don't mind, do you?"

"I probably should, but I don't. Take a whole muffin. It's so rich, I'll never finish all of it."

"Thank you." He moved the egg I hadn't touched onto his plate and tasted it. He closed his eyes in pleasure. "So good." He took another bite. "So, I know I put the rule in place, but am I allowed to try to guess what you do for a living?"

"Sure, go ahead."

"Something with boxes, so . . . Amazon fulfiller?"

I felt a nervous flutter in my stomach, thinking about the shipment waiting for me at home. "Ha, no."

"Mover?"

"Wrong again." I doubted he'd be able to guess.

I work for BookBox, a curated book-of-the-month club where I'm in charge of the rom-com selection. It wasn't a genre I read much before I took the job, and some days the contrast between what I read and the reality of my dating life was too stark. But I knew a book was good if I could still root for that happily-ever-after ending regardless of how many *Hey, baby*s I'd received in my Insta DMs that day.

"No one ever gets it right."

"Well, now you're challenging me to a duel."

"You forget I know what you do." I picked up my phone. "Which reminds me, I should let Kit know you arrived." I tapped out a quick text. *He showed.*

And? she wrote back. *Was I right?*

We'll see!

The servers are still down! He's going to be in the doghouse. DOWNWARD DOGGIE STYLE.

"Are you telling Kit that I'm cute?" Jack tipped my phone toward him, trying to read what I'd written. His eyebrows rose as he caught sight of my last text.

"I can explain."

"You don't have to."

"It's this thing Kit and I do, turn ordinary words into porny titles."

He snapped his fingers. "Like Pulp Friction?"

"Yes."

"Game of Bones."

I suppressed a laugh. "You got it."

"Horny Potter."

"You're a natural." I put my phone away. "Probably shouldn't be the only thing we talk about, though."

"I agree."

My mind whirred. How had this conversation gotten so off track? "How about . . . what's the worst date you've ever been on?"

Jack frowned. "Is that your way of saying this is the worst date *you've* ever been on?"

"Far from it."

"Oh?"

"Well, it's hard to pick just one, but if I put the guys who exposed themselves aside, top honors probably goes to—"

"Wait, you're putting the flashers *aside*?"

I shrugged. "A girl has to, these days. Have you not been online for the last ten years?"

"Well, not much. But also, I don't think guys mind getting flashed. Not that I'd know." Jack stopped, flustered. "This actually happens to you? Like on a regular basis?"

"Sadly, yes."

He shook his head. "Men kind of suck, huh."

"A lot of them."

"Well, I'm sorry."

"You don't have to apologize for your gender. But I appreciate the sentiment." I took a sip of my coffee but it had gone cold. "Your turn. Worst date ever."

Jack cocked his head to the side. "Names changed to protect the guilty?"

"Of course."

"Hmmm. Well, it was a long time ago, but probably the one where the girl—let's call her Debbie—brought her mom along."

"No."

"Yes."

I tried to imagine it and couldn't. "Wait, wait, wait. How old were you when this happened?"

His mouth twisted. "Fifteen."

"That puts a different spin on it."

"You've obviously never been a fifteen-year-old boy."

"And thank god for that." He touched my hand, then pulled back quickly, but it was long enough to register.

I cleared my throat. "So, things didn't work out with Debbie?"

9

"No, they did."

"No way this counts, then."

Janie slapped the bill down on the table. "Sorry, but I need the table."

"We just got here," Jack said.

"*You* just got here."

"Ah, right, well, okay. We'll pay up."

She tapped her foot impatiently. I could see the people who had the eleven-thirty reservation glaring at us from the doorway.

"Let's split it," I said.

"No, let me." Jack patted himself down, looking for his wallet, which he located in his front pocket. He pulled it out, then hesitated. "Remember how you said I wasn't the worst date?"

"Um, yes?"

"Someone charged a bunch of stuff on my card last week, and I'm waiting for a replacement. I have enough cash to cover the meal but not the tip."

Janie clearly wanted to retract her endorsement from earlier.

"Why don't you give me the cash and I'll put it on my card so I can tip?" I said.

"Sure, that'd be great." He handed me forty bucks and I gave Janie my card. I completed the transaction quickly, making sure to tip her generously.

She checked the receipt as it came out and smiled. "Thank you, Chloe. *You* have a good day, now."

I put my card away and we stood up.

"Thank you, Chloe," Jack said. "I feel like an idiot."

"I don't think Janie wants to see you back here again, but it's fine." I didn't care who paid for breakfast. He'd shown up, we'd had a nice conversation, he hadn't talked about his needs as a lover (true story) or been on his phone the whole time (also true, twice). It was enough.

As we walked to the exit, Jack placed his hand on the small of my back. It was a gesture I normally hated, but it felt comfortable with him. It had been a long time since I'd been intimate with another person, but it wasn't just that. Something about Jack felt different, and that was a pleasant surprise.

Outside, I turned my face up to the sun. It was a beautiful day. The cherry blossoms were in bloom and the sky was a deep blue and cloudless. It had been a cold, wet spring, and it was nice to feel the sunshine. I decided to fight the temptation to return to my apartment and hermit inside for the rest of the day. Central Park wasn't far. I should walk around. Maybe Kit would meet me.

"You find something you like up there?" Jack asked.

I brought my chin down. "A beautiful day. I'm always looking for a beautiful day."

Our eyes met. He gave me a look that felt appreciative, as if he understood me. "I like that."

"Thank you for brunch, it was nice, if brief."

He touched his chest above his heart. "Ouch. I'll have to make it up to you."

"I'd like that, Jack."

A shadow passed over his face, then lifted. "This has been great, Chloe. I was having a crappy morning and . . . well, let's just leave it at that."

"Sure." I extended my hand and he took it, then pulled me in for a hug.

I hadn't had time during our theatrical greeting to appreciate how well we fit together, but we did. I breathed in his smell of soap and the light spice of his aftershave as his arms tightened around me. I leaned in, then came to my senses and pulled away.

My dry season had gone on way too long.

"Talk soon?" I said.

He nodded and I smiled, then turned and walked away with a skip in my step. I was proud of myself for not trying to prolong the date. I felt pretty sure Jack would reach out soon, but if he didn't, that was okay. He was a good icebreaker, and proof that dating wasn't futile.

He was the start of something, and I was excited to find out what.

Chapter Two

Kit called me a block later, as if she had some sixth sense that my date was over.

"So? How was it?"

"How do you know I'm not still with him?"

"Are you?"

"Well, no, but I could be." The light changed and I stopped at the corner, standing too close to the curb, which is a habit I've had trouble breaking since I moved to New York. In Cincinnati it had never been a problem. But the crazy drivers in this city make getting too close to an intersection life-threatening. "Wait, did he call you?"

"Nope."

"You're clairvoyant?"

"Potentially."

"Pretty sure I'd know this by now."

She laughed. "How about I tell you where you are?"

The light changed and I crossed the street. "I don't even know where I am."

It was partly true. I've never been great at directions, and I still had no sense of the points on the compass in New York, despite it being on a grid that was supposed to be easy to learn. It was embarrassing how many times I took out my phone to figure out if I should turn left or right, particularly when I was in Manhattan. I didn't like looking like a tourist in the city I lived in.

"You're about to hit Central Park West."

I checked the street sign ahead of me. She was right. "How did you know that?"

"We have Find My Friends on our iPhones, remember?"

"Oh, right." Kit had insisted I install it when I moved to New York because she was worried I'd get lost. "But that's kind of creepy that you're checking on me."

"Well . . ."

"What?"

"I might have an alert set up that tells me every time you're on the move."

This stopped me in my tracks. A man slammed into to me, then cursed me out as he hurried away. "What?"

"You'd just moved to the city! I was worried about you."

"And the reason you never turned it off is?"

"I got used to the reminders of where you were. It was out of love, I promise."

Was it that big a deal? It wasn't as if I didn't tell Kit everything that was going on in my life anyway. "Okay, but turn it off now, all right?"

"I will. Hey, you know what? You're so close to the Met. You should go."

"We were supposed to go together."

"I know, but I'm tied up with John today and it's like fate that you're right there after talking about it so much."

I gazed into Central Park, thinking about the Met sitting across the lawn from where I was standing. At least, I thought that was where it was. I'd check the minute we got off the phone. "It's nice out. I was going to hang in the park."

"So do that after. Go to the museum already. You won't regret it."

"Why do you care so much?"

"I want you to finally start exploring this place."

Now I got it. "You're worried I'm going to move back to Ohio."

"Well, yeah. Obvi."

"Love you, Kit."

"Love you too."

I put my phone away with a smile after checking that yes, in fact, I could go straight through the park and get to the Met. I resolved to make it without checking my phone for directions as I set out, taking in the park, the cool of the trees, the people buzzing along the paths, pushing carriages, riding scooters, or jogging on the internal road. As I walked past the Jackie O. Reservoir, I watched the sunlight glint off the water and listened to the happy shouts of children running across the fresh green grass. Kit was right to worry I might leave. My apartment was small, everything was expensive, and I often felt anonymous and overwhelmed.

But right at that moment, I only saw the positives, and it felt like a place I'd be happy to stay in forever.

It didn't take long to get to the Met. I stared at the building for a moment, taking in the triple porticos and the wide sandstone stairs. I felt the same prick of excitement I got whenever I was about to enter somewhere new. I liked my routine, but there was something about the unknown that always got me excited.

"Pretty nice, right?"

I started, then turned toward the familiar voice. "Jack? What are you doing here?"

"Going to the Met?"

I tried to steady my heart. I was happy to see him, but the conversation with Kit had unsettled me. Was Jack following me? Exactly how many people did I have on my tail? "Odd coincidence."

"Is it?" He shrugged and his complete nonchalance reassured me. Jack wasn't following me. He wasn't crazy like Kit. "We were close by, and it's one of my favorite places. I try to get here three or four times a year. You?"

"It's my first time, actually."

"How is that possible?"

"I only moved to New York a year ago, and it took me a while to settle into my job. It's been on my list forever, but somehow I never make it here. Until today."

I watched a large family make their way up the stairs, the

mother anxious, the father holding one little girl on either side of him. They were wearing bright floral dresses that matched their mother's, and when they got to the top of the stairs one of them stopped and executed a perfect pirouette.

"Well, that settles it then," Jack said. "I'll be your tour guide."

"You don't have to do that."

"Trust me, you want this tour."

I was amused by his earnestness. "Okay, you convinced me. Lead the way."

We walked up the steps and I resisted the urge to execute my own (bad) pirouette at the top. Kit was right. The Met had been on my top ten list of places to visit when I came to New York. I was glad she'd pushed me to go.

We went inside and stepped up to the ticket window. While we were able to get in for free as New York residents, Jack insisted on paying for our tickets. He'd gone to the ATM after we'd separated and now had enough cash.

"We should pay for the arts," he said. "They're important."

"I agree. But you don't have to buy my ticket."

"It's the least I can do after this morning. Besides, I need to earn back your goodwill."

"Good Will Humping," I blurted.

"A Few Hard Men," Jack replied without missing a beat.

"Buffy the Vampire Layer."

Jack took our tickets and a museum map from the woman behind the counter, who was now giving us a funny look. "Impressive."

"I've had a lot of practice."

He chuckled as we walked away from the ticket window. "It shows. So . . . we're in one of my favorite places and I get to show it to you for the first time." He rolled up the map and tapped me on the arm excitedly. "I mean, look at this place. Isn't it great?"

We were in the main hall, a vast expanse of white marble and soaring pillars. Light flowed in from the glass rosettes in the coffered ceiling and the arched windows below them. Families with excited children and older couples wearing serious walking shoes were milling around us, the children's pitter-patter echoing off the walls. It was a happy space.

"It's beautiful."

"Right? Designed in 1902 by Richard Morris Hunt in the neoclassical style—"

I burst out laughing.

"You don't appreciate my tour guide knowledge?"

"You actually were a tour guide? I thought that was just a figure of speech."

He clasped his hands behind his back. "I guided a few summers when I was a teenager. My mom worked here and kind of insisted I do it. College applications, blah, blah, blah. But to be honest, I ended up loving it."

"That's adorkable."

He didn't look so sure. "My ex thought it was lame."

And there she was. His ex. I wanted to ask a million questions—who she was, how long they'd dated, when had they broken up and why?—but I squashed it. Not the time.

"Well, it's good she's your ex, then."

Jack nodded, but some of his enthusiasm had seeped away.

"Where should we go?" I asked. "What are your favorite spaces? Tour guide me."

"You sure?"

"One hundred percent."

"Okay, we definitely need to see the temple. And the armor is cool."

"Those sound great. But I have one request. Can we see the bed where Claudia slept? You know, *From the M—*"

"Oh, you're one of those!"

"What?"

"A *Mixed-Up Files* girl."

He was right. *From the Mixed-Up Files of Mrs. Basil E. Frankweiler* was one of my favorite books. I loved Claudia and Jamie's story, two siblings who ran away from home and ended up hiding in the Met.

"Is that a bad thing?"

"Depends. How well do you take disappointment?"

I scrunched up my face. "I can't see the bed?"

"Dismantled, I'm afraid."

"The chapel where she prayed?"

"Closed in 2001."

"You seem to know a lot about it."

He lifted his left shoulder. "Girls used to come in all the time with their favorite passages marked and it was my job to tell them that the museum was a lot different than when the book was written."

"Ten-year-old girls came into the Met alone?"

"They were usually with their parents. Sometimes an older sister."

"Ah. And you were how old? Seventeen, eighteen?"

"Where are you going with this?"

I tapped him on the chest with my index finger. "I bet the big sisters found you pretty irresistible."

Jack smiled impishly. "Seventeen-year-old me is feeling judged."

"How different was he from fifteen-year-old you?"

"He of the bad first date? Well, the seventeen-year-old version probably should be judged. He made some stupid decisions. And before you ask, no, I don't want to talk about them."

He said it lightly, and I got it. No way I wanted to tell Jack the stupidest things I'd done at seventeen. Not even the tenth-stupidest thing, which had been Gerry Bush, the lead in the school play, who had a way of memorizing swoony speeches from Shakespeare and using them when you were weakened by a few hits from his flask.

"You said something about a temple?"

"The Temple of Dendur!"

"That sounds like something from *The Lord of the Rings*."

"Is that bad?"

"Not necessarily."

Jack clicked his map against his palm. "I see . . . likes books, just not *those* kinds of books."

"I've read them."

"And they're awesome?"

"If you're into reading eight-hundred–page books."

"With all three volumes it's about twelve hundred pages, but—"

"I rest my case."

"Are we in court?"

I laughed. "We're in the Met."

He shook his head, a smile on his lips. "You want to see that temple or what?"

I crooked my arm out. "Lead the way."

He put his hand through the space I'd made, forming a link. It felt good to have that point of connection.

"Stick close to me," Jack said. "There are monsters ahead."

The Temple of Dendur was nothing like *The Lord of the Rings*. Where Middle Earth was dark, the temple was in a light-filled room, surrounded by a quiet pool. The sunlight streamed in through a wall of slanted windows, reflecting off the gleaming stone. When you walked in, the present fell away. It was easy to imagine yourself two thousand years earlier, in another place, another time.

"Did they sacrifice virgins in here?" I asked.

Jack snorted. "Not to my knowledge."

"Why did they build it?"

"You want the long version or the short version?"

"You still remember the long version?"

"You really are going to think I'm a massive dork."

I put my hand on his forearm. "I won't. I'll be impressed."

"That's because you haven't heard it." He touched my hand briefly, trailing his finger along the tendon as our eyes locked.

"Tell me."

He dropped his hand and cleared his throat. "It's basically a cult to the leader combined with religious and mythological elements."

I knelt down and examined a relief of figures on one of the walls to hide my blushing face. "This detail is fantastic."

"You can buy a rubbing in the gift shop."

I stood up. "I just might do that. Where to next?"

"Knights in shining armor?"

"That's right up my alley."

We made our way to the Arms and Armor galleries. Once inside, we stood in front of a long procession of knights on horseback and examined their gleaming armor.

"I used to love coming here as a kid," Jack said. "I'd spend hours in here when I had the day off from school."

"Why this room in particular?"

"Not sure. I guess because the armor was worn by real people, once. I used to imagine being in battle, how close you had to get to your opponent. You would've been surrounded by smells—horses, sweat, fear, mud. And there would've been so much noise—cries of pain, hoofbeats, the clang of the armor . . ." Jack trailed off, a tinge of red on his cheeks. "Sorry, I get carried away."

"I like when you get carried away."

"Oh?"

"You must've been a great tour guide."

"I enjoyed it. But wait, 'must have'? Am I failing today?"

"Not at all. This is the most fun I've had in a museum in a long time."

He grinned. "I'm glad."

I turned back to the knights. "It's funny, I probably had my face buried in a book while you were imagining the battles. A different kind of escape."

"Romance novels?"

"I was more into V. C. Andrews, though I guess you could say that those books had romantic elements if you're completely twisted?"

"I remember my sister reading those. They were awful."

"They were. I would've been better off reading romances."

He shook his head. "I don't get why women want to read books about being saved by a man."

"It's a fantasy. No matter how bad things are in real life, you always know that there's going to be a happy ending."

Jack touched the side of my face, his fingers moving gently on my skin. "That's—"

"Sammy, no!" A harassed-looking mother tried to catch her four-year-old boy before he climbed onto the plinth that held the soldiers.

Sammy clenched his fists and boosted himself up. He was wearing overalls and yellow rain boots. "Wanna ride the horsies!"

Jack's hand dropped and he bolted after the boy, scooping him up right before his little hand clasped the tip of one of the knight's swords. "No touching, little buddy."

"But I wanna! I wanna ride the horsie!"

Jack jumped off the plinth with Sammy in his arms. He delivered him to his mother, who thanked Jack profusely before she pulled a howling Sammy away from the knights.

"My hero!" I said to Jack as he walked back to me, the feel of his touch still lingering.

"All part of the training. I'd like to show you one more place. But it's a surprise."

"Should I close my eyes?"

"Not necessary. Follow me."

He turned on his heel with military precision and strode out of the gallery. I trailed along, wondering where he was leading me.

"Wait up," I called.

"Come on now, almost there." He had a laugh in his voice as he turned into the Greek and Roman art gallery. He moved purposely until he got to a large sarcophagus.

He opened his arms. "Ta-da!"

"Is that where—"

"Claudia hides her violin case? Yes!"

I touched its smooth surface. I loved books in general, but the *Mixed-Up Files* had saved me. It was the first book I'd read after my sister died, and I'd tell myself that she'd just gone to the museum, like Claudia and Jamie had. That she'd be back.

"Thank you, Jack."

"There used to be a large wishing pool that had something in it called the Fountain of the Muses."

It was in the book, too, described so vividly that it was easy to conjure a large fountain with bronze sculptures rising out of it. Visitors grasping pennies, warm in their hands, taking an important moment to wish for something.

Love, happiness, a dream come true.

"Do you have something you wish for, Chloe?" Jack said beside me, standing close, his tone intimate.

"Doesn't everyone?" Our eyes locked again. "Do you?"

"I do."

I felt the heat of his gaze and my hands started to tingle. Something was happening between us—but wait. We'd only met a few hours ago. I was getting carried away by nostalgia and the novelty of being on a real date.

"It's a shame the pool's not here anymore, then," I said, breaking eye contact. "But what about the statue? Where's that?" The statue had fascinated Claudia and her brother while they hid in the museum.

"It's always surrounded by a million people, but we can go see it if you like. Or . . ." He checked his watch.

"You have somewhere you need to be?" I said as gently as possible, masking my disappointment.

"You promise not to laugh?"

"How can I promise when I have no idea what you're about to say?"

"How do you feel about boats?"

"What do you mean?"

"It's not far, just in the park, but it'll be easier to take you there than to describe it."

The ground felt uneven beneath me. It wasn't a rational response to what he was saying, but I couldn't control how my body reacted. "What am I getting myself into?"

"It'll be fun, I promise."

"And if it isn't?"

"Then lunch is on me."

Chapter Three

We left the museum and walked south on Fifth Avenue. He seemed excited, and I couldn't imagine what we were headed to. I only hoped it wasn't something that would expose my worst fears.

"You have to tell me where we're going," I said after a few minutes of fretting. *Boat* was a scary word in my life, and though I knew that there was nothing to fear in Central Park, I couldn't shake the feeling of dread.

Jack looked shy. "More fodder for the Jack-is-a-complete-dork file."

I shook my fears away. "The tour was great. I'm glad my first time was with you."

"So, it was good for you?"

I swatted his arm. "Quit it. Where are we going?"

"It's for my nephew."

"It's a *bit* early to introduce me to the family."

"Ha. No, no, I'm doing this *for* my nephew. He won't be there today. Just be patient. We're almost there."

He directed us back into the park at East 72nd. There was a pond up ahead with a small crowd gathered in front of a brick structure.

"Are those remote-controlled sailboats?"

"Yep."

I smiled in relief as I watched the colorful boats sailing around the pond. "Thank goodness."

"What is it?"

"I thought it had something to do with actual boats. You know, human-sized, not for Stuart Little."

"Maybe some other time. For today, I present you the Central Park Model Yacht Club and one of their weekly regattas." He swept his arms wide, taking in the pond and the delighted faces of those watching. There were twenty boats in the water, each about two feet high. A line of men and boys stood on the side of the pond, behind a small rope.

"How do the remotes work?"

"They're wind powered. They can adjust the trim of the sail and the rudder's direction. Many of the boats are handmade."

"You seem to know a lot about it."

He kicked at the ground with his shoe. "My nephew, he's six and obsessed with sailboats. He's wanted to come here since he heard about it, and we've spent hours researching it together. I'm going to surprise him for his birthday."

"So this is a reconnaissance mission?"

"You could say that. I want to make sure it's safe for him.

He's on the spectrum and there are lots of places that trigger him. Before I bring him anywhere new, I check it out first, look for warning signs, where the exits are, that sort of thing."

How cute was this man? "You're a great uncle."

"Yeah, well, it's a lot on my sister and her wife, especially recently, and . . . anyway, you want to watch the regatta?"

"Definitely."

We walked closer and watched as the boats lined up at the starting line, a rainbow of primary blue, red, and yellow, with white sails trimmed in matching colors. There were several buoys in the water, and as far as I could tell the boats had to do some sort of lap between them. The *starter's gun* went off, and there was a lot of excited yelling from the men and boys controlling the boats, some more accurately than others. The race ended with much cheering, and the boats were retrieved by their owners.

"You want to take a turn?" Jack said. "It's an open competition now. Anyone can enter. We just have to rent a boat."

I scanned the boat club building. There was a line of people at the rental window. "What if they're sold out?"

"I'm willing to chance it if you are."

I smiled. "Sure."

Jack pointed to a roped-off area where the previous group of captains had been standing. "Why don't you go over there and hold our place by the starting line, and I'll get the boat?"

"Sounds good."

We parted and I walked to where the competitors were gathering.

"Only participants, miss," an older man in his seventies said to me in a gruff voice. He had a whistle around his neck like a referee and was wearing a white polo shirt with a yacht club logo on it. All he was missing was the captain's hat.

"Oh, my, uh, friend, is just getting our boat."

"All right, miss. You stand over there."

I moved to where he was pointing, quickly realizing that the other participants were all kids with a max age of ten and their parents. One of them, a boy of about nine with black hair and pale skin, gave me an intense look as I stood next to him. He was dressed like one of the royal children, in short pants with socks pulled up to his knees and a cream-colored crew sweater.

I scanned the line for Jack. He'd gotten a boat and a controller and was walking back to me.

"Looks like we're a bit older than the competition," I said when he was by my side.

"I did tell you it was for my nephew."

"I guess we have to let the kids win?"

"We definitely do." Jack bent down and put the boat in the water. It was painted a dark blue and had white sails with matching trim. He gave it a little shove to get it going, then stood up.

"Cheating!" the black-haired child said, pointing at Jack. "Daddy, he's cheating!"

A larger and older version of the kid appeared from behind him and put his hand on the little yeller's shoulder. The dad was wearing a matching outfit, though he'd also tied an ascot around his neck and his pants reached his ankles. "Now, Kenny, the race hasn't even started yet."

"He pushed his boat!"

Jack gave them a wide smile. "I was just getting it into position."

"Yes, well, you see, Kenny here is very particular about the rules being followed."

"Well, as you said, the race hasn't started yet, and it's my first time doing this so . . ."

Kenny glared at Jack.

"Can you tell us what the rules are, Kenny?" I said, stooping down so my eyes were level with his. "So we don't make a mistake again?"

Kenny scowled and held his remote control tightly to his chest.

"Come on, son." His dad encouraged him. "Tell the nice lady how it works."

"You can only use the *wind*!"

"Okay, sport, we got that," Jack said. "Won't happen again."

Kenny didn't look like he believed him, but his dad turned him away gently. I walked back to Jack. He had a remote in his hands. "You know how to work that thing?"

"They gave me a short demo at the booth, but I figure if a kid can do it, then how hard can it be?"

"Kenny seems pretty sure of himself," I whispered.

"Eh. I can take him." He fiddled with the remote and the boat started moving as it caught a small breeze. With some grunting and a lot of frustrated expressions, he got the boat to go to the rough approximation of the starting line, though it took tacking back and forth a couple of times to get there. By that time Jack was red in the face. "Don't laugh."

"I'm admiring your dedication to giving your nephew a good time."

"Thank you. You have any nieces or nephews?"

I watched the water dance in the sunlight. "No. I guess

I'm kind of an only child. I had a sister, but she died when I was ten."

"I'm so sorry, Chloe."

"It was a long time ago."

"How did she—" Jack stopped himself. "Sorry, I shouldn't pry, it's just . . . my mom is sick, and she's in the hospital, and . . ."

The starter made his way into the crowd. "Two-minute warning! Two minutes to get into position."

"Shit," Jack muttered. "How am I supposed to keep the boat here for two minutes?"

"Put it into the wind and let the sails go."

"You a sailor?"

"I was. I—" God, I never talked about this, and certainly not on a first date. "My sister and I, growing up in Ohio, we spent our summers at sailing camp in Kentucky. But that's how she died, and I haven't been sailing since."

Jack's hands dropped and he almost let go of the remote. "I am so, so sorry. You should've said something."

"It's fine."

"It's not fine. This must bring it all back, and then I go prying and . . ."

I touched his hand. "It was a long time ago, and this is just an innocent activity on a beautiful day."

"You sure?"

"One hundred percent. And I'm sorry about your mom too. That must be a lot."

"It is." A cloud raced across his face. "Look, I should've said something before, and I don't know why I didn't, but—"

"We're starting in ten seconds! Boats in position!" the starter bellowed next to us, then raised his arm above his head with his starter's gun. "Five, four, three, two . . ." *Boom!* The gun went off and the boats started moving slowly past the starting line.

"Come on, Jack, catch the wind!"

Jack was momentarily stunned, then concentrated on the controller and got the boat going slowly.

"Open up the mainsail some more," I said, long-buried knowledge coming back to me. "Let it go out as far as you can."

Jack fiddled with the controls and the sail went into position. "This is much harder than it looks."

"It's easy!" Kenny said, a smirk on his face. "You're bad at it."

"Kenny," his father warned, then gave us a bemused expression. "Kids."

"Right," I said, then muttered to Jack, "That's not a kid. He's the devil."

"I'm glad Tyler's not here."

Jack's boat gained some speed as a gust of wind spread across the pond. He was still pretty far behind the other boats.

"Aim for that red buoy," I said. "Then you'll want to try to tack around it and get going back in the other direction."

"In English, please."

"Try to turn the boat around that buoy and get going in the other direction. Like the other boats are doing."

He tried to hand me the remote. "You should do it."

"No, you're doing great. Besides, you wanted to impress your nephew, right? He'll be so excited when you win next time."

"Good point." Jack fiddled with the controls again, then made it to the buoy and around it. He gained on two of the other boats that were having a harder time with the maneuver. Once he was around the buoy, he opened his sail and caught a good wind, picking up speed.

"That's great! Keep trying to stay straight and you should overtake that other boat." I pointed to a red sailboat that was a few feet in front of him.

He held the remote tightly as he approached the other boat. "I can't believe how stressed I am."

I giggled. "You're in a full sweat. What about letting the kids win?"

"I know. It's silly. I have this competitive streak—"

"Watch out!"

The red boat swerved to the left and rammed into ours, knocking it almost over onto its side. The offending boat didn't seem to be affected and sailed away quickly as our boat started spinning in a circle.

"What the hell?" Jack said. "What happened?"

I searched for the culprit and made eye contact with Kenny. He was grinning like a maniac.

"I thought you were against cheating, Kenny?" I said gently.

"I didn't cheat! Daddy! She accused me! She made an accusation!"

"He rammed our boat," I said to Kenny's father.

"He's just a kid!" Kenny's father said.

"It's fine, forget it."

"She has to apologize!"

Jack was shaking with laughter. It was contagious, and I started laughing too. Meanwhile, our boat looked like it might go down the drain.

"Daddy! They're laughing at me! Daddy!"

I turned away from Kenny and his dad and bent down to take off my shoes.

"What are you doing?" Jack asked.

"Rescuing our boat."

I pulled off my shoes and socks, then rolled up my jeans. I hopped over the small concrete wall and waded into the water. I could hear the shouts of others telling me to get out, but I ignored them. Then the referee started blowing his whistle at me like I was a kid at the community pool who'd broken the rules. I reached our boat, picked it up, and carried it back to the side of the pond. The water was deeper than I'd thought and my jeans were soaked to the knees.

"You're disqualified!" Kenny said, pointing at me.

"No shit, kid."

"She sweared! Daddy!"

Jack was hovering at the edge and held out his hand. He helped me out, and I handed him the boat. Jack shook his head but his grin was wide, his eyes dancing. "I think we're out of the race."

"I'm thinking yes."

"I'm sorry, Chloe."

"What are you apologizing for? This was the most fun I've had in a long time."

"Really?"

"Honestly."

"I'm glad to hear that."

"Why don't we get that boat back and find somewhere where I can dry off?"

"Sounds like a plan."

Jack quickly returned the boat and came back with a towel.

"Where did that come from?" I asked.

"The gift shop." He handed it to me. It was white and had a sailing logo on it.

"Thank you."

Jack pointed to a bench not far away. "Why don't we go sit there?"

"Good idea." I slipped my feet into my shoes, and we walked to the bench, my wet jeans tugging on my legs. I took a seat and used the towel to dry off. "I'm glad we did that."

Jack sat next to me. "It didn't bring up too many bad memories of your sister?"

I put my legs out in front of me, letting the sun dry them, and kicked off my shoes. "No. Honestly, I mostly only have good memories of her."

"We don't have to talk about it."

"I know. I don't usually." I glanced at Jack. "I'm surprised I told you." I kicked myself for saying that last part. "Anyway, it reminded me of how much I used to love sailing. I should go back to it. Conquer my fears and all that."

"It's okay to be afraid. Some things are scary."

"Kenny was scary."

Jack chuckled. "He was. But I guess some people might find Tyler like that too."

"Is he a lot?"

"Sometimes. It's been hard on my sister and her wife. Especially with my mom sick."

I touched his knee. "I am so sorry about that."

"One day she seems fine, and the next . . . This has been a great distraction." He stopped, and shook his head. "That came out wrong. I just meant it's been fun to hang out."

"It has."

He stood up.

My heart sank. "Do you have to go?"

"What? No, no, I'm just hungry. That friends with eggs benefits or whatever was good, but it feels like we ate a thousand years ago."

"A thousand, huh?"

"A hundred at least."

I shaded my eyes from the sun. "I could eat."

He pulled out his phone and tapped at it. His eyes lit up. "Perfect."

"What?"

"Do you trust me?"

"Should I?"

"About this, definitely."

"It would help if you told me what *this* is."

"Only the best food truck in New York."

"Oh yeah?"

"I promise you. Any food allergies I should be aware of?"

"Nope."

"Great. Wait here. I'll be right back."

I watched Jack lope off toward the street and smiled to myself. For a day that had started with the near certainty of being stood up, it had taken a fantastic turn. I pulled out my phone and texted Kit.

Thank you.

For what?

Jack. He's great.

Not so great for me. Still no email. Wait, you're still with him?

I wasn't but we ran into each other at the Met.

I TOLD YOU TO GO THERE!

Yes, yes.

And yet you doubt my powers.

I don't. Magical Kit. It's your new name forever.

She sent me a praying hands emoji and I tucked my phone away. I knew it was a dangerous thing to think, but I couldn't keep my mind from going there. Everything about this day felt perfect. I could already imagine telling the girls at work about it—how we'd gone from worst date status to best, just like in the books we curated.

I stopped myself. This wasn't high school, and I didn't need to be mentally writing my name and his in intertwined hearts.

That could wait until the second date at least.